OSWALD'S GAME

OSWALD'S GAME

Jean Davison

FOREWORD BY NORMAN MAILER

W· W· NORTON & COMPANY   New York, London

Many thanks to my editor, Kathy Anderson, for her invaluable assistance and advice.

The text of this book is composed in Times Roman, with display type set in Melior Semibold. Composition and manufacturing by The Haddon Craftsmen, Inc. Book design by Nancy Dale Muldoon.

First Edition

Library of Congress Cataloging in Publication Data

Davison, Jean.
   Oswald's game.

   Includes index.
   1. Oswald, Lee Harvey. 2. Kennedy, John F. (John Fitzgerald), 1917–1963—Assassination. 3. Assassins—United States—Biography. I. Title.
E842.9.78D38 1983 364.1'524.1'0924 [B] 83-8351

ISBN 0-393-01764-8

W. W. Norton & Company, Inc., 500 Fifth Avenue, New York, N. Y. 10110
W. W. Norton & Company Ltd., 37 Great Russell Street, London WC1B 3NU

1 2 3 4 5 6 7 8 9 0

Contents

Foreword

IN field artillery, forward observers are told to bracket a target. If, in their estimation, the first shot falls three hundred yards short, they call for the next to be six hundred yards farther. They want to be certain to land on the far side; that way, by comparing the near and the long, they can approach a direct hit. The target is not found as well creeping toward it. One wants to make certain that errors fall to opposite sides of the mark.

Oswald's Game by Jean Davison fulfills such a purpose. Considering the difficulties surrounding one lonely researcher, she does it well, and here I may as well confess that the author came to my attention when she wrote me a letter full of gentle but determined criticisms to *Conspiracy* by Anthony Summers (McGraw-Hill 1980). I suggested then that she write her own book. Indeed, she has, and I think it may enter the small canon of acceptable words about Lee Harvey Oswald and the Kennedy assassinations, and say this although I am still not sympathetic to her point of view which would argue that Oswald was not an agent for the KGB, CIA, or FBI, nor any part of an anti-Castro Cuban conspiracy with the Mafia to kill Jack Kennedy (which possibilities are carefully investigated in Anthony Summers's book) but to the contrary, Davison here makes the case that Oswald was what he purported to be, an isolated Marxist, half-crazed, who killed for his ideas—in other words, we are given the Warren Commission

...7

revisited. While their august labor now resides in our minds as a congeries of evasions, replete with bad conscience (for the Warren Commission cut off more interesting possibilities than it opened) Jean Davison has gone through the forest and settled on a string of trees that offer a path. Her product, as a result, has lucidity and Oswald emerges as the protagonist of a novel, rather than as a set of forced conclusions by committee. Her work, in short, has conviction, and offers us a recognizable Oswald, a desperately fouled-up young psychopath, full of brilliance, arrogance, cruelty, and bad spelling all in one. So *Oswald's Game* presents a thesis that is unpleasant but not to be ignored, for it is possible. The merit is that Ms. Davison lands on the other side of the target.

When we treat such enigmas as assassination and the possible implication of secret police, we never know whether to give such agents credit for too much intelligence or too little—the crucial question is always: are they as stupid as they seem? Or do they pretend to such incompetence in order to conceal exceptional plans and works? Of course, both may be true. Some of the brightest and some of the most stupid (let us say blindly stubborn) men among us go into secret police work. Short of a solution to the Kennedy assassination, we do have to live, therefore, with two notions of Oswald—that he was the focus, the pawn, and the plaything of more than one intelligence organization, most specifically the CIA and the KGB (and on this is much intriguing evidence that Summers presents, and Davison all but ignores) or, to the contrary, these services were surprisingly benign in their treatment of Oswald—which is not inconceivable given the peculiar reflexes of bureaucracy—but is certainly suggestive of intense incompetence. It is not easy to believe that the KGB would accept an American defector without scrupulously analyzing the possibility that he was a young CIA plant, or without trying to turn him into an agent for themselves. At the least, to make him a double agent would be a game of much interest to them. In turn, on Oswald's voyage back to America, we are also asked, via Davison, to believe that the CIA never debriefed Oswald, or made any attempt to use him as a counter in a game with the KGB. It is hard to believe all those intelligent, game-hardened Ivy League classmates of mine were not seizing the rare opportunity that Oswald presented. Still, Davison takes the benign view. Somehow or other, Oswald slipped through. They did not bother with him. They were out to lunch when he came along. It is conceivable, but it is a point of view that must ignore much, particularly that the genial and urbane George de Mohrenschildt featured in her pages was not conceivably debriefing Oswald for the CIA.

If we are willing to accept Jean Davison's portrait of Oswald as a psychopath, and to a great degree I am, it becomes difficult to see him pursuing one course to the exclusion of all others. Psychopaths have a prodigious sense of their own talents, of their speed of mind and essential importance—so they see opportunities everywhere. Given their enormous sense of the present, their lack of loyalty to the past, and their taste for action, it is natural for psychopaths to attach themselves to every opportunity even when their aims are contradictory. The clue to much of Oswald's behavior, and Davison leads us to it even at damage to her thesis, is his psychopathy. He would not have been out of his element leading eight lives at once. To assume, however, that none of these eight lives was dictated by the KGB, CIA, FBI, Mafia may be to insist on a valley in this fog where others sense a mountain range. Davison does not even seem aware that Marina Oswald's uncle, Ilya Prusakov, was a lieutenant colonel in the MVD and a leading light of Minsk. He gave approval to her marriage to Oswald. The Marina Oswald that Jean Davison offers us does not present such fine connections.

No matter. I return to the first dilemma. The net of conspiracy is always *more* or *less* finely woven than what we do perceive of it. Coincidence often creates the facsimile of evidence for many a conspiracy. To give my own example, I remember that I worked through most of the Fifties in a small studio building on Fulton Street in Brooklyn, and on the floor below worked Colonel Abel, undercover head of a vast net of Soviet espionage in America. For years Abel and I must have gone up and down in the elevator together many times. Then, too, in the late Forties, I subscribed for a little while to the *Daily Worker,* and since I was staying with my parents at the time, my father was brought up before a Loyalty Board and almost lost his governmental job. Finally I wrote a novel called *An American Dream* and in the first paragraph Jack Kennedy is mentioned not ten lines away from the name of the villain whom I chose to call Barney *Oswald* Kelly. I wrote that paragraph in September, 1963, two months before the assassination.

Conceive of those items as they must look on a computer readout in some Intelligence shop. Then add to them that in 1965 I exhorted Berkeley youth to hang posters of LBJ upside down as a protest against the war in Vietnam, and in truth was so demagogical that a standing ovation rewarded me. I am struck how full of profile many a dossier can seem if we are not alert to these unfathomable powers of coincidence. So I can read *Oswald's Game* as a most legitimate attempt to perceive the terrain on that other side of the moon where people's lives are always less interesting than they ought to be, and less sinister, less manipulated. Though I belong to the Summers's school of conspiracy, I still think Jean Davison has delivered an invaluable tool, a corrective, a clear measure of the other possibility to be kept in mind by all us other amateur and professional investigators of the great American mystery. From my side of the debate, I choose then to greet her work.

Norman Mailer

Vladimir Ilyich and I recalled a simile L. Trotsky used somewhere. Once when walking, he spotted in the distance the figure of a man squatting on his haunches and moving his hands about in an absurd way. *A madman!* he thought. But on drawing nearer, he saw that it was a man sharpening his knife on the paving-stone.

—Lenin's wife, quoted in Bertram D. Wolfe's
Three Who Made a Revolution

Introduction

PRACTICALLY everybody who can remember November 22, 1963, remembers the exact moment when he or she heard that President John F. Kennedy had been shot while riding in a motorcade in Dallas. I was sitting in a staff office at the University of Georgia, getting ready to teach a class of freshmen, when I saw a knot of students in the hall huddled around a transistor radio. One glanced up at me with the fiercely introspective look survivors of a natural disaster often have and said, "Somebody shot President Kennedy."

I didn't believe it. An hour or so later, after news came that he had died, I walked outside the building and noticed the intense green of the lawn and trees and the sudden weight of the air. Down the hill, a long line of cars was backed up leaving the campus—all classes had been canceled. The cars moved foot by foot, but very quietly and patiently, like a funeral procession.

People too young to remember may find it hard to credit the degree of shock and disbelief that was the almost universal reaction. No American leader had been assassinated since McKinley in 1901, and Kennedy was no ordinary leader, as even his adversaries agreed. More than a popular president, he was fortune's child, having wit, elegance, wealth, and a style that made his admirers talk, even while he lived, of the Kennedy myth and the legend of Camelot. He had been destroyed in an instant by a bullet to the brain, and for no apparent reason.

At first, because Dallas was a notorious center of right-wing extremism, many people assumed Kennedy had been attacked by a right-wing fanatic—someone who opposed his civil rights program or his efforts to relax tensions with the Soviet Union. The news that the suspect who had been arrested—a 24-year-old named Lee Harvey Oswald—was a Marxist and a former defector to the Soviet Union struck many as a grotesque twist of fate. When Robert Kennedy told his brother's widow, Jacqueline, that Oswald was a Communist, her reaction was, "Oh my God, but that's absurd. . . . It even robs his death of any meaning." A Marxist killing a liberal president made no sense.

Under arrest, Oswald maintained he hadn't shot anybody. Two days later, when the police attempted to transfer him from one jail to another, he was gunned down by Jack Ruby, a Dallas nightclub owner, before a national television audience.

Over the next few weeks the public's impression of Oswald solidified around the bits of information that came out through the news media. Oswald never held a steady job and he had marital problems. He seemed erratic and aimless. Having defected to Russia, he returned to the United States and later tried to go to Cuba. In April of 1963 he had reportedly taken a shot at retired Major General Edwin A. Walker, a prominent right-winger—Walker was one of Kennedy's bitterest political enemies. Many editorials blamed the vicious anti-Kennedy atmosphere in Dallas for inciting a confused misfit to violence.

In 1964 the Warren Commission published the results of the official investigation—a summary that came to be known as the Warren Report, followed by twenty-six volumes of testimony and exhibits that sold mainly to libraries. The report presented strong circumstantial evidence that Oswald had fired three shots at the motorcade from the sixth floor of the Texas School Book Depository, striking Kennedy twice and Governor John Connally once, and that during his attempt to escape he had shot and killed Patrolman J.D. Tippit. Among other things, the rifle found in the School Depository had been mailed to Oswald's post office box, and the order blank and money order bore his handwriting. When he was arrested at a movie theater, he held in

his hand a pistol that matched the bullet casings found near Patrolman Tippit's body—and Oswald reportedly exclaimed, "It's all over
now." But perhaps the most telling was a small symbolic gesture.
Before Oswald went to work at the Depository on the morning of the
assassination, he took off his wedding ring and left it on his wife's
dresser, something he had never done before.

And yet, although the Warren Commission concluded that Oswald
shot Kennedy, it was unable to say why:

> Many factors were undoubtedly involved in Oswald's motivation for the
> assassination, and the Commission does not believe that it can ascribe
> to him any one motive or group of motives.

The Warren Report spoke of his troubled personal life, his hostility
to American society, his interest in Marxism, and his alleged propensity for violence. None of this seemed adequate to explain what had
been called the crime of the century. It seemed to many Americans
that the reason Kennedy was murdered would never be known.

Some felt, in fact, that there *was* no reason. If Oswald was a lone
gunman with no motive, then the assassination was an event without
meaning. It was as though Kennedy had been struck by a bolt of
lightning, or by a brick that happened to fall from a construction site
as the motorcade passed by. In their view, it amounted to the same
thing: the course of history had been changed by a freak accident.

Others suspected a conspiracy from the very beginning. They
pointed out that the murder of any head of state is a political crime.
If the assassin wasn't a raving lunatic—and Oswald certainly wasn't
that—then there must have been a political motive. The Warren
Commission's critics began asking the old legal question, *Cui bono?*
Who stood to gain by Kennedy's death? If Oswald had no obvious
motive, there were others who did—CIA operatives and Cuban exiles
who felt Kennedy had double-crossed them at the disastrous Bay of
Pigs invasion of Cuba, and Mafia dons who were feeling heat from
Kennedy's Justice Department, to name a few. As many of the critics
saw it, one had only to discover the links between these groups and
their patsy, Lee Harvey Oswald, to determine a motive. The result

would be a multitude of assassination books attacking the Warren Report and offering new theories about how and who and why. The prospect of a widespread, high-level conspiracy entered America's consciousness, as did a new suspicion about the way our world worked. In these books, Oswald is merely a pawn, and the real assassins are the unidentified men who successfully plotted to control and change American history.

It has been said that there are only two theories of history: blunder and conspiracy. Broadly speaking, these were the only theories about Dallas, as well. It was an act of random violence or a plot. Choose the first, and you run head on into the conclusion that history—life itself—is chaotic and meaningless. Choose the second, and history is a racket run by unseen, all-powerful conspirators.

In the mid-1960s I didn't take an interest in this controversy. Like a lot of people I had formed an immediate impression of the alleged assassin: he was "some kind of nut" who probably didn't know himself why he did what he did. As far as I was concerned, the case was closed. In 1965 I left my teaching job and got married, moved north, and began working as a free-lance writer.

Then in 1968 I happened to read an article about Oswald in *The Westwood Village Square,* a conservative, youth-oriented magazine that has since folded. The article was written by an anti-Communist propagandist named Ed Butler, who said he had faced Oswald in a New Orleans radio debate on Cuba in August 1963. That surprised me, since I found it hard to imagine Oswald, who apparently couldn't even hold a menial job, holding his own in a public debate. But according to Butler, he was a well-informed and articulate debater who was dedicated to the cause of Castro's Cuba. Butler produced testimony and documents from the Warren Commission records to bolster his belief that Oswald had been "conditioned to kill" by the Communist propaganda he'd been reading since he was a teenager. That didn't seem likely, to put it mildly, but even taking Butler's political bias into account, I couldn't reconcile this picture of Oswald as a skilled public debater with the one I had previously been given of him as a hapless drifter. Although I didn't realize it, I was getting bitten by one of the central mysteries of the Kennedy assassination—

the question of who Oswald really was.

On a later trip to the library I checked out Mark Lane's *Rush to Judgment,* one of the first attacks on the Warren Report. Lane had been retained by Oswald's mother to represent her son's interests before the Commission. His argument was that Oswald had been framed. Almost nothing was said about Oswald's personal background, his political commitment or lack of one. Like the defense attorney he was, Lane tore into virtually every piece of evidence in the case against his client—the shell casings found near Patrolman Tippit's body, the famous snapshots showing Oswald holding the rifle found in the Depository, and much more. Lane portrayed the Warren Report as a farce, a calculated attempt to conceal a conspiracy. By the time I had finished this angry book, I wondered if Oswald was involved in the assassination at all.

I now had *three* pictures of Oswald to choose from: those of the Warren Commission, Butler, and Lane. All had relied on evidence contained in the Commission's twenty-six volumes. Everybody had read the same material and arrived at wildly different conclusions. How was that possible? More to the point, who was telling the truth? At the time, it seemed simple enough to find out. I would read the twenty-six volumes myself.

I found the blue-bound *Hearings* in a local university library. Volumes I–XV contained the testimony of witnesses who appeared at the Commission's hearings or gave depositions before a Commission lawyer. The question-and-answer format made the transcripts read like the text of a play. The remaining volumes contained exhibits entered as evidence—FBI reports, photographs, and similar documents. The first thing that struck me was how disorganized this material was. An FBI report on ballistics might be followed by a psychiatric report on Jack Ruby's mother or a description of the preparations for the motorcade. And there was no index. I began taking notes, wondering if I could ever find an underlying order in this jumble of information.

During the reading I checked some of Mark Lane's footnotes. The testimony he had cited as evidence that the Warren Report was a cover-up had often been quoted out of context, so that what he quoted changed the meaning of what had actually been said. For example, the

way Lane wrote about Jack Ruby's testimony led readers to believe
that Ruby was denied the opportunity to reveal the existence of a
conspiracy.

After Ruby had been convicted of Oswald's murder and sentenced
to death, Warren Commission members Earl Warren and Gerald R.
Ford questioned him at the Dallas jail. For many months, there had
been rumors that Ruby was a hit man whose job had been to silence
Oswald. To hear Lane tell it, Ruby seemed eager to disclose his part
in this conspiracy:

> Ruby made it plain that if the Commission took him from the Dallas
> County Jail and permitted him to testify in Washington, he could tell
> more there; it was impossible for him to tell the whole truth so long as
> he was in the jail in Dallas. . . . "I would like to request that I go to
> Washington and . . . take all the tests that I have to take. It is very
> important. . . . Gentlemen, unless you get me to Washington, you can't
> get a fair shake out of me."

After quoting similar statements by Ruby, Lane continued:

> Representative Ford asked, not a little redundantly, "Is there anything
> more you can tell us if you went back to Washington?" Ruby told him
> that there was, and just before the hearing ended Ruby made one last
> plea to the Chief Justice of the United States.
> RUBY: But you are the only one that can save me. I think you can.
> WARREN: Yes?
> RUBY: But by delaying minutes, you lose the chance. And all I want
> to do is tell the truth, and that is all.

But Warren didn't take him to Washington. Reading Lane's account,
one is horrified. His implication is clear: Ruby was begging to be
allowed to expose the conspiracy, and the Chief Justice of the Supreme Court wouldn't listen.

Everything Lane quoted was in the record. What he *didn't* say,
however, was that the "tests" Ruby wanted to take were simply a lie
detector test—and the reason Ruby wanted to take one was to prove
that he was *not* part of a conspiracy.

After his arrest, Ruby had been diagnosed as a "psychotic depressive." His testimony to the Commission indicates that he believed he was the victim of a political conspiracy by right-wing forces in Dallas. He suggested that the John Birch Society was spreading the falsehood that he, a Jew, was implicated in the president's death in order to create anti-Jewish hysteria. "The Jewish people are being exterminated at this moment," Ruby insisted. "Consequently, a whole new form of government is going to take over our country." To foil this supposed plot, Ruby repeatedly asked to be given a lie detector test. At various points in their conversation Ruby told Warren:

> No subversive organization gave me any idea. No underworld person made any effort to contact me. It all happened that Sunday morning. . . . If you don't take me back to Washington tonight to give me a chance to prove to the President that I am not guilty, then you will see the most tragic thing that will ever happen. . . . All I want is a lie detector test. . . . All I want to do is tell the truth, and that is all. There was no conspiracy.

The following month Ruby was allowed to take a polygraph test in his jail cell, and he showed no signs of deception when he denied being part of a conspiracy. Because of the doubts about his sanity, however, the test results were considered inconclusive.

The only part of this background that appears in Lane's book is Ruby's statement, "All I want to do is tell the truth, and that is all." Had he presented the accompanying material, Lane might have argued that Ruby was faking. Instead, Lane cheated. He transformed a man who seemed pathetically anxious to prove his innocence into an honest conspirator desperate to reveal everything he knew. And this was only one of many similar distortions in *Rush to Judgment.*

I remember feeling outraged when I realized what Lane had done. Evidently, the Warren records were like a vast lumberyard. By picking up a few pieces here and there, and doing some cutting and fitting, any theory could be built for which someone had a blueprint.

Meanwhile my impression of Lee Harvey Oswald was changing. I was surprised by the sheer amount of material the Commission had collected on his background. Much of this information was new in the sense that it had never been published anywhere except in the *Hearings*. There was testimony from dozens of witnesses who had known Oswald at each stage of his life from birth to death—they described him and his activities and recounted numerous conversations they had had with him. And there was a good deal more: Oswald's personal papers and letters; detailed evaluations by social workers and a psychiatrist who had interviewed him when he was a junior high school truant; a diary and manuscript he had written that purported to show his experiences in the Soviet Union; his school, Marine, and work records—even lists of the books he checked out of libraries, the magazines and newspapers he subscribed to, and the reading material found among his effects.

A transcript of the radio debate Ed Butler had written about was included, and Oswald did indeed appear to be an able debater. The moderator, a reporter named William Stuckey, testified that he thought Oswald was impressive, almost like a young lawyer. And Stuckey's judgment was not unusual. Virtually everyone who knew Lee Oswald thought he was intelligent, rational, and dedicated to his brand of left-wing politics. The people who knew him best described him as a revolutionary. (This was in 1964, when most Americans thought revolutionaries existed only in banana republics or in Russia before 1917.) On the other hand, people also felt that he was bitter, secretive, and—the most frequent description of all—"arrogant." Testimony about his troubled personal life, beginning when he was a child, was presented in great detail as well.

And yet, if the impression Oswald gave his relatives and acquaintances was clear, some of his political activities were not. He went to the Soviet Union as a 19-year-old defector and lived there for almost three years. The particulars of his life during that period are, and probably always will be, sketchy. He had given political reasons for his defection, but were they the only reasons? After he returned to the United States, he supported Castro both publicly and privately, but he also made contact with anti-Castro groups. These clouded areas of activity raise questions about which side he was really on. After the assassination, there had been heavy speculation that he may have actually been working for the CIA or the FBI. (Although I didn't like

Mark Lane's methods, I could see that he and the other more responsible critics did have a point.)

But no one's explanation encompassed all the available material. The authors of the Warren Report had emphasized Oswald's personal life, while turning aside important questions about his political associations. Ed Butler ignored everything except Oswald's evident obsession with left-wing politics. The shadowy aspects of his record were left to the Commission's critics, who talked about little else.

Not that I was doing any better. Without ever having made a conscious decision to do so, I was becoming an assassination researcher. Reading the testimony, I was learning more about Lee Harvey Oswald than I ever wanted to know, and I couldn't understand his motivations either. I began putting the details of his life into chronological order, hoping to catch the drift of his thinking in the way events unfolded. Leaning first toward one theory, and then another, I soon discovered that it was possible to manipulate the evidence to support any position I took (whether it was, for example, that Oswald worked for the FBI or that he did *not* work for the FBI.) Unfortunately, whichever stand I chose, there was always evidence left over that seemed to contradict it. The simple idea of coming up with a theory and finding evidence to support it was obviously the wrong way to go about finding out the truth.

I gave up the research for a while and turned to other things. When I went back to it I made a deliberate effort to cover as much ground as I could without looking for patterns of evidence to convince me of any particular theory. Eventually the research involved substantially more than the Commission's twenty-six volumes. I read a biography of Oswald written by his brother and many other books and articles on the assassination. I went through contemporary newspapers and magazines, concentrating especially on those Oswald subscribed to and presumably read. I visited the National Archives to examine still other Commission records. Later, I read Senator Frank Church's senate committee reports on the CIA plots to murder Castro, and the 1979 hearings and report of the House Assassinations Committee. In 1978, a new study describing the personality traits of career criminals gave me additional insight into Oswald's character. The project, started on a whim, lasted, off and on, for thirteen years.

During that time, as I acquired more knowledge about Oswald and the times he lived in, explanations for some of his mysterious activities suddenly emerged. Since I had not been pursuing any particular theory by looking for evidence to support what I already believed, I was often surprised by what I found. I don't claim to have solved all the questions surrounding the assassination, but I believe I have found an answer to one of the most elusive: Oswald's motive.

The motive was one suspected by Lyndon Johnson, President Kennedy's successor. Shortly before he died, Johnson told journalist Leo Janos that after he took office he discovered "we were operating a damn 'Murder Inc' in the Caribbean." He said that a year or so before Kennedy's death a CIA-backed assassination team had been picked up in Havana. Although he couldn't prove it, Johnson believed that Dallas had been a retaliation for this thwarted attempt on Castro's life. On another occasion Johnson told columnist Marianne Means that he thought Oswald had acted "either under the influence or the orders" of Cuban Premier Fidel Castro. More recently, several writers—former CBS reporter Daniel Schorr, among others—have echoed LBJ's dreadful suspicion that American plots to kill Castro had somehow backfired in Dallas.

Writing in the *New York Review of Books* in 1977, Schorr pointed out that Oswald could have become aware of these plots, and Castro's reaction to them, from an article that appeared in his local newspaper some ten weeks before the assassination. The article was based on an impromptu interview American reporter Daniel Harker had had with Castro in September 1963, and Castro was quoted as saying, "We are prepared to fight them and answer in kind. United States leaders should think that if they are aiding terrorist plans to eliminate Cuban leaders, they themselves will not be safe." (This newspaper article appears in the Warren Commission's published exhibits. It *wasn't* mentioned in the Warren Report, however.)

Is it possible that Castro's warning to American leaders gave Oswald the idea that Kennedy should be killed? Daniel Schorr thought so. He revealed that just three weeks after the Harker interview was published, Oswald reportedly made threatening statements about

Kennedy when he visited the Cuban Embassy in Mexico City to apply for a visa to enter Cuba. Oswald was quoted as telling a consular official that he wanted to "free Cuba from American imperialism." Then he said, "Someone ought to shoot that President Kennedy. Maybe I'll try to do it." Schorr had uncovered two sources that reported Oswald's threat. One was a top-secret letter FBI director J. Edgar Hoover had sent to the Warren Commission in 1964, the other a tabloid article in 1967 that quoted Fidel Castro.

Considering the timing of Oswald's outburst, Schorr concluded that it was likely Castro had influenced Oswald, as Lyndon Johnson had suspected. Schorr wrote, "The 'influence' may have been as simple as reading Castro's public denunciation of attempts on him and the warning of possible retaliation." Schorr believed that "the possibility Oswald acted on his own, inspired by Castro's statement, cannot today be proved." Even so, he ended by saying, "An arrow launched into the air to kill a foreign leader may well have fallen back to kill our own."

By the time Schorr's article appeared, my research had already led me to a similar conclusion. This book will present evidence that Castro's public warning did, in fact, inspire Oswald to assassinate the president. Furthermore, the full context of Oswald's life directed him toward this reaction. In the final analysis, the assassination was a natural outgrowth of Oswald's character and background—and of the American-backed plots to kill Castro.

The reader will probably be skeptical, for there have already been two official investigations and scores of books, each claiming to have uncovered the truth about Dallas. He or she may well ask: If what you say is true, why hasn't this solution been discovered before now? In large part, American authorities have been understandably reluctant to suggest that Cuba or any other foreign government was involved—however indirectly—in the assassination of the president.

One of the authors of the Warren Report, attorney Wesley J. Liebeler, told writer David S. Lifton in 1965 that he "suspected Cuban involvement." Writing in *Best Evidence,* Lifton said that Liebeler then "dwelt at great length on a speech Castro had made in September 1963 and the possibility that this speech may have influenced Oswald."

(This "speech" was the newspaper article quoted above.) Lifton only mentioned this conversation in passing and said nothing further about it. But there was no hint of Liebeler's suspicion in the Warren Report. According to records in the National Archives, Liebeler had argued that Castro's warning should be included in the report, but he was overruled by the chief counsel of the investigation, J. Lee Rankin, who contended that there was no evidence Oswald had seen it. Liebeler wrote a memo protesting this decision, noting that the same could be said of certain anti-Kennedy propaganda distributed in Dallas, which *was* discussed in the report. Liebeler added, "Our discussion of the possible inclusion of the Castro quote had obvious political overtones."

Hoover's top-secret letter was also withheld from the report. After the assassination a Communist party informant for the FBI had gone to Cuba and met with Fidel Castro. The informant said that Castro had told him about a threat Oswald had made against the president in Mexico City—Castro explained that the Cubans had considered this a provocation and would have nothing to do with him. Hoover passed this information along in his letter to the Commission, but the matter was dropped. Nowhere in the report is there any indication that Oswald might have threatened Kennedy's life in the presence of a Cuban official. On the contrary, the report states that the Commission had found *no evidence* "that Oswald's trip to Mexico was in any way connected with the assassination of President Kennedy." The author of that section of the report, W. David Slawson, apparently never saw Hoover's letter.

Thus, the Warren Report omitted two significant pieces of evidence: (1) Castro's warning that he was ready to "answer in kind" to American-backed assassination plots, which appeared in Oswald's hometown paper on September 9; (2) a report that some three weeks later Oswald told the Cubans he was ready to kill the president. Had the Warren investigation put together these and other clues available to it, Oswald's probable motive might have been explained back in 1964.

However, there was one piece of information the Commission didn't have. It didn't know the CIA had been trying to murder Fidel

Castro. If these plots had been common knowledge in November 1963, as they are today, the announcement that the accused assassin was a militant supporter of Castro would have suggested a retaliation from the start. But the Warren Commission investigators didn't know about about our "Murder Incorporated" in the Caribbean—the CIA officials who had that knowledge didn't tell them. With that path kept in the dark, the Commission looked for Oswald's motivation down several better-lighted dead ends.

Having failed to provide a motive, the Warren Report soon fell prey to the proponents of a conspiracy, who dismissed Oswald as a pawn and looked for a motive in the minds of Mafia dons and CIA operatives. It is one purpose of this book to show how some of the most widely read conspiracy books have presented what amounts to an imaginary history. The argument that Oswald was the tool of a high-level conspiracy does seem plausible, until one tries to fit it into the context these theorists always leave out—the personality and background of Lee Harvey Oswald, the individual.

Jean Davison

OSWALD'S GAME

1... A Most Unusual Defector

ON a crisp, clear day in October, 1959, advisers and allies of the Kennedy family gathered for an important meeting at Robert Kennedy's house on Cape Cod. Seated in front of a fireplace, they listened as Senator John Kennedy talked about his decision to make a run for the 1960 Democratic presidential nomination. This election would mark the end of the Eisenhower era, a period of deceptive tranquillity compared to the raucous decade that lay ahead. The country was at peace, although the Cold War continued, as both sides tested intercontinental ballistic missiles and began putting unmanned satellites into orbit. In Cuba, Fidel Castro's revolution was less than a year old. There was a small group of U.S. military advisers in South Vietnam, but this would not be a campaign issue. Earlier that year the milestone of first American casualties—two GIs killed by a Vietcong bomb—made front-page news. However, the conflict there soon dropped to the back pages. At home, the civil rights movement was quietly gaining momentum. It was the year of "Father Knows Best" and "Leave It to Beaver," the TV quiz show scandals, and the kitchen debate between Premier Nikita Khruschev and Vice-President Nixon.

During the same month the Kennedy forces assembled to map strategy, a young ex-Marine named Lee Harvey Oswald entered the Soviet Union on a six-day visa. Soon after he reached Moscow he informed his female Intourist guide that he wanted to become a Soviet citizen. She helped him draft a letter to the Supreme Soviet and put him in touch with the appropriate officials—who were not encouraging. On October 21 he was informed that since his visa had expired, he would have to leave the country that evening. Oswald went back to his hotel room and cut his left wrist about an hour before his guide was scheduled to arrive. She found him in time, and he was taken to a hospital where his minor wound was stitched up and he was held for observation. The ploy of a suicide attempt apparently turned the Soviet bureaucracy around. According to Oswald's Russian diary, a new group of officials interviewed him and told him that his request to stay in the country was being reconsidered and that he would hear from them, but "not soon."

After waiting in his hotel room for three days, Oswald decided a "showdown" was needed to give the Russians a sign of his faith in them. On October 31 he took a taxi to the American Embassy, slammed his passport down on Consul Richard Snyder's desk, and announced that he wanted to give up his American citizenship. Oswald gave Snyder a signed, handwritten note:

> I, Lee Harvey Oswald, do hereby request that my present citizenship in the United States of America be revoked.
> I have entered the Soviet Union for the express purpose of applying for citizenship in the Soviet Union, through the means of naturalization. My request for citizenship is now pending before the Supreme Soviet of the USSR.
> I take these steps for political reasons. My request for the revoking of my American citizenship is made only after the longest and most serious consideration.
> I affirm that my allegiance is to the Union of Soviet Socialist Republics.[1]

The note showed that Oswald understood the legal procedure for renouncing his citizenship. Snyder observed at a glance that Oswald was "wound up like six watch springs." He later said, "You could tell he'd been rehearsing this scene for a long time."

When Oswald demanded that he be allowed to sign the necessary papers then and there, the consul stalled. The month before, another American had formally renounced his citizenship and had been accepted by the Soviets. It turned out that the man had been discharged from the armed forces with a 100% mental disability. When the mental problem became obvious, the Soviets had reacted as though they had purchased damaged goods. They contacted the embassy and ordered the Americans to "get him out of here." With that incident in mind, Snyder, who had once worked for the CIA, tried to get more information from Oswald. He asked his reasons, and Oswald launched into a condemnation of American military imperialism.

When Oswald declared, "I am a Marxist," Snyder joked that he was going to be a very lonesome man in the Soviet Union. Evidently, Oswald didn't get it. He replied that he had been warned the consul would try to talk him out of his decision, and he didn't want any lectures. Snyder quizzed him about his knowledge of Marxist theory. He later remembered asking him "if he could tell me a little bit about the theory of labor value." Oswald didn't have the faintest notion of what he was talking about. When he wrote to Washington about this incident two days later, he said that Oswald had "displayed all the airs of a new sophomore party-liner." The overall impression Snyder got was one of "overbearing arrogance and insufferable adolescence." He thought Oswald was intelligent and mentally competent—but unintellectual, intense, and humorless.

Sometime during their conversation, Oswald dropped another hot potato in his lap. While Oswald was in the Marines he had been a radar operator at a U.S. base in Japan from which America's secret U-2 planes made reconnaissance flights over the Soviet Union. He had tracked the high-altitude U-2s on his radar screen. When Snyder asked him if he was actually prepared to serve the Soviet state, Oswald told him about his duty as a radar operator and that he had informed Soviet officials he was ready to give them any military information he could recall concerning his specialty. He hinted he might know something of special interest.

Richard Snyder's assistant, John McVickar, was in the same room listening to this. The business about giving away secrets "raised hackles," he later testified. He thought Oswald made the threat in order to shock Snyder into taking prompt action on his renunciation of citizenship. The tone of the meeting was so unpleasant that McVickar and two other people who were in and out of the room during part of it—a receptionist and an American exchange student—still remembered it years later.

Finally Snyder told Oswald that the embassy staff would need some time to prepare the necessary papers and that he would have to come back. Oswald stalked out, leaving his passport behind. Snyder immediately drafted a wire to the Department of State reporting Oswald's visit, including his threat to reveal military information. Copies of the telex were sent to the CIA, FBI, and the Office of Naval Intelligence.

Someone at the embassy alerted the press, and the next day the *New York Times* ran a small story at the top of page 3:

EX-MARINE REQUESTS SOVIET CITIZENSHIP

MOSCOW, Oct. 31 (AP)—A former marine from Texas told the United States Embassy today that he had applied for Soviet citizenship.

"I have made up my mind, I'm through," said Lee Harvey Oswald, 20 years old of Fort Worth, slapping his passport on the desk.

The embassy suggested that he withhold signing papers renouncing his citizenship until he was sure the Soviet Union would accept him.

Mr. Oswald is the third American in recent months to apply for Soviet citizenship upon arriving in Moscow. . . .

Mr. Oswald's mother, Mrs. Marguerite Oswald, lives in Fort Worth. His sister-in-law, Mrs. R. L. Oswald of Fort Worth, said he got out of the Marines about a month ago and returned to Fort Worth for a visit.

After the news broke, Oswald was besieged by reporters at his hotel room. He refused all interviews, as well as telephone calls from his mother and brothers back home. His brother Robert found out when a reporter from the Fort Worth *Star-Telegram* confronted him at work with a telex from Moscow. He told the reporter, "Lee is awfully young, looking for excitement. I don't believe he knows what he is doing." As soon as Robert got home he telegraphed his brother: *"Through any possible means contact me. Mistake."*

On November 3 Oswald wrote to the American ambassador, going over Snyder's head as it were, to repeat his request for a revocation of his citizenship and to protest Snyder's refusal to grant his "legal right" to sign the papers. The letter concluded by saying that in the event his application for Soviet citizenship was accepted, "I will request my government to lodge a formal protest regarding this incident."

Five days later, he wrote Robert:

> Well, what shall we talk about, the weather perhaps? Certainly you do not wish me to speak of my decision to remain in the Soviet Union and apply for citizenship here, since I'm afraid you would not be able to comprehend my reasons. You really don't know anything about me. Do you know for instance that I have waited to do this for well over a year, do you know that I [phrase in Russian] speak a fair amount of Russian which I have been studying for many months.
>
> I have been told that I will not *have* to leave the Soviet Union if I do not care to. This then is my decision. I will not leave this country, the Soviet Union, under any conditions, I will never return to the United States which is a country I hate.

Reading these cold words, one wonders what there was in Oswald's past that led him to reject not only his country but his brother as well. Others—especially people who have followed the controversy about the Kennedy assassination—may suspect that Oswald was insincere and ask: *Who sent him? What was the real purpose behind his coming to the Soviet Union?* Certainly there was more to Oswald's defection than appeared on the surface.

Two weeks after his confrontation with Snyder, Oswald changed his mind about talking to the American press corps. He gave two interviews in which he elaborated on his reasons for defecting. On November 13 he called Aline Mosby, a UPI correspondent, who came to his room on the second floor of the Metropole Hotel. It was a large room overlooking the Bolshoi Theater, with ornate furniture and blue walls and she thought he looked totally out of place there, "like some Okie from the boondocks." Mosby asked questions and took notes in shorthand, and Oswald talked "non-stop" for two hours. He seemed a little stiff at first, but the longer he talked, the more confident, even smug, he became.

Aline Mosby was a veteran reporter, originally from Montana. (It was she who revealed, in 1952, that Marilyn Monroe had once posed for a nude calendar photo.) She had questioned other American defectors during her assignment in Moscow, but as the interview progressed she could see that Oswald was an anomaly. The others, as she perceived them, fell into one of two categories—either a "high-level official who had played an important role in his country and decided to transfer his knowledge to the Soviet side" or someone "of the romantic variety who flees behind the Iron Curtain in the hopes of escaping personal problems." Oswald claimed that his reasons were ideological. When Mosby heard him using phrases like "capitalist lackeys," she thought it sounded "as if it were all being given by rote, as if he had memorized *Pravda.*" She got very few glimpses of the person behind the political talk.

Mosby asked him how he had become a Marxist, and he told her, "I became interested about the age of 15. From an ideological viewpoint. An old lady handed me a pamphlet about saving the Rosenbergs. . . . I looked at that paper and I still remember it for some reason, I don't know why."[2] He was living with his mother in New York City at the time. The Rosenberg pamphlet introduced him to socialist literature. He began observing the "class struggle" in New York, "the luxury of Park Avenue and the workers' lives on the [Lower] East Side." Nobody had influenced him, he said and insisted that it was only through his reading and personal observation of American society that he had become a Marxist. "I guess you could say I was influenced by what I read, and by observing that the material was correct in its theses."

Serving in the Marines had strengthened his beliefs, particularly his view of American imperialism: "Like Formosa. The conduct of American technicians there, helping drag up guns for the Chinese. Watching American technicians show the Chinese how to use them —it's one thing to talk about communism and another thing to drag a gun up a mountainside." On guard duty at night, he said, he would dream about getting out of the Marines and going to Russia—it would be, he thought, "like being out of prison."

About his decision to leave America he said, "I would not care to live in the United States where being a worker means you are exploited by the capitalists. If I would remain in the United States, feeling as I do, under the capitalist system, I could never get ahead. . . . I would have a choice of becoming a worker under the system I hate, or becoming unemployed. . . . One way or another I'd lose in the United States. In my own mind, even if I'd be exploiting other workers." Evidently, it was fairly important to him to get ahead and not lose.

He presented himself as a struggling idealist: "I'm sincere in my ideal. This is not something intangible. I'm going through pain and difficulty to do this." But even an idealist can be aggressive, and he seemed to believe he had chosen the winning side. At one point he said, "Communism is an aggressive ideal as well as an economic system. . . . The forces of communism are growing. I believe capitalism will disappear as feudalism disappeared." He also talked about armchair socialists. "You don't just sit around and talk about it," he said. "You go out and do it."

The next day Aline Mosby's UPI story was picked up by a Fort Worth newspaper and run under the headline "Fort Worth Defector Confirms Red Beliefs." After reading her account in another paper available in Moscow, Oswald telephoned Mosby to complain about what he considered to be distortions, saying that his family had not been poverty-stricken, as she had said. True, he told her how he had seen the "impoverishment of the masses" in his own mother, but he felt that Mosby had put her emphasis in the wrong place. He reiterated that his defection wasn't prompted by personal hardship, but was "a matter only of ideology."

On November 16, 1959, Priscilla Johnson stopped by the American Embassy to pick up her mail. She had just returned from the United States, where she was covering the Camp David summit meeting between President Eisenhower and Premier Khruschev. Her first job, ironically enough, had been in Washington as a researcher for the newly elected senator from Massachusetts, John F. Kennedy. In the winter of 1954–1955 she had gotten to know him well. She had left Washington and was working in New York as a Russian-language translator when he was hospitalized there for two operations on his spine. She visited him occasionally during his recovery, posing as one of his sisters. In 1958 she went to Moscow as a correspondent for the North American Newspaper Alliance and *The Progressive* magazine. (In 1977, as Priscilla Johnson McMillan, she would publish a book with Oswald's widow called *Marina and Lee.*)

At the embassy that day she had run into John McVickar, who told her, "Oh, by the way, there's a young American in your hotel trying to defect. He won't talk to any of *us,* but maybe he'll talk to you because you're a woman." When she knocked on the door of Oswald's room later that day, he came out into the hall to speak with her instead of inviting her in, but readily agreed to come up to her room on the floor above for an interview that evening.

Oswald arrived dressed in a dark flannel suit. With his "pale, rather pleasant features," he resembled "any of a dozen college boys I had known back home." They talked for about five hours, from nine until two in the morning. Like Aline Mosby, she had also seen other defectors, and she too found Oswald hard to figure. Oswald had just turned 20, and she had never known anyone "of that age . . . , or that generation, taking an ideological interest to the point where he would defect." He reminded her of the leftists who had emigrated to Russia for political reasons in the 1930s. The reasons Oswald gave—unemployment in the United States, racial inequalities—sounded "nineteen-thirtyish."

He began by complaining about the runaround he had gotten at the embassy, insisting that the American officials were "acting in an illegal way." He told her he had decided to grant the interview because, now that Soviet officials had assured him he would not be forced to return to the United States, he felt "it was safe to tell his side of the story." He wanted to counter the American Embassy's statements about his defection because, he said, "I would like to give people in the United States something to think about."

After that, he seemed mainly interested in discussing economic theory. Like Richard Snyder, Priscilla Johnson got the impression that Oswald didn't fully understand Marxist economics. When she pointed out that the Soviets made a large profit from their workers in order to accumulate capital for the state, Oswald agreed. What was important, he said, was that the profit was used to benefit *all* the people, emphasizing this concept with a sweep of his arm. Asked about the difference in the living standards of the two countries, he replied, "They don't have as many hot water heaters and meat pies here but they will in 20 years, through an economic system that is leaving the United States far behind." At another point he told her, "I believe sooner or later communism will replace capitalism. Capitalism is a defensive ideology, whereas communism is aggressive." A recent meeting of the Supreme Soviet had taken no action on Oswald's request for citizenship, and Johnson thought he seemed disappointed and worried by that. But he told her he hoped that his experience as a radar operator would make him more desirable to them.

Oswald's account of how he became a Marxist was virtually the same as the one he had given Mosby. He reiterated his belief, from his observations in New York, that the workers were exploited and explained once more how he had discovered socialist literature and saw that the description it gave of capitalist society "was quite correct." He told her, "I had been brought up like any Southern boy to hate Negroes. Socialist literature opened my eyes to the economic reasons for hating Negroes: so the wages could be kept low."

Listening to him, Johnson felt "it was as though Oswald wanted to convince us both that he had never had a childhood, that he had been all his life a machine, calibrating social justice."

He repeatedly said that his decision to defect was "unemotional." But she noticed that his voice seemed to tighten when he talked about his mother, whom he described as a victim of the capitalist system. In contrast, his voice sounded cold and considerably more distant when he answered a question about his father's line of work: "I *believe* he was an insurance salesman." (In fact, his father had died before Oswald was born.) Oswald told her he had joined the Marines "because we were poor and I didn't want to be a burden on my family." By his account, he'd been making plans to defect for two years, finding out how to go about it mostly by reading. "I have had practical experience in the world," he said. "I am not an idealist completely. I have had a chance to watch American imperialism in action."

Shortly after the assassination, Priscilla Johnson would write, "If there was one thing that stood out in all our conversation, it was his truly compelling need . . . to think of himself as extraordinary." When she asked him if he recommended defection to others, he said he did not. The course he had chosen was not for everyone. Defection meant "coming into a new country, always being the outsider, always adjusting, but I know now that I will never *have* to return to the United States. I believe what I am doing is right."

And later, in *Marina and Lee,* she wrote, "Our evening was like a seesaw, with me trying to get Lee to talk about himself and Lee trying to talk about his 'ideology.' I would say that Lee won." Before he left, he told her he had never talked about himself so long to anyone before, and she felt a twinge of pity, "for if this was his idea of openness, then I thought he must never have talked about himself to anyone at all."

Ten days after his interview with Priscilla Johnson, Oswald wrote a second, remarkable letter to Robert, who had responded to his first one by telling Lee he hadn't renounced him. Robert was still puzzled about why his brother wanted to live in the Soviet Union. Oswald's lengthy reply began like a political tract and ended with a threat— the tone was much more hostile than the one he had used with the women reporters.

He began by explaining "Why I and my fellow workers and communists would like to see the capitalist government of the U.S. overthrown." He instructed Robert that the American government "supports an economic system which exploits all the workers, a system based upon credit which gives rise to the never-ending cycle of depression, inflation, unlimited speculation (which is the phase America is in now) and war. . . . Look around you, and look at yourself. See the segregation, see the unemployment and what automation is. Remember how you were laid off at Convair?"

He continued:

Ask me and I will tell you I fight for *communism*. . . . I will not say your grandchildren will live under communism, look for yourself at history, look at a world map! America is a dying country, I do not wish to be a part of it, nor do I ever again wish to be used as a tool in its military aggressions.

This should answer your question, and also give you a glimpse of my way of thinking.

So you speak of advantages. Do you think that is why I am here? For personal, material advantages? Happiness is not based on oneself, it does not consist of a small home, of taking and getting. Happiness is taking part in the struggle, where there is no borderline between one's own personal world, and the world in general. . . .

I have been a pro-communist for years and yet I have never met a communist, instead I kept silent and observed, and what I observed plus my Marxist learning brought me here to the Soviet Union.

I want you to understand [that] what I say now, I do not say lightly, or unknowingly. . . .

He advised his brother of the following.

1. In the event of war I would kill *any* American who put a uniform on in defense of the American government—any American.
2. That in my own mind I have no attachments of any kind in the U.S.
3. That I want to, and I shall, live a normal, happy and peaceful life here in the Soviet Union *for the rest of my life.*
4. That my mother and you are (in spite of what the newspaper said) *not* objects of affection, but only examples of workers in the U.S.

On December 17 Robert received a third letter in which Oswald said he wouldn't write again and didn't want Robert to continue writing to him. The letter concluded: "I am starting a new life and I do not wish to have anything to do with the old life. I hope you and your family will always be in good health." It would be hard to imagine a more extreme rejection of his past.

On January 4, 1960, Oswald was informed that his request for

Soviet citizenship had been denied. He was issued an "identity document for stateless persons" and sent to Minsk to start work in a radio factory. If Oswald's statements are to be believed, he never intended to see the United States or his family again.

Although the reasons Oswald gave for his defection were political, his letters to Robert—as well as the undercurrent of his interviews with Aline Mosby and Priscilla Johnson—suggest that there was something highly personal behind his ideology. One of the most curious things about Oswald's sketchy account of his past was his statement concerning the Save the Rosenbergs pamphlet. During the early 1950s American soldiers were fighting a bloody stalemate in Korea and anti-Communists like Senator Joseph McCarthy were riding high. This was the political atmosphere of Oswald's childhood. When the Rosenbergs were executed in 1953, Lee Oswald was *not* about 15 years old, as he had said, but 13. He had been born into an apolitical family in the conservative South. How could a pamphlet about saving the Rosenbergs have gotten this 13-year-old interested in Marxism "from an ideological viewpoint"?

2 ... Marguerite's Son

ARLY one hot August morning in 1939, Robert Edward Lee Oswald was mowing his lawn in New Orleans when he felt a sharp pain in one of his arms. His wife Marguerite gave him an aspirin and called a doctor, but he was dead of a heart attack before the doctor could get there. Marguerite arranged to have him buried the same afternoon —she was seven months pregnant and wanted to avoid any undue strain. Some of her in-laws were appalled by her "coldness" and never spoke to her again.

Lee Harvey Oswald was born on October 18, two months later. Marguerite was 32 years old.

Oswald never spoke much about his childhood. What he did say bore more than a trace of resentment and self-pity. In an autobiographical paragraph he wrote in 1962 he described himself simply as "the son of an Insurance Salesman whose early death left a fair mean streak of independence brought on by neglect." As in many statements people make about themselves to explain who they are, this one may reflect more than he realized. What Richard Snyder and others saw as his insufferable arrogance, Oswald evidently regarded as a "mean streak of independence," a more admirable quality, a proud, deliberate separation from other people. And ultimately he felt he was the person he was because his father died before he was born. If his mother neglected him, this was secondary: she too was a victim of circumstance. And this was precisely the way Marguerite saw herself.

The most significant and revealing thing about Oswald's childhood is how much his personality resembled his mother's. Robert Oswald saw some of Marguerite's worst traits repeated in Lee. Their mother had, as Robert once put it, "an extraordinary idea of her ability and her importance." If she didn't get everything she thought she deserved, it was because circumstances or individuals were against her. Throughout his youth Robert had heard her talk about the hidden motives and malicious actions of other people. She was the type, her older sister Lillian Murret testified, who in any disagreement would always insist she was right. Whenever they quarreled, Lillian wouldn't hear from her again until Marguerite needed "assistance or a place to stay." Lillian explained, "You see, I am forgiving, but she is not." People would say much the same things about Lee Oswald.

Marguerite had also once observed that Robert was like his easygoing father: "He is not opinionated like I am. My older son and Lee are my disposition." And to writer Jean Stafford she admitted, "I should say I'm very outspoken, I'm aggressive, I'm no dope. Let's face it, if you step on my toes I'm gonna fight back, and I don't apologize for that." This was, she added, the way she wanted her boys to be.

When Lee was born, Marguerite already had two sons—John Pic, from her first marriage, who was 8 and Robert who was 5. Her late husband, a collector of insurance premiums, had left her a $10,000 policy, and she began thinking about how she was going to get by once that was gone. In early 1941 she sold her house and bought a smaller one, where she opened Oswald's Notions Shop in the front room, selling sewing supplies and grocery items. This venture failed, and the following year she placed John and Robert in the Bethlehem Children's Home so that she could find work. Lee was too young to be accepted, so she boarded him with Lillian, who was married and had five kids of her own. Lillian liked her nephew, but he was unusual in one respect. Sometimes he would sneak out of her house at night in his pajamas, to be found later in a neighbor's kitchen. "He could slip out of the house like nobody's business," she said. "You could have everything locked up and he would still get out."

After one of her many quarrels with Lillian, Marguerite took Lee out of the Murret home and found a babysitter for him. She told the Warren Commission at one of its hearings, "War had broken out and the Negroes in New Orleans were going into factories and so on and so forth so there is many a job I had to leave in order to stay home and mind Lee until I could get help. . . . So, then at age 3 Lee was placed in the home. I waited patiently for age 3 because I wanted naturally for the brothers to be together."

Oswald was at the children's home with his brothers for thirteen months. The Lutheran orphanage had a relaxed atmosphere and its own school, and the two older boys would remember their stay there as a relatively happy time. Robert, who thought of Lee as his "kid brother" and "stayed pretty close to him," said Lee seemed happy there, too. Marguerite visited often and brought them home on weekends. One day she came by to introduce her sons to an older man she had been dating—Edwin A. Ekdahl from Boston, who was working in New Orleans as an electrical engineer. John Pic recalled, "He was described to us as Yankee, of course. Rather tall, I think he was over 6 feet. He had white hair, wore glasses, very nice man."

Not long after this, Marguerite took Lee out of the home and moved to Dallas, where Ekdahl had been transferred, leaving his brothers to finish the school year. After she and Ekdahl were married in May 1945, he tried to be a father to the boys, and Lee in particular became quite attached to him. That September John and Robert went off for the first of three school years at a military academy in Mississippi. Lee stayed behind, and frequently accompanied Marguerite and Ekdahl on his business trips to places like Boston and Arizona. Ekdahl was making $1000 a month, and they had moved to a comfortable house on a large plot of land in Benbrook, a Fort Worth suburb. But the Ekdahl marriage was shaky from the start. Marguerite complained that her husband was stingy and expected her to account for every penny. There were noisy arguments and several separations. Every time they got back together, Lee seemed elated. Then in the summer of 1947 Marguerite found out that her husband was seeing another woman.

Her reaction was pure Marguerite.

Ekdahl had sent her a telegram saying he'd be late getting back from a business trip. Marguerite told the Warren Commission, "So, I called his office, I . . . knew his secretary, and I was going to tell her that Mr. Ekdahl would be delayed 3 or 4 days. But immediately she said, 'Mrs. Ekdahl, Mr. Ekdahl is not in, he has gone out to lunch.' So, I said . . . 'When will he be back' and so on."

Not having let on to the secretary, Marguerite drove her car that evening to the building where her husband worked, watched him come out, and followed him to an apartment building. She went home and told her son John and a friend of his what had happened. Then she called John McClain, an attorney who lived next door, told him what she had seen, and asked his advice. Marguerite reported:

"He said, 'Mrs. Oswald, just ring the phone. Do you know the woman?'

"And I said, 'Yes.'

" 'Just ring the phone and let him know that you know he is there. . . .' "

She thought about it, but decided against it because "he could leave and say he was just there on business and I wanted to catch him."

"So the kids and I planned that we would say she had a telegram . . . we went up the stairs, I believe it was the second or third floor, and [John's friend] knocked on the door and said, 'Telegram for Mrs. C____. . . .'

"She said, 'Please push it under the door' and I told him no; he said, 'No, you have to sign for it.'

"So with that she opened the door . . . [and] I, my son, and . . . the other young man walked into the room . . . Mrs. C____ had on a negligee, and my husband had his sleeves rolled up and his tie off sitting on a sofa . . . he said, 'Marguerite, Marguerite, you have everything wrong, you have everything wrong.'

"He says, 'Listen to me.'

"I said, 'I don't want to hear one thing. I have seen everything I want to see, this is it."

It might have been a scene from a bedroom farce, but Marguerite's devious and vindictive personality was behind it, manipulating her oldest son and another teenager into taking part in the subterfuge.

According to Robert, "Lee's imagination and love of intrigue was a lot like Mother's. She always had a wild imagination and I think it influenced Lee's view of the world."

In 1948 Ekdahl filed suit for divorce and, Marguerite said, "I thought I was sitting pretty. He didn't have anything on me. I had him for adultery with witnesses and everything and I didn't have an idea that he could sue me for a divorce, but [he] did. . . ." John Pic had to testify for Marguerite and, as he remembers it, Lee was called to the stand but excused by the judge as being too young—he was eight—to know "right from wrong and truth from falsehood." In his complaint, Ekdahl charged that his wife argued incessantly about money, flew into "uncontrollable rages," and threw cookie jars, glasses, and bottles at him. The jury found Marguerite guilty of these "outrages" and granted the divorce, awarding her a mere $1500 settlement.

Although Marguerite attributed their breakup to disagreements over money, a friend of hers, Myrtle Evans, thought her attachment to Lee had something to do with it. She thought Marguerite "spoiled him to death." According to Evans, Marguerite wouldn't discipline Lee or let Ekdahl do it, and Lee demanded so much of her attention that she and Ekdahl never had a chance to be alone. But this mother-son relationship was oddly detached. Lee would go his own way, as she did, and she would observe from a distance. After telling Jean Stafford she had taught her sons to fight back, Marguerite said,

Let me give you one little instance with Lee and the next-door neighbor boy. They were approximately the same age, and if not, they were the same height, and Lee had a dog. He loved his shepherd collie dog. It was named Sunshine. He used to romp in the back yard with his dog and took him every place he went, and this little boy was throwing rocks over the fence at Lee's dog. Well, my kitchen window had a view to the back yard. And I watched my son Lee for approximately three days telling the little boy over the fence he better stop throwing rocks at his dog. Well, I was amused, and I was just waiting to find out what happened. Finally, one day when I came home from work the father called me on the phone. It seemed his son was very badly beaten up— in a child's way. My son Lee had finally taken upon himself, after much patience, I thought, to confront the little boy enough to fight him, and the father didn't approve. I told the father what happened, and since the boys were approximately the same age and height, let them fight their own battles.

While she was at work, Marguerite encouraged Lee to come straight home after school instead of playing with other children. Marguerite insisted he had always been solitary by nature, as she was, and preferred to play alone. "I am not lonely," she said. "But I live to myself." The picture she gives of Oswald at this age—and of her attitude toward him—is vivid and worth closer inspection:

Lee had a normal life as far as I, his mother, is concerned. He had a bicycle, he had everything that other children had.

Lee had wisdom without education. From a very small child—I have said this before, sir, and I have publicly stated this in 1959 [when she was interviewed after his defection]—Lee seemed to know the answers to things without schooling. That type child, in a way, is bored with schooling, because he is a little advanced.

Lee used to climb on top of the roof with binoculars, looking at the stars. He was reading [astronomy]. Lee knew about any and every animal there was. He studied animals. All of their feeding habits, sleeping habits. . . . And Lee read history books, books too deep for a child his age. At age 9—he was always instructed not to contact me at work unless it was an emergency, because my work came first—he called me at work and said, "Mother, Queen Elizabeth's baby has been born."

He broke the rule to let me know that Queen Elizabeth's baby had been born. Nine years old. That was important to him. He liked things of that sort.

He loved comics, read comic books. He loved television programs. But most of all he loved the news on radio and television. If he was in the midst of a story, a film—he would turn it off for news. That was important. . . . Lee read very, very important things. . . .

Yet he played Monopoly, played baseball.

He belonged to the Y. He used to go swimming. He would come by work with his head wet, and I would say, "Hurry home, honey, you are going to catch cold."

And I considered that, sir, a very normal life.

While the divorce was pending, Marguerite moved to a small house next to the railroad tracks. For John, it meant they "were back down in the lower class again." Soon they relocated, first to a one-bedroom house where John and Robert slept in a screened-in porch while their mother and Lee shared the bedroom, and then to another house in Fort Worth, so that Marguerite could be nearer her job at a department store. Later she began selling insurance.

Marguerite had taken the older boys out of the military academy. They could have stayed on with the aid of scholarships, and wanted to, but their mother reminded them that they were orphans and she could no longer afford it. Robert later wrote, "We learned, very early, that we were a burden. By the time we were teenagers, she felt that we should take over some of her burden." John was 16 when she told him to quit school and get a job. Eventually, she talked him into joining the Marine Corps Reserve to bring in a little more income. He was still under age, but she signed an affidavit giving him an earlier date of birth. As John saw it, "Money was her God," and "Every time she met anyone she would remind them she was a widow with three children. I didn't feel she had it any tougher than a lot of people walking around."

According to Robert, John Pic was "so resentful of Mother that he simply ignored her as much as he could." He went back to high school on his own, signing his report cards himself and working at a shoe store part-time. Three days before he was to graduate in 1950, he enlisted in the Coast Guard. During the following year Marguerite wrote him several letters containing a repetitive theme: "Try and help as much as possible. After all, my struggle to keep what we have will also help you boys," and "I have four more payments on the car and then that struggle will be over."

With John gone, it was Robert's turn to quit school and go to work. He, too, went back to school and completed his junior year, working after school and Saturdays at the A&P. In July 1952 he joined the Marines. Soon after he left, Lee bought a copy of the Marine Corps handbook and began studying it. He was only 12, but he planned to join the service too, as soon as he was old enough.

The month after Robert left home, Marguerite and Lee Oswald

loaded their belongings into her 1948 Dodge and moved to New York City. John was stationed on Ellis Island and was living with his wife, a woman from New York, and their infant son in her mother's apartment on East 92nd Street. Marguerite said she wanted to meet her new daughter-in-law and first grandchild. John recalled that the day they arrived, Lee was waiting for him at the subway exit about ten blocks from the apartment and seemed glad to see him. He took a few days' leave to show him around the city, and during that time he noticed a change in his younger brother: Lee had definitely become "the boss." If he decided to do something, he did it. Pic thought he had no respect for his mother at all.

As time went by, tension developed at the Pics' apartment when Marguerite made no move to help pay the grocery bills or find a place of her own. When Pic's wife was interviewed by the FBI after the assassination, she still remembered how Lee kept damaging their bookcase by putting beverage glasses down on it. She also remembered that one day she asked Lee not to turn on a TV set Marguerite had brought with them and Lee pulled out "a small pocketknife with a blade opened." He moved toward her, she said, and she backed off. When Pic got home that night, she told him about it. Marguerite claimed it wasn't anything serious, simply a misunderstanding. John asked Lee what had happened and immediately "he became real hostile toward me." After that, whenever John tried to talk to him "he ignored me, and I was never able to get to the kid again." Warren Commission lawyer Lee J. Rankin questioned Marguerite about the incident:

"Was there any time that you recall . . . a threat of Lee Oswald against Mrs. Pic with a knife or anything like that? Do you remember that?"

"Yes, I do," she replied. "I am glad you said that. My daughter-in-law was very upset. The very first time we went there . . . we were not welcome. And immediately it was asked what did we plan to do as soon as we put our foot in the house. . . . I had made it plain to John Edward that I was going to have a place of my own, that we were just coming there to get located.

"My daughter-in-law resented the fact that her mother—this went on before I got there—that her mother had to leave the house and go visit a sister so I could come. . . . I had never met my daughter-in-law. She didn't like me and she didn't like Lee.

"So she—what is the word to say—not picked on the child, but she showed her displeasure. . . .

"So there was, I think now—it was not a kitchen knife—it was a little pocketknife, a child's knife that Lee had. So she hit Lee . . . I remember this distinctly, because I remember how awful I thought Marjory was about this. Lee had the knife in his hand. He was whittling, because John Edward whittled ships and taught Lee to whittle ships. He puts them in the glass, you know. And he was whittling when this incident occurred. And that is what it occurred about, because there was scraps of wood on the floor.

"So when she attacked the child. . . . she made the statement to my son that we had to leave, that Lee tried to use a knife on her.

"Now, I say that is not true, gentlemen. You can be provoked into something. And because of the fact that he was whittling, and had the knife in his hand, they struggled.

"He did not use the knife—he had an opportunity to use the knife.

"But it wasn't a kitchen knife or a big knife. It was a little knife. So I will explain it that way, sir. So immediately then I started to look for a place."

She found a job as assistant manager of a Lerner dress shop and took a basement apartment, one big room, in the Bronx. As soon as she could find a larger place they moved again, to East 179th Street. Originally, Lee Oswald was enrolled in a Lutheran private school and then switched, after several weeks of irregular attendance, to a seventh-grade class in Junior High School No. 117. By the following January he had been absent 47 out of the 64 school days, and he finally stopped going entirely. He later explained that he preferred being by himself and had "many more important things to do."

At first he would get dressed as though he were going to school, but after his mother left for work he would stay home all day reading or watching television. Sometimes he would go to the public library or ride the subways. Once he was picked up by a truant officer at the Bronx Zoo—he was reportedly surly and called the officer a "damn

Yankee." When a teacher came to the Oswald apartment to ask him to return to class, he said he would think about it.

Eventually, truancy charges were brought against him, and in March 1953 he was ordered to appear before a juvenile judge. On the appointed day, Marguerite showed up at court alone and told Judge Delany her son had refused to come with her. As a result, a warrant was issued, and at a hearing in April, at which he did appear, Lee Harvey Oswald was remanded to Youth House, a juvenile detention center, for three weeks of evaluation so the court could determine whether or not he needed psychiatric help.

The old Youth House was on Manhattan's Lower East Side between First and Second avenues on Twelfth Street, among tenement buildings. Oswald was examined by a physician and then a psychologist. The latter, Irving Sokolow, reported:

> He achieved an I.Q. of 118 on the Wechsler Intelligence Scale for Children (abb.) indicating present intellectual functioning in the upper range of bright normal intelligence. All his scores were above the average for his age group, appreciably so in the verbalization of abstract concepts and in the assembly of commonly recognizable objects. His method of approach was generally an easy, facile and highly perceptive one. Although presumably disinterested in school subjects he operates on a much higher than average level. . . .
>
> The Human Figure Drawings are empty, poor characterizations of [a] person approximately the same age as the subject. They reflect a considerable amount of impoverishment in the social and emotional areas. . . . He exhibits some difficulty in relationship to the maternal figure suggesting more anxiety in this area than in any other.
>
> Under conditions of emotional stress and strain he appears increasingly defensive . . . and in general incapable of constructing an effective ego-defense.

Afterward, a social worker named Evelyn Strickman talked to him at length and wrote an insightful report in which we are able to see Oswald's own assessment of his situation, and hers. She began by describing him as "a seriously detached, withdrawn youngster of thirteen" who answered questions, "but volunteered almost nothing about himself spontaneously."

By persistent questioning, the information received from Lee was as follows: his father died before he was born and he doesn't know a thing about him. He has no curiosity about his father, says he never missed having one, and never thought to ask about him. His mother was left with three children. . . . Lee said his mother supported them by working as an insurance broker and she was on the go all day long. He doesn't remember anyone else taking care of him and he thinks she either left him in the care of his older brothers or . . . that he shifted for himself. She would leave early in the morning and come home around seven or eight at night after a hard day's work. Occasionally she took Lee with her on these trips, but he wrinkled his nose and said it was very boring because she was always making stops, going into houses and trying to sell people things, while he waited for her in the car.

He told her that after his brothers went into the service, his mother decided to move to New York "to be near John." His story of their stay with the Pics was similar to his mother's, but he didn't tell her why they left.

Questioning revealed that while Lee felt John was glad to see them, his sister-in-law . . . was unhappy about their sharing the apartment until they could find a place of their own and she made them feel unwelcome. Lee had to sleep in the living room during this period although there were five rooms in the apartment and he admitted that this made him feel as he always did feel with grownups—that there was no room for him.

After they relocated, the report continued, "He withdrew into a completely solitary and detached existence where he did as he wanted and he didn't have to live by any rules or come into contact with people."

When questioned about his mother's reaction to this he said she told him to go to school, "but she never did anything about it." When he was asked if he wished that she would do something he nodded and finally emerged with the fact that he . . . felt his mother "never gave a damn" for him. . . . When Lee and his mother are home together, he is not uncomfortable with her, but they never have anything to say to each other. She never punishes him because she is the kind of person who just lets things ride. It was hard for him to say whether she acted the same way towards his brothers, because he never noticed. Although his brothers were not as detached as his mother was, he experienced rejection from them, too, and they always pushed him away when he tried to accompany them. They never met any of his needs. He said he had to be "my own father" because there was never any one there for him.

When Miss Strickman expressed her understanding of his lonely situation, he denied he really felt lonely, and she noted, "Questioning elicited the information that he feels almost as if there is a veil between him and other people through which they cannot reach him, but he prefers this veil to remain intact." When this revelation prompted her to inquire about his fantasy life, he responded by pointing out "this is my own business."

He agreed to answer questions if he wanted to, rejecting those which upset him and acknowledged fantasies about being powerful, and sometimes hurting or killing people, but refused to elaborate on this. None of these fantasies involved his mother, incidentally. He also acknowledged dreaming but refused to talk about the dreams other than to admit that they sometimes contained violence, but he insisted that they were pleasant.

Asked about his future, he told her he wanted to return home, and assured her that he would run away if he were placed in a boarding school as an alternative. He admitted that home "offered him very little," but he said that's how he wanted it. Being away from home meant "a loss of his freedom and privacy." Miss Strickman wrote, "If he could have his own way, he would like to be on his own and join the Service. While he feels that living that close to other people and following a routine would be distasteful he would 'steel' himself to do it."

Miss Strickman also interviewed Marguerite—she described her as a "smartly dressed, gray-haired woman, very self-possessed and alert and superficially affable," but essentially a "defensive, rigid, self-involved person" who had almost no understanding of Lee's behavior and of the "protective shell" he had drawn around himself. She wrote, "I honestly don't think that she sees him as a person at all but simply as an extension of herself." When she remarked to Marguerite "that it must have been difficult for her to be both parents as well as the breadwinner, proudly she said she had never found it so. She felt she was a very independent, self-reliant person, who never needed help from anyone, and who pulled herself up by her own bootstraps. Her mother died when she was only two, and her father raised six children with the help of housekeepers in a very poor section of New Orleans of mixed racial groups. She always had 'high-falutin' ideas and managed to make something of herself."

Marguerite made it clear she believed her son Lee had been treated unjustly:

> Mrs. O. railed and railed against NYC laws which she felt in a large measure were responsible for the way Lee acted. She said that when he first began to truant, the truant officer picked him up in a police car and took him back to school and she thought that was just atrocious. . . . She said she felt Lee could be stubborn and defiant . . . as she would be if someone kept stressing with him the way the truant officer had with Lee that he had to go to school because the NYC law said so.

When it came time to write her recommendation, Evelyn Strickman faced a dilemma. She felt that if he returned home and got counseling, his mother's "attitude about social workers, probation, etc., would inevitably communicate itself to the boy" and that if he started showing improvement in therapy she was "one of these mothers who would have to break it up." On the other hand, Lee was so strongly against placement she doubted much could be accomplished by sending him away, either. She noticed that he had become totally withdrawn at Youth House: "I have spent some time watching him with other boys and he doesn't participate or mingle in any way but keeps himself completely aloof."

The following day Oswald was seen by the chief psychiatrist, Renatus Hartogs, who had gathered the reports on his desk and whose task it was to put a label on Oswald's behavior and decide what to do with him. Hartogs found him to be a tense and evasive boy who disliked talking about himself and his feelings. Lee repeated to Hartogs his belief that his mother and brothers showed little interest in him, and he remarked, "I dislike everybody." In Hartogs' view, Lee Oswald was quite disturbed emotionally—but definitely not psychotic: "He was in full contact with reality," and there was "no indication of psychotic mental changes." Lee's problem, he believed, came from the impact of his "emotional isolation and deprivation." The psychiatrist's diagnosis was "a personality pattern disturbance with schizoid features and passive–aggressive tendencies." As he later explained,

> The "schizoid features" were apparent in his extreme withdrawal and the depth to which he seemed to live in fantasy. "Passive–aggressive tendencies" is a term used to describe an apparently compliant manner which hides, however, deep anger.

Hartogs recommended that Oswald be allowed to go home on the condition that both he and his mother seek help from a child guidance clinic. If that didn't work out, placement in a juvenile home for further treatment could come later.

Released from Youth House on May 7, 1953, Oswald appeared in court again and was put on parole with the understanding that he would return to school and attend regularly. Mrs. Oswald was told that the case had been referred to a family agency for counseling, and Lee's probation officer recorded, "Both mother and boy promised to cooperate."

The Save the Rosenbergs pamphlet probably fell into Oswald's hands three days later—ironically, on Mother's Day.

Julius and Ethel Rosenberg were on death row in upstate New York. Their execution was set for June 19. During May and June, supporters of *The Worker,* the Communist party daily, were canvassing neighborhoods all over the city in a subscription drive. They gave away copies in a housing project in the Bronx and simultaneously tried to enlist help in the Rosenberg campaign. On Mother's Day, May 10, women who had been recruited through an ad in *The Worker* passed out leaflets for the New York Committee for Clemency for the Rosenbergs on city street corners. (This was the only instance I could find, in back copies of the *New York Times* and *The Worker,* of city-wide distribution of leaflets on the streets—there may have been others. But the fact that women volunteers were specifically recruited for this one suggests, at least, that this may have been the day the "old lady" handed him a pamphlet. Possibly Oswald was on his way to the Bronx Zoo or the library or the subway station that Sunday—the entrance to any of those places would probably have been a good spot for a demonstration.)

It isn't known exactly what was in the pamphlet, but the campaign for clemency had only two themes. The first was that the Rosenbergs were innocent victims of an unjust court. In *The Worker* they were described as martyrs who were being lynched by a hanging judge and by President Eisenhower, who refused to commute their sentences. The other theme was implicit in the choice of women for a Mother's Day demonstration—implicit, too, whenever the names of the Rosenbergs' sons Michael and Robert were mentioned. Michael was 10; Robert was four years younger. Their parents were going to be executed, leaving them orphans. It's unlikely that a campaign could have been designed any better to strike Oswald's nature and circumstances. "I looked at that paper," he told Aline Mosby six years later, "and I still remember it for some reason, I don't know why."

It wasn't that he had compassion for the Rosenbergs. Oswald never had a talent for empathy. An acquaintance of his in Dallas, an intelligent and sensitive man, believed that Oswald saw people as cardboard figures, with the single exception of his daughter June. There is evidence for this in the Youth House records. He had no curiosity about his dead father. He didn't know how his mother treated his brothers because he never noticed. If Robert and John, five and eight years older, respectively, didn't always want a kid brother tagging along, they were rejecting him. They "never met any of his needs." Whether through force of example or inherited disposition, Lee Oswald had acquired an egocentricity resembling his mother's. What made the

Rosenberg pamphlet memorable to him, surely, was that he saw *himself* in it—the "innocent victim" of a New York court. He held in his hand a message that said to him: Here are allies you can identify with. Here are people who feel as you do about the legal system.

The more one takes this period of his life into account, the more plausible the story he told in Moscow becomes. The pamphlet got him started reading socialist literature, he said, and he saw that the description it gave of capitalist society matched his own observations. When he talked about "watching the treatment of workers in New York and observing the fact that they are exploited," we may assume he was speaking primarily about Marguerite. During the year and a half they lived there, she resigned or was fired from at least three different jobs. When Evelyn Strickman saw him at Youth House, his resentment was aimed at his mother. She was always busy selling insurance and when she came home she didn't even make him a decent supper. She never gave a damn for him. By the time he spoke with Priscilla Johnson, his view of Marguerite had changed, and his explanation of why he became a Marxist shifted the blame to her employers: "At 15 I was looking for something that would give me the key to my environment. My mother has been a worker all her life. All her life she had to produce profit for the capitalists. She is a good example of what happens to workers in the United States." It was as though new battle lines had been drawn. The uncaring mother had become a "good example" of what capitalism does to people. It followed that if he could see her as the victim of a political system, he now had a more secure emotional footing—and a way to fight back. Thus, Oswald's anger and resentment were easily subsumed by a radical political outlook.

Oswald would always be reluctant to talk about himself and his feelings, but he would become articulate and combative about politics. In his second letter to Robert from Moscow, he rejected not only capitalism but his family as well, vowing to kill any American who fought against Russia. The glaring ideology of that letter initially hides the person who wrote it, but using his past as a filter, we see the detached 13-year-old who resented his mother's financial struggle, who felt without reason that his brothers had neglected him, who admitted having fantasies about being powerful and sometimes hurting and killing people. He would insist the Rosenberg pamphlet got him interested in Marxism from "an ideological viewpoint." He would protest that his decision to defect was unemotional, that it was motivated by ideology alone, not by personal hardship. This was a sore point with him. But if this reconstruction is correct, his turn toward politics could hardly have been more firmly entangled in his emotional life.

That is not to say that he was insincere when he said he defected for political reasons, or that he wasn't actually committed to Marxism, as he understood it. On the contrary, one of his Marine Corps buddies, Kerry Thornley, said he thought Oswald had an "irrevocable conviction" when it came to his political beliefs:

> I think you could sit down and argue with him for a number of years . . . and I don't think you could have changed his mind . . . unless you knew why he believed it in the first place. I certainly don't. I don't think with any kind of formal argument you could have shaken that conviction. And that is why I say [it was] irrevocable.

Oswald's chance encounter with the Rosenberg pamphlet just after he got out of juvenile court is the sort of coincidence any decent novelist would scorn as being too melodramatic, too pat. Evidently, history doesn't make that type of editorial judgment. When I was doing some background reading on the Rosenberg case, I ran across another coincidence, another one of history's whims—Julius Rosenberg's account of his own introduction to politics, at age 15 in New York:

> I stopped to listen to a speaker at a street corner meeting. . . . His topic was to win freedom for Tom Mooney, [a] labor leader who was imprisoned on a frame-up.
> That night I was reading a pamphlet I bought from the speaker giving the facts of this case and the next day I went and contributed 50 cents. Then I began to distribute the pamphlets and collect signatures on a Mooney petition from school friends and neighbors.

In *The Implosion Conspiracy,* Louis Nizer quoted the passage above and remarked, "It is curious how a purely accidental incident can change the course of a person's life. If Julius Rosenberg had not stopped to listen to the Mooney orator, he may not have been seated in a defendant's chair in the courtroom eighteen years later."

We return now to the summer of 1953, to pick up Oswald's trail. In July Robert Oswald came to New York City on a ten-day furlough to visit his family, and Lee showed him around. After taking him by subway from the Bronx to Times Square, Lee guided him to the top of the Empire State Building and mapped a tour for him from Wall Street to the Museum of Natural History. Typically, Lee didn't open up to him about his recent troubles. Nobody else in the family mentioned Lee's confinement or his clash with Mrs. Pic to Robert, either. (As far as one can tell from the Warren records, Oswald never talked about his court appearances and his stay at Youth House with anyone, ever. As he wrote Robert from Moscow, "You really don't know anything about me.") Robert noticed some tension between John and their mother, but that was nothing unusual, no different from their past relationship.

Earlier that year, Marguerite had told John that the school authorities suggested Oswald be seen by a psychiatrist but that she couldn't get him to go. She said he refused to see a "nut doctor or head shrinker." John advised her to just *take* him, but he never heard any more about it.

In September 1953 Lee Oswald entered the eighth grade in the Bronx. The following month one of his teachers reported:

> During the past 2 weeks practically every subject teacher has complained to me about the boy's behavior. He had consistently refused to salute the flag during early morning exercises. . . . He spends most of his time sailing paper planes around the room. When we spoke to him about his behavior, his attitude was belligerent. [When] I offered to help him, he brushed out with, "I don't need anybody's help!"

Another court hearing was scheduled on October 29, but Marguerite telephoned the probation officer to say she couldn't make it. (The hearing had already been postponed once for the same reason, and the

Warren Report notes that she was apparently afraid that Lee might be "retained in some sort of custody" if he showed up.) Justice Sicher continued his parole and suggested a referral to the Berkshire Industrial Farm or Children's Village. At about the same time, Marguerite went to talk to school authorities about Lee, and subsequently his classroom behavior improved.

On January 4, 1954, a representative of the Big Brothers organization came to the Oswald apartment to offer its help. He reported that Mrs. Oswald was cordial but informed him that Lee was doing fine, going to the Y every Saturday, and needed no further counseling. She told him she was considering returning South, and he reminded her she would have to get the court's consent before leaving its jurisdiction. Several days later, Marguerite packed and left with her son for New Orleans.

3...Dropping Out, Joining Up

ON arriving in New Orleans that January, Marguerite and 14-year-old Lee moved in with her sister, Lillian, until they found another place to live—an apartment managed by Marguerite's old friend Myrtle Evans. To Marguerite's way of thinking, bringing Lee back to the South had averted a tragedy. The anger he had revealed in New York receded from view. To his relatives and Evans, Oswald seemed quiet and studious, often going off into his bedroom to read or listen to the radio. His cousin Marilyn Murret, who was 25, recalled seeing him read encyclopedias "like somebody else would read a novel." He returned to school, and the disciplinary problems didn't reappear.

But Lillian noticed a strange aloofness. The Murrets were Catholic, and on Fridays he came over to have seafood, which he liked. Then on Saturdays he came back, and Mrs. Murret would give him money to rent a bike even though he could have borrowed one from her children. "My children had a bike, but it seemed like he wanted to go up in the park rather than ride their bicycles, and sometimes I would have to . . . give him more money so that he could keep his bike another hour." She bought him some school clothes "so he would look presentable to go to school, you know, whatever a boy needs, and when we gave them to him, he said, 'Well, why are you all doing this for me?' And we said, 'Well, Lee, for one thing, we love you, and another thing we want you to look nice when you go to school, like the other children.' " But he offered no thanks, and later on he told her, "I don't need anything from anybody." Another time he told her he didn't want to go to school anymore because he already knew everything they had to teach him. Like his mother, Lillian thought —Marguerite "didn't think she needed anybody either."

Sometime after returning to New Orleans Oswald was beaten up by a gang of white boys for sitting in the black section of a city bus. Marguerite and Lillian assumed he must have forgotten the buses were segregated while he was in New York, and the Warren Report says he probably acted "out of ignorance." But Marilyn Murret thought it was possible he had acted "defiantly."

After a falling-out with Myrtle Evans in the spring of 1955, Marguerite moved to an apartment in the French Quarter. There Oswald spent time playing pool and darts with a junior high classmate named Edward Voebel, but made no other friends. In Voebel's opinion, "people just didn't interest him generally" because he was "living in his own world."

One day Oswald shocked Voebel by showing him a plastic gun and glass cutter and outlining a plan to steal a pistol from a store on Rampart Street. When Oswald went to reconnoiter the store, Voebel tagged along and pointed out a burglar alarm wire running through the shop's plate glass window. Afterward Oswald said no more about his idea. Since there had recently been several jewel robberies on Canal Street in which store windows were cut, it occurred to Voebel that Lee wanted to "look big among the guys" by doing something similar.

Had he gone ahead with this scheme, it would have been what policemen call a copycat crime. Voebel's testimony thus provides a revealing glimpse of young Oswald's thinking. At age 15 one of his fantasies was to imitate a daring crime described in the local press.

In June Oswald filled out a personal history form at school, listing his plans after high school as "military service" and "undecided." That summer he joined the Civil Air Patrol and attended several meetings at which one of the leaders was an eccentric pilot named

David Ferrie. Ferrie would become a central figure in many conspiracy theories.

It was during this period, when Oswald was evidently looking for excitement, that he began to think of himself as a Marxist. In Moscow he would tell Aline Mosby:

> Then we moved to New Orleans and I discovered one book in the library, "Das Kapital." It was what I'd been looking for.
> It was like a very religious man opening the Bible for the first time.
> I read the "Manifesto." It got me interested. I found some dusty back shelves in the New Orleans library, you know, I had to remove some front books to get at the books.
> I started to study Marxist economic theories. I could see the impoverishment of the masses before my own eyes in my own mother, and I could see the capitalists. I thought the worker's life could be better.
> I continued to indoctrinate myself for five years. My mother knew I was reading books but she didn't know what they were about.

(In fact, Marguerite did know, but said nothing to him about it.) At this point Oswald's only work experience consisted of about ten Saturdays as a stock boy in a shoe store where his mother worked.

In the fall of 1955 Lee entered 10th grade at Warren Easton High School, but dropped out after his birthday a month later. He wrote a letter to school authorities to which he signed his mother's name:

> To whom it may concern,
> Because we are moving to San Diego in the middle of this month Lee must quit school now. Also, please send by him any papers such as his birth certificate that you may have. Thank you.
> Sincerely,
> Mrs. M. Oswald

As he often did, Oswald had woven a part of the truth into a deception. He was planning to join the Marines and go to their training center in San Diego. Since he was just 16, Marguerite signed a false affidavit saying he was a year older. But the recruiting officer must have seen through the ruse, for Oswald had to wait another year to get out on his own.

Early in 1956 Oswald went to work for the Pfisterer Dental Laboratory making deliveries around town with an 18-year-old named Palmer McBride. The two young men shared an interest in classical music and astronomy and would visit one another after work. McBride soon learned that Lee Oswald "was very serious about the virtues of Communism, and discussed these virtues at every opportunity." Oswald's "central theme seemed to be that the workers in the world would one day rise up and throw off their chains." Oswald showed McBride the library copies of *Das Kapital* and the *Communist Manifesto* he kept in his room, and McBride thought he "seemed quite proud to have them." On another occasion, after they began discussing President Eisenhower, McBride recalled, "He then made a statement to the effect that he would like to kill President Eisenhower because he was exploiting the working class." McBride added, "This statement was not made in jest."

In April 1956 Senator James Eastland of Mississippi held lengthy subcommittee hearings in New Orleans to investigate alleged Communist activity in the area. The hearings were covered by the local press, especially after a defense attorney was ejected from one of the sessions. Eastland told a television interviewer that there were, or had been, Communist cells in Louisiana.

It was apparently about this time that McBride and Oswald got to know William Wulf, a history major and president of an astronomy club they were interested in joining. During a visit to Wulf's home Oswald, who had been looking at some of the books in Wulf's library, started talking about communism. McBride recalled that Oswald began telling Wulf "about the glories of the Worker's State and saying that the United States Government was not telling the truth about Soviet Russia." As Wulf remembered it, Oswald

started expounding the Communist doctrine and saying that he was highly interested in communism, that communism was the only way of life for the worker, et cetera, and then came out with a statement that he was looking for a Communist cell in town to join but he couldn't find any. He was a little dismayed at this, and said that he couldn't find [one] that would show any interest in him as a Communist.

According to Wulf, Oswald "was actually militant on the idea, and I can repeat that he expressed his belief that he could be a good Communist, he could help the Communist Party out, if he could find the . . . Party [and] join it." At this point,

we were kind of arguing back and forth about the situation, and my father came in the room, heard what we were arguing on communism, [saw] that this boy was loudmouthed, boisterous, and asked him to leave . . . and that is the last I have seen or spoken with Oswald.

Wulf concluded that Oswald was "looking for something to belong to."

On another occasion Oswald had tried to talk McBride into joining the Communist party with him.[1] At a time when most adolescent males were thinking about cars and girls, Oswald's fantasy life involved a pistol and an unrequited romance with the Communist party. As a child, one of his favorite TV shows had been "I Led Three Lives," an anti-Communist program that stressed the supposedly clandestine and subversive nature of Party work. This kind of life—being an outsider and secretly fighting the authorities—would likely have appealed to him.

The patterns laid down during adolescence shaped Oswald's later behavior. Evidently, he had already begun to identify more closely with the political world than with his immediate environment. One might wonder why this should be so. Psychiatrist and author Edwin Weinstein believes that many potential assassins take up a political cause to give themselves a sense of identity. Several other American assassins have identified strongly with a political group—John Wilkes Booth with the Confederacy, Sirhan Sirhan with the Palestinians, and so on. This identification may take the place of close relationships with relatives and friends—in effect, the cause becomes the assassin's family or "pseudo-community." More important, however, the typical assassin often has a grandiose self-image that allows him to see himself as a player on the world political stage. For most people, President Eisenhower was a remote figure somewhere above them; Oswald projected himself onto Eisenhower's level, as someone who wanted to punish what he saw as an abuse of power.

And yet, classifying Oswald as a typical assassin doesn't go very far toward explaining him. There is another model that may throw more light on his character, or at least one side of it. The episode Voebel recounted about the pistol foreshadowed the fact that Oswald ended his life as someone accused of committing two murders with firearms. In 1978 there was a brief stir in the press about a three-volume work entitled *The Criminal Personality* by psychiatrist Samuel Yochelson and his associate, psychologist Stanton Samenow. The work was the result of a study Yochelson had instituted at St. Elizabeths Hospital in Washington, D.C., a federal psychiatric hospital where felons judged to be criminally insane are treated. (John Hinckley, Reagan's attacker, is now confined there.) Yochelson and Samenow examined 250 young men who were habitual felons, having them record their thoughts daily on tape and interviewing both the inmates and their relatives. *The Criminal Personality* presents their provocative conclusions, which I'll attempt to summarize.

Yochelson and Samenow contend that all habitual criminals, of whatever category, share many specific character traits from early childhood. In their view, the typical felon is unusually self-centered and secretive. At an early age the criminal-to-be "wraps himself in a mantle of secrecy," as Samenow puts it, and "sees himself as unique." He conceals his ideas and activities from his family because he doesn't want to be interfered with. He is chronically restless, dissatisfied, and angry. He often gets into trouble for school truancy. Violation becomes a means of getting excitement; normal life seems boring. Listening to the tapes, the authors discovered that their subjects spent a good deal of time fantasizing about potential crimes they would never commit—merely thinking about a crime was itself exciting.

Whatever crimes they did commit, Yochelson and Samenow's subjects saw themselves as good, decent people. An inmate would usually justify his behavior by describing himself as a victim of his environment. He sees himself as superior to others, capable of great things.

He wants to be Number One, to come out on top, but he expects instant success and considers schoolwork and most jobs beneath him. If he joins a sports team, he wants to be the captain and run the show. (The authors describe a prison football team as consisting of eleven quarterbacks.)

Highly manipulative, the criminal described here sees other people as pawns. Even as a child, he rejects close personal relationships. He is basically a loner, because his view of reality is totally egocentric. He feels he owns the world. The world must conform to his demands, not the other way around. Lying comes as naturally as breathing. "If he goes to a grocery store," says Samenow, "he will say it's the Safeway even if he intends to go to Grand Union." He feels he is right, and others must see things on his terms. As one inmate wryly put it, paraphrasing Descartes, "I think; therefore, it is."

When held accountable, "the criminal believes he has been wronged, that he has been obstructed in the exercise of his rights and privileges."

Although he has broken the law, the law now must be inviolate when invoked in his behalf. The breaker of laws becomes a constitutionalist. There is *no inconsistency* in this, from the criminal's viewpoint. In breaking the law, he exercised the freedom to do as he wanted. He will now use the law to achieve the same freedom, which is being denied him [emphasis in the original].

Assuming that this unflattering portrait is accurate, how did the St. Elizabeths inmates get this way? Yochelson and Samenow could find no cause. Although they had expected to find the root cause in family or social influences, they discovered that their subjects came from all kinds of backgrounds and, in many cases, had siblings who were "straight." These authors concluded that the criminal freely chooses his way of life in his unending quest for power, control, and excitement. They noted that some people with this type of personality were attracted to radical political movements of the left or the right—in their view, for the same reasons they were drawn to crime. "Although he may forcefully present himself as a spokesman for the oppressed, he is using his cause as a vehicle for self-aggrandizement. . . . For those who take direct action, the excitement of the event outweighs the merit of the cause."

The St. Elizabeths study is highly controversial and its findings have been rejected by many criminologists. One suspects there is something more than "free choice" involved in the criminal lifestyle. But the personality profile outlined above appears to describe Lee Oswald remarkably well. For one thing, this model at least provides a framework for looking again at Oswald's breathtaking arrogance— for instance, the manner in which he threatened to give away military secrets at the U.S. Embassy and then loudly complained that the embassy had acted illegally in refusing to let him sign away his citizenship. Oswald expected his adversaries to abide by the letter of the law, whereas he did as he pleased.

However, despite the foregoing analysis, it ought to be remembered that Oswald was an individual, not a type. Throughout his life, none of his acquaintances saw him as dangerous or as a criminal. For the most part, his teenage years were mundane—he often rode a bike in the park or went to museums. Even McBride remained friendly, despite Lee's hangup on Marxism. The cumulative details of his life reveal more about him than any category we might use to explain him.

In July 1956 Marguerite took Lee to live in Fort Worth with Robert, who had just gotten out of the Marines. That fall he entered the 10th grade for the second time, and a classmate recalled that Oswald tried to get him interested in Marxism, too. Oswald went out for the B football team, but was kicked off the squad for refusing to run laps with the other players. (Robert later commented, "He usually wanted to be 'the boss' or not play at all. He was like Mother in this respect.") Soon he dropped out of school again.

On October 3, 1956, young Oswald wrote the Socialist Party of America:

Dear Sirs;
    I am sixteen years of age and would like more information about your youth League, I would like to know if there is a branch in my area, how

to join, etc. I am a Marxist, and have been studying socialist principles for well over fifteen months. I am very interested in your Y.P.S.L.[2]

Later that month, after his seventeenth birthday, he enlisted in the Marines.

4 . . . The Marxist Marine

SOME critics of the Warren Report have found it strange indeed that
an avowed Marxist should want to join the U.S. Marine Corps. Robert thought his brother saw "an escape from the drabness of school,
a chance to lead his own life, and an opportunity to impress the world.
. . . To him, military service meant freedom." John Pic was blunter.
He thought his half-brother joined up largely to get out from under
"the yoke of oppression from my mother." Oswald himself once said
that he enlisted not because he was a patriot but because he wanted
"to get away from the drudgery" and see the world.

Whatever his reasons for enlisting, Oswald's career in the Marines
would show a development of the same pattern of behavior we've
already seen—problems with authority, a good deal of secretive
scheming, and dramatic incidents in which he tried to manipulate or
outwit the system.

On aptitude tests during basic training Oswald scored significantly
above the Corps average in reading and vocabulary, and significantly
below in arithmetic and pattern analysis. In a six-week course on
aviation fundamentals, he finished forty-sixth in a class of fifty-four.
As usual, he kept to himself, doing a lot of serious reading. During
combat training in early 1957 Oswald shared a tent with Allen R.
Felde, who recalled that Oswald constantly talked about politics. He
said that Oswald espoused "the cause of the working-man" and be-

lieved the American intervention in Korea had resulted in one million needless deaths for which he held Presidents Truman and Eisenhower responsible.

After being trained as a radar controller, Oswald was shipped overseas to Japan in September. At the Atsugi base twenty miles west of Tokyo he began work in the radar room, where he often plotted the course of America's U-2 planes. The U-2 was an extremely light jet that could achieve altitudes close to 100,000 feet. U-2s were then operating at American bases in Europe and the Far East, ostensibly to collect weather information. Their principal purpose, however, was to gather military intelligence. Lone U-2s began "straying" over Communist territory in 1956—at the touch of a button seven cameras, mounted under the plane, took continuous, high-resolution pictures of the ground below. They were doing the work eventually taken over by spy satellites. Several of Oswald's co-workers later remembered seeing these strange-looking glider-like planes take off and land. In their briefings, Oswald and the other men were told that the U-2 was a top-secret reconnaissance project which they were not to discuss with anyone outside their unit.

Oswald seemed to take pride in his work and would bristle whenever a young officer tried to second-guess or correct him. Being resentful of authority was almost second nature among the enlisted men, but Daniel Patrick Powers, who had been with Oswald since their technical training, thought Oswald wasn't resentful of authority *per se:* "he was resentful of the position of authority that he could not command."

Oswald began gathering with his fellow Marines in some of the cheap bars near the base and apparently had his first sexual experience with a Japanese bar girl. Then he started dating a beautiful young Japanese woman who was a hostess at a Tokyo bar. When the time approached for his unit to be shipped out to the Philippines in November 1957, Oswald grazed his left arm with a .22 caliber bullet from a derringer he had kept in his locker. A barracks-mate, George Wilkens, heard the shot and rushed in to find Oswald sitting quietly on a bunk holding the gun. Wilkens had seen the gun a few weeks before when Oswald showed it to him and said he had bought it from a mail-order company in the United States. Others rushed in, and Wilkens left.

At the hospital Oswald claimed his minor wound had been caused accidentally when he dropped his government-issue .45. But the .22 bullet was found, and the incident was reported as a breach of regulations concerning private firearms. The scuttlebutt afterward was that Oswald had deliberately shot himself to avoid leaving Japan to go on maneuvers. If that was his plan, it failed—he was shipped out to the Philippines five days after he was released from the hospital.

After his unit returned in the spring of 1958, Oswald was court-martialed for possessing an unauthorized weapon. He was fined $50 and sentenced to twenty days at hard labor, but the confinement was suspended for six months. Two months later, however, he was court-martialed again. This time he was charged with attempting to provoke a fight with Sergeant Miguel Rodriguez at the Bluebird Cafe in Yamato, and for assaulting Rodriguez by pouring a drink on him. (Oswald evidently bore a grudge because the sergeant had kept him on mess duty.) After electing to serve as his own defense counsel, Oswald cross-examined Rodriguez and persuaded the court he was drunk that night and had spilled the drink by accident. (Years later, Rodriguez would still insist Oswald had been sober and knew exactly what he was doing.) But despite this minor victory, Oswald was found guilty of using "provoking words" and sentenced to the brig. He served eighteen days in a tough military prison.

His fellow Marines noticed a change in Oswald when he got out. He seemed bitter and more withdrawn than he had been before. One man remembered Oswald telling him, "I've seen enough of a democratic society here. . . . When I get out I'm going to try something else." Oswald would later claim that he met a few Communists in Japan who got him interested in going to the Soviet Union to see what a socialist country was like. There may be some truth in this—it would have been in character for him to try to make contact with a Communist group, as he had in New Orleans. The court-martial may have helped make up his mind. In any case, it was during this period that Oswald began studying the Russian language.

In September 1958, a month later, the Chinese began shelling the offshore islands of Quemoy and Matsu, which were controlled by the Nationalist government on Formosa (now Taiwan), and Oswald's unit was sent to Formosa to set up a radar base. Shortly after they arrived, Oswald was on guard duty one night when the officer in charge heard four or five shots at Oswald's position. Running over, he found Oswald "shaking and crying." Oswald told him he was seeing things and that he couldn't stand being on guard duty. After Rhodes reported what had happened, Oswald was sent back to Japan on a military plane. Rhodes believed Oswald was faking. He told Edward Jay Epstein, "Oswald liked Japan and wanted to stay. . . . I know he didn't want to go to Formosa, and I think he fired off his gun to get out of there. . . . There was nothing dumb about Oswald."

At the end of his overseas duty in November 1958 Oswald was transferred to the El Toro base in Santa Ana, California. He became part of a radar crew with about seven other enlisted men and three officers. One of the officers, Lieutenant John E. Donovan, was a recent graduate of the Foreign Service School. He found Oswald to be "very competent," "brighter than most people," and surprisingly well-informed about foreign affairs. He recalled that Oswald

> would take great pride in his ability to mention not only the leader of a country, but five or six subordinates. . . . He took great pride in talking to a passing officer coming in or out of the radar center, and in a most interested manner, ask him what he thought of a given situation, listen to that officer's explanation, and say, "Thank you very much." As soon as we were alone again, he would say, "Do you agree with that?" In many cases it was obvious that the officer had no more idea about [what he was saying] than he did about the polo . . . matches in Australia. And Oswald would then say, "Now, if men like that are leading us, there is something wrong—when I obviously have more intelligence and more knowledge than that man."

If the officers weren't too high in rank, Oswald would point out their mistakes. One of the enlisted men, Nelson Delgado, enjoyed the way Oswald baited them: "Oswald had them stumped . . . four out of five times. They just ran out of words. . . . And every time this happened, it made him feel twice as good. . . . He used to cut up anybody that was high ranking . . . and make himself come out top dog."

Donovan also recalled that Oswald thought the poverty he saw in Asia was unjust and that he took a special interest in Latin America. At a Warren Commission hearing, Donovan was asked, "Did he ever have any specific suggestions as to what should be done about problems in Asia or Latin America?" Donovan answered, "No. His only solution that I could see was that authority, particularly the Marine Corps, ought to be able to recognize talent such as his own, without a given magic college degree, and put them in positions of prominence." As Donovan recalled, this attitude carried over to the squadron football team, on which Lee played end:

> [H]e often tried to make calls in the huddle—for better or worse . . . a quarterback is in charge of the team and should make the calls. . . . And I don't know if he quit or I kicked him off. . . . at any rate, he stopped playing.

He felt that Oswald's only common bond with the other enlisted men was a desire to get out, but that the others respected his intelligence and admired his ability to "pursue Russian on his own and learn it."

At the El Toro base Oswald flaunted his admiration for all things Russian, playing Russian music in the barracks and putting his name in Russian on one of his jackets. He subscribed to a Russian-language newspaper and to the *Daily Worker.* Some of his barracks-mates kidded him, calling him "comrade," or accused him jokingly of being a Russian spy. Oswald seemed to enjoy these comments immensely.

Some critics of the Warren Report have argued that Oswald couldn't have gotten away with this ostentatious pro-Russian behavior without official sanction. They contend that Oswald was merely pretending to be pro-Russian, while he was, in fact, working for American intelligence. As it often happens, a more reasonable explanation is less exciting, but more suited to his character. Oswald was apparently not as open about his political beliefs with the officers as he was with the enlisted men. Lieutenant Donovan, for instance, never heard Oswald "in any way, shape or form confess that he was a Communist, or that he ever thought about being a Communist." He thought Oswald subscribed to the Russian newspaper to learn the language and to get another view of international affairs. Oswald's behavior evidently attracted official interest just once, when a mail-room clerk reported that he had been receiving leftist literature. When Captain Robert E. Block questioned Oswald about this literature, Oswald replied, in a typically disingenuous fashion, that he was indoctrinating himself in Russian theory in conformance with the Marine Corps policy (of getting to know the enemy). Although Block wasn't satisfied with that explanation, he let the matter drop. According to Thornley, Oswald believed he was being watched because of his politics and felt "unjustly put upon."

In December 1958, when Fidel Castro was on the verge of defeating Batista in Cuba, Oswald began spending more time with Nelson Delgado, a Puerto Rican who agreed with him in supporting Castro. While Delgado was on leave in January Castro took power, and when he returned Oswald joked that he must have been down in Cuba helping Castro win. The Cuban revolution fired Oswald's imagination, especially when it appeared that other Latin American countries might follow suit. In June, Dominican exiles based in Cuba launched an invasion of the Dominican Republic in an unsuccessful attempt to overthrow Trujillo. Later that summer there were similar exile raids against Nicaragua, Guatemala, and Haiti. Oswald's hero during this time was William Morgan, a former sergeant in the U.S. Army who had become a major in Castro's army. That August Morgan received considerable press coverage when he lured some anti-Castro rebels into a trap by pretending to be a counter-revolutionary.

Delgado recalled that Oswald wanted to emulate Morgan. They began talking about going to Cuba to join the revolutionary forces as officers and "lead an expedition to some of these other islands and free them too." They talked about how they would "do away with Trujillo." With Delgado's help, Oswald learned some elementary Spanish.

After the Cuban government started sending hundreds of Batista supporters before the firing squad, Delgado lost his enthusiasm for

Castro, but Oswald defended him. He argued that in all new governments some errors were bound to occur, but he was certain that these people had been investigated prior to their executions and that the American press wasn't publicizing those investigations. For Delgado, leaving for Cuba had been barracks talk, mostly, but Oswald still wanted to go. He asked Delgado for ideas about how an Anglo-American like himself could, in Delgado's phrasing, "get with a Cuban, you know, people, be part of that revolutionary movement," and Delgado suggested he get in touch with a Cuban embassy. He believed that Oswald later made contact with the Cuban consulate in Los Angeles and received mail—perhaps pro-Cuban literature—from there. But for some reason Oswald abandoned the idea of going to Cuba, at least for the moment.

Delgado also remembered that Oswald had no use for religion—"He used to laugh at Sunday school . . . mimic the guys that fell out to go to church. . . . Oswald told him that "God was a myth or a legend, that basically our whole life is built around this one falsehood." The Bible was simply "a novel." Oswald preferred *Das Kapital* and other political books like George Orwell's *Animal Farm.* Through Delgado, we are able to see that Oswald had little sense of irony. As he described *Animal Farm* to Delgado, the farmer represented the imperialistic world, and the animals were the workers or socialist people, and "eventually it will come about that the socialists will have the imperialists working for them." When he was asked if Oswald had explained that after the pigs took over the farm they became like the farmers, Delgado replied, "No; just that the pigs and animals had revolted and made the farmer work for them." Oswald had read the book literally and obviously missed Orwell's point.

Nelson Delgado's name appears in many conspiracy books, but mainly because he testified that Oswald was a poor rifle shot when he was in the Marines:

Q. Did you fire with Oswald?
A. Right; I was in the same line. . . . It was a pretty big joke, because he got a lot of "Maggie's drawers" [a red flag indicating the shot had missed the target], you know, a lot of misses, but he didn't give a darn.

Q. Missed the target completely?
A. He just qualified, that's it. He wasn't as enthusiastic as the rest of us. We all loved—liked, you know, going to the range.

The key element in this account is that Oswald wasn't enthusiastic —he didn't give a darn. He scored just one point above the score necessary to qualify. As a raw recruit he had done better. And according to a report in *Time,* his Marine rifle-score book showed him "making 48 and 49 points out of a possible 50 in rapid fire at 200 yards from a sitting position, without a scope."

In the spring of 1959 Oswald struck up an acquaintance with Kerry Thornley, another young radar operator, who would be so impressed by Oswald that he would write a novel about him after his defection. As in the case of Delgado, Oswald became interested in Thornley after Thornley seemed to agree with some of his ideas—beginning with an admiration for the new Cuban leader. They met at a bull session during which Oswald learned that Thornley, too, was an atheist. "What do you think of communism?" Oswald asked him. When Thornley replied he didn't think much of it, Oswald told him, "Well, I think the best religion is communism." At first Thornley felt that Oswald was merely playing to the crowd, but he later decided that Oswald sincerely believed "communism was the best system in the world." Although he noticed some gaps in Lee's knowledge, Thornley considered him to be "extremely intelligent," and was surprised on learning after the assassination that Oswald had never finished high school. He thought the news media underestimated Oswald's understanding of Marxism:

I certainly think he understood much more than many people in the press have seemed to feel. I don't think he was a man who was grasping onto his particular beliefs . . . trying to know something over his head, by any means.

He also thought Oswald "could analyze what he read very well, but it was a very subjective impression."

Thornley said, "I think in his mind it was almost a certainty that the world would end up under a totalitarian government or under totalitarian governments." With that future in mind, Oswald seemed to be "concerned with his image in history":

> He looked upon history as God. He looked upon the eyes of future people as a kind of tribunal, and he wanted to be on the winning side so that 10,000 years from now people would look in the history books and say, "Well, this man was ahead of his time. . . ." He wanted to be looked back upon with honor by future generations. It was, I think, a substitute in his case for traditional religion.
>
> The eyes of the future became what to another man would be the eyes of God, or perhaps to yet another man the eyes of his own conscience. . . .
>
> I don't think he expected things to develop within his lifetime. I am sure that he didn't. He just wanted to be on the winning side for all eternity.

Oswald's view of history wasn't as unusual as it might appear. In a book on the ideological battles of the McCarthy period, Victor S. Navasky wrote, "Ernest Becker has argued that what man really fears is not so much extinction but extinction with insignificance. Man wants to know that his life has somehow counted, if not for himself then at least in a larger scheme of things, that it has left a trace, a trace that has meaning." In wanting his name to live on, young Oswald was not very different from a philanthropist who endows a library in his name or a politician who hopes to be remembered. But Oswald was staking his hopes in what has been called "revolutionary immortality." And in that particular system of belief, there is a catch. In order to be remembered, his side has to win. If the revolution he supported prevailed, he would live on. If it didn't, he would end up in the dustbin of history. Fighting for the revolution thus meant fighting for his own immortality.

For someone who defines himself and his hope of immortality through his politics, as Oswald did (thus making politics his religion), ideological disputes are quite literally a matter of life and death. As Navasky wrote, "No wonder men go into a rage over fine points of belief: if your adversary wins the argument about truth, *you die.* Your immortality system has been shown to be fallible, your life becomes fallible."

One day Oswald was complaining to his buddy Thornley about the stupidity of a ceremonial parade they were preparing for, and Thornley happened to joke, "Well, come the revolution you will change all that," at which point Oswald looked at him "like a betrayed Caesar," in Thornley's words, "and screamed . . . 'Not you too, Thornley.' . . ." They never spoke to each other again.

5... The Defection

Even before he met Kerry Thornley, and while he was daydreaming with Delgado about Cuba, Oswald was making concrete plans for his defection. He had been thinking about it long enough to anticipate a problem he would have to face. After his discharge he was required to serve three more years in the inactive Marine Reserves. How was a member of the Reserves going to explain applying for a passport for a trip to Europe and the Soviet Union, without arousing suspicion?

To get around this difficulty, Oswald worked out an elaborate cover story. He was due to be discharged from active duty in December 1959. In March he passed a high school equivalency exam and applied for admission to the Albert Schweitzer College in Switzerland for the spring 1960 semester. On his application he indicated that he planned to attend a summer course at the University of Turku, Finland, before returning to America to pursue his "chosen vocation." Turku is 100 miles west of Helsinki, the city through which he would enter the Soviet Union. After his application to Schweitzer College was accepted, he had an alibi. If anyone questioned him before he entered the Soviet Union, he could say that he was traveling to Finland to enroll at Turku and would be visiting Russia as a sidetrip. (Soon after the defection, Robert Oswald realized this was his cover story and mentioned it to a reporter.)

Oswald must have spent a good deal of time working out this

scheme. The trips that Delgado noticed he took alone into Los Angeles may have involved visits to libraries or consulates there to find out about European colleges and routes to the Soviet Union. The plan suggests that he feared someone in authority might spot him as a potential defector and pick him up. He talked with Delgado about extradition treaties and the countries that were "extradition-free," like Cuba, Russia, and Argentina. Oswald told him about a route to get to the Soviet Union, in Delgado's words, "bypassing all U.S. censorship. . . . And he definitely said Mexico to Cuba to Russia. . . . I remember him at the time mentioning two men that had defected, and we were wondering how they got there." Later on, Delgado asked Oswald if he still intended to go to Cuba. Oswald grimaced and acted as if he didn't know what he was talking about. "When I get out," he said, "I'm going to school in Switzerland."

In June 1959 he wrote Robert, "Pretty soon I'll be getting out of the Corps and I know what I want to be and how I'm going to be it, which I guess is the most important thing in life."

Later that summer—five months before he was due to be discharged—he saw an opportunity to expedite his departure. In December 1958 Marguerite had been hit on the nose by a jar that fell off a shelf at the store where she worked. She went from doctor to doctor trying to obtain evidence with which to sue her employer and wrote Oswald about her troubles. On August 17 he wrote back saying that he had applied for a hardship discharge

> *in order to help you.* Such a discharge is only rarely given, but if they know you are unable to support yourself then they will release me from the U.S.M.C. *and I will be able to come home and help you* [his emphases].

He cautioned her to make the "right" impression when the Red Cross representative arrived to ask questions about her capacity to support herself. Marguerite came through. She somehow got letters from an attorney, a doctor, and two friends—plus one from herself—all saying she had been injured at work and was unable to support herself. Because of this documentation, Oswald's petition for discharge was approved fairly quickly.

Oswald's letter to Marguerite says quite a bit about his nature, for he never intended to live in Fort Worth and help support his mother. Immediately after his discharge was approved he applied for a passport, indicating he planned to sail from New Orleans within three weeks to attend the colleges in Europe. Under countries to be visited he listed Cuba, the Dominican Republic, England, France, Switzerland, Germany, Finland, and Russia. Before being discharged he signed the customary statement promising not to divulge any secret or confidential information he may have gained during his military service.

The day after he arrived at his mother's one-room apartment in Fort Worth, he informed her that he was going to "board a ship and work in the export–import business." When she tried to talk him out of it, he told her his mind was made up and, "If I stay here, I will get a job for about $35 a week, and we will both be in the position that you are in." He visited Robert and his family at their home— where he altered his explanation somewhat by saying he had plans to go to New Orleans and "work for an export firm." He said nothing about boarding a ship. After two days at home he left for New Orleans, where he booked passage on the freighter *Marion Lykes* bound for France. On the steamship company's application form he described himself as a "shipping export agent." From New Orleans he wrote Marguerite:

I have booked passage on a ship to Europe. I would have had to, sooner or later, and I think it's best I go now. Just remember above all else that my values are different from Robert's or yours. It is difficult to tell you how I feel. Just remember this is what I must do. I did not tell you about my plans because you could hardly be expected to understand.

During the first days at sea Oswald spent most of his time pacing back and forth on deck. There were only three other passengers aboard: a retired army colonel and his wife, and a 17-year-old student, Billy Joe Lord. They found their fellow passenger to be vague about his travel itinerary and bitter about life in the United States. He complained about his mother's circumstances, the fact that she had to work in a drugstore to get by. When he saw that Billy Joe, his roommate, had brought a Bible, he said he couldn't see how anyone could believe in God in light of the findings of modern science, since "anyone with intelligence would recognize there was only matter."

From Le Harve, France, Oswald sailed to Southampton, England, where he told customs officials he planned to stay in Britain for one week before proceeding to school in Switzerland. On the next day he flew to Helsinki.[1]

Oswald arrived in Moscow around the time of his twentieth birthday, in October 1959. Shortly thereafter, he told his Intourist interpreter, Rimma Shirokova, that he wanted to become a Soviet citizen. She helped him write a letter to the Supreme Soviet requesting citizenship. But at that point the Soviet bureaucracy took control. When his six-day visa expired, Oswald was informed he would have to leave the country immediately. And since the Russians were not interested in him, he would have to return to the United States. Oswald went back to his hotel room, considered the situation for a few hours, and cut himself above his left wrist.

Although the Warren Report cautiously called it "an apparent suicide attempt," there is reason to believe that this incident was another one of Oswald's dramatic manipulations. He knew that Rimma was scheduled to arrive at his hotel room within the hour and would find him. The hospital records, provided by the Soviets after the assassination, state that his injury was "light" and that Oswald told his doctor he had cut his wrist to "postpone his departure" from the Soviet Union. In fact, this "apparent suicide attempt" was similar to the minor gunshot wound Oswald had inflicted on himself in Japan. Each incident seemed to have had the same purpose—to avoid being sent where he did not want to go. The emotion expressed was probably not suicidal despair but an extraordinary willfulness—a determination to act decisively and even violently to manipulate events.

The strategem worked, at least for a while. After being released from the hospital, Oswald was transferred to another hotel, although his tourist visa had expired. His diary claims he was interviewed by a new set of Soviet officials the same afternoon. They asked him to describe the other officials he had seen, and took notes. But these bureaucrats also put him off. Several factors must have entered into their decision—among them, Oswald's evident unpredictability and the overall political situation. While Oswald was sailing to Europe, Soviet Premier Nikita Khrushchev had been touring the United States after meeting with President Eisenhower at Camp David. The world press was heralding a potential thaw in the Cold War.

Priscilla Johnson thought the Soviets were suspicious of all foreigners, including those whose ideological credentials were unquestionable—as, of course, Oswald's were not. Having never joined the Communist party, he had no ideological record. One of the questions the second group of officials asked him was, "What documents do you have to show who and what you are?" The only thing Oswald could produce was his Marine Corps honorable discharge.

After waiting for three days without getting an answer, Oswald decided to take action again. He went to the American Embassy and attempted to sign away his citizenship. As a non-American he couldn't have been forced to return to the United States—it would have made it impossible for Soviet officials to tell him, as one already had, "Go home." Although he didn't get to sign the papers that day, he eventually got what he wanted. When he spoke to Priscilla Johnson two weeks later, he said the Russians had assured him he would be allowed to stay.

Toward the end of November the embassy lost track of him in Moscow. He surfaced in Minsk the following January. Some writers suspect that during the interim Oswald was being questioned by the KGB.

Like his fellow radar operators, Oswald had a low security clearance. In 1964 John Donovan, his former crew chief at El Toro, listed the confidential information Oswald was known to have had access to: the location of every base in the West Coast area, their radio frequencies and call signs, their radar capabilities, and the relative strengths of all squadrons. (The radio frequencies and call signs were changed after Oswald's defection.) He also had some knowledge of the U-2 and of a device called TPX-1, which was used to transfer radio and radar signals several miles away from their source, diverting missiles set to home in on them. And he had received instruction in the then-new MPS 16 height-finding radar equipment, which could locate planes, such as the U-2, at extremely high altitudes. But he would not have had the technical expertise to reveal very much about those devices.

When Oswald hinted to Snyder that he knew something of special interest, he may have been talking about the U-2. But the Russians already knew a good deal about the American "mystery plane." One intelligence observer has said that the Soviets may have first learned about the U-2 from a Ukrainian-born scientist and aerial photography specialist who defected from the United States in 1956. The existence of the plane was no secret. In March 1958 the Japanese magazine *Air Review* published photographs of U-2s taken by a 16-year-old boy standing off-base near a runway of an American installation.

It was apparently standard practice for the Soviet intelligence services to debrief defectors, especially military personnel. As one CIA officer has remarked, if nothing else, "they will talk to a Marine about close order drill." We may assume Oswald was debriefed. The important thing for our purposes, however, is not that he may have given away secrets but that he didn't receive the favorable treatment he had clearly expected as a reward.

According to his wife Marina, he had come to her country hoping to get an education. He applied for admission to the Patrice Lumumba University of Friendship of Peoples in Moscow, where students from Third World countries learned Marxist ideology. He wanted to study philosophy, economics, and politics. But in May 1961 his application was turned down. Looking back, Kerry Thornley thought Oswald must have assumed that the Russians would accept him in a "much higher capacity" than they did. He thought Oswald expected them, "in his own dreams, to invite him to take a position in their government, possibly as a technician, and I think he then felt he could go out into the world, into the Communist world and distinguish himself and work his way up into the party, perhaps."

This hope was, of course, completely unrealistic. Even the most celebrated defectors were never given significant positions in the Soviet Union. Guy Burgess and Donald MacLean, high-level members of British intelligence who had been KGB agents for many years, defected after learning they were under suspicion by the British. After being feted in Moscow, they were given work at the English Department of a government publishing house. Another defector, Morris Block, was sent to Odessa to work as a shipfitter. Lee Harvey Oswald was sent to Minsk to work in a radio factory. He lived there from January 1960 until May 1962, and for more than half of that time, he was trying to get out.

When Richard Snyder appeared before the Warren Commission he was asked what his reaction was when he heard Oswald had been sent to live in Minsk. Snyder, who had once taken a walk around the town while waiting for a train, replied, "Serves him right." Minsk was heavily industrialized and unattractive. Its winters were long and severe, quite different from anything Oswald had ever experienced. He was given an expensive apartment and a monthly stipend—he lived well, by Russian standards—but he was assigned manual labor, which he disliked. The records supplied by the Soviet government indicate that he made a familiar impression on his employers: "Citizen Lee Harvey Oswald reacts in an over-sensitive manner to remarks from the foremen, and is careless in his work. Citizen L. H. Oswald takes no part in the social life of the shop and keeps very much to himself."

While Oswald was in Minsk, the American plots to assassinate Fidel Castro began. The idea originated during the planning stages of the Bay of Pigs invasion, while Eisenhower was still in office. Just a few CIA officials were involved. The rationalization then was that Castro's elimination might make the invasion less costly in lives, or possibly unnecessary.

From the moment President John F. Kennedy took office, Cuba was a troublesome burden. In his first State of the Union message he said, "In Latin America, Communist agents seeking to exploit that region's peaceful revolution of hope have established a base on Cuba. . . . Our objection with Cuba is not over the people's drive for a better life. Our objection is to their domination by foreign and domestic tyrannies." He warned that such domination in Latin America "can never be negotiated." The public was alarmed by this new Soviet ally —"only 90 miles from Miami," as the popular expression went. A month after the Bay of Pigs debacle, the House of Representatives passed a resolution declaring that Cuba was "a clear and present danger" to the Western Hemisphere. Editorial writers cited the Monroe Doctrine and demanded that the administration do all it could to get rid of the Castro government. When other methods failed, the assassination idea bobbed to the surface again.

Nobody knows precisely who ordered the assassination attempts. Despite a thorough investigation in 1975, Senator Frank Church's senate committee on intelligence activities couldn't determine whether the CIA acted on its own or on orders from above. During the investigation Church predicted to the Baltimore *Sun,* "The people will recognize that the CIA was behaving during those years like a rogue elephant rampaging out of control," and the phrase "rogue elephant" quickly embedded itself in the public mind. But that was not the conclusion reached by Church's committee in its report four months later:

> The picture that emerges from the evidence is not a clear one. . . . The Committee finds that the system of executive command and control was so ambiguous that it is difficult to be certain at what levels assassination activity was known and authorized. This situation creates the disturbing prospect that Government [i.e., CIA] officials might have undertaken the assassination plots without it having been uncontrovertibly clear that there was explicit authorization from the Presidents. It is also possible that there might have been a successful "plausible denial" in which Presidential authorization was issued but is now obscured.

One committee member has said that pinning down responsibility for these activities was "like nailing Jello to a wall." The committee ended up criticizing CIA officials for failing on several occasions "to disclose their plans and activities to superior authorities, or to do so with sufficient detail and clarity." But it also criticized administration officials "for not ruling out assassination, particularly after certain Administration officials had become aware of prior assassination plans."

That last statement was a reference to former Attorney General Robert Kennedy, who served as a liaison with the CIA on Cuban policy for the White House. On May 7, 1962, Kennedy had been informed by CIA general counsel Lawrence Houston and another CIA officer, Sheffield Edwards, that an intermediary for the CIA had contacted Mafia leader Sam Giancana before the Bay of Pigs with a proposition of paying $150,000 to hire some hit men to go into Cuba and kill Castro. Kennedy was led to believe that this plot had been terminated, but that was untrue. Since Giancana's association with the CIA complicated the attorney general's ongoing attempt to prosecute Giancana, he was furious. Houston recalled Kennedy's response: "If you have seen Mr. Kennedy's eyes get steely and his jaw set . . . his voice get low and precise, you get a definite feeling of unhappiness."

One of the few things made clear by the Church committee report was that, following the Bay of Pigs humiliation, the Kennedy administration put considerable pressure on the CIA to "do something about Castro." Robert Kennedy's notes of a White House meeting on November 4, 1961, indicate that he wanted stronger covert action against Cuba: "My idea is to stir things up on [the] island with espionage, sabotage, general disorder, run and operated by Cubans themselves with every group but Batistaites & Communists. Do not know if we will be successful in overthrowing Castro but we have nothing to lose in my estimate."

On November 16 President Kennedy delivered a speech at the University of Washington in which he said, "We cannot, as a free nation, compete with our adversaries in tactics of terror, assassination, false promises, counterfeit mobs and crises." But at the end of that month, the president authorized a major new covert action program called MONGOOSE, the purpose of which was to "use our available assets . . . to help Cuba overthrow the Communist regime." It was a project designed to use Cuban exiles in intelligence and sabotage activities aimed toward an internal revolt against the Castro government—the same idea Robert Kennedy had outlined earlier.

On January 19, 1962, a meeting of MONGOOSE participants was held in the attorney general's office, and the notes taken by a CIA executive assistant contain the following account of what Robert Kennedy told them:

Conclusion Overthrow of Castro is Possible

". . . a solution to the Cuban problem today carried top priority in U.S. Govt. No time, money, effort—or manpower is to be spared."

"Yesterday . . . the President had indicated to him that the final chapter had not been written—it's got to be done and will be done."

Former CIA Director Richard Helms told the committee that during the MONGOOSE period "it was made abundantly clear . . . to everybody involved in the operation that the desire was to get rid of the Castro regime and to get rid of Castro . . . the point was that no limitations were put on this injunction." As the pressure increased, he said, "obviously the extent of the means that one thought were available . . . increased too." He added, "In the perceptions of the time and the things we were trying to do this was one human life against many other human lives that were being lost . . . people were losing their lives in raids, a lot of people had lost their life at the Bay of Pigs, agents were being arrested left and right and put before the wall and shot." Helms testified that he received no direct order to assassinate Castro, but he told the committee: "I have testified as best I could about the atmosphere of the time, what I understood was desired, and I don't want to take refuge in saying that I was instructed to specifically murder Castro."

Other administration officials backed up Helms's picture of the crisis. Former Secretary of Defense Robert McNamara testified, "We were hysterical about Castro at the time of the Bay of Pigs and thereafter, and . . . there was pressure from [President Kennedy and the attorney general] to do something about Castro." But he added, "I don't believe we contemplated assassination. We did, however, contemplate overthrow."

Nevertheless, talk of assassination was in the air in 1961. George Smathers, former senator from Florida and an old friend of the president's, told the Church committee that the subject came up during a conversation he had with Kennedy on the White House lawn. He testified that the president asked him "what reaction I thought there would be throughout South America were Fidel Castro to be assassinated." After Smathers told him that it would only result in unfavorable publicity for the United States, Kennedy agreed with him. (It was Kennedy's habit to ask people all manner of questions to obtain information.)

Later on, Kennedy let Smathers know he didn't want to hear any more about Cuba. One evening when Smathers was a dinner guest:

> I just happened to mention . . . something about Cuba, and the President took his fork and cracked the plate . . . and says, for Gods sakes, quit talking about Cuba.

On November 9, 1961, reporter Tad Szulc was asked by Robert Kennedy to meet with the president, off the record, to discuss the situation in Cuba. The president asked Szulc a number of questions about conversations he had had with Castro and what he thought the United States might do about Cuba, either in a hostile way or in establishing some kind of dialogue. Kennedy then asked, "What would you think if I ordered Castro to be assassinated?" Taken aback, Szulc told him he would strongly disapprove of the idea for both ethical and pragmatic reasons. Szulc said that Kennedy replied, "I agree with you completely." The notes Szulc wrote shortly after the meeting continue:

> JFK said he raised question because he was under terrific pressure from advisers (think he said intelligence people, but not positive) to okay a Castro murder, said he was resisting pressure.

Officially, the CIA was against the idea as well. Only the month before, its Board of National Estimates had prepared a paper for the president which concluded that "it is highly improbable that an extensive popular uprising could be fomented" against Castro and that Castro's death "would almost certainly not prove fatal to the regime."

After hearing this sometimes contradictory testimony, some committee members came to feel that a Becket-like situation may have developed in which CIA officials carried out what they believed to be the wishes of their superiors. At one point, Senator Charles Mathias questioned Richard Helms:

Q. Let me draw an example from history. When Thomas Becket was proving to be an annoyance, [like] Castro, the King said who will rid me of this man. He didn't say to somebody, go out and murder him. He said who will rid me of this man, and let it go at that.

A. That is a warming reference to the problem.

Q. You feel that spans the generations and the centuries?

A. I think it does, sir.

Q. And that is typical of the kind of thing which might be said, which might be taken by the Director or by anybody else as Presidential authorization to go forward?

A. That is right. But in answer to that, I realize that one sort of grows up in [the] tradition of the time and I think that any of us would have found it very difficult to discuss assassinations with a President of the United States. I just think we all had the feeling that we're hired . . . to keep those things out of the Oval Office.

Q. Yet at the same time you felt that some spark had been transmitted, that that was within the permissible limits?

A. Yes, and if he had disappeared from the scene they would not have been unhappy.

The first known CIA plot to assassinate Fidel Castro was set into motion in August 1960, when an official in the CIA's Office of Medical Services was given a box of Castro's favorite cigars and asked to treat them with poison. After being doctored, the cigars were handed over to an unidentified conspirator on February 13, 1961.

6... Getting Out

Fᴇʙʀᴜᴀʀʏ 13, 1961: At the American Embassy in Moscow, Richard Snyder found on his desk a letter from Lee Harvey Oswald, whom he hadn't seen or heard from in over a year. Oswald had decided to return to the United States, but he was worried about the reception he might get from the American authorities. He wrote, "I desire to return to the United States, that is if we could come to some agreement concerning the dropping of any legal proceedings against me." He asked to have his passport returned and concluded, "I hope that in recalling the responsibility I have to America that you remember yours in doing everything you can to help me since I am an American citizen."

On February 28 Snyder replied. He asked Oswald to come to Moscow for an interview to determine his citizenship status. Unsure about the reference to "legal proceedings," Snyder also sent a dispatch to the State Department about Oswald's letter, asking whether he might face prosecution on his return, and if so, should Snyder tell him that? The State Department responded by saying it had no way of knowing whether Oswald had broken any laws and could offer him no guarantees. It cautioned Snyder not to return his passport through the Soviet mails under any circumstances.

Oswald didn't want to go to Moscow to be interviewed—he was afraid he might be arrested the minute he set foot on American territory at the embassy. On March 12 he wrote Snyder again saying he found it "inconvenient" to come to Moscow:

> I see no reason for any preliminary inquiries not to be put to me in the form of a questionnaire and sent to me. I understand that personal interviews undoubtedly make the work of the Embassy staff lighter than written correspondence; however, in some cases other means must be employed.

Snyder replied on March 24, restating the need for him to come to Moscow. And there the matter rested, for the moment—a standoff.

Meanwhile, something else was going on in Oswald's life. On March 17 he had met Marina Prusakova, an attractive 19-year-old girl, at a dance at the Minsk Palace of Culture. He saw her once more at another dance the following week. Soon after, Oswald went into the hospital for an adenoid operation, and Marina visited him there several times. After just these few meetings—and a stolen kiss on a hospital stairway—Oswald proposed. Marina, an orphan, lived with her Aunt Valya and Uncle Ilya, sleeping in their living room. When Oswald was released from the hospital on April 11, she invited him home for dinner. Oswald told her relatives he had come to Russia to learn the truth about it, not just the "truth" shown to tourists. He told them he was happy there. As he was leaving for work, Ilya put his arm around Oswald's shoulders and told him, "Take care of this girl. She has plenty of breezes in her brain."

Marina had not yet decided to say yes. She would later admit that she had been attracted to Oswald because he was an American, someone out of the ordinary compared to her Russian boyfriends. The fact that he had a private apartment was appealing, as well. But Marina has also said, "I fell in love with the man." In her biography of Marina, Priscilla Johnson McMillan noted that the ideal man of Marina's imagination was Pechorin, the protagonist of Mikhail Lermontov's story "A Hero of Our Time." She wrote, "Vengeful and cold, Pechorin is forever spinning webs of intrigue that destroy all those whose lives touch his own." McMillan pointed out that Pechorin shunned emotional contact with other people and boasted, "How many times have I played the part of an axe in the hands of fate? Fame is a question of luck. To obtain it, you only have to be nimble."

On April 18 Oswald proposed again and insisted that they be married right away or break up—he couldn't go on seeing her, he said, without having her. They were married as soon as it could be arranged, on April 30. They had known each other for six weeks.

Could there have been some reason other than passion for Oswald's sudden decision to marry? He later claimed that he had proposed to another Russian girl, Ella German, and had been turned down—he married Marina on the rebound, he said, to hurt Ella and didn't fall in love with Marina until after their marriage. That may have been true. But it would have been unusual for Oswald to take a step like marriage without considering how it would affect his plans to leave Russia. Eventually he would have to go to the embassy. Did it occur to him that if the Americans intended to arrest him it might be to his advantage to have a Russian wife? Before his wedding Oswald, having cut himself off from his family, was completely alone. If the Americans had wanted to take him into custody at the embassy and whisk him away to the United States to stand trial, no one but Oswald would have protested. Marrying a Russian citizen gave him some leverage. If he were arrested now, his wife could protest to the Soviet government—thus raising the specter of an "international incident."

Although Marina didn't realize it until after their marriage, Oswald had told her many lies during their courtship. He had said he was 24, increasing his age by three years. He told her his mother was dead. And he maintained that he had renounced his American citizenship and could never go back to the United States. Having grown up in the Soviet Union, Marina could understand someone wanting to keep secrets from potential informers. But as McMillan put it, "Marina soon realized that her husband's secretiveness was of another kind entirely. He told lies without purpose or point, lies that were bound to be found out. He liked having secrets for their own sake. He simply enjoyed concealment."

A few weeks after their wedding they went to see a Polish spy movie. Coming out of the theater Lee remarked, "I'd love a life like that." When Marina expressed surprise, he explained, "I'd love the danger."

During their courtship Marina also began to notice Oswald's interest in Cuba. In mid-April an army of Cuban exiles supported by the United States invaded Cuba at the Bay of Pigs and was quickly defeated. Marina heard Oswald condemn the invasion and American policy toward Cuba and Fidel Castro in general. He took her to see a Soviet film about Castro and afterward spoke of him as "a hero" and "a very smart statesman." Oswald sought out the Cuban students living in Minsk—there were about three hundred of them—to find out more about Castro's revolution. The students he met were disappointed in Russia, as he was. According to Marina, he felt the Cubans would succeed in creating an egalitarian society where the Russians had failed.

On May 16, less than three weeks after his marriage, Oswald wrote the American Embassy in a familiar vein:

> I wish to make it clear that I am asking not only for the right to return to the United States, but also for full guarantees that I shall not, under any circumstances, be prosecuted for any act pertaining to this case. . . . Unless you think this condition can be met, I see no reason for a continuance of our correspondence. Instead, I shall endeavour to use my relatives in the United States, to see about getting something done in Washington.

He informed the embassy he had gotten married: "My wife is Russian . . . and is quite willing to leave the Soviet Union with me. . . ." He said he would not leave without her, adding, "So with this extra complication, I suggest you do some checking up before advising me further."

Earlier that month Oswald had written a letter to his brother Robert, his first since 1959, when he told Robert he never wanted to hear from him again. Acting as though nothing had happened, Lee informed Robert of his marriage and invited him to visit him in Russia sometime. Testing the waters, he said nothing about his plans to return. He also wrote to his mother for the first time in a year and a half. After Robert answered in a friendly manner, Oswald wrote a second time on May 31: "I can't say whether I will ever get back to the States or not, if I can get the government to drop charges against me, and get the Russians to let me out with my wife, then maybe I'll be seeing you again. *But* you know it is not simple for either of those two things."

When he had received no response to his most recent letter to Snyder by July, Oswald decided to take his vacation and fly to Moscow. He still suspected he was walking into a trap. He told Marina the embassy was entitled to arrest him because, "I threw my passport on the table and said I didn't want to be a citizen anymore." Always sensitive to his legal rights, Oswald must have known that that action wasn't enough to put him in jail. More likely, he was worried he would be accused of giving the Soviets military information, as he had threatened to do.

Since Oswald hadn't let the embassy know he was coming, Richard Snyder was surprised to see this bad penny turn up. Snyder remembered him as one of the most obnoxious young men he had ever known. Since it was a Saturday, the consular offices were closed, and Snyder suggested he return the following Monday. Oswald telephoned Marina and asked her to join him, assuring her, "It's okay. They didn't arrest me." She flew to Moscow on Sunday and accompanied him to the embassy the next day.

To determine whether Oswald had committed any expatriating acts, the embassy personnel questioned him at length about his activities since he had come to the Soviet Union. Was he a Soviet citizen, they asked? No. Had he applied for citizenship? No. Had he taken an oath of allegiance to the Soviet Union? No. Had he made any statements for the Soviet press or for audiences? No. Had he joined a Soviet trade union? No. When he was asked whether he had given the Russians information he had acquired as a radar operator, he replied

That he was never in fact subjected to any questioning concerning his life or experiences prior to entering the Soviet Union, and never provided such information to any Soviet organ. . . . that he doubted in fact that he would have given such information if requested despite his statements made at the Embassy.

The Warren Report noted that some of these answers were undoubtedly false. Oswald had almost certainly applied for Soviet citizenship, he had a membership card in a Soviet trade union, and "his assertion to Snyder that he had never been questioned by Soviet authorities concerning his life in the United States is simply unbelievable." But at the time, since Oswald's answers indicated he was still an American citizen and there was no way of proving otherwise, the embassy had little choice but to conclude that he had not expatriated himself. In a dispatch to the State Department, Snyder reported Oswald's many denials and added:

Oswald indicated some anxiety as to whether, should he return to the United States, he would face possible lengthy imprisonment for his act of remaining in the Soviet Union. Oswald was told informally that the Embassy did not perceive, on the basis of the information in its possession, on what grounds he might be subject to conviction leading to punishment of such severity as he apparently had in mind. It was clearly stated to him, however, that the Embassy could give him no assurance as to whether upon his desired return to the United States he might be liable to prosecution for offenses committed in violation of laws of the United States or of any of its States. Oswald said he understood this. He had simply felt that in his own interest he could not go back to the United States if it meant returning to a number of years in prison, and had delayed approaching Soviet authorities concerning departing from the Soviet Union until he "had this end of the thing straightened out."

Snyder concluded:

Twenty months of the realities of life in the Soviet Union have clearly had a maturing effect on Oswald. He stated frankly that he had learned a hard lesson the hard way and that he had been completely relieved of his illusions about the Soviet Union at the same time that he acquired a new understanding and appreciation of the United States and the meaning of freedom. Much of the arrogance and bravado which characterized him on his first visit to the Embassy appears to have left him.

When McMillan read that last passage to Marina Oswald after the assassination, Marina burst out laughing and remarked that "without an ulterior purpose he would never have said any such thing."

It now appeared that he would be allowed to go home. But despite the assurances Snyder had given him, Oswald remained wary. Upon returning to Minsk with his wife, he began preparing a cover story to protect himself, just as he had done when he planned his defection.

After the assassination one of the items found among Oswald's belongings was a twelve-page handwritten account of his life in Russia which he had grandly entitled "Historic Diary." When portions of the diary appeared in the news media, Oswald's melodramatic tone made it appear as if he were a highly emotional young man who had become thoroughly disillusioned with the Soviet Union. What no one realized then was that the "Historic Diary" was not a diary at all—that is, it was not a daily, spontaneous account of his experiences in Russia. It had been written up *after* his July interview at the embassy.[1]

The Warren Commission staff noticed anachronisms in the diary. Entries for particular days sometimes alluded to events that hadn't yet occurred. Because of these discrepancies, the Warren Report noted that Oswald had apparently written many entries at a later date, possibly with "future readers in mind," and that it wasn't an accurate guide to the details of his activities. Despite this skepticism, however, the report relied on the diary to establish Oswald's state of mind when he decided to return to the United States. It quoted an entry dated January 4–31, 1961:

> I am starting to reconsider my desire about staying. The work is drab, the money I get has nowhere to be spent. No night clubs or bowling alleys, no places of recreation except the trade union dances. I have had enough.

The report concluded that "a great change must have occurred in Oswald's thinking to induce him to return to the United States," and suggested that he came back chastened—his return "publicly testified to the utter failure of what had been the most important act of his life." The idea that Oswald had learned his lesson and was humbled was, of course, the same impression he had created with Richard Snyder.

But Oswald's actual purpose in writing the diary is suggested by its contents. Point by point, the diary covered most of the questions he had been asked at the embassy. It begins with his arrival in Moscow full of hope and idealism. It describes his attempt to renounce his citizenship—omitting his threat to give away secrets. A November entry mentions the interview he had with Aline Mosby, which he knew had been published in the United States: "I give my story, allow pictures, later story is distorted, sent without my permission, that is: before I ever saw and O.K.'ed her story." His questioning by Soviet officials is made to appear extremely perfunctory.

The diary claims he was offered Soviet citizenship but turned it down. It says he was asked to address a meeting of workers in Minsk but politely refused. It says nothing of his joining a trade union. After recording his growing disillusionment with the Soviet system, he wrote:

> *Feb. 1st [1961]* Make my first request of American Embassy, Moscow for reconsidering my position. I stated "I would like to go back to U.S."
>
> *Feb. 28th* I receive letter from Embassy. Richard E. Snyder stated "I could come in for an interview anytime I wanted."
>
> *March 1–16* I now live in a state of expectation about going back to the U.S.

Oswald didn't mention his concern about the possibility he would be arrested. The rest of the diary depicted a continuing disillusionment with the Soviet Union and an uncharacteristic silence about politics.

In short, the "Historic Diary" was a self-serving account that could be used as evidence that he had violated no American laws. It may also have served to get his story straight in his own mind, in case he was questioned by the authorities after he arrived in the United States, as indeed he would be.

By January 1962 the only hitch remaining was getting the Americans to agree to let Marina come into the country. The embassy wrote

Oswald suggesting that he precede his wife to the United States, but he refused. Sometimes he would tell Marina, "If it hadn't been for you, I could have gone to America long ago." And she would counter his accusation with perhaps more truth than she realized, "The only reason you're waiting for me is—you're afraid they'll arrest you if you're alone."

During January Oswald got troubling news from his mother, who wrote him that the Marines had changed his honorable discharge to a dishonorable (in fact, an "undesirable") discharge. He must have suspected this change was a prelude to criminal charges, for on January 30 he wrote Robert:

> You once said that you asked around about whether or not the U.S. government had any charges against me, you said at that time "no," maybe you should ask around again, it's possible now that the government knows I'm coming they'll have something waiting. . . . If you find out any information about me, please let me know. I'd like to be ready on the draw so to speak.

On the same day he also wrote John Connally, who he believed was still secretary of the navy. (Connally was by that time governor of Texas.) Oswald's letter to him was a shrewd mixture of gall and dissembling:

> I wish to call your attention to a case about which you may have personal knowledge since you are a resident of Ft. Worth as I am. In November 1959 an event was well publicized in the Ft. Worth newspapers concerning a person who had gone to the Soviet Union to reside for a short time (much in the same way E. Hemingway resided in Paris).
>
> This person, in answers to questions put to him by reporters in Moscow criticized certain facets of American life. The story was blown up into another "turncoat" sensation, with the result that the Navy department gave this person a belated dishonourable discharge, although he had received an honourable discharge after three years service on Sept. 11, 1959 at El Toro Marine Corps base in California.
>
> These are the basic facts of *my* case.
>
> I have and always had the full sanction of the U.S. Embassy, Moscow USSR and hence the U.S. government. Inasmuch as I am returning to

the U.S.A. in this year with the aid of the U.S. Embassy, bringing with me my family (since I married in the USSR) I shall employ all means to right this gross mistake or injustice to a boni-fied [sic] U.S. citizen and ex-service man. The U.S. government has no charges or complaints against me. I ask you to look into this case and take the necessary steps to repair the damage done to me and my family. For information I would direct you to consult the American Embassy, Chikovski St. 19/21, Moscow, USSR.

Conally referred his letter to the Department of the Navy, which informed Oswald that it contemplated no change in his undesirable discharge.

On February 15 Oswald wrote Robert once more. After indicating that he and Marina had received their Soviet exit visas, he said:

> The chances of our coming to the States are very good. . . .
> How are things at your end? I heard over the voice of America that they released Powers, the U2 spy plane fellow. That's big news where you are I suppose. He seemed to be a nice, bright, American-type fellow, when I saw him in Moscow.
> You wouldn't have any clippings from the November 1959 newspapers of Ft. Worth, would you?
> I am beginning to get interested in just what they *did* say about me and my trip here.
> The information might come in handy when I get back. I would hate to come back completely unprepared.

Oswald may have had a particular reason for mentioning Francis Gary Powers.

The Russians had created an international sensation by shooting down Powers's U-2 plane in May 1960. Powers cooperated with his captors by revealing what he knew, and President Eisenhower was forced to admit that the United States had been conducting reconnaissance flights over Soviet territory. It was one of the Soviets' most impressive propaganda coups ever. That August, Powers went on trial in Moscow. Oswald couldn't have missed hearing about it—excerpts from the trial became daily fare on Soviet television, and a movie of the trial made the rounds at neighborhood theaters. During his trial

Powers's defense attorney, Mikhail Griniev, had emphasized that "the divulgence of state secrets in the United States is punishable by ten years' imprisonment, or a fine of ten thousand dollars, or both." Griniev pointed out that Powers had said: "I know that I shall be tried in your court, but if I happen to return home I shall be tried there as well." In February 1962 Powers was exchanged for an imprisoned Russian spy, Colonel Rudolf Abel.

The ten-year sentence for divulging state secrets may have been the kind of lengthy prison sentence Oswald was worried about. Over and over he had asked Robert to look into certain unspecified charges he might be faced with. Robert apparently didn't know what he was talking about. He may have wanted Robert to send him the newspaper clippings so he could find out whether anything had been said about his threat to expose military secrets. In any case, the Powers case stayed on his mind, for two weeks later he wrote Robert: "In another month or so it'll start to thaw out here although I suppose it's already hot in Texas. I heard a "voice of America" program about the Russians releasing Powers. I hope they aren't going to try him in the U.S. or anything."

By May the paperwork was finally completed and the Oswalds and their infant daughter June left the Soviet Union. It had taken Oswald fifteen months to get out. On board the SS *Maasdam* Oswald found some stationery and spent hours in the ship's library writing about politics. Still worried about his reception, he prepared himself for the hostile questions American reporters might ask a returning defector. He compiled a list of possible questions and answers—one giving sanitized responses reminiscent of his diary and the other giving what was evidently the truth. Here are some of the dual answers he gave.

Why did you go to the Soviet Union? One response was that he went as a tourist "to see the land, the people and how their system works." The other, that he went "as a mark of disgust and protest against American political policies in foreign countries, my personal sign of discontent and horror at the misguided line of reasoning of the U.S. Government."

What are the outstanding differences between the Soviet Union and the United States? Answers: "freedom of speech, travel, outspoken opposition to unpopular policies, freedom to believe in god," and "None, except in the U.S. the living standard is a little higher, freedoms are about the same, medical aid and the education system in the USSR is better than in the USA."

Are you a Communist? "No, of course not. . . ." and "Yes, basically, although I hate the USSR and [its] socialist system I still think Marxism can work under different circumstances."

The defector was coming home, essentially unchanged.

7... Homecoming

ON June 8, 1962, a Fort Worth newspaper carried a photograph of Lee Harvey Oswald and an article headlined, "Ex-Marine Reported on Way Back from Russia." Six days later the Oswalds arrived at Love Field, the Dallas airport. Robert and his family met them and brought them home to stay until they could get settled—they would live at Robert's for about a month. Oswald had cautioned his brother to make no statements to the press before he got home—"None at all!"—and now, when reporters called the house Oswald refused to talk with them. A week later a *Fort Worth Press* writer sent him a letter asking for an interview, saying that Oswald's story might be salable to a magazine or book publisher or possibly even to the movies. The writer warned Oswald he might have trouble finding a job in Fort Worth: "You would be surprised how many people still link the name Lee Oswald with 'traitor' and 'turncoat.' " Oswald never answered.

Marina enjoyed her first taste of American life. Robert's wife, Vada, cut her hair and gave her a permanent, and Marina seemed delighted with the way she looked. She bought her first pair of shorts and was overwhelmed by the supermarkets. Before long Oswald would begin speaking disparagingly of his wife as a typical American girl, someone more interested in material things than in important political issues. He would complain that he had thought he married a different sort of girl, "a Russian girl."

On June 19 Oswald called on Peter Gregory, a Siberian-born petroleum engineer who taught Russian at the Fort Worth Public Library. Oswald asked if Gregory would write him a letter of recommendation, certifying his competence in the Russian language, so that he might try to get a job as a translator. (Oswald was by this time fluent in Russian.) Gregory opened a book at random and had Oswald read for him, then gave him the letter he wanted. Through Gregory, Oswald would meet other members of the Russian-speaking émigré community in the area.

Meanwhile, the Fort Worth FBI had taken note of Oswald's return. Special Agent John Fain saw Oswald's picture in the paper and called Marguerite, and then Robert, to locate Oswald and arrange for an interview. Oswald went down to the FBI office and spoke to Fain and another agent for about two hours. Fain found him to be "insolent and tense." When Fain asked him why he went to Russia, Oswald said "because I wanted to" and "to see the country."

For the past five years it had been part of the FBI's job to interview returning defectors and report any significant findings to the CIA.[1] The FBI agent also wanted to make sure Oswald wasn't going to be recruited by Soviet intelligence, and on this point Oswald "seemed to be just a little bit derisive of our questions, and hesitated to bring out whether or not the Soviet intelligence officials might have been interested in him or might have contacted him. . . . He just didn't think he was that important; in other words, that they would want to contact him." According to Fain's written report, Oswald denied that he had tried to renounce his American citizenship or that he had said he would reveal radar secrets to the Soviets. Fain asked Oswald to take a lie detector test on whether he had dealings with Soviet intelligence and Oswald refused.

In mid-July he got a job as a sheet-metal worker for a manufacturer of louvers and ventilators and moved his family to an apartment on Mercedes Street, in a low-income area of Fort Worth. He spent much of his free time reading books on history and politics he'd checked out of the library. As soon as he had settled, he sent an airmail payment to *The Worker* for renewal of his subscription. On August 12 he sent a letter to the Socialist Workers party asking for information, and the party sent him some literature. He also wrote to the Fair Play for Cuba Committee in New York and received some pamphlets.

Agent Fain hadn't been satisfied with Oswald's responses in their first meeting. He decided to interview Oswald again on August 16, and went to the Mercedes Street address. The interview went over the same ground and yielded similar denials. Marina recalled:

> Lee had just returned from work and we were getting ready to have dinner when a car drove up and [a] man introduced himself and asked Lee to step out and talk to him. There was another man in the car. They talked for about two hours and I was very angry, because everything had gotten cold. . . . I asked who those [men] were, and he was very upset over the fact that the FBI was interested in him. . . . Lee said that the FBI had told him that in the event some Russians might visit him and would try to recruit him to work for them, he should notify the FBI agents. I don't know to what extent this was true. . . . he said that they saw Communists in everybody and they are much afraid . . . inasmuch as I had returned [with him] from Russia.

The FBI's concern was that the Soviets might be able to coerce Oswald into intelligence work because Marina had relatives in Russia. Oswald quickly developed what an acquaintance would call an "extreme allergy to the FBI." Fain had gotten Oswald's new address from Robert, and from that point on, whenever Oswald moved, he rented a post office box and refused to give Robert his home address. After this FBI visit, Marina says he remained nervous and irritable for some time. If the past is any guide, his fear of being arrested must have been renewed.

Oswald didn't know it, but before Fain retired in October, he determined that Oswald wasn't working in a sensitive industry, and decided to close his case, at least temporarily.[2]

Many of the Russian-speaking émigrés in the Dallas–Fort Worth area had heard about Oswald's arrival, and they were eager to find out about current conditions in the Soviet Union. Peter Gregory gave a dinner party to introduce the Oswalds to George Bouhe and Anna

Meller. Like most of the émigrés, Bouhe and Meller were strongly anti-Communist. They quickly discovered they had nothing in common with Oswald politically. When Bouhe asked about the living standards of the Russian worker, Oswald told him he had made 90 rubles a month and had a rentfree apartment. Pressed about other costs, Oswald said a pair of boots cost about 19 rubles, cafeteria food about 45. Bouhe said, "90 minus 45, minus 19, what is left?" Oswald didn't respond. Bouhe soon stopped discussing the Soviet system with him.

Bouhe later visited the Oswalds at their apartment, and when he saw what few things they had, he collected clothes for the whole family and bought some groceries and a crib for the baby, who had been sleeping on the floor in a suitcase. Oswald was furious. He picked up a shirt Bouhe had brought him and measured and remeasured it. Finally Bouhe said, "Lee, this is to go to work. Wear them 3 or 4 days, get them dirty, then throw them away." Oswald folded the shirt and gave it back to him. He said, "I don't need any." The other gifts were tacitly accepted, however. Anna Meller visited, too, and was shocked to see Marxist books in the living room. She thought Oswald was extremely irresponsible in not taking better care of his family and in refusing to let Marina learn English. (Oswald wanted to retain his Russian and wanted June to learn the language.) From his point of view, he was eminently responsible: he was pursuing important political concerns that they were too self-centered and bourgeois to recognize. But the way he criticized both the Soviet Union and the United States made Meller think he was mentally ill. She told the Warren Commission, "He had always something hidden; you [could] feel it."

That summer Gregory's son Paul, a student, paid Marina to tutor him in Russian for a couple of months. Sometimes he would drive the Oswalds to the grocery store, and he was amazed at how little Lee bought. Oswald would get the cheapest possible cut of meat and then haggle to make sure they gave him the best of the lot. Paul remembered that once when they were coming out of the store Marina missed the step down and fell with June in her arms. Oswald rushed over to make sure the child was all right, ignoring his wife, and then gave her a tongue-lashing.

Paul Gregory believed that Oswald considered him a friend, while other people were "beneath him." The two young men discussed politics, and Oswald expressed admiration for Castro and for President Kennedy, whom he called "a good leader." He told Paul the Party leaders in Russia were " 'ruining the principles which the country should be based on.' In other words, they were not true Communists." When Paul mentioned his interest in going to the Soviet Union as an exchange student, Oswald advised, "Just go over there. Don't get on a waiting list. You will never get there. If you want to do something, go ahead and do it. You will get involved in red tape." After recalling this conversation for the Warren Commission, Gregory added, "And I think that was possibly the way he thought about everything." After the assassination, Paul told the FBI that Oswald was "arrogant, stubborn, and would not discuss anything but his particular type of politics, which was definitely radical."

Before long, other members of the Russian-speaking community were offering their help. Meller and Bouhe noticed that Marina's teeth were in very poor condition and sought out the assistance of another émigré, Elena Hall, a dental technician, who directed Marina to a low-cost clinic and began collecting money and clothes for the family. Elena's husband John drove her to the Mercedes Street apartment, and on the way over she told him how destitute the Oswalds were. When they walked in, John Hall remembered, Oswald had just been to town to buy "this 50-cent magazine on Russia, which of course I thought, to myself, here they are destitute and he is spending 50 cents on a magazine, especially about Russia." Oswald seemed to him "a so-called egghead." At a later meeting Hall, who was a Baptist and owned his own dental lab, tried to convince Oswald that "our system was a tremendous enterprise, was the best." But to Hall's mind, this young man was "completely out in left field in politics" and "you just didn't have any idea at all that you were going to change him." Elena thought the same thing. Her attitude was that after seeing what Russia was like he should have learned his lesson.

Oswald resented the émigrés' help, never thanked anyone, and showed his contempt for these middle-class anti-Communists. Marina told the Commission, "Well, he thought that they were fools for having left Russia, they were all traitors." He said that they only liked money, and that everything is measured by money in this country. There was only one exception to his general dislike of this group —George de Mohrenschildt, a petroleum engineeer from Dallas. Almost thirty years Oswald's senior, de Mohrenschildt had a flamboyant personality and a colorful past. Born in Russia in 1911, de Mohrenschildt had been an officer in the Polish Army and a roughneck in the Louisiana oilfields. In 1941 he had worked for a French intelligence agent collecting information on people involved in pro-German activity in the United States. Nicknamed "The Mad Russian," de Mohrenschildt was a nonconformist. It was said of him that he might show up at a formal dinner in a bathing suit or come to a church function and announce that he was an atheist. George, who had the reputation of being a "leftwing enthusiast" of some kind, was the one émigré who would listen to Oswald's political ideas and take him seriously. For this reason, Oswald looked up to him, and apparently was more open with him than he was with most people. The older man would be Oswald's confidant until de Mohrenschildt left Dallas in April 1963.

De Mohrenschildt told the Warren Commission, "I could understand his point of view, because that is what happens exactly in the whole world with dissatisfied people. If they are constructive, they study more and try to get good jobs and succeed. The [others] try to form a revolutionary party. And he was one of them." He described Oswald as "an idealistic Marxist" who "had read and created some sort of a theory, a Marxist theory for himself. . . . he was building up a doctrine in his head." He testified that when he asked him why he had left Russia, Oswald replied, "Because I did not find what I was looking for."

> Q. And did you ask him what he was looking for?
> A. A Utopia. I knew what he was looking for—Utopia.

A manuscript found among Oswald's belongings shows that he did, indeed, have visions of forming a party and was constructing his own Marxist doctrine. In a long, rambling discussion on politics, he wrote:

It is readily foreseeable that a coming economic, political or military crisis, internal or external, will bring about the final destruction of the capitalist system; assuming this, we can see how preparation in a special party could safeguard an independent course of action after the debacle.

He proposed a new system of pure communism controlled at the local level, with civil liberties, heavy taxes on profits but none on individuals, an abolition of fascist organizations and racial discrimination, and strict gun controls. His idealistic goals were teamed with a grandiose fanaticism that de Mohrenschildt apparently never detected:

> Resourcefulness and patient working towards the aforesaid goals are preferred rather than loud and useless manifestations of protest. Silent observance of our principles is of primary importance. But these preferred tactics now, may prove to be too limited in the near future, they should not be confused with slowness, indecision or fear, only the intellectually fearless could even be remotely attracted to our doctrine, and yet this doctrine requires the utmost restraint, a state of being in itself majestic in power. . . . Membership in this organization implies adherence to the principle of simple distribution of information about this movement to others and acceptance of the idea of stoical readiness in regards to practical measures once instituted in the crisis.

Years later, de Mohrenschildt wrote a manuscript about Oswald that was published in the House Assassinations Committee hearings. In it he said, "What I liked about him was that he was a seeker for justice —that he had highly developed social instincts. And I was disappointed in my own children for the lack of such instincts." His manuscript described many of their conversations, as de Mohrenschildt remembered them. Although his account may not be entirely reliable —de Mohrenschildt was known to exaggerate—it may still provide some revealing insights into Oswald's thinking.

De Mohrenschildt wrote that Oswald had been disappointed by his reception as a defector because he had naively expected "to be treated as a special person, a prominent refugee, and nothing happened." Oswald admitted that living conditions in Russia were poor. "But what does it matter," he said, "if everyone is in the same boat, if everyone suffers." At least there were no rich exploiters there, Oswald said, and no great contrasts between the rich and the poor. He said he got out of Russia "because all bureaucrats, all over the world, are stupid." Here, in de Mohrenschildt's words, are Oswald's statements on other subjects:

On integration: Lee's faith, his strongest belief was—racial integration. He told me on many occasions, "it hurts me that the blacks do not have the same privileges and rights as white Americans." "Segregation in any form, racial, social or economic, is one of the most repulsive facts of American life. . . . I would be willing any time to fight these fascistic segregationists—and to die for my black brothers." Because of his poor, miserable childhood, he probably compared himself to the blacks.

On world politics: "Under dictatorship people are enslaved but they know it. Here the politicians constantly lie to people and they become immune to these lies because they have the privilege of voting. But voting is rigged and democracy here is a gigantic profusion of lies and clever brainwashing. . . . Free people should not remain mere pawns in the world game of chess played by the rulers."

On J. Edgar Hoover: Also he said something about the FBI which did not strike me at the time as very clever, but history proved his judgment correct. "Knowledge is a great power, especially if you know it about very important people." Obviously J. Edgar Hoover's files must come to your mind.

On death: "I have had enough time in this short existence of mine. What shall I do with eternity? When a rich man dies, he is loaded with his possessions like a prisoner with chains. I will die free, death will be easy for me."

On Marina: "I never wanted a middle-class wife, mediocre, obscure, money loving. . . ."

George seemed to agree with this opinion of Marina. He wrote that he found no "substance" in her: "She was amusing sometimes, witty, naive mostly, like some Russian peasants, yet with a great deal of shrewdness underneath. My wife used to call her affectionately 'that rascal Marina'—and that description fitted her perfectly."

According to de Mohrenschildt, Oswald "thought that someday

there would be a 'coup d'etat' in this country organized by the Pentagon and that the country would become a militaristic, nazi-type dictatorship."

Concerning President Kennedy, de Mohrenschildt wrote, "Lee actually admired President Kennedy in his own reserved way." He recalled Oswald praising a picture of Kennedy on the cover of *Time* and remarking on how different he looked from "the other ratty politicos." He said that Oswald hoped Kennedy would accept coexistence with the Communist world after the Bay of Pigs.

De Mohrenschildt said he told Oswald, "If you want to be a revolutionary, you have to be a fool or to have an inspiration. And your actions will be judged by the success or failure of your life"—and Oswald agreed. But he also claimed that he urged Oswald to be more flexible, saying, "Live pleasantly and keep your own ideology to yourself." And to that Lee replied, "You are right. But this society we live in, it's so disgusting and degrading. How can you stand it?"

The approving audience Lee Oswald received from this eccentric but sophisticated man was undoubtedly encouraging to him. During this time, de Mohrenschildt spoke highly of Oswald to at least one acquaintance, who testified, "According to George, . . . he had great intellectual powers; he was a very clever person . . . and very well-read. . . . He told me on several occasions that '. . . he's just an idealistic Marxist.' "

In September 1962 a black student named James Meredith tried to enroll in the all-white University of Mississippi at Oxford. On the evening of September 30, a mob of segregationists rioted against the federal marshalls who were protecting Meredith on campus. Two people were killed, and after President Kennedy called out the National Guard, former Major General Edwin A. Walker, who was believed to have instigated the riot, was arrested for insurrection. This latest violence in the struggle for civil rights in the South made headlines around the world.

Walker had resigned from his army command in West Germany in 1961 after being reprimanded for trying to indoctrinate his troops with the rightist philosophy of the John Birch Society. Since then he had become a national political figure speaking against integration and Castro's Cuba. His home base was Dallas. Oswald was aware of Walker's history. At some point, when Oswald wrote up his theory that a military coup was possible in America, he argued that the army had too many conscripts and bases to lead a coup, and that "The case of General Walker shows that the Army . . . is not fertile enough ground for a far-right regime to go a very long way." He contended that the coup might come instead from the smaller Marine Corps—"a rightwing-infiltrated organization of dire potential consequences to the freedom of the United States." He concluded, "I agree with former President Truman when he said that 'The Marine Corps should be abolished.' "

After Walker's arrest, the news media followed him closely. He was released on $50,000 bond on October 7 and arrived at Love Field, where he was greeted by two hundred supporters. During the next few months, Walker would repeatedly make headlines as he prepared to stand trial in Mississippi.

As it happened, a group of the émigrés came to Oswald's apartment on the same Sunday Walker returned, and Oswald announced that he had been laid off from his job. (This was, in fact, untrue. His employer was satisfied with his performance. Oswald was simply planning to quit.) Feeling sorry for Marina and the baby, the émigrés offered to help. It was settled that Marina and June would move in with de Mohrenschildt's daughter Alexandra and her husband Gary Taylor for a few days, and then go to live with Elena Hall while Oswald went to Dallas to look for another job.

There were evidently several reasons behind his decision to move to Dallas. He probably wanted to live in a city where the FBI didn't know his address. And he wanted to get away from Marguerite, who had been visiting his family despite his strong objections. He didn't tell her where he was going and didn't see her again until after the assassination. And, just possibly, he may have already turned his attention to the right-wing leader, General Walker.

On arriving in Dallas the following Tuesday, Oswald rented a box at the main post office. A few days later he got a job at a graphic arts firm, Jaggars-Chiles-Stovall, as a trainee in photographic reproduction. Making no reference to Fort Worth, he told his new boss he had recently gotten out of the Marines.

Oswald began receiving his copies of *The Worker* at the post office. In the October 2 edition there was an appeal for support for two Communist party officials who were being prosecuted after failing to register under the McCarren Act. The article spoke of the work being done by the Gus Hall–Ben Davis Defense Committee with John Abt as chief counsel. The committee's address was given with the comment that it needed and invited financial support. After Oswald began working at Jaggars-Chiles-Stovall, he made up some poster-like blow-ups of an anti-McCarren Act slogan and sent them to the defense committee as a contribution. On the front page of the same issue, big headlines proclaimed: "Gen. Walker Arrested for Insurrection" and, alongside:

Nation Supports the President's Action
Punish the Guilty!
Gov. Barnett   Gen. Walker
White Citizens Council

> One year ago on Nov. 12, 1961 *The Worker* exposed the fascist character of Gen. Edwin A. Walker and warned the Kennedy administration and the American people of the need for action against him and his allies. A front-page article asserted:
> "The general thus becomes the first open candidate for leadership of the mass movement which the military–monopolist–pro-fascist plotters are now hoping to organize throughout the nation. . . .
> Critical of the "indecisiveness of the Kennedy administration in this situation," *The Worker* insisted last November that "firmness is essential" to defeat the ultra-Rights. . . .

In the October 7 issue another front-page story, headlined "Gen. Walker Bids for Fuehrer Role," again warned "the Kennedy Administration and the American people of the need for action against him and his allies." Two weeks later an article, headlined "Oxford Campus Plot for Bloodbath Bared," contained the assertion that "a coded file, arms and other materials" found in a car driven by one of Walker's cronies would reveal that "financial backers of extreme right wing groups" were "seeking the violent overthrow of the government."

Oswald probably read, and agreed with, a good deal of this. But nothing in *The Worker*'s call for political action advocated violence. Many other American newspaper editorials were saying much the same thing about Walker. Oswald already had his own ideas about the former army general. In his view, the man must have had three strikes against him—he opposed fair play for black Americans, he opposed Castro to the extent of calling for an invasion of Cuba, and he was a potential leader of a right-wing coup.

8... Taking Action

For most of October and part of November 1962, when Oswald was living alone in Dallas, Marina and June were dependent on the charity of the Taylors and the Halls. From this time onward his family would stay almost a third of the time with other people. When Oswald came to visit Marina at the Taylors, their relationship seemed so impersonal to Gary that he thought it was "like two friends meeting." Oswald would play with his daughter but never attempted to be alone with his wife. Taylor decided Marina's feelings simply weren't important to him.

In fact, the Oswald marriage had been strained ever since the couple arrived in the United States. In Fort Worth, Oswald had struck his wife, giving her a black eye, for allowing Bouhe to teach her some English. This was only one of the ways in which he tried to exert his control over her. He was often rude and overbearing to his wife in front of other people, ordering her around in a domineering voice. As a teenager, he had yelled orders at his mother in the same manner.

Most of their quarreling reflected their differences over his obsession with politics. Although Marina agreed with some of his views—she admired Castro, too—she felt the family should come first. To Oswald, such mundane concerns were bourgeois and stupid. She thought he had—as a later friend of Marina's would put it—"an overblown opinion of himself, and of what he could and should achieve in the world." He in turn complained about her lack of interest in politics. One of the émigrés, Katya Ford, was questioned about the Oswalds' relationship:

> Q. Did she tell you whether or not they discussed politics?
> A. She said she was arguing with him about that. Certainly, in fact, [as] he called her, she was a typical American girl, . . . not interested at all in politics. . . . She said she wanted a house and family and he said "All the American girls think that way". . . .

For the rest of their life together, Marina would continually wonder whether Lee loved her or not and would continue to hope he would give up this rival, politics, and settle down.

Occasionally Oswald would get into some friendly political arguments with the Taylors. He talked about the ideal society he had written about. Alexandra said, "He believed in the perfect government, free of want and need, and free of taxation, free of discrimination, free of any police force . . . total and complete freedom in everything." She felt he was "extremely devoted" to his ideas and "very, very rigid." And she found him persuasive: "He could almost make anybody believe what he was saying." But her overall opinion was negative. She thought he expected things to be given to him on a silver platter.

Gary Taylor was a Democrat who often expressed a strong disapproval of the John Birch Society, but there was little else he and Oswald could agree on. He gathered that Marina's husband was pro-Communist but anti-Russian, and that Oswald was disappointed when the Russians assigned him to a factory job instead of giving him "something important to do."

Max Clark, a Fort Worth attorney and friend of George de Mohrenschildt, met Oswald at about this time and got a similar impression about Oswald's ambitions and his reasons for leaving the Soviet Union. Oswald told him he had been unhappy about his work assignment in Minsk and had finally made up his mind that the Russian system was not "true communism" and that he would "never be able to get ahead or make his mark" in the Soviet Union. Clark told the Warren Commission that Oswald "seemed to have the idea that he was made for something other than what he was doing."

In October 1962 a serious international crisis developed over the introduction of Soviet nuclear missiles into Cuba. In a dramatic television appearance President Kennedy announced that he had ordered a naval blockade to prevent Soviet ships carrying more missiles from entering Cuban waters. After almost two weeks of worldwide fear of a nuclear war the confrontation ended on October 28, when the Soviet Union agreed to withdraw the missiles—over the strong protest of Fidel Castro.

We have only a glimpse of Lee Harvey Oswald's reaction to this crisis. According to one man who met him at a party the following February, after citing the Bay of Pigs and the missile crisis as examples of imperialist interventions, Oswald suggested that Kennedy's actions had set the stage for a nuclear holocaust. He added that even after the missiles had been withdrawn, American-sponsored acts of terrorism and sabotage against Cuba were continuing. This was presumably a reference to the sporadic paramilitary raids conducted by Cuban exile groups. (This account was, incidentally, the only report of Oswald's saying anything critical about President Kennedy before late September 1963.)

A day or two after the missile crisis ended, Oswald clipped a coupon from a pamphlet the Socialist Workers party had sent him, checked the box "I would like to join the Socialist Workers Party," and sent it via airmail to the New York headquarters. Writer Albert H. Newman has suggested that this action may be read as a sign of Oswald's feelings about the missile crisis. A Trotskyist group, the Socialist Workers party vehemently supported Castro and often criticized the Soviet Union for being too soft on Western imperialism. Since there were no chapters of the organization in Texas at that time, Oswald was unable to join. On the back of the coupon, now a Warren Commission exhibit, a portion of the party's message can be seen, and its tone suggests another reason Oswald may have been attracted to this group:

... that you are helping in the greatest cause ever undertaken, and that your weight really counts.

Socialism is the only road leading away from poverty, inflation, unemployment, imperialist war, totalitarianism—all the world-wide scourges of decaying capitalism. Socialism can save us from capitalist barbarism and open up a new world for humanity. The most courageous workers, those capable of the greatest sacrifices, those intelligent enough to see the task and endowed with the will to carry it out, must take the lead. That is our historic. . . .

In November Oswald finally rented an inexpensive apartment for his family on Elsbeth Street in the Oak Cliff section of Dallas. His landlady, Mrs. Mahlon Tobias, remembered that when he looked the place over, he particularly wanted to be shown the back entrance. Weeks later, when she rang his doorbell, Oswald came out the back and around the side of the building to see who it was. The Taylors helped the Oswalds move in on November 4, and for once Oswald thanked them. "Very briefly, thank you, and that was all," Alexandra said.

Before a week had passed the Oswalds were quarreling again. It had started over a trifle—or so Marina thought. Perhaps because he wanted no more visits from the FBI, Oswald had told Mrs. Tobias that his wife was from Czechoslovakia. Marina later wrote:

When the landlady asked me, I told her that I was from Russia, not knowing what Lee had told her. In this way a misunderstanding arose. I did not understand why Lee was hiding the fact that he was married to a Russian. . . . He got angry with me, said that I did not understand anything, and that I was not supporting him. I answered that it was hard to understand such stupidity, and that he was simply stupid. He told me that if I didn't like it I could go where I wanted. I was terribly hurt. I had no one there close to me except him and if this man rejected me, why should I stand in his way. I took June and left Lee to go to my Russian acquaintances.

Taking only her child, a few diapers, a shirt, and a baby bottle, Marina took a taxi to the Mellers' home. This time when the émigrés got together and agreed to look after her, it was with a condition.

George Bouhe told her he didn't think Oswald would ever treat her as he should and, "If you leave him, of course we'll help. But if you say one thing now and then go back, next time no one will help." Marina assured him she would never go back "to that hell."

Bouhe took her to stay at the home of Katya and Declan Ford. Oswald found out where she was living and called asking her to come home. He had been invited to his brother Robert's for Thanksgiving and wanted her with him—it would be humiliating if he had to go alone. Marina was curt with him at first but soon began to relent. A few days later Valentina Ray offered to let Marina live with her until she could learn enough English to find a job. Marina agreed, but she told her husband where she was, and when he telephoned her there, she consented to see him.

At the Rays' home they went into a bedroom to talk, and Marina reported that only after he begged her to return did she give in: "We talked alone in the room, and I saw him cry for the first time. What woman's heart can resist this, especially if she is in love? Lee begged me to come back, asked my forgiveness, and promised that he would try to improve. . . . Knowing Lee's character, I can say that this is perhaps the first time in his life that he had to go and ask someone a favor, and what is more, show his tears. . . . Lee was not particularly open with me about his feelings, but always wore a mask."

Whether the scene represented his true feelings or was just another manipulation to get what he wanted, he recovered his composure very quickly. What Valentina Ray remembered from that day was Oswald arguing politics with her husband. He offered to drive the reconciled couple home, and the political lecture continued en route. Valentina said her husband came home "huffing, puffing, said he never met anybody dumber in his life, doesn't understand simple economics or how anything works in this country."

After Marina moved back, most of the émigrés threw up their hands. Only the de Mohrenschildts remained friendly, exchanging visits and taking them to a few parties. For a short while, the Oswald household was peaceful. Marina said of this period, "He used to bring home dozens of books from the library and just swallowed them down. . . . Sometimes it seemed to me that he was living in another world which he had constructed for himself, and that he came down to earth only to go to work, to earn money for his family, to eat, and to sleep."

In early December 1962 Oswald began making use of the Jaggars-Chiles-Stovall facilities and materials for his own purposes when he was working overtime. Using the photographic techniques he'd learned, he made some advertising posters for the Socialist Workers party and *The Worker,* as well as the Hall–Davis Defense Committee. (*The Worker*'s poster said, "READ THE WORKER / If you want to know about / PEACE / DEMOCRACY / UNEMPLOYMENT / ECONOMIC TRENDS.") Along with the blowups, he sent letters offering to do further photographic work at no charge. Each organization wrote a polite letter of acknowledgment, and Oswald carefully saved these replies—he would find a use for them in the months ahead.

In mid-December he took out a subscription to *The Militant,* the Socialist Workers' newspaper. Like *The Worker,* it was critical of General Walker and of Kennedy's policies on Cuba and the civil rights struggle. One of the first issues he would have received in January commented on the speech President Kennedy gave in the Miami Orange Bowl on December 29. Before a crowd of 40,000 Cuban exiles, Kennedy greeted a group of Bay of Pigs veterans who had just been ransomed from their imprisonment in Cuba. When the president was presented with the Cuban brigade's battle flag, he spontaneously declared, "I can assure you that this flag will be returned to this brigade in a free Havana"—a prediction that drew tumultuous cheers from the audience. *The Militant* called it "the most barefaced and disgusting display of immorality, ignorance and bad taste ever put on by a U.S. President." In its January 21 issue, *The Militant* published Castro's response to Kennedy's Miami appearance, a speech headlined, "We Will Not Stop Being Revolutionists." Castro said Kennedy had "conducted himself like a pirate." After citing the Bay of Pigs and the Cuban citizens who had been killed in exile raids and in internal counter-revolutionary attacks, he declared, "Mr. Kennedy, too much blood has flowed between you and us."

At the beginning of 1963 Oswald began making specific plans to assassinate General Walker. The final decision apparently came after

January 21, when a federal grand jury in Mississippi released Walker after declining to indict him. The next day, the Dallas *Morning News* quoted Walker: "I am glad to be vindicated. . . . Today my hopes returned to the Cubans and millions of others who long to return to their homes. . . ." On January 27, Oswald ordered a Smith & Wesson .38 snub-nosed revolver from a Los Angeles mail-order firm, using "A. J. Hidell" as an alias.

This was his first known use of the Alek James Hidell alias. "Alek" had been his nickname in Russia. "Hidell" was probably an altered "Fidel," embraced by two of his own initials. The "James" is less certain but may have come from a fictional character he was known to have admired—James Bond.

It was apparently around this time that he printed up a phony ID in the name of Alek James Hidell—perhaps he thought he might need identification to pick up the gun at the post office. He also began studying a city map and a bus schedule to lay out an escape route from Walker's home on Turtle Creek Boulevard. And he began putting pressure on Marina to return to the Soviet Union with June. The Warren Commission evidently never realized why Oswald wanted to send his family to Russia. Marina testified, "Lee wanted me to go to Russia . . . and I told him that if he wanted me to go then that meant he didn't love me and . . . in that case what was the idea of coming to the United States in the first place. Lee would say that it would be better for me to go to Russia. I did not know why. I did not know what he had in mind. He said he loved me but it would be better for me if I went to Russia."

Q. Did he have a job then?
A. Yes.
Q. Did you feel that you were getting along on what he was making?
A. Of course. . . .
Q. Did you understand when he suggested you return to Russia that he was proposing to break up your marriage?
A. I told him that I would go to Russia if he gave me a divorce, but he did not want to give me a divorce.
Q. Did he say why?

A. He said that if he were to give me a divorce that would break everything between us, which he didn't want. That he wanted to keep me as his wife.

When she was asked if she now understood why Oswald wanted her to return to the Soviet Union, she said, "Yes . . . I think I know why[;] he had in mind to start his foolish activity which could harm me, but, of course, at that time he didn't tell me the reason. . . . At that time when I would ask him he would get angry because he couldn't tell me."

While he was waiting for the pistol to arrive, something happened to delay his plans. On February 14 the *Morning News* announced that Walker would be going out of town on a nationwide tour, dubbed "Operation Midnight Ride," from February 27 to April 3 to make speeches warning about the dangers of Castro and communism. Three days later Oswald forced the reluctant Marina, who wanted to stay in America, to sit down and write the following letter to the Soviet Embassy in Washington:

I beg your assistance to help me to return to the homeland in the USSR where I will again feel myself a full-fledged citizen. Please let me know what I should do for this, i.e., perhaps it will be necessary to fill out a special application form. Since I am not working at present (because of my lack of knowledge of the English language and a small child), I am requesting you to extend to me a possible material aid for the trip. My husband remains here, since he is an American by nationality. I beg you once more not to refuse my request.

It is not too difficult to see Oswald's hand in this, especially in the phrase "full-fledged citizen" and in the request for "material aid." Since he couldn't afford to send his family to Russia, he expected the Russians to take care of it.

On February 22 Lee and Marina went to a party given by Everett Glover, a friend of de Mohrenschildt's. One of the guests was Ruth Paine, a Quaker who had recently separated from her husband Michael and who was studying the Russian language. Ruth was eager to meet someone who spoke modern Russian because she hoped to be able to learn the language well enough to teach it. She and Marina began a friendship that evening which Oswald encouraged for his own reasons. Marina said later that "from the moment he met Ruth, Lee [thought] only how to use her."

Marina would remember February 1963 as by far the worst month of their marriage. Oswald often flew into a rage and beat her whenever she seemed to go against his wishes. Their landlady noticed that Marina was always quiet around Oswald and that he never seemed to want her to be out of his sight when he was home. She thought Marina seemed "very lonely." During this period Oswald sometimes wouldn't come home until seven o'clock or later, and Marina never knew where he was. On one such night in late February, Mrs. Tobias testified that Marina came knocking on her door:

> . . . and wanted to know if she could use the phone. She said, "I don't know where my husband is." . . . I said to her, "Mrs. Oswald, Marina, can you read English?" She said "Yes"—and I went and got a tablet of paper. . . . took a pencil and wrote "When he gets home give him a good kick in the shin." And she started laughing . . . and she said she would.

Marina then called several numbers and spoke in Russian but, said Mrs. Tobias, "She never did find him." One of Marina's calls was to George de Mohrenschildt, who telephoned Jaggars-Chiles-Stovall for her and found out Lee wasn't there. Oswald, of course, was angry when he discovered she'd been checking up on him. Later that week their fighting got so noisy the owner of the building told Oswald he would have to stop fighting or move. Oswald decided to move.

On March 3 they carried their belongings to another furnished apartment several blocks away at 214 West Neely Street, using June's stroller as a carrier. Mrs. Tobias watched them go: "They moved away in that stroller. . . . They didn't have very much—all he had was books and what little dishes they had, and that wasn't very many, and the baby bed." The new apartment had a small room Oswald appropriated for a study—it had an interior door that could be locked and another door leading to the outside. Now he could come and go without Marina's knowledge, and he could have privacy while he worked out his plans.

At least some of Oswald's mysterious activities undoubtedly had to do with General Walker. He may have rehearsed his route by riding the buses he intended to use to and from Walker's home. At any rate, it is certain that after Walker left town, Oswald undertook a reconnaissance. On the weekend of March 9–10 he used his Imperial Reflex camera to photograph the alley behind Walker's house and an area near a railroad where he would hide the weapon. (The pictures, found among Oswald's possessions, could be dated because of some construction work going on in the background.) He recorded a detailed description of the house and its surroundings in a notebook he kept in his study.

Evidently his survey of Walker's property changed his mind about the appropriate weapon, for on March 12 he ordered a Mannlicher-Carcano rifle from Klein's Sporting Goods in Chicago, again using the Hidell alias. By coincidence both weapons were shipped on March 20 and arrived about five days later. When Walker returned to Dallas, he'd be ready.

It was during this month that the FBI took a renewed interest in the Oswalds. It was FBI practice to interview immigrants from the Soviet bloc countries on a selective basis, and Marina was one of those selected. When John Fain retired he left her case marked pending inactive. On March 4 Fain's successor, James P. Hosty, Jr., obtained Marina's Elsbeth Street address from the Immigration and Naturalization Service records. On the 11th, the day before Oswald ordered his rifle, Hosty drove over and spoke to Mrs. Tobias, who told him that they had moved. Hosty obtained the Oswalds' new address. But having learned of their frequent quarrels from Mrs. Tobias, he decided to allow them a certain "cooling off period," as required by FBI regulations, before he talked to Marina. (Even though he was going by the book, this decision would ultimately earn him a reprimand and the eternal wrath of J. Edgar Hoover.) Hosty checked Lee Oswald's file and found that he was on *The Worker*'s mailing list. At Hosty's request, Oswald's case was reopened on March 26. But when he finally went to the Neely Street apartment in late May they had moved without leaving a forwarding address.

Would it have made a difference if agent Hosty had caught up with Oswald before he attacked Walker? Probably not. Oswald already knew the FBI was interested in him, and the watchful eye of the authorities had never stopped him in the past.

On Sunday, March 31, Oswald had Marina take several pictures of him in their backyard. Dressed in black, he wore a pistol on his belt, holding the rifle in one hand and a recent copy of both *The Militant* and *The Worker* in the other. He told her he wanted photographs to send to *The Militant*. Oswald was clearly proud of what he was about to do. He inscribed one of the prints "For Junie from Papa" and gave it to Marina as a keepsake for their daughter, so that "maybe someday June will remember me." Marina put this print and one like it in June's baby book.

Oswald obviously believed that *The Militant* would applaud his attack on Walker. He undoubtedly got this idea from the general editorial line of the newspaper, which advocated revolutionary violence where necessary. In the February 25 issue there was a review of a book by Robert F. Williams that called for blacks to arm themselves. The review noted, "John Brown and the Abolitionists did not fight slavery with prayers but with armed struggle against the evil system. Williams thus stands in the American tradition of struggle for freedom, the best of our heritage and legacy. [Martin Luther] King's Gandhiism runs counter to this spirit. . . . [and] is racist in its outlook." The review spoke of the "inadequacy of narrowly conceived tactics of non-violence."

On April 2 Ruth Paine invited the Oswalds to dinner and had her husband Michael pick them up at their apartment. An engineer with Bell Helicopter, Michael was an intelligent and well-educated man whose father had been a Trotskyite after leaving the Communist party in the 1940s. Michael could remember being taken to Party meetings as a child and being bored by them. Like Ruth, he was tolerant of political dissidents even when he disagreed with them. That night one of the few things he and Oswald could agree on was their opinion of General Walker—they both criticized the Far Right. Naturally Oswald said nothing about his secret plan. At the Oswalds' Neely Street apartment, Paine was shocked by Oswald's rudeness to his wife. At Ruth's, he became annoyed when he tried to include Marina in their conversation and Oswald seemed to resent having to translate for her. But Oswald was pleased with the evening, for he saw once more how Ruth's interest in Marina could serve his purposes. The Russian visas hadn't come through, and if he went ahead with his plan to kill Walker, Marina might need a friend who spoke Russian. During the week Oswald practiced with the rifle.

On April 6 he lost his job. He never held any job for very long, mostly due to his attitude. He resented his employers—any employers. As he had said in Moscow, if he lived in the United States he would face the choice of being an exploiter or one of the exploited, and rather than assume either role he would end up being one of the unemployed. Oswald appeared to like his job at Jaggars-Chiles-Stovall, but eventually began to show his resentment by reading Russian magazines at work—it was reminiscent of the way he had openly read Russian newspapers in the Marines. His employer noticed it, and he also noticed that Oswald's work often had to be redone. Around the first week of April he informed Oswald he would have to let him go.

To help Oswald find another job, de Mohrenschildt referred him to a friend, Sam Ballen, a native of New York who served on the boards of several Dallas corporations. During a two-hour interview with Ballen, Oswald didn't mention his recent employment and instead claimed to have learned reproduction work in Russia and New Orleans. Inevitably the conversation drifted into Oswald's politics: his opposition to racial prejudice and what Ballen later called his "compassion for mankind generally." Oswald complained that he too was the victim of prejudice because of his stay in the Soviet Union. Although sympathetic, Ballen decided that this young man wouldn't fit into a team operation—he was "too hard-headed, too independent." Ballen considered Oswald to be "a truth-seeking decent individual with a bit of Schweitzerian self-sacrifice in him—so much so that I didn't want him working for me." For his part, Oswald seemed uninterested in a position that required conformity. He told Ballen, "Don't worry about me."

Sometime in early April—the exact time isn't certain—Oswald staged his first pro-Castro demonstration. With a placard saying "Hands Off Cuba! Viva Fidel!" hanging on his chest, he handed out Fair Play for Cuba literature briefly on a downtown street. Two policemen later reported seeing the demonstration. According to a passerby, when Oswald spotted them coming toward him he muttered, "Oh hell, here come the cops," and ducked into a nearby store. He wrote the Fair Play for Cuba Committee in New York to report his demonstration (omitting the appearance of the police) and asked the group to send him "40 or 50 more" of their pamphlets.

Having completed his speaking tour, General Walker came home. Oswald may have been following his progress in the Dallas newspapers. On March 6 the *Times Herald* had reported on a speech Walker gave in Savannah in which he challenged President Kennedy to take "one U.S. Army division . . . and liquidate the scourge that has descended upon the island of Cuba." This was only a few days before Oswald reconnoitered the Walker house and grounds and ordered his rifle.

On the evening of April 10 Oswald went to Walker's home with the Mannlicher-Carcano, which he had concealed under a raincoat. He took a position in a dark alley behind a stockade fence, 120 feet from the back of the house. Inside he could see Edwin A. Walker through a lighted window sitting at his desk. The light obscured a strip of the window casing and the bullet missed, striking the wall just above Walker's head and leaving bits of wood and glass in his hair. Oswald ran without waiting to see the result. He hid the rifle and escaped on a city bus (exactly as he would do after the assassination of President Kennedy).

Around 10 o'clock that evening Marina grew restless wondering where he was. She went into his study and found a key and a note of instructions written in Russian:

1. This is the key to the mailbox which is located in the main post office in the city on Ervay Street. This is the same street where the drugstore, in which you always waited is located. You will find the mailbox in the

post office which is located 4 blocks from the drugstore on that street. I paid for the box last month so don't worry about it.

2. Send the information as to what has happened to me to the Embassy and include newspaper clippings (should there be anything about me in the newspapers). I believe that the Embassy will come quickly to your assistance on learning everything.

3. I paid the house rent on the 2d so don't worry about it.

4. Recently I also paid for water and gas.

5. The money from work will possibly be coming. The money will be sent to our post office box. Go to the bank and cash the check.

6. You can either throw out or give my clothing, etc. away. Do not keep these. However, I prefer that you hold on to my personal papers (military, civil, etc.).

7. Certain of my documents are in the small blue valise.

8. The address book can be found on my table in the study should you need same.

9. We have friends here. The Red Cross also will help you (Red Cross in English) [sic].

10. I left you as much money as I could, $60 on the second of the month. You and the baby can live for another 2 months using $10 per week.

11. If I am alive and taken prisoner, the city jail is located at the end of the bridge through which we always passed on going to the city (right in the beginning of the city after crossing the bridge).

Marina testified that when her husband got home that night he was pale. He told her what he had done, and defended his action by describing General Walker as "the leader of a fascist organization." She responded by saying even though that might be true, he had no right to take his life. She made him promise never to do such a thing again, and tucked the note of instructions he had left her into one of her books. She told the Assassinations Committee that Oswald "felt quite strongly that he was doing a justice to the people" and considered her a fool for not understanding him. She quoted Oswald: "Well, what would you say if somebody got rid of Hitler at the right time? So if you don't know about General Walker, how can you speak up on his behalf?" She reported that after reading the news accounts the next day Oswald was "kind of angry" that he missed him, but at the same time "kind of pleased with himself, with the clever fellow he was" in getting away with it.

Oswald destroyed the notebook he'd used for the planning, but kept the photographs of Walker's house and its surroundings and the photographs of himself holding the rifle. He evidently wanted a record of the attempt for some future use. It's possible he was even considering another attempt to kill Walker, at some later date after the police attention subsided.

One may ask why Marina didn't immediately go to the Dallas police. In retrospect it is easy to condemn her. But Marina evidently didn't leave her husband or go to the police for much the same reasons other battered wives often choose to stay with their husbands—at times, she was afraid of him. Someone on the Assassinations Committee asked her, "What do you think he would have done if you had gotten rid of the rifle?" And she answered, "Well, he probably would have got rid of me." She had no one else, no way of supporting herself and June; and she was three months into a second pregnancy. But despite everything she still loved him and hoped he would change.

Marina did not realize that Oswald could not change without giving up the image he had of himself as an idealist who *acted* on his principles. His feelings of self-worth derived not from his work or personal relationships, but from his ideology. The assassination attempt against Walker, like his defection, revealed Oswald's extreme dedication to his political beliefs. All else was secondary to him—his family, even the question of whether he lived or died. At the same time, Oswald expected and craved recognition as a revolutionary hero. Both these events were clearly designed to attract worldwide attention to himself as well as to his cause. Giving up these ideas, as Marina wanted, would have meant scrapping his identity and constructing a new one—or becoming a hypocrite in his own eyes, someone who sat around and talked but did nothing.

The attack on Walker resembled his defection in another respect: it was carefully planned. Part of the excitement must have been in the detailed anticipation. The note he left Marina indicates that he had considered every eventuality—that he might be killed or arrested, or that he might escape, possibly to another country. Albert Newman believes that had Oswald assassinated Walker he intended to go to the Cuban Embassy in Mexico City, tell the officials there what he had done—proving it with his notebook and photographs—and ask for asylum in Cuba, an "extradition-free" country. McMillan suggests that in the event of an arrest he might have used his trial as a forum to denounce American fascism, before asking for asylum in *Russia*. At any rate, as Marina later said of the backyard photographs, "He must have had something in his mind—some grandiose plans."

On April 21 Oswald staged another dramatic scene. After reading the morning newspaper he got dressed and put his Smith & Wesson pistol into his belt. He informed Marina that former Vice-President Richard Nixon was coming to town and that he wanted "to go and have a look." Marina has testified that she replied, "I know how you *look*"—and physically restrained him from leaving the apartment. (In fact, Nixon was *not* coming to Dallas, but that day's *Morning News* reported a speech he had made in Washington. The banner headline read, "Nixon Calls for Decision to Force Reds Out of Cuba/Open U.S. Support of Rebels Urged.")

When skeptical Commission members questioned her about this incident, Marina admitted that she could not have kept her husband from leaving their apartment if he had really wanted to go. She said that at first he was angry and told her, "You are always getting in my way," but then rather quickly gave in. "It might have been," she continued, "that he was just trying to test me." (Thinking back on it, Marina saw the incident as a "kind of nasty joke," an example of a sadistic streak he had. She also told the Commission that when he made her write letters to the Russian Embassy asking to be allowed to return to the Soviet Union, "He liked to tease me and torment me in this way . . . especially if I interfered in any of his political affairs, in any of his political discussions.")

It isn't clear why Oswald now decided to move to New Orleans. Marina has said it was her suggestion that he go to his hometown to find work, because she wanted to get him away from the temptation of trying to kill Walker again. But it also appears that Oswald had, as usual, some political goal in mind. When Ruth Paine visited the Oswalds on April 24, she found them waiting with their bags packed ready to be driven to the bus station. Rather than see the pregnant Marina make the long bus trip with a small child, she offered to let them stay with her while Lee went ahead to look for a job. This was evidently exactly what Oswald had intended all along. She drove him to the terminal to check his baggage, and the next day Oswald took a bus to New Orleans.

9...The Activist

FROM our perspective twenty years later, America's undeclared war on Cuba looks like a hysterical overreaction. It did not seem so to most Americans at the time. The Kennedy administration was under intense public pressure to do something about Cuba. Thousands of refugees had fled to the United States bringing horror stories about life under communism, and many of them were prepared to fight to liberate their country. (Other refugees, according to the *New York Times*, were Castro agents who were sent to create disunity and promote agitation against the U.S. government among the exiles.) Castro had proclaimed himself an ally of the Soviet Union and was boasting that his revolution would spread throughout Latin America. Occasionally it looked as though his dream might come true. Shortly after the missile crisis, for example, pro-Castro guerrillas knocked out one-sixth of Venezuela's oil-production capacity.

The White House was still uncertain what to do about Cuba. After the October crisis, the MONGOOSE operation was disbanded, and the Special Group committee, chaired by presidential assistant McGeorge Bundy, took control of covert actions in Cuba. On January 4, 1963, and again in April and June, Bundy proposed to the president the idea of opening communications with Castro with an eye to taking Castro "out of the Soviet fold." This option was to be explored on a "separate track," however, while other proposed actions, such as sabotage, were going on. In February 1963 *Time* carried an article called "The Hardening Soviet Base in Cuba," which quoted a top administration official as saying that present U.S. policy toward Cuba was "not containment; it's getting rid of Castro"—through economic and political pressures. It stated that the administration was hoping for an uprising against Castro and quoted President Kennedy on what his reaction might be: "Probably the first U.S. response would be diplomatic. . . . But a real uprising in Cuba would not be like a Bay of Pigs invasion financed from abroad. It would be a cry for help which the U.S. could not afford to ignore." Another report on a Kennedy news conference that month quoted him as conceding "that Soviet troops in Cuba are surely being used to train Cubans to export revolution and sabotage throughout Latin America." One White House estimate reported that at least 13,000 Latin American students were being trained.

Early spring brought the first public talk about the possibility that Fidel Castro might be assassinated by someone dissatisfied with his rule inside Cuba. On March 15 the *Wall Street Journal* quoted un-named Washington officials as declaring that Castro's assassination had become "the major U.S. hope for de-communizing Cuba"—explaining that "rising public discontent in Cuba" was "bound to bring a successful assassination attempt sooner or later." This item was picked up for brief mention by both *The Worker* and *The Militant.* Both papers omitted the reference to rising discontent in Cuba. At approximately the same time an exile group called Alpha 66 raided a Cuban port and shelled a Russian ship, eliciting a strong protest from the Soviet government. The FBI and Coast Guard responded with an official crackdown nationwide on exile raiders starting the first week of April. This new policy, in turn, brought protests from the exiles and Republican leaders.

In an April 19 speech President Kennedy attempted to counter demands for a second invasion of Cuba by predicting that "in five years" Castro would likely no longer be in power and that ultimately the United States would be seen to have contributed to his downfall. In recent years this speech has sometimes been interpreted as a sign that Kennedy was aware of a CIA effort to kill Castro. But he was clearly referring to the *long-term* effect of administration pressures on Cuba in general, which he hoped would eventually result in Castro's overthrow. It would have been illogical for him to suggest that an American contribution to Castro's murder would someday be applauded—none of the plotters wanted the U.S. role ever to be revealed. Moreover, according to the Church committee investigation, there were no ongoing assassination plots during this period. The plots involving members of the Mafia had been terminated in February after producing no results whatsoever. (It appears that the Mafia participants weren't seriously interested in eliminating Castro but were stringing the CIA officials along for their own purposes.)

But at the time, Fidel Castro apparently saw the president's statements as a threat. His response came two days later in an April 21 *New York Times* headline that today seems startling:

CASTRO SAYS U.S. PLANS SLAYINGS
Declares Assassination Plot Replaced Second Invasion

The story began, "Premier Fidel Castro said today that the United States had abandoned plans for a second invasion of Cuba in favor of a plot to assassinate Cuban leaders." Castro then gave his version of recent Cuban–American history, asserting that after the Bay of Pigs the Soviets had introduced missiles into Cuba to prevent a second invasion attempt, and had withdrawn them in return for Kennedy's promise that Cuba would not be invaded. The American government, said Castro, understood that new military attacks on Cuba would provoke a world war. But, Castro added, "We cannot rest on our laurels. . . . They are now making plans to assassinate the leaders of the revolution."

(This story was picked up by the Dallas *Times-Herald* the same afternoon, but Lee Oswald almost certainly didn't see it. This was the day of Oswald's "nasty joke" about shooting Nixon, and therefore the events of April 21 were vividly impressed on Marina's memory. She testified that Oswald didn't leave their apartment after going out for the morning newspaper, and if she is right, Oswald couldn't have bought a *Times-Herald* that afternoon.)

In May 1963, the National Security Council's Standing Group discussed several contingencies, and found that the prospect of Castro's death resulting in favorable developments inside Cuba was "singularly unpromising." The CIA's Office of National Estimates agreed. The memorandum it prepared concluded that Castro would be replaced by his brother Raul or someone else who had Soviet backing, and warned, "If Castro were to die by other than natural causes the U.S. would be widely charged with complicity. . . ."

The president's speech on April 19 and the negative conclusions of the Standing Group and the CIA may be taken as further evidence of the administration's continuing sense of frustration concerning Cuba. The tension of those times was reflected in an April 29 issue of *The Militant* which quoted a statement Robert Kennedy had made on April 22: "We can't just snap our fingers and make Castro go away. But we can fight for this. We can dedicate all our energy and best possible brains to that effort."

Lee Oswald hadn't been in New Orleans since 1959 when he had passed through on his way to the Soviet Union. The city was much the same. In late April it was already getting hot and humid. During the months ahead there would be frequent afternoon thunderstorms, and swarms of mosquitos blown in from nearby salt marshes would attack pedestrians on downtown streets. One could still get off a streetcar in the middle of Canal Street and walk into the French Quarter, with its carnival atmosphere of jazz and strip shows, tawdry souvenir shops, sidewalk artists, and occasional young black boys offering a quick softshoe routine in exchange for money. But there *had* been a considerable influx of Cuban exiles, some of whom were active in anti-Castro organizations.

Oswald called his Aunt Lillian from the Greyhound Bus station. She was surprised to hear from him, since she didn't know he had returned from the Soviet Union, nor did she know he had married and was a father. She agreed to put him up while he looked for a job. He stayed with her family for a couple of weeks.

Oswald applied for and received unemployment benefits from Texas, and then found a job as a maintenance mechanic at the William

B. Reily Company, a distributor of Luzianne coffee. Lillian remembered him coming home excited.

. . . and he grabbed me around the neck and he even kissed me and he said "I got it; I got it!" . . . I said, "Lee, how much does it pay" and he said, "Well, it don't pay very much but I will get along on it." . . . I said, "Well, you know, Lee, you are not really qualified to do anything too much. If you don't like this job why don't you try to go back to school again at night time and see if you can't learn a trade or whatever you think you can prepare yourself to do." And he said, "No, I don't have to go back to school. I don't have to learn anything. I know everything." . . .

Q. Did you get the impression . . . that he really believed he was that smart?

A. He believed he was that smart, yes, sir.

Q. You don't think he was spoofing you?

A. No; I think he really thought he was smart, and I don't think he envied anybody else, because he thought he knew it all, I guess.

That same morning Oswald began looking for a place to live. He went to see his mother's old friend Myrtle Evans, who was still managing apartments. She had nothing available, but they drove around in search of "For Rent" signs. They found a vacant apartment at 4907 Magazine Street for $65 a month, and Oswald took it. That evening he called Marina at Ruth's house in Irving, Texas, to tell her the news. Marina had been spending a lot of time discussing with Ruth the question of whether Lee loved her or not, and now, after hanging up the phone, she kept repeating to her daughter, June, "Papa nas lubet . . . Daddy loves us, he got work and he wants us to come." The next day Ruth, Marina, and their children left Irving to drive to New Orleans.

Seeing the Magazine Street apartment with its dark rooms and roaches was a bitter letdown for Marina, and Ruth noticed that Oswald seemed disappointed by her reaction. Although their meeting had been cordial, the Oswalds began quarreling almost immediately, and Ruth decided to leave earlier than she had planned. The fighting stemmed from the problem they had always had: their priorities were not the same. For after his family was settled, Oswald turned to political activities.

On May 14 he mailed a change-of-address card to the Fair Play for Cuba Committee, and eight days later the National Director, Vincent T. Lee, wrote a routine reply: "We received your notice of change of address. . . . We hope to hear from you soon so that we may again have your name amongst those who continue to support the efforts of our Committee." Much to Vincent Lee's subsequent regret, Oswald needed no encouragement. He responded quickly:

I am requesting formal membership in your organization.

In the past I have received from you pamphlets etc., both bought by me and given to me by you.

Now that I live in New Orleans I have been thinking about renting a small office at my own expense for the purpose of forming a F.P.C.C. branch here in New Orleans.

Could you give me a charter?

Also I would like information on buying pamphlets etc. in large lots, as well as blank F.P.C.C. applications etc.

Also a picture of Fidel, suitable for framing would be a welcome touch.

Offices down here rent for $30 a month and if I had a steady flow of literature I would be glad to take the expense.

Of course I work and could not supervise the office at all times but I'm sure I could get some volunteers to do it.

Could you add some advice or recommendations?

I am not saying this project would be a roaring success, but I am willing to try.

An office, literature, and getting people to know you are the fundamentals of the F.P.C.C. as far as I can see so here's hoping to hear from you.

Why this sudden burst of political activism? Albert H. Newman has suggested that Oswald wanted to establish a pro-Castro record in New Orleans so he could attain a visa to Cuba which he could then use as an escape route after he returned to Dallas to make another attempt on Walker's life. Newman pointed out that during his stay in Dallas

Oswald had gone out of his way to conceal his whereabouts. On his job applications and correspondence, he had given a box number, not a home address. And as far as Oswald knew, the FBI hadn't tracked him from Fort Worth to Dallas. In New Orleans, however, he made no secret of his Magazine Street address, and he would soon become engaged in political activities that would inevitably draw the attention of the local police and FBI. Oswald wanted visibility in New Orleans, but had wanted to stay hidden in Dallas. Newman believes that the sentence in the letter above beginning, "Now that I live in New Orleans . . ." reflects this change in tactics. But it doesn't necessarily follow that Oswald planned to go back to Dallas. It may be that he simply realized he would have to establish his reputation as an activist somewhere else—making himself known as a Castro supporter in Dallas might have made him a suspect in the still-unsolved Walker shooting.

The first part of Newman's theory is well established. There's little doubt that Oswald's pro-Castro activities were designed to help him get into Cuba and be warmly received once he got there. Marina has testified that although her husband wanted to help the Cuban revolution, she knew "that his basic desire was to get to Cuba by any means and that all the rest of it was window dressing for that purpose." There is more than Marina's testimony to support this. Oswald's attempt to enter Cuba would be a repetition of his earlier defection, but with a difference. He had had some difficulty being accepted by the Soviets because he carried no credentials. They had asked for papers to show who and what he was, and he had none. This time he would have plenty of papers showing his ideological record. Throughout that summer he would write to the Fair Play Committee, the Communist party, and *The Worker* telling them of his political work, and he would save their replies. He would write up the details of his work under such headings as Marxist, Street Agitation, Radio Speaker, and Lecturer. In the fall he would present this material when he applied for a Cuban visa in Mexico City. (We know this because the résumé material was found among Oswald's belongings after the assassination, and an employee at the Cuban Embassy described some of these credentials to the Mexican police.)

What did Oswald hope to do after he got to Cuba? Certainly, he didn't expect to be given factory work or be sent to a Cuban equivalent of Minsk. Oswald had a rigid and willful personality, seemingly incapable of fundamental change; he kept repeating the same patterns over and over. Disappointed by his reception in Russia, he probably expected that the Cubans would recognize his abilities and give him the important assignment he thought he deserved.

It may be that he returned to the dream he had discussed with Nelson Delgado just four years before—becoming an officer in Castro's army to lead a revolution in another country. This was not as fantastic an ambition as it might seem. In 1963 it was illegal for Americans to travel to Cuba. But during March there had been a flurry in the press about a so-called "subversion airlift" flying between Mexico City and Havana. Some of these stories appeared in *Time,* a publication Oswald subscribed to (although it isn't known whether he saw them). On March 29, for instance, the magazine reported that there were twice-weekly flights from Mexico City and that, in 1962 alone, approximately 1500 Latin Americans and others had been taken to Cuba for "indoctrination and guerrilla warfare training." *Time* claimed that "thousands of students, small-time labor leaders, intellectuals and professional men" were getting "all-expense-paid tours" of Cuba and that many returned to their countries to become "terrorists, guerrillas, and Communist party workers." The article said that until February 15 "it was no trick to fly to Mexico, where the Cuban embassy issued a visa on a slip of paper. No telltale stamp marred the passports. Now the Mexicans stamp passports 'Salió a Cuba' in bold letters. But, of course, passports can be conveniently 'lost,' destroying the evidence." *Time* also noted that the airlift had figured prominently in the questions and answers at President Kennedy's press conference a week earlier.

During the summer a group of 58 students sponsored by the Fair Play for Cuba Committee defied the U.S. ban on travel to Cuba. President Kennedy publicly condemned their action, and the State Department lifted their passports when they returned. In July Edwin E. Willis, the chairman of the House Un-American Activities Committee, gave a speech in New Orleans in which he charged that many of the travelers had Communist backgrounds and had returned to this country "to lecture on the glories of Castro's Cuba."

At some point Oswald considered hijacking a plane to Havana. He studied airline schedules and maps, and when Marina refused to go along with the scheme, he told her he would go ahead on his own. On July 30 the *Times-Picayune* covered the Cuban flights from Mexico City and noted, "Any American with a valid passport and a clean criminal record can enter Cuba via Mexico without State Department authorization provided he is acceptable to Cuban authorities and aerial transportation is available." After this—Marina thought it was in late August—Oswald burst into the apartment with the news that he had found a legal way to get to Cuba. According to McMillan, he told her, "There's a Cuban Embassy in Mexico. I'll go there. I'll show them my clippings, show them how much I've done for Cuba, and explain how hard it is to help in America. And how above all I want to help Cuba."

In late May Oswald's campaign to establish his pro-Castro credentials was just beginning. He was also trying to get Marina to answer a letter she had received from the Soviet Embassy in Washington in April, asking her to state her reasons for wanting to go back to the Soviet Union. On the same weekend that Oswald wrote the Fair Play for Cuba Committee asking for a charter, Marina sent a plaintive letter to Ruth (in Russian): ". . . As soon as you left all 'love' stopped, and I am very hurt that Lee's attitude towards me is such that I feel each minute that I bind him. He insists that I leave America, which I don't want to do at all. I like America very much and think that even without Lee I would not be lost here. What do you think. This is the basic question which doesn't leave me day or night."

Without waiting for a reply from the Committee, Oswald dropped by the Jones Printing Company opposite his workplace. Using the alias "Osborne," he ordered, for $9.89, one thousand copies of a handbill reading:

HANDS OFF CUBA!

Join the Fair Play for Cuba Committee
NEW ORLEANS CHARTER MEMBER BRANCH

Free Literature, Lectures
LOCATION:
[space left blank]
EVERYONE WELCOME!

In the meantime, Vincent T. Lee had written a cautious reply to Oswald's requests, and sent him a membership card, but not the charter or application forms he had wanted. The Fair Play director said that although the Committee would like to see a New Orleans chapter opened, "It would be hard to conceive of a chapter with as few members as seem to exist in the New Orleans area." He added, "You must realize that you will come under tremendous pressures with any attempt to do FPCC work in that area." He told Oswald that most chapters operated semi-privately out of a home using a post office box for mailings to avoid violent opposition from "the lunatic fringe." Vincent Lee advised against taking an office so soon, suggesting that Oswald wait and see how he could operate in the community through several public experiences first.

Oswald was, of course, not prepared to "wait and see." On June 3 he rented Post Office Box 30061, listing his own name and that of A.J. Hidell and Marina Oswald as persons authorized to pick up mail. In addition, he gave Fair Play for Cuba as an organization receiving mail at that box. He visited another printer and ordered five hundred offset copies of a membership application form he had made up. A few days later Oswald responded to Vincent Lee and enclosed one of the handbills:

I was glad to receive your advice concerning my try at starting a New Orleans F.P.C.C. chapter. I hope you won't be too disapproving of my innovations but I do think they are necessary for this area.

As per your advice, I have taken a P.O. Box (No. 30061).

Against your advice, I have decided to take an office from the very beginning.

[As] you see from the circular I had jumped the gun on the charter business but I don't think it's too important, you may think the circular is too provocative, but I want it to attract attention, even if it's the attention of the lunatic fringe. I had 2,000 of them run off. . . .

In any event I will keep [you] posted, and even if the office stays open
1 month more people will find out about the F.P.C.C. than if there had
never been any office at all, don't you agree?
Please feel free to give advice and any other help.

Not surprisingly, the national director thought better of offering any
more advice. Although Oswald would continue sending reports of his
activities throughout the summer, hoping to get some favorable response, Vincent Lee never again wrote back.

On June 10 Oswald wrote *The Worker:*

. . . . I have formed a "Fair Play for Cuba Committee" here in New
Orleans. I think it is the best way to attract the broad mass of people
to a popular struggle.

I ask that you give me as much literature as you judge possible since
I think it would be very nice to have your literature among the "Fair
Play" leaflets (like the one enclosed) and pamphlets in my office.

Also please be so kind as to convey the enclosed "honorary membership" cards to those fighters for peace Mr. Gus Hall and Mr. B. Davis.
Yours Fraternally,

The "membership cards" were evidently two copies of the forms he
had printed. If the Party officials Hall or Davis happened to send even
a perfunctory letter of thanks, it would look good in his résumé. They
did not. (As far as the FBI could later determine, Oswald never rented
an office, as he claimed.)

On June 16 an FBI informant in New York reported that Oswald
had written a letter to *The Worker.* The information may have come
from someone in the New York post office who made a note of his
return address on the envelope. In any case, the information was sent
to the FBI in New Orleans, which relayed it to Dallas, where agent
James Hosty had recently lost track of him. In early July Hosty asked
the New Orleans office to verify Oswald's presence there. It wasn't
until August that the office confirmed Oswald's residence in that city.
Keeping track of Oswald was apparently not high on the FBI's list
of priorities, but the agency didn't have, at this point, any reason to
believe that it should be.

During the second week of June there was a drumbeat of political developments in the news. On the 11th newspapers across the country carried reports of Governor George Wallace's flight to the University of Alabama to block the admission of a black student, and of a South Vietnamese monk who had burned himself to death to protest the anti-Buddhist policies of Premier Ngo Dinh Diem. A day later, civil rights activist Medgar Evers was killed by a right-wing sniper in Mississippi. On June 14, a front-page headline in the *Times-Picayune* played up a local story. It announced the arrival of the U.S. carrier *Wasp* at the Dumaine Street wharf, where it was greeted by state dignitaries and relatives of the 2800 officers and men on board. The accompanying story also mentioned that the *Wasp*'s planes had provided aerial reconnaissance during the October naval blockade of Cuba.

This news gave Oswald an idea. That weekend he appeared at the Dumaine Street dock and began handing out his "Hands Off Cuba" handbills and a Fair Play pamphlet called "The Truth About Cuba is in Cuba." One of the enlisted men he solicited complained to a patrolman, who approached Oswald and told him he needed a permit and would have to leave or be arrested. Oswald argued strenuously, but he left.

During this period Oswald was still greasing and oiling machinery at Reily's coffee company. It was the sort of dirty manual work he hated. A fellow worker named LeBlanc remembered that Oswald approached him one day on the job:

> . . . and I asked him, I says, "Are you finished all your greasing?" He said yes. So he asked me . . . "Well, can I help you?" I said, "No, what I am doing I don't need no help." So he stood there a few minutes, and all of a sudden he said, "You like it here?" I says, "Well, sure I like it here. I have been here a long time, about 8½ years or so." He says, "Oh, hell, I don't mean this place." I said, "Well, what do you mean?" He says, "This damn country." I said, "Why, certainly, I love it. After all, this is my country." He turned around and walked off.

Oswald spent a large portion of his work time at the Crescent City Garage next door looking at gun magazines in their waiting area. The garage owner later said they had talked about rifles—trajectory and feet per second and the supposed deadliness of a small-caliber bullet.

On June 24 Oswald applied for a new passport in New Orleans and was routinely issued one the next day.[1] Later that week Marina noticed that he seemed depressed. He stole a glance in her direction, then put aside something he was writing and went into the kitchen. She found him seated on a chair in the dark, his head down. When she embraced him, he began to sob. He told her he was lost and didn't know what to do, and then asked, "Would you like me to come to Russia, too?" Marina was delighted. He held her by the shoulders and told her to write the Soviet Embassy and say he would be coming back with her. He said he would add his own request to her letter. That weekend he helped her compose her second letter to the embassy. This time she requested visas for the entire family, explaining that she was homesick and her husband was frequently unemployed. ("More tears and fewer facts," Oswald directed.)

Marina didn't discover until she was questioned by the Warren Commission that before Lee mailed her letter, he had included the following note.

Dear Sirs:
Please *rush* the entrance visa for the return of Soviet citizen, Marina N. Oswald.
She is going to have a baby in *October*, therefore you must grant the entrance visa and make the the transportation arrangements before then.
As for my return entrance visa please consider it *separately*.

His major concern was the same as before—to get Marina and June back to Russia.

For the past few weeks Ruth Paine had been considering Marina's predicament, and on July 11 she wrote to tell her friend that if Lee insisted she go back to Russia alone, she could come and live with her instead. They both had small children, and Marina could keep her company now that Michael had moved out, and help her improve her Russian. Later Ruth wrote that she would be making a trip east and would stop by for a visit around September 18. Ruth's offer would fit neatly into Oswald's plans.

Because of his general lack of interest, the William B. Reily Company fired him on July 19. Oswald again signed up for unemployment benefits from Texas. He now had more time for reading. Among the library books he read that summer were a biography of John Kennedy, a book on communism by J. Edgar Hoover, *Russia Under Khruschev, Brave New World, The Huey Long Murder Case,* and four James Bond spy novels. The first book he had checked out was *Portrait of a Revolutionary: Mao Tse-tung.* He was also subscribing to some Russian magazines (including *Agitator,* a Party manual on the techniques of propaganda and agitation), as well as *The Worker, The Militant,* and *Time.*

In July Oswald's cousin Gene Murret, who was studying to become a priest at a Jesuit college in Mobile, Alabama, invited Oswald to come to the college to give a talk on his experiences in the Soviet Union. The Murrets drove the Oswalds to Mobile, and by all accounts, Oswald handled himself well. His audience of students and faculty had expected to hear a man who had been disillusioned by Soviet communism. Instead, Oswald implied that he was disappointed in Russia only because the full principles of Marxism weren't being lived up to. He criticized capitalism, claiming its foundation was based on the exploitation of the poor. Perhaps to draw a laugh, he said, "Capitalism doesn't work, communism doesn't work. In the middle is socialism, and that doesn't work either." Yet he told them he still believed in the Marxist ideals. During the question and answer session, Oswald seemed reluctant to discuss religion with the Jesuit students, but when one asked what atheism in Russia does to morality, he answered, "No matter whether people believe in God or not, they will do what they want. . . ."

While Charles Murret and his son attended Oswald's all-male lecture, Robert J. Fitzpatrick, a student who spoke Russian, showed Marina and Lillian around the seminary grounds. It had been several months since Marina had been able to converse with anyone except Lee in her native tongue, and her remarks to Fitzpatrick were more revealing than anything her husband had to say to his audience. She told him that she liked the United States, but that at least in Russia people had no difficulty making a living. Then she told him about Lee's troubles. He was out of work and they were having financial problems. He did a lot of haphazard reading. She told him her husband was away from home a great deal and she did not know any of his associates or any of his activities. She said she had no opportunity to learn English because Oswald kept her away from other people. Fitzpatrick thought she appeared to be happy with Oswald, but that he "was definitely the head of the family."

The young defector: Lee Harvey Oswald in September 1959, a photograph taken for Moscow newspapers. *(SOURCE: National Archives.)*

Marguerite Oswald and Edwin A. Ekdahl after their marriage in 1945. *(SOURCE: National Archives.)*

Oswald, in dark glasses, and several co-workers at the Minsk Radio factory. *(SOURCE: National Archives.)*

Lee and Marina Oswald after their wedding, April 1961. *(SOURCE: National Archives.)*

At the Minsk railroad station, the Oswalds are seen off by Russian friends as they leave for the United States in May 1962. *(SOURCE: National Archives.)*

March 1963: Posing in his backyard in Dallas, Oswald holds the rifle later found in the School Book Depository. *(SOURCE: Jeanne de Mohrenschildt.)*

The back of George de Mohrenschildt's copy of this photograph, showing Oswald's inscription, "To my dear friend George, from Lee," and a message in Russian, apparently in Marina's hand: "Hunter of fascists ha-ha-ha!!!" *(SOURCE: Jeanne de Mohrenschildt.)*

In August 1963 Oswald distributes Fair Play for Cuba leaflets in front of the New Orleans Trade Mart. *(SOURCE: WDSU-TV, New Orleans.)*

Castro Blasts Raids on Cuba

Cuba. We will know how to defend ourselves, and we will not be afraid to face him, but, in any case. I am not interested in getting involved in U.S. domestic politics."

Says U.S. Leaders Imperiled by Aid to Rebels

EDITOR'S NOTE — Prime Minister Fidel Castro turned up at a reception in the Brazilian Embassy in Havana Saturday night and submitted to an impromptu interview by Associated Press correspondent Daniel Harker. Harker's account of the interview reached New York Sunday afternoon.

By DANIEL HARKER

HAVANA (AP)—Prime Minister Fidel Castro said Saturday night United States leaders" would be in danger if they helped in any attempt to do away with leaders of Cuba.

Bitterly denouncing what he called recent U.S.-prompted raids on Cuban territory, Castro said: "We are prepared to fight them and answer in kind. United States leaders should think that if they are aiding terrorist plans to eliminate Cuban leaders, they themselves will not be safe."

Speaking with this correspondent at a Brazilian National Day reception in the Brazilian Embassy, Castro also disclosed that Cuba has not made up its mind about signing the limited nuclear test-ban treaty drawn up last month in Moscow.

RUSSIANS PUZZLED

(A recent dispatch from Moscow indicated the Russians themselves have been puzzled by Cuba's silence in connection with the treaty. Speculation there was that Castro was holding out for more Soviet economic aid and threatening to cast his lot with the Red Chinese.)

Castro said Cuba is studying the [illegible] "This is an important decision. and we are not ready yet to make up our minds," he added. The prime minister did not explain which points in the treaty are being given most considera-

tion. But he said: "We are taking into account the current world situation, which of course involves the Caribbean situation, which has been deteriorating in the last few days due to piratical attacks by the United States against the Cuban people."

TREND CHANGED

World affairs, he said, "seemed to be entering a more peaceful climate a few days ago, but now this trend has changed with attacks."

He accused the United States of carrying out "double-crossing and shifting policies."

He added: "The United States is always ready to negotiate and make promises which later it will not honor. This has happened to promises made during the October crisis. They have been broken, as can be seen with new attacks. But I warn this is leading to a very dangerous situation that could lead to a worse crisis than October's."

Castro then launched into a discussion of the U.S. political scene, saying he expects no change in Washington's foreign policy even if there is a change in administrations after the 1964 presiden-

tial election.

BOTH 'CHEAP, CROOKED'

"I am sure it will be a fight between (President) Kennedy and (Sen. Barry) Goldwater (R-Ariz.). Both are cheap and crooked politicians." Castro said.

"We have heard Goldwater is tough. Well, if he ever is elected, let him try his tough policies on

Castro's warning to American leaders about assassination plots, as reported in the New Orleans *Times-Picayune*, September 9, 1963.

Opposite page: Two other views of the Trade Mart demonstration, showing Oswald with a Latin American helper (indicated by an arrow in *top photo*, at far left in *bottom photo*). This man has never been identified. (*SOURCE: WDSU-TV, New Orleans.*)

Top: **Ruth Paine's home in Irving, Texas.** *(SOURCE: National Archives.)*

Bottom: **The Dallas rooming house where Oswald was living at the time of the assassination.** *(SOURCE: Wide World Photos.)*

10... "Street Agitation . . . Radio Speaker and Lecturer"

SUMMER, 1963: The Cuban exile community in New Orleans was the largest in the United States outside of Miami. One of the militant groups represented in the city was the Cuban Student Directorate, or DRE, which had claimed responsibility for an offshore shelling of Havana in 1962.

On August 1 the official crackdown on such raids, begun in April, reached New Orleans. A front-page story in the *Times-Picayune* announced that FBI agents had impounded a large cache of dynamite and bomb casings in nearby Mandeville. A follow-up story indicated that the ammunition belonged to an unnamed Cuban exile. The *Picayune* said that the FBI was investigating a possible plan "to carry out a military operation against a country with which the United States is at peace"—a violation of the U.S. Code. The implication was clear that there was Cuban exile paramilitary activity going on in the area. In fact, as it later came out, the cache had been earmarked for a ragtag group of volunteers who had assembled at a secret guerrilla training camp near Mandeville. After the FBI raid on their depot, the group quickly disbanded.

It was apparently common knowledge that some of the exile groups were looking for ex-GIs to train their guerrillas. In the June 8 *Satur-*

day Evening Post, for instance, a story called "Help Us Fight" reported that, following the Bay of Pigs, exile leaders had asked the CIA for money and "a few tough men in green berets from the U.S. Special Forces to train leaders in the techniques of guerrilla war." The exiles complained about being turned down: "They told us that Fidel's spies would infiltrate our movement." The article concluded, "The pin prick raids have been outlawed. . . . There is still work, however, that brave men could do—as they were doing in small independent groups before the suppression came. It is the silent, dangerous work of organizing an underground." (It isn't known whether Oswald saw this article, but it's conceivable that the *Post*'s cover photo of Fidel Castro with the caption "The Mounting Chaos in Castro's Cuba" may have caught his eye.)

In any case, it was evidently the discovery of this exile ammunition dump near New Orleans that inspired Oswald's next move.

Oswald made some inquiries. On page 87 of his notebook, there appears:

Cuban Student
Directorate
107 Decatur St.
New Orleans La.
Carlos Bringuier

This was followed by the names of a local "City Editor" and a reporter—and two other street addresses labeled "Cuban exile stores."

Carlos Bringuier, the Directorate's only official in New Orleans, ran the Casa Roca clothing store in the French Quarter. In the front window he displayed a 3 × 4-foot sign showing the Statue of Liberty being stabbed in the back. The hand holding the dagger was connected to a long chain wrapped around Cuba. The sign said, "Danger! Only 90 Miles from U.S.A., Cuba Lies in Chains." Although his organization wasn't associated with the Mandeville training camp, Bringuier had heard about it when two of their volunteers came to him seeking transportation back to Florida.

On August 5 Bringuier was in his store speaking with two teenaged boys who had been trying to collect donations for his organization by selling so-called "war bonds." The boys had brought the bonds back when they found out Bringuier didn't have the required city permit. As they were talking, Oswald walked in and eased into their conversation. He introduced himself to Bringuier and said he was an anti-Castro ex-Marine who wanted to fight Castro. He said he had been trained in guerrilla warfare and was willing not only to train exile guerrillas but to lead their raiding parties into Cuba.

Bringuier was immediately suspicious. He thought Oswald might be an agent of either Castro or the FBI. He had heard rumors that there was a Castro agent in the Mandeville camp. Bringuier told him he wasn't interested because he wasn't involved in any paramilitary activity.

At some point, apparently while Bringuier was waiting on a customer, Oswald had a talk with the two anti-Castro boys. He told them how to make gunpowder and a zipgun, how to derail a train by locking a chain around one of the rails—and how to blow up the New Orleans Huey P. Long Bridge. One of the boys testified, "He told us to put powder charges at each end of the bridge from the foundation to where the foundation meets the suspension part . . . blow that part up and the center part of the bridge would collapse."

Before he left, Oswald offered Bringuier a cash contribution, but the Cuban refused it by saying he had no city permit to accept money. The next day Oswald returned to the store and left his Marine Corps guidebook with Bringuier's brother-in-law.

In his political résumé, Oswald wrote.

I infiltrated the Cuban Student Directorate and then harassed them with information I gained including having the N.O. City Attorney General call them in and put a restraining order pending a hearing on some so-called bonds for invasion they were selling in the New Orleans area.

So far as is known, there was no such restraining order. Oswald was puffing up his résumé with a false claim. The important thing here is that he stated his purpose: to infiltrate and harass the Directorate.

This entry also seemed to explain why he offered Bringuier a contribution—that is, to get him into trouble with the law for raising money illegally.

The résumé didn't mention the other tactics he used—posing as a guerrilla trainer and suggesting violent activities to the boys. Probably he didn't want to put anything in writing that was potentially incriminating. But his evident intention was to cause as much damage to the DRE as he could. The offer to lead guerrilla raids into Cuba may hark back to his old hero, William Morgan, who had posed as a counterrevolutionary to lead some anti-Castro rebels into a trap.[1] Had Oswald gotten that far, he could have made himself a hero by turning the raiding party over to the Cubans—or so he may have imagined. And even if he only got as far as the training camp, he might have gained some information he could pass along to the Cubans when he went to Mexico City—a nice boost for his credentials.

In any event, practically every source agrees that Oswald's approach to Carlos Bringuier was an infiltration attempt.

Oswald was not done with Bringuier yet, however. On August 9 a friend of Bringuier's came into the store and told him he had seen someone with a sign saying "Viva Fidel" and "Hands off Cuba" passing out literature a few blocks away on Canal Street. Bringuier grabbed his sign from the window, and then went with his friend and another Cuban to confront the pro-Castro demonstrator. They finally located him near Walgreen's Drug Store. To Bringuier's surprise, it was the same Lee Harvey Oswald who had offered his services to fight Castro. When Oswald saw him coming, he smiled and offered to shake his hand. Outraged, Bringuier called him a Castro agent and began to "blame him in the street." A crowd gathered and took Bringuier's side. According to Bringuier "they started to shout to him, 'Traitor! Communist! Go to Cuba! Kill him!' and some other phrases that I do not know if I could tell in the record."

A policeman came and asked Bringuier to keep walking and let Oswald hand out his literature, but Bringuier explained what Oswald had done to him a few days earlier and refused to go. When the policeman left to telephone headquarters, one of Bringuier's friends took Oswald's batch of handbills "and threw it on the air." Carlos took off his glasses and was about to hit Oswald:

but when he sensed my intention, he put his arm down as an X. . . .
Q. He crossed his arms in front of him?
A. That is right, put his face and told me, "O.K. Carlos, if you want to hit me, hit me." At this moment, that made me to reaction that he was trying to appear as a martyr if I will hit him, and I decide not to hit him, and just a few seconds later arrive two police cars. . . . When we were in the First District of Police, we were in the same room, one small room over there, and some of the policemen started to question Oswald . . . and Oswald at that moment—that was in front of myself —was really cold blood. He was answering the questions that he would like to answer, and he was not nervous, he was not out of control, he was confident of himself at that moment. . . .

The Cubans bailed themselves out, but Oswald spent the night in jail.[2] Marina stayed up until 3 A.M. not knowing where he was. Worried, she checked the closet where he kept his rifle and was relieved to see it was still there.

The next morning Oswald was questioned by police lieutenant Francis L. Martello of the intelligence squad. Among the ID cards Oswald produced at his request was his New Orleans Fair Play chapter membership card with the signature of A.J. Hidell shown as chapter president. (Marina had signed the name at his insistence, after she commented that the name was obviously an "altered Fidel.") Oswald led Martello to believe that the chapter was thriving. Oswald then asked to speak with someone from the FBI, and an agent named Quigley came over to see him. Oswald gave him a similar song and dance, showing him the card with Hidell's name.

Albert Newman has pointed out that Oswald told both Martello and Quigley that he had moved to New Orleans from *Fort Worth* about four months before. Oswald apparently wanted to accomplish several things by talking to Quigley: he wanted to be sure the FBI knew he was now living in New Orleans and that he had been in Fort Worth, not Dallas, when the Walker shooting occurred, and he wanted to give the impression that A. J. Hidell was a real person, not an alias.

After speaking to Quigley, he called the Murrets' number and reached his cousin Joyce, who came down to the police station but decided not to post bail when she realized what he was in for. But she did speak to Lt. Martello and told him that her cousin Lee had been in Russia and wouldn't let his wife learn English. That was the first Martello had heard about Oswald's stay in Russia, and he decided to question him again. Oswald admitted that he had lived in the Soviet Union, and when Martello asked him his opinion of Russian communism, he replied, "It stunk." Martello reported:

> He said they have "fat, stinking politicians over there just like we have over here" and that they do not follow the great precepts of Karl Marx, that the leaders have everything and the people are still poor and depressed. I asked Oswald why he would not allow members of his family to learn English. . . . He stated the reason why he did this was because he hated America. . . . I then spoke to him about the Fair Play for Cuba Committee again and asked him if he knew that Castro had admitted he was a Marxist-Leninist and he said he did. He was then asked if he truly believed Castro was really interested in the welfare of the Cuban people and he replied that he was not going to discuss the merits and demerits of Castro but was primarily concerned with the poor people of Cuba and that if this country would have good relations with the poor people of Cuba and quit worrying about Castro, that was his main concern. . . .

In two other comments Oswald seemed to be following his old practice of telling the literal truth, but with a secret twist. Martello asked him which country he would choose, Russia or America, if he had to place his allegiance and Oswald told him, "I would place my allegiance at the foot of democracy." As an example of Oswald's Marxist bias, Kerry Thornley mentioned that "he could look upon the Soviet system today as a democracy by, of course, giving a completely different definition to the word 'democracy.' " When Martello asked him what he thought about Kennedy and Khrushchev, he said he thought "they got along very well together." Khrushchev had recently come to an agreement with Kennedy on the Nuclear Test Ban Treaty, a conciliatory move that both China and Cuba had criticized.

After he got out of jail later that day, his uncle Charles ("Dutz") Murret paid him a visit and noticed a picture of Fidel on his living room mantel. As Lillian recalled it, Murret "asked Lee in a fatherly way, what was he doing, you know, who he was connected with, and so forth, and whether he was with any Commie group, and Lee said no, he wasn't, and Mr. Murret told him, he said, 'You be sure you show up at that courthouse for the trial,' and Lee said, 'Don't worry, I'll show up,' and he told Lee, he said, 'You ought to get out and find yourself a job.' " Oswald didn't attempt to argue, but after Murret left he told Marina, "Well, these are just bourgeois . . . only concerned with their own individual welfare."

Carlos Bringuier described their court appearance on August 12: "I came first with my friends, and there were some other Cubans over there and I saw when Oswald came inside the court. . . . See, here in the court you have two sides, one of the white people and one for the colored people, and he walked directly inside of the colored people and he sat directly among them in the middle, and that made me to be angry too, because I saw that he was trying to win the colored people for his side. When he will appear in the court, he will defend Fidel Castro, he will defend the Fair Play for Cuba, and the colored people will feel good for him, and that is a tremendous work of propaganda for his cause. That is one of the things that made me to think that he is really a smart guy and not a nut."

Oswald pleaded guilty and paid a $10 fine. He came home smiling. The next day the *Picayune* gave him a small write-up:

PAMPHLET CASE SENTENCE GIVEN

Lee Oswald, 4907 Magazine, Monday was sentenced to pay a fine of $10 or serve 10 days in jail on a charge of disturbing the peace by creating a scene.

Oswald was arrested by First District Police at 4:15 P.M. Friday in the 700 block of Canal while he was reportedly distributing pamphlets asking for a "Fair Play for Cuba."

Police were called to the scene when three Cubans reportedly sought to stop Oswald. Municipal charges against the Cubans for disturbing the peace were dropped by the court.

He cut clippings and sent one to Arnold Johnson, the information director of the Communist party, and another to Vincent Lee. To the latter, he wrote:

Continuing my efforts on behalf of the F.P.C.C. in New Orleans I find that I have incurred the displeasure of the Cuban exile "worms" here [the Cuban government's term for the exiles]. . . .

I am glad I am stirring things up and shall continue to do so. The incident was given considerable coverage in the press and local T.V. news broadcast.

I am sure it will be all to the good of the Fair Play for Cuba Committee.

Another clipping went into his pro-Castro file.

When Marina was questioned about the purpose of his pro-Castro activities in New Orleans, she said, "I think that Lee engaged in this activity primarily for purposes of self-advertising. He wanted to be arrested. I think that he wanted to get into the newspapers. . . ."

Q. Do you think that he wanted to be advertised and known as being in support of Cuba before he went to Cuba?
A. Yes.
Q. Do you think he thought that would help him when he got to Cuba?
A. Yes.
Q. Did he tell you anything about that, or is that just what you guess?
A. He would collect the newspaper clippings about his—when the newspapers wrote about him, and he took those clippings with him when he went to Mexico.

On August 16 Oswald staged another demonstration in front of the International Trade Mart. A friend of Bringuier's picked up one of the leaflets and saw that Oswald had his name and address stamped on it. They decided to turn the tables on him. The friend went to Oswald's house posing as a Castro sympathizer and talked to him for about an hour on his front porch. Oswald reportedly told him that the United States didn't have the right to invade Cuba or overthrow its government, and that if it tried to, he would fight for Castro. He wasn't taken in by the visitor. Afterward, Marina testified, "I asked Lee who that was, and he said it was probably some anti-Cuban, or perhaps an FBI agent."

The Oswalds were getting along better by this time. He no longer hit her—she was seven months pregnant—and he even confided in her to some extent. According to McMillan's book, Marina tried to tell Oswald he wasn't the outstanding man he thought he was. She reminded him that Cuba had gotten along without him so far, and told him, "Poor great man sits here all by himself. He's part of a great cause, and yet he has nothing to eat. Nobody sees that he's a genius."

"You laugh now," he replied, "But in twenty years, when I'm prime minister, we'll see how you laugh then." He told her Cuba was "a tiny country surrounded by enemies" and that he hoped his leaflets would help wake up the American people. When Marina commented that America obviously wasn't ready for a revolution, he agreed: "You're right. I ought to have been born in some other era, much sooner or much later than I was."

Marina explained to the Warren Commission, "I was not exactly happy with this occupation of his, but it seemed to me better than his 'games' with the rifle as in Dallas. To tell the truth, I sympathized with Cuba. . . . But I did not support Lee since I felt that he was too small a person to take so much on himself."

As a result of the publicity he'd been attracting, Oswald was invited to appear on a local radio show called Latin Listening Post. The moderator, William Stuckey, found him to be self-assured and "very well qualified to handle questions"—if his speaking style had a fault, it was that Oswald seemed "a little stiff" and too academic. On the air, Stuckey asked him about his background, and Oswald said that after he had been honorably discharged from the Marines as a buck sergeant, he had gone back to work in Texas, and had recently moved to New Orleans with his wife and child. No mention of Dallas or Russia. (Because of his court-martials he had never gotten above the rank of private first class.)

In response to Stuckey's questions, he denied that Castro was controlled by the Soviet Union, and pointed out that when Khrushchev had asked him to allow on-site inspections of his rocket bases during the missile crisis, Castro refused. He called Castro an "experimenter, a person who is trying to find the best way for his country." But he

insisted that the Fair Play Committee did not support Fidel Castro
as an "individual"—rather, it supported "the idea of an independent
revolution in the Western Hemisphere, free from American intervention."

> If [Castro] chooses a socialist or a Marxist or a Communist way of life,
> that is something upon which only the Cuban people can pass. We do
> not have the right to pass on that. . . . We cannot exploit that system
> and say it is a bad one, it is a threat to our existence and then go and
> try to destroy it.

According to Oswald, the "current of history" indicated that "countries emerging from imperialist domination" would choose socialism
in one form or another. "Cuba," he declared, "is irrevocably lost as
far as capitalism goes and there will never be a capitalist regime again
in Cuba." Here Oswald was repeating two themes expressed in a letter
to his brother Robert from Moscow four years earlier: opposition to
American imperialism and a classic Marxist belief in historical inevi-
tability.

When Stuckey asked him why so many people were fleeing Cuba,
Oswald mentioned the criminal class and said that many of them were
"the same people who are in New Orleans and have set themselves
up in stores with blood money." He said he thought that the Cuban
government's attitude was "good riddance." Stuckey pressed him on
this issue, asking why so many workers and peasants were leaving
Cuba while few were leaving dictatorships like Nicaragua, and Oswald turned the question to his advantage.

> Well, a good question. [The] Nicaraguan situation is considerably differ-
> ent from Castro's Cuba. People are inclined not to flee their countries
> unless some new system, new factor, enters into their lives. I must say
> that very surely no new factors have entered into Nicaragua for about
> 300 years, in fact the people live exactly as they have always lived in
> Nicaragua. I am referring to the overwhelming majority of the people
> in Nicaragua, which is a feudal dictatorship with 90 per cent of the
> people engaged in agriculture. These peasants are uneducated. They
> have one of the lowest living standards in all of the western hemisphere

and so because of the fact that no new factor, no liberating factor, has entered into their lives, they remain in Nicaragua.

He explained the flight of workers and peasants from Cuba this way:

You know, it's very funny about revolutions. Revolutions require work, revolutions require sacrifice. . . . These people are the people who do not remain in Cuba to be educated by young people, who are afraid of the alphabet, who are afraid of these new things which are occurring, who are afraid they would lose something by collectivization. . . . You know, it used to be that these people worked for the United Fruit Company or American companies engaged in sugar refining, oil refining in Cuba. They worked a few months every year during the cane cutting or sugar refining season. . . . They feel that now they have to work all year round to plant new crops, to make a new economy . . . they feel that they have been robbed of the right to do as they please. . . . What they do not realize is that they have been robbed of the right to be exploited, robbed of the right to be cheated, robbed of the right of New Orleanean companies to take away what was rightfully theirs. Of course, they have to share now. Everybody gets an equal portion. This is collectivization and this is very hard on some people, on people preferring the dog-eat-dog economy.

Oswald was good at this. When Stuckey brought up the lack of press freedom in Cuba, he compared it to the voluntary press censorship during wartime in the United States and complained about the *Times-Picayune* and *States-Item* syndicate, which he spoke of collectively as "the only newspaper we have in New Orleans and a very restricted paper it is." He said, "The Fair Play for Cuba Committee has often approached this paper with information or comments and this paper has consistently refused [to use it,] because . . . it is sympathetic to the anti-Castro regime. It has systematically refused to print any objective matter, giving the other man's viewpoint about Cuba." (This answer shows that he had been following the local newspapers' coverage of Cuba.) He also claimed that he had gone to their offices and asked for coverage of his Trade Mart demonstration and they refused.

The other answers he gave indicate that he was well-informed about Cuba. His reference to young people teaching the old was an allusion to the Alphabetization or Literacy Campaign of 1961, in which young Cubans went into rural areas to teach older people to read. Oswald also complained about the U.S. restrictions on travel to Cuba. And he referred to the anti-Castro underground—the "Batistaites" still in Cuba who had gone into hiding and had been "engaged in counter-revolutionary activities ever since the Bay of Pigs and even before that, just after the revolution. In other words, they have remained underground."

He probably obtained this information from a variety of sources, but primarily from his reading, including the pamphlets Fair Play had sent him and articles about Cuba in *The Militant* and elsewhere. He had also spent time with Cuban students in the Soviet Union—one of his best friends there was a Cuban student named Alfred. And although there's no direct evidence for this, he may also have been in contact with some other Cubans in New Orleans. (Back in Dallas, George de Mohrenschildt had noticed that Oswald knew quite a bit about the history of several Latin American countries. He later wrote that Oswald told him he'd learned a lot from talking with refugees from those countries when he was a teenager in New Orleans—"no better source of information.")

After this broadcast, Stuckey and the station manager decided to arrange a debate between Oswald, Carlos Bringuier, and another anti-Communist, Ed Butler. Oswald showed up promptly on the afternoon of August 21. He was wearing a Russian-made suit—heavy gray flannel, badly cut—a shirt and tie, and carried a black looseleaf notebook under his arm. Since the initial interview, Bill Stuckey had learned, through a telephone call to the FBI, that Oswald had lived in Russia. He confronted him with this on the air and caught Oswald offguard.

STUCKEY: You did live in Russia for three years?
OSWALD: That is correct, and I think that those, the fact that I did live for a time in the Soviet Union gives me excellent qualifications to repudiate charges that Cuba and the Fair Play for Cuba Committee is communist controlled.

Naturally, his opponents didn't agree.

Later in the debate Bringuier asked him if he concurred with Castro's recent characterization of President Kennedy as "a ruffian and a thief." Oswald replied, "I would not agree with that particular wording. However, I and the Fair Play for Cuba Committee do think that the United States Government through certain agencies, mainly the State Department and the CIA, has made monumental mistakes in its relations with Cuba." Bringuier was referring to recent press reports of a speech in which Castro charged that the United States hadn't delivered all the food and medical supplies it had promised Cuba in return for the release of the Bay of Pigs prisoners. Castro had said, "The ruffian Kennedy operates this way. We freed the mercenaries and already they are organizing new aggressions against Cuba."

Oswald's remark that he didn't agree with Castro's particular wording suggests that he may have instead agreed with the substance. But he went on to blame the State Department and the CIA, and this too may have reflected his attitude toward John Kennedy. Marina has said that he considered Kennedy the best American leader one could expect at that point in history. And he seemed to feel that Kennedy might have pursued a softer line on Cuba if it hadn't been for the political pressures he had to contend with. He explained how a president had to reckon with the opinions of others. His only negative comment was that Joe Kennedy had bought the presidency for his son —but this criticism was directed against capitalism. "Money paves the way to everything here," he said. Thus, he seemed to put most of the blame for America's policy toward Cuba on conservative elements, not on Kennedy himself. But it should be kept in mind that Oswald considered his wife unqualified to discuss political issues with him, and he knew she admired Kennedy.

Although Lee Harvey Oswald was a clever debater, the revelation about his defection won the debate for his opponents. Stuckey later said, "I think that we finished him on that program. . . . Oswald seemed like such a nice, bright boy and was extremely believable before this. We thought the fellow could probably get quite a few members if he was really indeed serious about getting members. We figured after this broadcast of August 21, why, that was no longer possible."

After the program Stuckey noticed that he looked "a little dejected" and invited him to a nearby bar for a beer. At the bar Stuckey thought he seemed to relax for the first time, and they talked for about an hour. When Stuckey asked if his relatives had influenced him to become a Marxist, Oswald seemed amused. No, he said, they were "pretty much typical New Orleans types." He told Stuckey that he had started reading Marx and Engels when he was 15 and that his service in Japan had convinced him that "something was wrong with the system," so he decided to go to Russia and see for himself how a revolutionary society operates. But he became disillusioned with Russia, he said, and he believed that Cuba was now the only revolutionary country in the world. Stuckey's impression was that Oswald regarded himself "as living in a world of intellectual inferiors." He thought Oswald knew he was intelligent and wanted "to have an opportunity to express his intelligence."

A week after the debate, Oswald wrote the Central Committee of the Communist Party USA:

Please advise me upon a problem of personal tactics.

I have lived in the Soviet Union from Oct. 1959 to July 1962.

I had, in 1959, in Moscow, tried to legally dissolve my United States citizenship in favor of Soviet citizenship, however, I did not complete the legal formalities for this.

Having come back to the U.S. in 1962 and thrown myself into the struggle for progress and freedom in the United States, I would like to know whether, in your opinions, I can continue to fight, handicapped as it were, by my past record, can I still, under these circumstances, compete with anti-progressive forces aboveground or whether in your opinion I should always remain in the background, i.e. underground.

Our opponents could use my background of residence in the U.S.S.R. against any cause which I join, by association, they could say the organization of which I am a member is Russian controlled, etc. I am sure you see my point.

I could of course openly proclaim (if pressed on the subject) that I wanted to dissolve my American citizenship as a personal protest against the policy of the U.S. government in supporting dictatorships, etc.

But what do you think I should do? Which is the best tactic in general?

Should I dissociate myself from all progressive activities?

Here in New Orleans, I am secretary of the local branch of the "Fair Play for Cuba Committee," a position which, frankly, I have used to foster communist ideals.

On a local radio show, I was attacked by Cuban exile organization representatives for my residence etc. in the Soviet Union.

I feel I may have compromised the F.P.C.C., so you see that I need the advice of trusted, long time fighters for progress. Please advise.

The information director of the party, Arnold Johnson, eventually replied on September 19, saying that, as an American citizen, "you have a right to participate in such organizations as you want," but that "often it is advisable for some people to remain in the background, not underground."

Marina has said that Oswald thought more highly of the American Communists than he did of the Party members in Russia. He showed her a letter from a Party official in New York—perhaps this one—and said in effect: see, here is someone important who understands what I'm trying to do. It must have seemed to him, after the debate, that he could no longer work openly as a pro-Castro organizer, certainly not in New Orleans—and that he would now have to remain in the background, i.e., underground.

In late August he began practicing dry-firing his rifle several times a week on his front porch. He explained the practice to Marina: "Fidel Castro needs defenders. I'm going to join his army of volunteers. I'm going to be a revolutionary."

During the second half of the summer, Oswald was seen with two Latin Americans who have never been identified. Dean Andrews, a New Orleans attorney, claimed that in July Oswald came to his office more than once in the company of a short, stocky Mexican, about 26 years old. He called the Mexican "Oswald's shadow." Although Andrews couldn't prove his story, one part of his testimony rings true. He said that Oswald came to see him about getting his less-than-honorable discharge upgraded. Oswald had been trying to get the Marines to reinstate his honorable discharge ever since he returned to the United States, and that month had received official notice that his request had been rejected. Considering Oswald's persistence when he believed he had been wronged, it makes sense that he might have then gone to an attorney. (Andrews said that since Oswald couldn't pay his fee, nothing came of it.)

Also, about this time, Oswald was reportedly seen in the Habana Bar with a Mexican or Cuban by both the bartender and Orest Pena, the owner. The Habana Bar was said to be a hangout for Spanish-speaking seamen, both pro- and anti-Castro. The man with Oswald was described as being approximately 28 years old, short and muscular, with very hairy arms and a receding hairline.

Finally, during the August 16 Trade Mart demonstration, Oswald was photographed by a local TV news crew while he was handing out his leaflets with two young men. One was a teenager Oswald approached and offered $2 for an hour's work. But the other was a Latin American who has never been identified. The House Assassinations Committee published a photograph taken from the news film and suggested that this second man should be investigated further.

Oswald was always on the lookout for people who agreed with his political ideas. Under a paragraph entitled "Organizer" in his résumé, he wrote: "I hired persons to distribute literature. I then organized persons who display receptive attitudes toward Cuba to distribute pamphlets. . . . I caused the formation of a small, active, FPCC organization of members and sympathizers where before there was none." It has been assumed that Oswald was lying when he claimed to have organized a small group of supporters. It may be that he was simply exaggerating—possibly his support consisted of only one or two unidentified Latin Americans.

The Warren Report described Oswald's completed résumé as consisting of

> . . . several sheets of notepaper which he presumably intended to call to the attention of Cuban and Soviet officials in Mexico City to convince

them to let him enter Cuba. On these sheets he had recorded facts about his Marine service, including the dates of his enlistment and discharge; the places where he had served, and the diplomas that he had received from military school. Recorded also were notes on his stay in the Soviet Union, his early interest in Communist literature, his ability to speak Russian, his organization of the New Orleans chapter of the Fair Play for Cuba Committee, his contact with police authorities in connection with his work for the Committee, and his experience in "street agitation," as a "radio speaker and lecturer," and as a photographer.

At the end of many of these sections Oswald attached some of the letters and other documents he'd collected. The handwritten sheets appear in the Commission's published exhibits.

This material is more revealing than the Commission realized. The section on his military service was probably intended to show that he was qualified to serve as a revolutionary soldier. There would otherwise seem to have been little point in giving so many details. The other material seems designed to demonstrate that he was versatile and well-qualified to serve the revolution in other capacities—as a political organizer or translator, for example.

Under the heading "Marxist," he wrote that he had attended "numerous Marxist reading circles and groups" at the factory where he worked in Minsk, "some of which were compulsory and others which were not," and indicated that he had learned still more about the works of Marx, Engels, and Lenin from Russian newspapers and TV, adding that "such articles are given very good coverage daily in the USSR." That last statement indicates that he wrote this résumé with the Cuban officials in mind and not the Russians, who would certainly have known about such articles.

In a brief section entitled "Russian" he said that he was "totally proficient in speaking conversational Russian" and appended the letter Peter Gregory had given him back in June 1962. Knowing that there were Russian technicians and advisers in Cuba, Oswald may have thought his knowledge of the language would be useful. Throughout, the document presents not only what he had done, but something of what he thought he was capable of doing. For instance, in phrasing similar to that of an ordinary job résumé, he wrote, "I am experienced in street agitation having done it in New Orleans. . . ."

But probably the most telling part of the résumé came under the heading "Photographer." It reveals a corner of Oswald's fantasy life that had first surfaced in 1961, when he told Marina he would have loved the dangerous life of a spy. When he worked at Jaggars-Chiles-Stovall, he struck up an acquaintance with a co-worker, Dennis Hyman Ofstein, who taught him how to use some of the photographic equipment. After they had become friendlier, Oswald asked him if he knew what the term "microdot" meant. He then explained to Ofstein that microdots were highly reduced photographs used to transmit secret information—and indeed they are, as any reader of spy novels knows. Very likely, Oswald was hoping Ofstein could teach him how to reduce a photograph to that size. But Ofstein had never heard the term, and the equipment at the plant wasn't capable of producing any such photographs. The word "microdot" also appears in a notebook of Oswald's next to the name Jaggars-Chiles-Stovall. In his résumé, Oswald wrote down the dates he had worked for them and that he was familiar with "blowups, miniaturization, etc."

Overall, this document suggests that Oswald didn't consider himself a miserable failure who, as the Warren Report put it, saw Cuba as "his last escape hatch, his last gambit to extricate himself from the mediocrity and defeat which plagued him throughout most of his life." Instead, these credentials indicate that he saw himself as an experienced political operative who was qualified to work for the Cuban revolution as a soldier, lecturer, organizer, agitator, translator, or spy. His ambition was evidently much the same as it had been in 1959. As Kerry Thornley had guessed, he expected to be welcomed aboard, and he would then go out and distinguish himself in the Communist world and work his way up—after twenty years, he might even get to be prime minister. For someone who couldn't hold a job in the United States, he had some extraordinary ambitions.

During the first six months of 1963 there had been little, if any, American sabotage activities against Cuba—the results were not considered worth the effort. But in June 1963 the Special Group of the

National Security Council decided, with the president's approval, to step up covert cperations inside Cuba.

Sabotage missions were carried out by Cuban exiles led by paramilitary specialists under contract to the CIA. Operating out of Florida, they ran boats to Cuba that dropped off agents and supplies. As in many other such underground operations, the chief purpose was to sabotage the economy and promote disaffection with the government among the people. But some of the raiders had ideas about more direct action. As far as they and their American advisers were concerned, there was a war going on. The CIA's deputy director of intelligence during that period, Ray Cline, later told a journalist, "I'm almost positive that there was no serious CIA-controlled effort to assassinate anybody, but I think the intention of some infiltration teams was to do it." And one of the Cuban raiders said, "The papers now want to say there were plots. Well, I can tell you there were plots. I took a lot of weapons to Cuba. Some of them were very special weapons for special purposes. They were powerful rifles with sophisticated scopes —Springfields with bolt actions, rifles only used by snipers. . . . Everyone in the underground was plotting to kill Castro, and the CIA was helping the underground." Occasionally some of the infiltrators and their supporters inside Cuba were captured and shot.

On August 18 anti-Castro commandoes shelled and machine-gunned a Cuban factory. On the 21st, the day of Oswald's radio debate, the *Times-Picayune* reported that the Cuban government had charged that the raid was planned, organized, and supplied by the CIA. Ten days later a front-page story headlined "Policy Changed on Cuba Attacks" quoted a *Washington Post* report that the new U.S. policy was to "neither encourage nor discourage" such raids, if they were militarily feasible and not carried out simply for publicity purposes. This change was seen as "an encouragement to activist exiles."

In early September the CIA renewed its contact with one of its informants, a high-level Cuban official codenamed AM/LASH. Although the CIA was primarily interested in keeping AM/LASH in place for intelligence purposes, AM/LASH now proposed that he engineer a coup involving, as a first step, Castro's assassination. The case officers who talked with him in Brazil cabled headquarters on

September 7 saying that AM/LASH was interested in attempting an "inside job" against Castro and was awaiting a U.S. plan of action.

Even while covert activities continued, however, the White House was considering an attempt to establish communications with the Cuban government. Beginning in September, an adviser to the American delegation to the United Nations, William Attwood, had a series of informal talks with the Cuban ambassador to the U.N. to try to open negotiations leading to an accommodation between the two countries. When Attwood individually informed Robert Kennedy and McGeorge Bundy of his effort, each agreed it was worth pursuing.

Thus, American policy was proceeding along two distinct and contradictory roads. Attwood had advised the White House of his diplomatic efforts, but the CIA officials involved with AM/LASH didn't inform the White House of theirs. Richard Helms testified that he didn't believe it was necessary,

> . . . given this Cuban of his standing and all the history . . . of trying to find someone inside Cuba who might head a government and have a group to replace Castro . . . this was so central to the whole theme of everything we had been trying to do, that I [found] it totally unnecessary to ask Robert Kennedy at that point [whether] we should go ahead with this.

Meanwhile, behind the scenes, Oswald was pursuing his own covert activities, evidently determined to play a role in the international chess game.

On September 5 two planes dropped bombs on Santa Clara, Cuba. Late in the evening of September 7 Premier Castro gave an impromptu, three-hour interview to Associated Press reporter Daniel Harker during a reception at the Brazilian Embassy in Havana. Two days later the *Times-Picayune* reported:

CASTRO BLASTS RAIDS ON CUBA
Says U.S. Leaders Imperiled by Aid to Rebels

Havana (AP)—Prime Minister Fidel Castro said Saturday night "United States leaders" would be in danger if they helped in any attempt to do away with leaders of Cuba. Bitterly denouncing what he called US-prompted raids on Cuban territory, Castro said, "We are prepared to fight them and answer in kind. United States leaders should think that if they are aiding terrorist plans to eliminate Cuban leaders, they themselves will not be safe."

Castro went on to accuse the United States of "double-crossing" policies and called President Kennedy a "cheap and crooked politician." A similar story appeared in the *States Item.*

What were these terrorist plans Castro referred to? Although it's possible that Cuban intelligence had learned of the AM/LASH operation, Castro implied that the plot was connected to the recent raids carried out by Cuban exiles. As the Church committee noted, talk of assassinating Castro was common among the more militant exile groups. It was "part of the ambience of that time" for militant exiles to say that the best way to get their country back was to shoot Fidel. The committee report says, "Castro's September 7 statement could have been referring to information he received relating to such assassination plots hatched by exile leaders. In addition there were paramilitary raids on Cuba by exile leaders shortly before Castro's interview." In any case, Raymond Rocca, a CIA official who had been assigned to work with the Warren Commission, wrote in 1975, "There can be no question from the facts surrounding the Castro appearance, which had not been expected, and his agreement to the interview, that this event represented a more-than-ordinary attempt to get a message on the record in the United States."

Castro was mistaken to assume, as a matter of course, that President Kennedy had ordered or had specific knowledge of any of these attempts. They grew out of the crisis atmosphere that prevailed, when it seemed to many people that Castro had to be removed by any means necessary. So far as anyone knows, the president never saw Castro's intended message. But among the potential readers was Lee Harvey Oswald, a disturbed young radical who had been following the local papers looking for a way to help Cuba. With his taste for violence and his subjective interpretations of everything he read, Castro's warning may indeed have seemed like the king's outcry against Becket quoted earlier by Senator Charles Mathias: "Who will rid me of this man?"

The irony is that the CIA plots may have evolved in the same manner.

During September Oswald eagerly awaited Ruth Paine's arrival. After Marina and June went to stay at Ruth's home in Irving, he would be free to go to Mexico City to apply for a Cuban visa. He informed his wife that he would also visit the Soviet Embassy in Mexico and try to speed up her return to the Soviet Union. He assured her that if everything worked out he would arrange for her to join him in Cuba or for him to visit her in Russia. When Ruth arrived he led her to believe that he was going to Houston or Philadelphia to look for work, and cautioned Marina not to tell her anything about his actual destination.

The women left for Texas on September 23. Oswald was seen hurrying out of his apartment, suitcases in hand, the following afternoon. After a gap of two nights and a day, he was spotted in south Texas on a Trailways bus headed for the Mexican border. During the intervening period, Oswald was reportedly in Dallas. His appearance there provides the first indication that Oswald had read Castro's warning and that he was responding to it with his own idea of political action, much as he had to other news reports about Cuba that summer.

11... The Troubling Testimony of Sylvia Odio—"A Matter of Some Importance to the Commission"

During 1963 Sylvia Odio, an attractive, 26-year-old Cuban exile, was a leader of the anti-Castro movement in Dallas. Mrs. Odio had a personal reason for wanting to see Fidel overthrown. She came from a wealthy Cuban family that had supported Castro before the revolution but later turned against him. Since 1961, her parents had been imprisoned in Cuba, her father at the prison on the Isle of Pines.

At about nine o'clock on the evening of September 25, 1963, the doorbell rang at Sylvia Odio's apartment in Dallas. Her sister Annie answered, then went to call Sylvia to the door. Standing under the outside light were three strangers. Keeping the chain latch on, Sylvia took a good look at them. Two were Latin Americans in T-shirts who looked tired and scruffy. One was taller and had an unusual bald spot on one side of his hairline. The other one—she thought he looked Mexican—was shorter, heavier, and "very hairy." The third man standing between them was an Anglo-American who vaguely needed a shave.

One of the Latins asked, "Are you Sarita Odio?"

She told him she was not. "That is my sister [who is] studying at the University of Dallas. I am Sylvia."

Then he asked, "Is she the oldest?"

"No, I am the oldest."

And he said, "It is you we are looking for."

He told her they were members of the Cuban Revolutionary Junta (JURE), the anti-Castro organization Sylvia Odio belonged to. Suspicious, she asked their names. She later recalled, "One of them said his name was Leopoldo. He said that was his war name. In all this underground, everybody has a war name. This was done for safety in Cuba. So when everybody came to exile, everyone was known by their war names." It was Leopoldo, the taller one, who did most of the talking. The other Latin gave his war name as something like "Angelo."

After she refused to let them in, Leopoldo told her, "We are friends of your father." He gave her "almost incredible details" about her father's past, which she believed only someone who knew him, or was very well-informed, would have known. Mrs. Odio later testified, "after they mentioned my father they started talking about the American. He [the Latin American] said, 'You are working in the underground.' And I said, 'No, I am sorry to say I am not working in the underground.' And he said, 'We wanted you to meet this American. His name is Leon Oswald.' He repeated it twice. . . . And they introduced him as an American who was very much interested in the Cuban cause."

The American attempted a few words in Spanish, "trying to be cute." She asked him if he had ever been to Cuba and he said he hadn't, but that he was interested in her movement. Afterward he stood silently, watching and listening—as Odio would put it, "sort of looking at me to see what my reaction was, like somebody who is evaluating the situation."

One of the Latin Americans took out a letter written in Spanish that requested money for her organization to buy arms to overthrow Castro. He asked if she would translate the letter into English for him and "send a whole lot of them" to American businessmen. Mrs. Odio refused. (She had been shown a similar petition by a Dallas leader of JURE, and had turned him down too.) She asked who had sent them, and Leopoldo told her that they had "just come from New Orleans," where they were trying to get their movement organized, and that they were doing this on their own. He apologized for the late hour, saying they were leaving on a trip that night or the next evening.

The entire conversation lasted about fifteen minutes. Sylvia told them she had to go and, still suspicious, she added that she was going to write to her father about their visit. As they were leaving, Leopoldo asked, "Is he still in the Isle of Pines?" Then they drove away in a red car, with Leopoldo at the wheel.

The next day Leopoldo telephoned her after she got home from work. It was a conversation Odio wouldn't be likely to forget. From what he said, it was clear he continued to believe she had contacts with the anti-Castro underground. Leopoldo asked her what she had thought of the American. When she replied, "I didn't think anything," he said, "Well, you know, he's a Marine, an ex-Marine, and an expert marksman. He would be a tremendous asset to anyone, except that you never know how to take him. . . . You know, our idea is to introduce him to the underground in Cuba, because he is great, he is kind of nuts." He said, "He could go either way. He could do anything—like getting underground in Cuba, like killing Castro."

Then, while Mrs. Odio listened uneasily, he raised the possibility of another assassination. "The American says we Cubans don't have any guts. He says we should have shot President Kennedy after the Bay of Pigs, because he is the one that was holding the freedom of Cuba actually. He says we should do something like that." He added that "Leon" had told him, "It is so easy to do it." He told her again that he and his friends were going on a trip, and that he wanted to talk to her again on their return. Their conversation ended, and she never heard from any of them again.

Alarmed, Odio had suspected at once "some sort of scheme or plot," though she didn't know what. There had been something too calculating about Leopoldo's approach: "When I had no reaction to the American, he thought that he would mention that the man was loco . . . and would be the kind of man that could do anything like getting underground in Cuba, like killing Castro. He repeated several times that he was an expert shotman. And he said, 'We probably won't have anything to do with him. He is kind of loco.'" He was feeling her out. Then, "When he mentioned the fact that we should have killed President Kennedy . . . he was trying to play it safe. If I liked him, then he would go along with me, but if I didn't like him, he was kind of retreating to see what my reaction was. It was cleverly done."

A few days later Odio wrote to her father describing her visitors. (His eventual response would be a warning to stay away from these men, because he didn't know them.) She almost succeeded in putting the incident out of her mind. On November 22 she was at work when word came that the president had been shot. Immediately she remembered what Leopoldo had said about the exiles taking revenge against Kennedy. After her boss sent everyone home, Sylvia fainted on her way to the parking lot and was taken to a hospital by ambulance.

In another part of town, Annie Odio had watched the Kennedy motorcade pass by on its way to the Book Depository around noon. An hour or so later, when she saw Oswald's picture on television, her first thought was, "My God, I know this guy and I don't know from where. . . . Where have I seen this guy?" After learning of her sister's collapse, Annie Odio visited her at the hospital and mentioned the feeling that she had seen Oswald before. Sylvia, who started to cry, reminded her of the three men who came to her apartment. There was a TV set in the room, and Oswald's picture came on. Sylvia later described their reaction: "Annie and I looked at one another and sort of gasped. She said, 'Do you recognize him?' She said, 'It is the same guy, isn't it?' I said, 'Yes, but do not say anything.'"

The women were too afraid to go to the authorities with their story, but Sylvia told another sister about it, who told an American friend. Eventually the information made its way to the FBI, who came to question Sylvia in mid-December and then relayed her story to the Warren Commission.

Odio's account of her meeting with Oswald was arguably the most important new information given to the Commission. Here was a witness who said she had seen Oswald with two unknown companions, one of whom reported a threat Oswald had made against the president's life—this scarcely two months before the assassination. Odio's experience might well provide the key to the mystery of why Kennedy was killed.

From the outset it was clear that Odio was a credible witness. The FBI checked her out, and her reputation was excellent. More important, her physician insisted that Sylvia had told him about her mysterious visitors soon after she saw them, well *before* the assassination. And she was able to produce the letter her father had written denying the visitors were his friends. Furthermore, the details of her account matched up with other evidence about Oswald she almost certainly couldn't have known about.[1] For instance, Leopoldo had said they had just come from New Orleans and were leaving on a trip—at a time when Oswald had left New Orleans and would soon be in Mexico. Her description of one of the Latin Americans was similar to that of the "Mexican" Oswald had reportedly been seen with in New Orleans. In short, Sylvia Odio's story held up, and she was, and still remains, quite certain the man she saw that night was Lee Harvey Oswald.

Even before Odio was called to testify before the Warren Commission, one of its staff lawyers, W. David Slawson, was trying to pin down Oswald's movements from the time when he was last seen in New Orleans by Marina and Ruth Paine on Monday, September 23, to the time when he was next spotted on the bus heading for Mexico shortly after 6 A.M. on Thursday, September 26. If Oswald's whereabouts during that period could be accounted for, Odio's story—and its disturbing implications—could be quickly disposed of.

As it turned out, this was not easy to do. There were no cyewitnesses who could establish Oswald's presence in New Orleans after neighbors saw him leave his apartment on the afternoon of the 24th, and no evidence could be found that he left the city by bus, train, or commercial airline. Thus, the evening of the 24th and the entire next day and night were a blank. Slawson had one slim piece of paper with which to bridge the gap—Oswald's weekly Texas unemployment check that was cashed at a Winn-Dixie supermarket on the 24th or 25th. The local postal officials told Commission investigators that the check probably would not have reached Oswald's post office box before the early morning hours of Wednesday, September 25. Slawson reasoned that if Oswald stayed over somewhere in New Orleans until Wednesday morning to wait for this check, and was next seen on his way to Mexico, he must have caught the connecting bus that left New Orleans for Houston on Wednesday afternoon.[2] And if he was on that bus, he could not have been at Odio's apartment.

Slawson's analysis seemed reasonable enough on the surface, but there were problems with it. No witness could be found who saw Oswald on the 10-hour bus ride from New Orleans to Houston—an unusual circumstance, since there were passengers who had seen him on every other leg of his bus trip to Mexico City and back to Dallas. Furthermore, the driver of the connecting bus said he had never seen Oswald "at any time."

There was also good reason to believe that the postal authorities had for once underestimated the efficiency of the U.S. mails. Marina testified that Oswald always picked up his weekly Texas unemployment checks on a *Tuesday*. Indeed, elsewhere in the Warren Report (in knocking down a rumor that Oswald had been in Mexico the preceding week), the Commission asserted that Oswald "cashed a check from the Texas Employment Commission at the Winn-Dixie Store no. 1425 in New Orleans" on "Tuesday, September 17." Thus it appears that Oswald could have cashed his *next* check on Tuesday the 24th and left town, perhaps in a private car, the same day.

Meanwhile, another staff lawyer, Wesley J. Liebeler, had by now taken Sylvia Odio's deposition, and Liebeler wasn't satisfied with Slawson's analysis. He wrote an internal memo saying, "There are problems. Odio may well be right. The Commission will look bad if it turns out she is." Liebeler pointed to the testimony of lawyer Dean Andrews and the bartender at the Habana Bar, who each said he had seen Oswald with a similar-looking Latin American. Liebeler noted that Oswald would have had time to travel to Dallas to see Odio and still get to south Texas in time to catch the bus to Mexico.

The response of the Commission's chief counsel, Lee J. Rankin, has often been quoted by critics of the Warren Report. He told Liebeler, "At this stage we are supposed to be closing doors, not opening them." The Commission's work was winding down, and President Johnson was pushing for the release of their report well before the November election to avoid having the investigation become a campaign issue.

Nevertheless, in August 1964 Rankin wrote FBI Director J. Edgar Hoover: "It is a matter of some importance to the Commission that Mrs. Odio's allegations either be proved or disproved." Rankin suggested that the two Latin Americans might have been either members of an anti-Castro group other than JURE or "pro-Castro individuals attempting to infiltrate the anti-Castro groups in Dallas."

Rankin asked Hoover to conduct the investigation necessary to find out who these men were. He continued, "We are also concerned about the possibility that Oswald may have left New Orleans on September 24, 1963 instead of September 25, 1963 as has been previously thought. In that connection Marina Oswald has recently advised us that her husband told her he intended to leave New Orleans the very next day following her departure on September 23, 1963." Rankin concluded that since Oswald was in Mexico after the 26th, "the only time he could have been in Odio's apartment appears to be the nights of September 24 or 25, most likely the latter."

Hoover subsequently reported back, saying the FBI had located an anti-Castro activist named Loren Hall who claimed that he had visited Mrs. Odio that September in the company of Lawrence Howard, a Mexican-American from East Los Angeles, and William Seymour from Arizona. Seymour was said to resemble Oswald. When the Warren Report was published a few days later, the doubts expressed in Rankin's letter were nowhere to be seen. Even though no other new evidence had turned up, the report asserted that Oswald probably left New Orleans by bus on the 25th. Its discussion ended: "While the FBI had not yet completed its investigation into this matter at the time the report went to press, the Commission has concluded that Lee Harvey Oswald was not at Mrs. Odio's apartment in September of 1963."

Before the ink was dry, the FBI's explanation collapsed. After both Lawrence Howard and William Seymour denied having visited Odio, Loren Hall retracted his story (he later claimed the FBI had misquoted him in the first place), and Mrs. Odio failed to recognize pictures of any of them.

The Warren Commission had not succeeded in closing the doors against its critics. Sylvia Odio's testimony, and its handling by the authorities, would be a central issue in nearly every conspiracy book. Clearly, the Odio incident—as it came to be called—could not be explained away as a simple case of mistaken identity because, as the critics were quick to point out, the report had left a huge question dangling in mid-air: If Oswald wasn't at Odio's apartment, *why was a look-alike using his name?*

The critics believed they knew the answer. In *Accessories After the Fact,* Sylvia Meagher presented a careful analysis of the Commission's evidence and demonstrated, almost beyond question, that Oswald *could have been* at Odio's apartment on the night of September 25. And since Odio's account "coincided with facts to which she had no access," the likelihood of fabrication was "thus virtually destroyed." However, Meagher then proceeded to a strangely narrowed conclusion. She wrote, "That leaves two possibilities open: that the real Oswald visited Mrs. Odio with two companions, one of whom deliberately planted highly incriminating information about him without his knowledge; or that a mock-Oswald visited her, to accomplish the same purpose." Either way, it was a frame-up, for, as she saw it, Leopoldo "took pains to plant seeds which inevitably would incriminate Oswald in the assassination carried out on November 22, so that an anonymous phone call would be enough to send police straight after him even if he had not been arrested within the hour."

Who was behind this scheme to frame Oswald? In Meagher's hypothesis, they were probably Cuban counter-revolutionaries and their ultra-right associates, who may have taken notice of Oswald after his attempt to infiltrate Carlos Bringuier's organization in New Orleans. Their purpose would have been "to revenge themselves not only against the President whom they considered a Communist and a traitor but also against a Marxist and suspected double-agent who had tried to infiltrate the anti-Castro movement."

Since it's true that the Far Right and many Cuban exiles were bitter about Kennedy's performance at the Bay of Pigs, this hypothesis has a certain appeal. But take a closer look.

What would Meagher's anonymous caller have told the police? Presumably, that they should question a woman named Sylvia Odio —who would then tell them what she later told the Warren Commission: that Oswald and his companions claimed to be members of an anti-Castro organization, that Oswald had been offered as a potential assassin of Castro, and that he said the exiles should kill the president because of the Bay of Pigs. How could this revelation, coming in the heat of the moment following Kennedy's death, have *helped* the anti-Castro movement or the Far Right? Indeed, Meagher's plotters had painted Oswald as a violent ally of the very factions that were supposedly trying to frame him. Meagher herself noted that Odio didn't call the police, perhaps because she "feared that the Cuban exiles might be accused of the President's death."

If this was an attempt by Cuban counter-revolutionaries to implicate a Marxist, it was a peculiar way to go about it.

Nevertheless, almost all of the theorists who came after her have followed the direction of Meagher's accusing finger. For the critics, the Odio incident could only have been an effort to frame Oswald. They assume that since Leopoldo's report of Oswald's remark about killing Kennedy was incriminating, it must have been *intended* as incriminating. This is a natural, common-sense view, and it's probably wrong. It's easy to forget that these events from the past, which are now set in concrete from our point of view, actually took place in the uncertain flux of the present. For some reason, since we know what was going to happen on November 22, we tend to assume Leopoldo did, too. But when these men visited Odio's apartment, Kennedy's trip to Dallas had not even been scheduled, let alone announced. Strange as it may seem, no one on earth could have known that Oswald would ultimately land a job in a building that would overlook a Kennedy motorcade.

But the frame-up theory's ultimate weakness involves the critics' conception of Lee Harvey Oswald. In every conspiracy book, Oswald is a piece of chaff blown about by powerful, unseen forces—he's a dumb and compliant puppet with no volition of his own. If the man Odio saw was an impostor, how could the plotters be certain no witnesses would be able to establish Oswald's presence somewhere else that evening—unless they ordered the unsuspecting patsy to stay out of sight? And if the real Oswald was used, how did the anti-Castro plotters get their Marxist enemy to stand at Odio's door to be introduced as a friend of the Cuban exiles? No one has come up with a plausible scenario that can answer those questions.

In years to come, Odio would be interviewed by two other government commissions—the Church committee and the House Assassinations Committee—and those investigators would also conclude that she was a truthful witness. After its relatively brief examination of the president's assassination, the Church panel reached no public conclusion—Odio's testimony wasn't mentioned in its final report. The Assassination Committee's report was hardly more helpful. It said, "The committee was inclined to believe Silvia [sic] Odio" and "did not agree with the Warren Commission's conclusion that Oswald could not have been in Dallas at the requisite time." But it could go no farther: "Based on a judgment of the credibility of Silvia and Annie Odio, one of these men at least looked like Lee Harvey Oswald and was introduced to Mrs. Odio as Leon Oswald." A fuller account of their indecision was later given by the Committee's chief counsel and director, G. Robert Blakey, who wrote:

> Based on all [the] evidence, we believed Silvia [sic] and Annie Odio:
> three men, who identified themselves as members of an anti-Castro
> organization, did visit their apartment in Dallas about two months prior
> to the Kennedy assassination; and one of them, who was either Lee
> Harvey Oswald or his look-alike, was introduced to them as Leon
> Oswald. Rather than dismiss the incident, as the Warren Commission
> had, we considered it a significant, if mysterious association of Oswald
> (or someone posing as Oswald) with two individuals who were engaged
> in anti-Castro activities, or acting as if they were.

To sum up, there have been only two explanations for Odio's disturbing testimony. It was a case of mistaken identity, as the Commission said, and a "Leon Oswald" and two other men visited her for unknown reasons. Or it was an attempt to frame Oswald by planting incriminating statements. The first is no explanation whatsoever, and the second is based on several unreasonable assumptions. The point to be stressed is this. Sylvia Odio gave testimony of obvious, even crucial importance, and no one could explain what it meant.

Some mysteries defy rational analysis. It takes a moment of unearned insight—or what has been called the Aha! reaction—to understand them. There is a picture psychologists use showing a white goblet on a black background. Stare at it long enough and, with lightning speed and no conscious effort, one sees that the background is actually the silhouette of two people facing one another. The goblet becomes merely the white background between them. *(Aha! Why didn't I see it before?)* When I first read Sylvia Odio's testimony, I was a long way from understanding Oswald's thinking, and no matter how I turned it, her testimony made no sense. All the other evidence said Oswald was a supporter of the Castro revolution. Yet here he was, apparently teamed up with two counter-revolutionaries.

One day I was reading a Secret Service report describing their questioning of Marina Oswald shortly after Oswald's death, when a single sentence brought me up short. Marina had remarked that her husband "was boastful that he was a good shot and that he learned this while in the military service." That was exactly the way Leopoldo had described "Leon Oswald" to Sylvia Odio: "He's a Marine, an ex-Marine, and an expert marksman." *They were talking about the same man.*

There was just one other witness who spoke of Oswald as an ex-Marine who bragged about his military expertise—and that was Carlos Bringuier, the exile leader whose organization Oswald had tried to infiltrate. I began to see how similar his encounters with Bringuier and Odio were. Oswald had approached each of them as an eager volunteer. With Bringuier, he was an ex-Marine who could train guerrillas and lead raids against Cuba. With Odio, he was an ex-Marine marksman who could knock off Fidel. (Although it was Leopoldo who voiced this proposal, it was the same general line Oswald had used with Bringuier.)

There were other similarities. Oswald had offered Bringuier a contribution, hoping to draw the exiles into a violation of the law. Odio's visitors asked her to distribute a letter appealing for funds to buy arms for the war on Cuba. A letter of this kind would probably have been illegal. Infiltration and harassment—this was how Oswald had described his encounter with Bringuier. ("I infiltrated the Cuban Student Directorate and then harassed them with information I gained including having the N.O. City Attorney General call them in and put a restraining order . . . on some so-called bonds for invasion they were selling in the New Orleans area.")

But a third tactic was used. While Oswald was in Bringuier's store, he gave two anti-Castro teenagers specific instructions on derailing trains and blowing up the Huey P. Long Bridge. With Sylvia Odio, he allegedly proposed a still more outrageous act of violence. It had been put almost in the form of a dare: the exiles "didn't have any guts. . . . It is so easy to do it." The age-old role of the provocateur is to encourage acts of violence that will discredit the group he has infiltrated. By goading the exiles into attacking the president, a pro-Castro provocateur might have hoped to destroy two threats to Cuba with one blow.

For a police detective, a criminal's M.O., his method of operating, is nearly as distinctive as his fingerprints. The Odio episode followed Oswald's M.O. In other words, the mysterious Odio incident was another of Oswald's attempts to infiltrate the anti-Castro underground. The intended victim of this enterprise was not Lee Harvey Oswald, but Sylvia Odio and the Cuban exiles. Oswald was plotting against the exiles, not the other way around. Unlike the explanations offered by the Warren Commission and its critics, this solution *fits the rest of the evidence about Oswald.* And it makes better sense, after all, that Oswald went to see Odio for some reason of his own, than that he was impersonated or duped by his enemies.

Having caught a glimpse of what Oswald was up to, I still had to ask why. Why was Oswald put forward as a potential assassin of Castro, and why the talk about killing Kennedy, as well? Again, Oswald's similar approach to Carlos Bringuier provides a clue. In

August Oswald was already planning to go to Cuban officials in Mexico and show them "how much he'd done to help Cuba." When he learned about the FBI raid on an exile arms cache, he saw a chance to bring the Cubans something special: valuable intelligence about the inner working of an exile training camp. But his infiltration attempt failed when Bringuier turned him down.

Then, on September 9, Castro's warning about assassination plots appeared in the *Times-Picayune*. He declared that United States leaders would be in danger if they aided terrorist plans to eliminate Cuban leaders.

It would have been fairly easy to read between the lines. These terrorist plans were obviously the work of the same exile groups that were conducting the raids with U.S. support. In the past, the Cuban government had blamed the CIA. Now Castro seemed to be pointing a finger directly at Kennedy and saying that two could play at that game.

Here was another danger to Cuba, and a new opportunity for Oswald to prove himself. He had already made one attempt to penetrate the enemy underground. Now, if he could just make contact with the exile leaders involved in these "terrorist plans," he might come up with an even bigger trophy: inside information about the plots to kill Cuba's leaders. Once again he would seek out an exile group and offer his help—not as a guerrilla leader this time, but as a marksman who could assassinate Fidel. He would try to infiltrate as a volunteer, as he had before. While he was at it, he'd plant another little seed of provocation. He'd attempt to goad the exiles into retaliating against Kennedy.

In other words, the Odio incident was Oswald's reaction to Castro's warning.

Although I was fairly convinced of this by 1976, I still didn't understand why Oswald and the others went all the way to Dallas to carry out this scheme. Why did they go to Sylvia Odio, in particular? An article in the *Saturday Evening Post* that year provided an answer. The authors, George O'Toole and Paul Hoch, had apparently discovered more about Odio's father from some of the large number of Warren Commission records that were declassified in 1976. It turns out that Odio's parents weren't ordinary political prisoners, as the Warren Report suggested. They had been indirectly involved in a spectacular plot to assassinate Castro in 1961.

The plot was the work of Antonio Veciana and Reinaldo Gonzales, members of the anti-Castro underground. Veciana's mother had rented an apartment near the presidential palace from which they planned to fire a bazooka to kill Castro and other officials. Before their plan could be carried out, however, word of it reached the Cuban police. Veciana and his mother escaped to Miami, while Gonzales fled to a farm that was owned by Sylvia Odio's parents. Gonzales was tracked down and arrested, as were the Odios. Castro himself announced the breaking up of this plot at a public meeting in Havana in October 1961. At the time, the Odio daughters were already out of the country.

Having somehow learned of her father's background, her visitors apparently concluded (however mistakenly) that Amador Odio's eldest daughter might be interested in introducing a volunteer hit man to the underground. Notice the chain of association in their approach to her. They talked first about the details of her father's activities in Cuba. Then, "after they mentioned my father they started talking about the American. He said, 'You are working in the underground.' And I said, 'No, I am sorry to say I am not working in the underground.' And he said, 'We wanted you to meet this American. His name is Leon Oswald.' . . . And they introduced him as an American who was very much interested in the Cuban cause." Oswald told her the same thing, then stood silently, evaluating the situation. The underlying logic seemed to be: *We know about your father's connection with a terrorist plot to kill Castro. We believe you have contacts with the underground. Here is an American you can use.* Had Odio invited them in, she might well have heard the rest of their proposal about Oswald that evening.

What did they want from Mrs. Odio? Apparently, they hoped she would know, and tell them, the name of the right person to see—the leader behind these new assassination plots. And, in fact, it appears that Odio may have had a reputation for being able to put people in touch with the anti-Castro underground. Mrs. Odio told the Commission that in June 1963 she had spoken with a Uruguayan named Johnny Martin who claimed he could provide the exiles with second-hand weapons if she could put him in touch with an appropriate leader. As she later said, she had "jumped at the opportunity that something could be done" and arranged a meeting between Martin and an exile leader in Miami.

Mrs. Odio believed it would not have been difficult for anyone to find her. She testified that shortly before the Oswald incident, a speaker at an anti-Castro meeting in Dallas had mentioned that he knew her father in Cuba and that Amador Odio's daughters were living in that city. Odio said she could have been located by calling the Catholic refugee relief agency or even by consulting the phone book.

Overall, one gets the impression that Cubans in this country formed a tightly knit community in which news got around easily and secrets were hard to keep. Oswald may have found Mrs. Odio the same way he apparently found Bringuier—simply by asking around. Another New Orleans anti-Castro exile, Ernesto Rodriguez, has recently claimed that Oswald had also visited *him* to offer his services as a guerrilla warfare specialist, and that it was he who sent Oswald to see Bringuier. Thus, it appears that Oswald made more forays into the anti-Castro camp than anyone realized, or wanted to admit.

The real names of the two Latin Americans will probably never be known. We know enough only to speculate about their roles. The evidence suggests they were not anti-Castro activists, as they claimed. Angelo was likely the Latin American of similar appearance that Oswald was seen with in New Orleans. Both men evidently lied when they said they were members of JURE and friends of Odio's father. (The other leaders of JURE said they had never heard of them, and Odio's father, now living in the United States, still insists they were no friends of his.) And if they were from New Orleans, as they said, they would almost certainly have known of the splash Oswald had made there in August as a Fair Play for Cuba activist. None of this rules out the idea that one or both of these men were anti-Castroites who had infiltrated Oswald's one-man operation. Leopoldo may have been an anti-Castro militant who truly believed Oswald would be an asset to his cause. But his telephone conversation with Odio followed Oswald's line with Bringuier so closely that this seems doubtful. And Leopoldo's parting shot about Amador Odio—"Is he still in the Isle of Pines?"—sounds almost like a jeer. It seems more reasonable that these three were birds of a feather than that they were working at cross purposes.

But let's pull back for a moment to get a broader view. Was there someone behind the scenes telling Oswald what to do?

Let's make that question more specific: Who would have had a reason to order Oswald to get inside the exile underground? Not the CIA, apparently, since the CIA already had plenty of contacts with that group—the CIA was, in fact, running the war against Cuba. The FBI? Maybe, though it's difficult to imagine that Hoover's boys would have wanted one of their operatives to go around suggesting that Castro's opponents should murder the president. Besides, it's hard to picture Lee Oswald working for the FBI or the CIA, unless we crop out everything else we know about him.

There is another possibility. Although the House Assassinations Committee concluded, "on the basis of the evidence available to it," that the Cuban government was not involved in the assassination, its report called the CIA investigation of the question of Cuban involvement grossly inadequate—and it attached a fine-print footnote:

> With respect to the incident at the home of Sylvia Odio in Dallas, the CIA had developed since 1963 the ability to identify from physical descriptions possible intelligence agents who may have been involved. In fact, at the committee's request, the CIA attempted to identify Odio's visitors, and it determined that they may have been members of Cuban intelligence. The committee showed photographs supplied by the CIA to Odio who stated they did not appear to be the visitors in question. The committee came to the conclusion that had she been shown photographs in 1963, when the event was clearer in her mind, she might have been able to make an identification. It is also regrettable that the CIA did not make use of a defector from Cuba who had worked in intelligence and who might have been able to identify the Odio visitors.

An extraordinary footnote. And yet, it's hard to believe that Leopoldo and Angelo were Cuban intelligence agents. Anything this trio hoped to get out of Mrs. Odio they must have hoped to get right away, before she could check their authenticity with her father. The whole affair had an improvised, amateurish flavor. As we'll see later on, although Oswald *wanted* to work for the Cubans, he apparently got no further with them than he did with the Russians.

"As far as taking orders," Marina told the House Assassinations Committee, speaking generally, "I knew him personally and he didn't like to take orders." There's no reason to assume that Oswald was following orders when he went to see Bringuier or Odio, because he had a motive of his own—or, rather, two motives. He wanted to help Cuba, and he wanted to make a name for himself as a Castro supporter and revolutionary. Oswald was on his way to Cuba, he hoped, and he evidently wanted to come bearing gifts—much as he had done when he went to Russia with his military information.

The simplest and most reasonable conclusion is that the Odio incident was Oswald's idea. Looked at more closely, each of the tactics used was typical of Oswald in some manner. It was like him to pose as a leader: the guerrilla warfare expert, the expert marksman. He was putting his military training to ironic use—as an enlisted man, Oswald had once complained that all the Marine Corps did was teach you to kill, and after you got out you might be a good gangster. The second tactic—trying to draw the exiles into a violation of the law—also sounds like Oswald, who often showed a tendency to be legalistic. And finally, the threat against a president's life was also in character, since he had already made a verbal threat against Eisenhower.

But it wasn't just the tactics. The entire incident had the imprint of Oswald's personality on it. Consider another remark of Marina's. She was asked if she thought her husband would have prepared for his defection by learning Russian: "Was that a trait of his . . . that when he got ready to do something he felt was important he spent a period of time preparing for it?" She answered, "I would say yes," and a few minutes later circled back to the same question: "Going back to say that Lee was always preparing for something, he not always prepared himself [sic], but he was quite calculating in that respect, and sometimes quite clever. He would masquerade somehow." George de Mohrenschildt, too, saw this trait of his. Concerning the theory of the conspiracists that Oswald was working for the anti-Castro side in New Orleans, he wrote:

> I cannot visualize Lee being in cahoots with these Cuban refugees in New Orleans . . . but he might have played his own game, meeting some of them, checking just for the hell of it what their motivations were.
> The amazing and attractive side of Lee's personality was that he liked to play with his own life, he was an actor in real life. A very curious individual.
> On the other hand, I can very easily visualize Lee joining a pro-Castro group.

The Odio incident was characteristic of Oswald. There was even, perhaps, a model for it from his childhood, although this was probably an event he had long forgotten. In Fort Worth sixteen years earlier, Marguerite had also stood outside a rival's door with two confederates. As the ringleader, she told one of them what to say— "Telegram for Mrs. C____."—to trap her wandering husband, Edwin A. Ekdahl. As Robert said, his brother's "imagination and love of intrigue" were a lot like his mother's.

The compelling aspect of Sylvia Odio's testimony is the window it provides on Lee Harvey Oswald's thinking just two months before Dallas. Up until then, there was little indication that Oswald felt any animosity toward John Kennedy. In fact, he seemed to favor him over the other politicians on the scene. In August he had publicly blamed the CIA and State Department for America's policy toward Cuba. But sixteen days after Castro's warning appeared, Oswald not only tried to penetrate the plots Castro spoke about, he suggested that Kennedy should be killed. The September 9 warning evidently had an effect: Oswald now believed that Castro was in danger and that the Cuban leader held Kennedy responsible.

This conclusion is admittedly based on inferences—I have deduced Oswald's thinking by reading Odio's testimony in light of his past behavior. The method I've used is an old one. During closing arguments in a trial, each attorney will attempt to weave the available evidence into a reconstruction of the events in question. It is then up to the jury to decide whose account is more likely to be true. I have presented the Odio incident within a narrative of Oswald's other activities, showing how the pieces mesh. Although I don't claim to have conclusive proof, I do maintain that my interpretation is more credible than the alternative theories.

Only two other explanations of this incident have been given—that it was an extraordinary case of mistaken identity, or a plot to frame a Marxist by presenting him as an anti-Castro hit man. Neither view can be totally disproved. But neither encompasses the other evidence about Oswald nearly as well as the solution I've proposed.

I found new support for my argument in 1977, when I learned that Lee Harvey Oswald had made a second threat against Kennedy's life just a few days after he left Sylvia Odio's doorstep. The man who revealed this threat was not an unknown named "Leopoldo," but Fidel Castro himself.

12... Castro's Revelations

ON Thursday afternoon, September 26, Oswald's bus crossed the Mexican border at Laredo, Texas. A fellow passenger, an Englishman named John McFarland, recalled that Oswald told him he was en route to Cuba and explained that he had to travel via Mexico because it was illegal to go there directly from the United States. When McFarland asked why he wanted to go to Cuba, Oswald replied, "To see Castro, if I could."

The bus arrived in Mexico City the following morning, and Oswald registered at the Hotel Comercio four blocks from the bus station using the alias Harvey Oswald Lee. He immediately set about arranging his travel plans. According to Marina, he went to the Soviet Embassy first. Exactly what he said there isn't known, since the Russians didn't allow the Warren Commission to interview its embassy personnel. However, from Marina's testimony and other evidence it's apparent that he asked them to expedite the visas he and Marina had applied for through the Washington embassy, and that he told them he would be going to Russia through Cuba. He also seemed to believe that the Russians could smooth his way at the Cuban Embassy.

A Commission lawyer later asked Marina, "Did he tell you why he went to Mexico City?"

"From Mexico City he wanted to go to Cuba—perhaps through the

... 205

Russian Embassy in Mexico he would be able to get to Cuba."
"Did he say anything about going to Russia by way of Cuba?"
"I know that he said that in the Embassy. But he only said so. I
know that he had no intention of going to Russia then."
"How do you know that?"
"He told me. I know Lee fairly well—well enough from that point
of view."

Next he went to the nearby Cuban Embassy, where he requested
an in-transit visa, that is, a permit to travel to Cuba en route to the
Soviet Union. The exact reason he didn't ask for a regular visa to Cuba
alone is puzzling, although an in-transit visa might have allowed him
to visit his family in Russia if their visas came through. On his
application, Oswald wrote that he wanted to leave for Cuba on September 30 and remain there for two weeks—or longer, if possible. He
was interviewed by Silvia Duran, a Mexican citizen and Castro supporter who worked in the consular section. After the assassination,
her name and office phone number were found in Oswald's notebook,
and she was brought in for questioning by the Mexican police. On
November 23, 1963, she gave them the following statement:

. . . . On the night of Nov. 22, Senora Duran heard over the radio the
name of LEE HARVEY OSWALD, which caused her to remember that
this name refers to a North American who in the last days of September
. . . appeared at the Cuban Consulate and applied for a visa to Cuba in
transit to Russia and based his application on his presentation of his
passport in which it was recorded that he had [lived] in the latter
country for a period of three years, his work permit from that same
country written in the Russian language and letters in the same language, as well as proof of his being married to a woman of Russian
nationality and being the apparent Director in the city of New Orleans
of the organization called "Fair Play for Cuba" with the desire that he
should be accepted as a "friend" of the Cuban Revolution, as a result
of which the speaker, in compliance with her duties, received all of his
data and filled out the appropriate application, and he left to return in
the afternoon, this time with his photographs [for the application], and
the speaker, recognizing that she [was exceeding] her duties, semi-
officially called the Russian Consulate by telephone because of her interest in facilitating the handling of the Russian visa for LEE HARVEY

OSWALD, but from there they answered her that the operation [of getting him a visa to Russia] would require approximately four months, which annoyed the applicant, since (as he affirmed) he was in a great hurry to obtain the visas which would permit him to travel to Russia, insisting that he was entitled to them because of his background and his partisanship and personal activities in favor of the Cuban movement, . . . [and] that his wife, of Russian nationality, was at that time in the city of New York from where she would follow him, although his place of origin was the aforementioned city of New Orleans; that as soon as Oswald understood that it was not possible to give him a Cuban visa without his previously obtaining a Russian one, because the former was for transit, he became highly agitated and angry, as a result of which the speaker called [Consul Eusebio] Azcue, who, at that time, was in his private office in company with his ultimate replacement, MIRABAL, but came out and began to argue in English with OSWALD in a very angry manner and . . . concluded by saying to him that, "As far as he was concerned, he would not give him a visa," and that "A person like him, in place of aiding the Cuban Revolution, was doing it harm." . . . that in spite of the argument the speaker handed to OSWALD a piece of paper . . . in which she recorded her name . . . and the telephone number of the Consulate . . . and, at any rate, she initiated the handling of the visa application by sending it to [Cuba, from which] a reply was received in the normal manner some fifteen to twenty days later approving the issuance of a visa, but conditioning it on his previously obtaining the Russian [one], although she does not recall whether OSWALD subsequently called her or not on the telephone. . . . and that upon seeing his photograph which appears in today's newspapers, specifically the newspaper "El Dia," she immediately recognized and identified it as being the same person she had been referring to as LEE HARVEY OSWALD.

Of course, Marina was not in New York—this was but a lie to heighten the sense of urgency, as was the statement that he was in a great hurry to reach *Russia*. But note that even after the scene with Azcue, Oswald took Duran's telephone number so that he could check back about his application. And despite the argument, Oswald kept trying. On Saturday and the following Tuesday, October 1, he made several visits to both the Russian and Cuban embassies, with a continued lack of results.

The Cuban government provided the Warren Commission with the application form which bore Oswald's photograph and signature, as well as its letter, dated October 15, which conditionally approved his in-transit visa. The Warren Report said that the CIA had been able to corroborate Duran's account through several means, adding, "By far the most important confirmation of Senora Duran's testimony, however, has been supplied by confidential sources of extremely high reliability available to the United States in Mexico. The information from these sources establishes that her testimony was truthful and accurate in all material respects. The identities of these sources cannot be disclosed without destroying their future usefulness to the United States."

The CIA's "confidential sources" in Mexico included wiretaps on the Soviet Embassy's phones. On Tuesday, October 1, Oswald returned to the Cuban Embassy. At his request Duran again called the Soviet Embassy and handed the receiver to Oswald. Speaking in Russian to a Soviet guard, he asked if there was any news concerning a telegram that had been sent to Washington. The guard asked to whom Oswald had spoken at the embassy. "Comrade Kostikov," Oswald replied, whereupon the guard suggested that he again speak in person to Kostikov. "I'll be right over," Oswald replied, and hung up.

The CIA recorded this conversation and a transcript was made, but the tape was retained for only a week or so. The reference to Kostikov had aroused the agency's interest, for in addition to his routine consular duties, Valery Vladimirovich Kostikov served as a KGB intelligence officer.

The agency's Mexico station also had surveillance cameras outside the Soviet Embassy, which was considered to be a center of espionage activity directed against the United States. After hearing the phone call, the CIA staff went through its photographs of persons recently entering and leaving the embassy, and found one of a blond, heavyset American type that it guessed might be the man who had identified himself as Oswald during the call. (This tentative identification would cause the CIA considerable embarassment later on. The man in the photo was never identified, but he evidently had no connection with Oswald whatsoever, and the Mexico station never came up with a picture of Oswald. This circumstance led to a theory that the heavyset man had impersonated Oswald at the Soviet Embassy.)

Meanwhile, CIA headquarters was alerted, and on October 10 the agency informed the FBI, the State Department, and the Office of Naval Intelligence of Oswald's contact with the Soviet Embassy. The notification omitted Oswald's reference to Kostikov, however.

In 1976 David Phillips, a CIA official who was serving in Mexico at the time, added an important detail about Oswald's conversations with the Russians. Phillips told the *Washington Post* that, in a phone call to the embassy, Oswald had tried to make a deal. (Whether this was the call mentioned earlier or another one isn't clear.) According to Phillips, Oswald said in effect, "I have information you would be interested in, and I know you can pay my way [to Russia]." The translator and typist who had worked on the transcript of the conversation confirmed Phillips's story. This sounds like Oswald, since he had already asked the Washington Embassy to make travel arrangements back to Russia for his wife and child. By the Commission's estimate, Oswald had only about $214 on hand when he left New Orleans, hardly enough to pay transportation costs for the trips he had in mind. Furthermore, Phillips's story would help explain the CIA's interest in Oswald's contact with Kostikov.

But what information could Oswald have had of interest to the Soviets? A possible answer came in 1975 from a second Ernesto Rodriguez—not the New Orleans Cuban exile mentioned earlier, but another man who was a former CIA contract agent in Mexico City. Rodriguez claimed that Oswald had told both the Soviets and the Cubans that he had information about a new CIA attempt to kill Fidel Castro. According to Rodriguez, Oswald offered the details in return for a Cuban entry visa. He said that Oswald had also talked about this planned assassination attempt in conversations with Fair Play for Cuba members in Mexico City.

Rodriguez's story is uncorroborated and should be approached with caution, but in light of Oswald's known activities, it is not implausible. This wouldn't have been the first time Oswald offered secrets to get what he wanted. More important, he had recently tried to penetrate the exile plots through Sylvia Odio. We have learned of only two infiltration attempts Oswald made—there may have been others. Anyone who had told him about a plan to kill Castro would have been understandably reluctant to come forward with his testimony after the president's death. We know from Odio's testimony that this was the kind of information Oswald was seeking. Thus, it's conceivable that he did find out details of a Castro assassination plot from some unknown source, or that he at least *claimed* that he had.

Another question that remains unsettled is what Oswald did with the rest of his time in the city. Silvia Duran told the House Assassinations Committee that she had suggested to Oswald that he might be able to get a Cuban visa if he could obtain a letter of recommendation from a Mexican in good standing with the Cuban government. From other evidence the Committee concluded that she had referred him to a philosophy professor at the local National Autonomous University who had held seminars on Marx in her home. In late September Oswald was reportedly sighted at the university, where he approached four left-wing philosophy students. One of them, Oscar Contreras, who had contacts in the Cuban Embassy, later said that Oswald had introduced himself and told them that he wanted to go to Cuba because the FBI was bothering him and life in the United States was not for him but that the Cuban consulate was refusing to give him a visa. He asked if they could help him out, and the students agreed to try. According to Anthony Summers, who interviewed Contreras in 1978, Contreras then got in touch with his contacts at the embassy, including Consul Azcue and an intelligence officer—who told him that Oswald was suspected of being a provocateur "sent by the United States to go to Cuba with evil intent."[1] Although Contreras's story is also uncorroborated, his statement about the Cuban officials' reaction to Oswald should be kept in mind.

What else did Oswald have to say to Cuban officials in Mexico City? We should remember that he was angry at being denied a visa, and made some comments to Azcue that provoked the Cuban to say that someone like him was actually hurting the revolution, not helping it. Azcue evidently considered him to be a hothead.

In 1964 new evidence turned up about a statement Oswald had

made at the Cuban Embassy. After the assassination an American Communist party member—who was also an FBI informant—made a trip to Havana and spoke with Fidel Castro. On June 17, 1964, J. Edgar Hoover sent a top-secret letter by a special courier to the Warren Commission's chief counsel, J. Lee Rankin. Hoover wrote that "through a confidential source which has furnished reliable information in the past, we have been advised of some statement made by Fidel Castro, Cuban Prime Minister, concerning the assassination of President Kennedy." The existence of this letter didn't come to light until 1976, when it was declassified along with many other Commission papers in the National Archives—but the crucial paragraph containing what Castro said had been deleted from the declassified copy. The following year, however, TV newsman Daniel Schorr obtained the deleted passage from his own sources. In his book *Clearing the Air* (excerpted in the *New York Review of Books*), Schorr revealed that the missing paragraph quoted Castro as saying "that Oswald, on his visit to the consulate, had talked of assassinating President Kennedy. The consul had taken this as a deliberate provocation. The Cuban ambassador in Mexico City had reported the incident to Havana. It had not been taken seriously at the time, but after Kennedy's assassination, Castro had come to suspect that the effort to get Oswald into Cuba was part of a right-wing conspiracy. Oswald would return from Cuba, then assassinate the president, and it would look as though Castro had been responsible."

This information was never pursued by the Commission or mentioned in its report. In fact, two of the staff lawyers, W. David Slawson and David Belin, don't recall ever having seen Hoover's letter. But the FBI informant's account would be supported by another report three years later.

While Hoover's letter lay buried, time passed. In early 1967 New Orleans' flamboyant district attorney, Jim Garrison, announced to the world that he had uncovered a conspiracy behind the assassination of the president. His chief suspect was David Ferrie, Oswald's old Civil Air Patrol instructor. But Ferrie, in poor health, died of a cerebral hemorrhage on February 22. Undaunted, Garrison soon arrested a prominent New Orleans businessman, Clay Shaw. Garrison charged that Ferrie, Oswald, and Shaw had plotted the assassination at a party in Ferrie's apartment and that the murder itself had been carried out by a team of anti-Castro Cubans. Eventually the conspirators he mentioned would include Minutemen, CIA agents, Dallas oil men and policemen, arms dealers, White Russians, and a host of other reactionaries.

The more publicity Garrison got, the wilder his charges became. In May 1967 Garrison issued a subpoena for CIA director Richard Helms, demanding that Helms produce a photograph showing Oswald in the company of a CIA agent in Mexico. Garrison apparently reasoned it this way. The CIA had never produced a photograph of Oswald taken by their surveillance cameras stationed outside the Cuban and Russian embassies. Therefore, they must have taken a photograph that showed Oswald in the company of someone whose identity they did not want to be revealed. Who could Oswald's supposed companion have been? Obviously, a CIA agent.

By this time the press was calling the Garrison investigation a three-ring circus. In June an hour-long NBC documentary charged Garrison with attempting to bribe and intimidate witnesses and using other questionable tactics. When NBC gave Garrison air time to reply on July 15, Garrison once again asserted that Oswald was without question "in the employ of U.S. intelligence agencies." He did not, however, produce any evidence.

Meanwhile, Fidel Castro was evidently watching the Garrison case with interest. In July 1967 scores of foreign reporters went to Cuba to cover an international conference in support of revolutionary groups in Asia and Latin America. At an official reception in mid-July, Castro met an American reporter named Laura Bergquist and gave her a lengthy impromptu interview which she later wrote about in *Look* magazine. (It must be understood that Castro likes to talk—Turner Catledge of the *New York Times* once said of him that he made the garrulous Senator Hubert Humphrey look like Silent Cal Coolidge.) Castro surprised Bergquist by admitting he had made a mistake in making his famous attack on the Moncada barracks in 1953. Castro spoke with her for two or three hours, until he was finally drawn away by an aide tugging on his sleeve. For our purposes the most important thing he said to her that evening was a reference to the Garrison case. He asked her if Garrison's theory of the assassination was supportable. The reason for his interest seems clear. Ever since Oswald's pro-Cuba background had been revealed in late 1963, Castro's public position was that Cuba had been set up and that the murder was a plot by right-wing forces. Now there was a New Orleans prosecutor saying the same thing.

A British journalist, Comer Clark, later claimed that he had also gotten an impromptu interview with Castro in July 1967, perhaps during this same week. And Clark's version of what Castro told him was the same story J. Edgar Hoover had reported in his then still-classified letter of 1964. According to an article by Clark published that October—in, of all places, the *National Enquirer*—Castro told him that Oswald had come to the Cuban consulate twice, each time for about fifteen minutes. Clark quoted Castro as saying, "The first time—I was told—he wanted to work for us. He was asked to explain, but he wouldn't. He wouldn't go into details. The second time he said he wanted to 'free Cuba from American imperialism.' Then he said something like, 'Someone ought to shoot that President Kennedy.' Then Oswald said—and this was exactly how it was reported to me —'Maybe I'll try to do it.' "

Castro added that he had not alerted the United States government because Oswald had been considered a "wild man" and was not taken seriously: "We didn't have any relations with the American government anyway. If I'd taken it seriously I might have informed the United Nations or some other official agency like that. But who would have believed me? People would have said that Oswald was just mad, or that I'd gone mad." Clark also quoted him as saying, "I thought the visits might be something to do with the CIA—whether anything eventually happened or not. . . . Then, too, after such a plot had been found out, we would be blamed—for something we had nothing to do with. It could have been an excuse for another invasion try. In any case, people would have tried to put it at my door. I was not responsible for Kennedy's death, I will tell you that. I think he was killed by U.S. fascists—right-wing elements who disagreed with him." (Since Jim Garrison also thought that Oswald's trip to Mexico had "something to do with the CIA," Castro was in effect supporting that theory.)

These statements attributed to Castro by Clark tally point for point with the private conversation reported in Hoover's letter to the Commission. This may be better appreciated if we look at the two accounts side by side.

FBI informant's report:	*Comer Clark interview:*
At the consulate Oswald had talked of assassinating President Kennedy.	"Then he said something like, 'Someone ought to shoot that President Kennedy. . . . Maybe I'll try to do it.' "
The consul had taken this as a deliberate provocation, but it had not been taken seriously at the time.	Oswald had been considered a "wild man" and was not taken seriously.
After Kennedy's assassination Castro had come to suspect that the effort to get Oswald into Cuba was part of a right-wing conspiracy. . . . it would look as though Castro had been responsible.	". . . after such a plot had been found out, we would be blamed—for something we had nothing to do with. . . . I think he was killed by U.S. fascists—right-wing elements. . . ."

There are several good reasons for believing that Castro did in fact make these statements to Hoover's informant and to Comer Clark. First, the general interpretation of the assassination attributed to him in both accounts is exactly what he has expressed on other occasions. In 1974, for instance, he told Frank Mankiewicz and Kirby Jones: "[T]his man—Oswald . . . applied for a permit at the Cuban embassy to travel to Cuba, and he was not given the permission. We had no idea who he was. But I ask myself why would a man who commits such an act try to come here. Sometimes we ask ourselves if someone did not wish to involve Cuba in this, because I am under the impression that Kennedy's assassination was organized by reactionaries in the United States and that it was all a result of a conspiracy.

"What I can say is that he asked permission to travel to Cuba. Now, imagine that by coincidence he had been granted this permit, that he had visited Cuba for a few days, then returned to the United States and killed Kennedy. That would have been material for a provocation."

But more important, the statements attributed to Oswald sound authentic. Clark's more detailed account fits in perfectly with Oswald's past record and with his known situation at the time he appeared at the Cuban Embassy. For instance, Castro quoted Oswald as saying he wanted to work for the Cubans. It now appears that this was indeed Oswald's ambition, but few people realized that in 1967. There was certainly no hint of this in the Warren Report or the early conspiracy books. Furthermore, if we accept that Castro's warning and the Sylvia Odio incident were fresh in his mind, it is reasonable that Oswald might have said, "Someone ought to shoot that President Kennedy," and then add—as though the possibility had just occurred to him—"Maybe I'll try to do it." Less than a week before this, Leopoldo had relayed a similar message to Odio. Oswald's statement to the Cuban official that he wanted to "free Cuba from American imperialism" sounds familiar as well. Leopoldo had quoted him as saying that Kennedy was the one "who was holding the freedom of Cuba, actually." And Oswald had been speaking out against "American imperialism" ever since his interviews with Johnson and Mosby in Moscow.

These threats echo similar statements he had made about Eisenhower and General Walker. To Oswald, these dissimilar men were identical in one respect—they were leaders who abused their power to exploit and oppress, or threatened to do so: Eisenhower was "exploiting the working class," Walker was potentially another Hitler— and he thought he would be "doing a justice to the people" if he got rid of him. And now, President Kennedy, who Oswald had once believed might accept the status quo after the Bay of Pigs, had been unmasked in Oswald's mind as a danger to Cuba, someone who ought to be killed.

Finally, there is another reason to believe that Clark was telling the truth. It appears that Consul Azcue did indeed consider Oswald a "wild man"—otherwise, why would he have told Oswald that a person like him was hurting the Cuban revolution rather than helping it?

Thus, Comer Clark's story contained a rich subtext that neither

Clark nor Castro could have known about. It doesn't seem likely that Clark could have fabricated this story with its myriad of reflections of Oswald's character and background. But after his free-lance account of Castro's revelation was published in the *National Enquirer,* it sank without a trace until it was brought to light by Daniel Schorr in 1977.

By 1978 the situation had changed. The Garrison investigation had long since collapsed into a fiasco, and the recent revelations about CIA plots to murder Castro had given impetus to a new theory—that Kennedy's death had been a Cuban retaliation for the murder plots. Early that year the House Assassinations Committee sent a delegation to Havana to meet with Castro. The congressmen and staff members wanted to ask him about two incidents in particular: the warning he had given to Daniel Harker about assassination plots in September 1963, and Comer Clark's report.

When the delegation finally got to see him, Castro appeared to be cooperative. Concerning the 1963 impromptu interview with Harker, Castro insisted he had been misunderstood: "I did not mean to threaten by that. . . . but rather, like a warning that we knew; that we had news about it; and that to set those precedents of plotting the assassination of leaders of other countries would be a very bad precedent. . . . I didn't say it as a threat. I did not mean by that that we were going to take measures—similar measures—like a retaliation for that. . . . For 3 years, we had known there were plots against us. So the conversation came about very casually, you know; but I would say that all these plots or attempts were part of the everyday life." He added, "We were constantly arresting people trained by the CIA . . . with explosives, with telescopic target rifles."

Castro again made the reasonable argument that it would have been madness for the Cubans to have plotted Kennedy's death, saying, "That would have been the most perfect pretext for the United States to invade our country which is what I have tried to prevent for all these years, in every possible sense"—an argument that was also implied in a comment Clark quoted him as having made: "It could have been an excuse for another invasion try." In addition, Mankiewicz and Jones had quoted him as saying "That would have been material for a provocation." The Committee had no trouble accepting this. A Cuban plot would have indeed been a reckless adventure, and its discovery would probably have destroyed Cuba. Had Castro been planning a retaliation in September 1963, he would hardly have talked about it ahead of time to an American reporter.

But Castro's response to their second question took the delegation by surprise. When he was asked about Oswald's reported threat against President Kennedy at the embassy, Castro said, "This is absurd. I didn't say that. It has been invented from beginning until the end." Castro denied that the interview ever took place. He suggested that the journalist's reputation should be investigated. (Clark had by this time died.) Castro argued that Clark's story was implausible because, had the threat occurred, "it would have been our moral duty to inform the United States."

The Committee disagreed that Cuba would have been obligated to report such a threat. Furthermore, it had access to "a highly confidential, but reliable source" that disputed Castro's testimony. The source reported that Oswald had "vowed in the presence of Cuban Consulate officials to assassinate the President." Nevertheless the Committee ultimately accepted Castro's denial. It decided "on balance" that Oswald didn't voice a threat to Cuban officials. Its reasoning was somewhat peculiar. The Committee argued in its report that Castro probably would not have lied to American congressmen, because being caught in a lie would have raised sinister implications of direct Cuban involvement.

Castro may have figured the odds differently. For if he had admitted that the Clark interview was authentic he would have been lending support to Schorr's theory that his own warning about assassination plots may have inspired Oswald. Thus, while it would have been in Cuba's interest to reveal Oswald's threat at the time Jim Garrison was arguing that the CIA had sent Oswald to Mexico City, it was now in Cuba's interest to deny it.

Maurice Halperin has written of Fidel Castro, "Like all successful political leaders. . . . he has been a disciple of Machiavelli, capable of inconsistency, opportunism, and deceit but not for their own sake and always weighing anticipated profits against costs in any political operation." Halperin also noted that Fidel often said, "We are not afraid of danger. As a matter of fact, we thrive on it. And besides, everyone has to die sooner or later."

Had the Cuban premier been an ordinary witness, the Committee might have checked his story more carefully. To back up his argument that the Clark interview never took place, Castro contended that it wasn't easy to get an interview with him, that even a well-known reporter like Bill Moyers had had difficulty arranging a meeting. While this may well have been true of formal interviews, lengthy impromptu conversations were something else again, as the Daniel Harker and Laura Bergquist interviews demonstrate. (As a matter of fact, it is odd that Castro should have made this argument during the same meeting at which he explained that the warning Harker reported was part of a conversation that "came about very casually.")

Second, to refute Comer Clark's claim that he had spoken with him at a Havana pizzeria, Castro told the Committee delegation that he never went to public restaurants. Whether or not this was true when he said it in 1978, it was certainly not true in earlier years. In 1974 Castro took the visiting writers Mankiewicz and Jones to an Arab restaurant "in the middle of nowhere" and table-hopped to greet all the patrons. And in *Castro's Cuba, Cuba's Fidel,* published in 1967, Lee Lockwood described how Castro drove around a Havana suburb after midnight until he found an "all-night pizzeria" where Castro, Lockwood, and the Swiss ambassador talked for an hour and a half.

Mankiewicz and Jones later wrote, "Fidel is a former trial lawyer and he shows it. All his arguments follow a carefully structured presentation. By the time he has built his case, if you do not watch out, he has you convinced of things you do not believe."

13... October 1963—Reading between the Lines

ONE can only guess at Oswald's thoughts on the long bus ride back to Dallas. It seems clear that he was genuinely disappointed and angry about the red tape he had run into at the Mexican embassies.

Oswald's life was a constant circling over the same ground. His quarrel with Azcue might have reminded him of the trouble he'd had getting the Russians to accept him—or of the angry scene at the American Embassy when he tried to give up his citizenship. Bureaucrats were always blocking his path, and whenever he was thwarted he usually reacted with outrage or with some kind of dramatic manipulation. But apparently nothing he tried in Mexico worked.

When his first defection hadn't given him what he wanted he came back, much the same as he was, and tried again. One might expect a similar reaction to this latest setback. Oswald seldom gave up on an idea. Faced with an obstacle he maneuvered around it, but he had never reversed his direction.

But first, there were other matters to attend to. The Warren Commission calculated that Oswald had about $129 left when he returned from Mexico. As soon as he arrived in Dallas on October 3, he filed a claim for his last unemployment check. He spent the night at the Y, and the next day began looking for work. He applied for a job with the Padgett Printing Corporation, and only afterward did he call Marina and hitchhike out to the Paine house in Irving. When they were alone he told Marina about his recent disappointment at the Cuban Embassy: "Ah, they're such terrible bureaucrats that nothing came of it after all." He gave her the impression he'd changed his mind about going to Cuba and sending her to Russia.

It was agreed that Marina would stay on at Ruth's until after the baby was born while Oswald took a room in Oak Cliff. The Padgett company job fell through when one of the owners of Jaggars-Chiles-Stovall recommended against him, saying he was a troublemaker with "Communist tendencies," and several other applications brought no offers. At the end of his first week at the rooming house, Oswald's landlady decided she didn't want to rent to him any longer. ("I didn't like his attitude. He was just kind of like this, you know, just big shot. . . . Just didn't want him around me.") When Oswald moved into another rooming house, he signed the register as O.H. Lee.

In a letter to her mother on October 14, Ruth mentioned that Lee was looking for work in Dallas.

> . . . He spent last weekend & the one before with us here and was a happy addition to our expanded family. He played with Chris [Ruth's son], watched football on TV, planed down the doors that wouldn't close, and generally added a needed masculine flavor. From a poor first impression I have come to like him. . . .
>
> If Lee can just find work that will help so much. Meantime, I started giving him driving lessons last Sunday (yesterday). If he can drive this will open up more job possibilities & more locations.
>
> I feel committed to seeing Marina & Lee through this difficult period in their lives. This may mean (tho' I think it somewhat unlikely) having her & the babies here until spring if Lee has to go East or somewhere looking for work.
>
> What I would like most is Marina to stay through Christmas (which she has never celebrated—at least American style) then have you in Feb.

Later that day she and Marina had coffee at a neighbor's house, and one of the women there, hearing that Lee needed a job, suggested he might try the place where her brother, Wesley Frazier, worked—the

Texas School Book Depository. When Oswald telephoned that evening, Ruth told him about this possibility, and he applied the next day. The superintendent, Roy S. Truly, later said, "He looked like a nice young fellow to me—he was quiet and well mannered. He used the word 'sir,' you know, which a lot of them don't do at this time." Truly told him he could start work the following day as temporary help, filling book orders at $1.25 an hour.

In the days ahead Oswald would often read a local newspaper during his break in the Depository lunchroom. One of his co-workers once noticed him reading something about politics. On the weekends he got a ride to Ruth's house with Wesley Frazier, and he would read newspapers there, as well. There was a good deal going on that might have interested him. On October 8 President Kennedy signed the Nuclear Test-Ban Treaty with the Soviet Union. Cuba immediately denounced the treaty, contending that while the U.S. was making an agreement with the Soviet Union, it was increasing its acts of sabotage against Cuba. Kennedy was meanwhile trying to prod the Russians into getting their troops out of Cuba. There were also several newspaper reports on pro-Castro terrorist attacks going on in Venezuela. In South Vietnam the political situation was deteriorating. For some time the American government had been attempting to get Premier Ngo Dinh Diem to make peace with his Buddhist opponents and get on with the real war against the Communists.

During the weekends Oswald spent at Ruth's he sometimes talked with Michael Paine, who, although separated from his wife, spent part of his weekends there. Michael didn't notice any change in Oswald's political views since he last saw him in April. Oswald's major theme remained the exploitation of man by man, which he called an unforgivable moral sin. Not only did Oswald feel that American workers were exploited, Paine said, but "he also thought they were brainwashed . . . that churches were all alike, all the religious sects were the same and they were all apparatus of the power structure to maintain itself in power." When Paine pointed out that his church was financed by people like himself, Oswald merely shrugged. Paine said, ". . . his views still stood and it also permitted him, I think, gave him the moral ground to dismiss my arguments because I was here just a product of my environment . . . and therefore I was just spouting the line that was fed me by the power structure."

Despite Lee's pious concern for the working man, Michael observed that, with the exception of his daughter June, "people were like cardboard" to him. People were either stupid or malicious—the exploited or the exploiters. As for the president, he got the impression that Oswald "didn't like anybody," but that he disliked Kennedy less than the politicians to the right of Kennedy. (After one of their conversations, Oswald told Marina that Michael didn't understand anything about politics. Michael had religion, he said, but he had no philosophy.)

Like de Mohrenschildt, Paine saw Oswald as a revolutionary—someone who assumed that "the church and the power structure and our education was all the same vile system and therefore there would have to be an overthrow of the whole thing." Michael thought Oswald had "unreasonable and unrealistic and pervasive" feelings of hostility toward American society in general. He testified, "I thought that he was of the mind that something small or evolutionary changes were never going to have any effect. It had to be, though he never revealed to me what kind of actions or policies he would have advocated or did advocate . . . it had to be of a rather drastic nature, where kindness or good feelings should not stand in the way of those actions." When Paine felt moved to say that his own values were diminished in a situation of violence, Oswald, in obvious disagreement, remained silent.

Michael also noticed that Oswald sometimes got "hot under the collar" but exerted self-control as though he had had considerable practice in holding his position firmly and not getting ruffled. It reminded him of the movie about Lawrence of Arabia, when Lawrence held a match while it burned down to his fingers and said that "you just learn how to stand the pain."

Despite the theoretical talk about violence and revolution, neither Michael nor Ruth had any idea that Oswald was capable of acting on these beliefs. They had no idea he had once tried to assassinate Walker —or that the weapon he used now lay disassembled and wrapped in a blanket among other belongings of the Oswalds in their garage.

Michael had moved the bundle out of his way a couple of times and imagined that it contained camping equipment.

When Oswald left New Orleans he had given Ruth's address to the post office as his forwarding address, where he continued to receive his copies of *The Worker* and *The Militant* as well as the Russian magazines he subscribed to, and *Time.* The Commission asked Michael Paine if he had ever discussed these publications with Oswald.

> A. Yes, we talked with regard to the . . . *Worker.* He said that . . . you could tell what they wanted you to do by reading between the lines, reading the thing and doing a little reading between the lines. He then gave me an issue to look and see.

Michael took the paper and glanced over it, thinking to himself, "Here is a person who is pretty, well, out of it again if this is the way he gets his communications from headquarters." It suggested to him that Oswald "wanted to be a party to something or a part of a group that had objectives." This conversation happened "fairly soon after his coming back, so let's say the middle of October." He didn't remember which issue of *The Worker* it was.

The Commission questioned him further about the incident.

> Q. Did you draw any inference at the time as a result of this conversation with Oswald?
> A. Well, it made me realize that he would like to be active in some kind of—activist. It made me also feel that he wasn't very well connected with a group or he wouldn't have such a tenuous way of communication, and I thought it was rather childish . . . to think that this was his bona fide way of being a member of this Communist cause or something

This was the situation Oswald was in—the situation he had been in since he tried to join the Communist cause in New Orleans when he was sixteen. He had recently failed to reach "headquarters" in Cuba. Operating on his own, he had to obtain his ideas by reading between the lines of *The Worker* and other newspapers. Not that he saw these ideas as literal messages to him—Paine did not think he was irrational. Oswald simply thought he was smart enough to deduce what was going on in the world and decide what to do about it. But Oswald's statement about *The Worker* suggests that he believed the newspaper's call to political action had given him a sanction of some kind to act against Walker.

The call to revolutionary violence was not entirely in Oswald's imagination. An October 1963 issue of *The Militant* contained a major speech by Castro entitled "What is Our Line? The Line of Consistent Anti-Imperialism." Speaking just after the failure of a leftist coup attempt in Santo Domingo, Castro pointed to "a great lesson for the Dominican people and for all the peoples, that there is only one way, there is only one remedy: to liquidate the militarists, to fight the militarists, to defeat the militarists and shoot their leaders. . . . We must know how imperialism is trying to tighten the knot, when the imperialists are launching a counter-revolutionary offensive. They do not impress us. We are already veterans in this struggle. . . . But we must know what our duties are in the struggle against the counter-revolutionary offensive of imperialism and in the struggle for the economy. With the rifle and the work-tool, the work-tool and the rifle, with these, with both, we must bring our victory."

Friday, October 18, was Oswald's twenty-fourth birthday, and when he arrived in Irving, Marina and Ruth surprised him with a cake and wine. He seemed touched and self-conscious. Lee and Marina were getting along well. Michael noticed that she sometimes sat in his lap and whispered "sweet nothings" in his ear. On the day following his birthday they went into the living room after supper to watch television together. Marina lay with her head in his lap, half-asleep, while he watched two old movies. Occasionally she felt him sit up straight and strain toward the television set, greatly excited.

What was he watching that caused this unusual reaction? By an eerie coincidence, the double feature he had chosen echoed the theme of Castro's public warning: murder plots against Cuban leaders could lead to a retaliation.

The first movie was *Suddenly,* in which Frank Sinatra played an ex-GI who planned to shoot an American president. Sinatra's character took over a house overlooking a railroad station. Holding a rifle, he waited at a window for the president's train to arrive. But at the end, the train passed by without stopping and Sinatra was killed. The second movie, *We Were Strangers,* was based on the overthrow of Cuba's Machado regime in 1933. John Garfield played an American who had gone to Cuba to help a group of rebels assassinate the Cuban dictator by digging a tunnel and planting explosives.

Oswald's strong reaction to these films made an impression on his wife. A Secret Service report two weeks after the assassination quotes her as saying that her husband had seen a movie on TV "depicting a plot to kill a Cuban dictator with a bomb where the plotters had to dig a tunnel and that Lee did not like the picture as he said that was the way they did it in the old days." She later testified, "One film about the assassination of the president in Cuba, which I had seen together with him, he said that this was a fictitious situation, but that the content of the film was similar to the actual situation which existed in Cuba, meaning the revolution in Cuba."

Q. Do you recall anything else he said about either of these films?
A. Nothing else. He didn't tell me anything else. He talked to Ruth a few words. Perhaps she knows more. . . . They spoke in English. [So far as the record shows, Ruth was never asked about this.]

After Marina's testimony was revealed, the movie dealing with an American president's assassination, *Suddenly,* received considerable attention in the press. But the other movie—the one Oswald commented on—did not. Since the Commission staff was unaware of the plots to murder Castro, Oswald's statements attracted no further attention. Apparently even Marina didn't fully understand what he meant. For Oswald, however, "the revolution in Cuba" was the Castro revolution, not only his takeover of power but the continuing social revolution. The most reasonable explanation for Oswald's remarks is that he saw the parallels between this movie and the American-backed plots against Castro. The movie was a fictionalized account of the actual situation which existed in Cuba—except that the methods shown were out of date. That observation, in turn, suggests that Oswald somehow knew of the methods being used in *ongoing* plots.

I believe that, together with the two recent threats he made against President Kennedy's life, this excited reaction and his comments indicate that Oswald was, in fact, aware of Castro's warning about American-backed plots to assassinate him. He was excited because the double feature had practically read his mind.[1] Coincidences like this one can make almost anyone believe that fate has intervened. If I'm right, these two movies must have seemed like a tug at his sleeve.

On the next night, a Sunday, Marina's labor pains began. Ruth drove her to the hospital while Oswald stayed behind to babysit June and the Paine children. When Ruth returned, the children were in bed and Oswald was in his room. Although his light was still on, he didn't come out to ask her about Marina. Shortly after eleven Ruth called the hospital and was told that Marina had delivered a girl. By then, Oswald's light was out. Much annoyed, Ruth decided he might as well wait until the following morning to hear that he was a father again. Evidently, Oswald was extremely preoccupied.

Even at this point, there are signs that Oswald hadn't yet made his decision. The president's tentative plans to visit Dallas had been announced, but the visit would not be made definite until November 8, and even then there was no word of a motorcade.

During the next two weeks Oswald resumed his old routine of building his political credentials, and he once again turned his attention to Edwin A. Walker. On Wednesday, October 23, he attended a large right-wing rally at which Walker spoke. The next evening some of Walker's followers created a national furor by jostling and spitting on the U.S. ambassador to the United Nations, Adlai Stevenson. Over dinner at the Paines' that Friday, Oswald mentioned going to the Walker rally. Michael, who was also interested in finding out more about the Far Right, gathered that Lee was going around to right-wing groups to familiarize himself with them. That evening Michael was going to an American Civil Liberties Union meeting and invited Oswald to come along.

During the meeting one of the speakers made the remark that all members of the John Birch Society shouldn't be considered anti-Semitic. "Lee at this point got up," Paine recalled, "speaking loud and clear and coherently, saying that . . . he had been to this meeting of the right-wing group the night before or two nights before and he refuted this statement, saying names and saying how . . . people on the platform speaking for the Birch Society had said anti-Semitic things and also anti-Catholic statements." One of the names Oswald mentioned was Walker's.

A friend and co-worker of Paine's, Frank Krystinik, was at the ACLU meeting and heard Oswald's remarks. He got the impression that Oswald was "stirring in dirty thoughts that you shouldn't like General Walker. He didn't say General Walker is a bad guy. He just made comments that General Walker is anti-Semitic and anti-Catholic and he was spreading a little seed of thought."

After the formal meeting broke up, discussion continued over coffee. Krystinik joined Oswald and Paine at the back of the room, and approached Lee by saying that Michael had told him a bit about his political background. Knowing that Frank was about to defend free enterprise, Michael excused himself, because he had heard it all before. Krystinik asked Oswald what Russia had to offer that was better than he could find in the United States, and recalled, "He kind of shrugged his shoulders and didn't make any particular comment then." Frank mentioned that he had met Marina and June at the Paines' and told him he should be "real proud of them"—to which Oswald replied that they were nice, and let it go at that. Soon they were debating about capitalism. Krystinik told him he was an employer and paid two men $3 an hour and made $4, but he bought the machinery and material. Oswald said he was exploiting labor but, "That is all right for you. In your society it is not a crime."

Frank sensed that Oswald was talking down to him and acting "as if he had complete command of the argument." He felt that there were moments in the discussion when he had him practically beaten but Oswald wouldn't accept his opinion. Lee "turned his back and would go down a different avenue." Frank agreed with Michael, who had told him that Oswald was interesting to talk to but that once he had said his piece, he got very repetitive—he "had a certain fixed image in his mind, and was reluctant to have it improved or changed."

The only time President Kennedy's name was mentioned Oswald had said he thought Kennedy was doing "a real fine job" in civil rights —Krystinik noticed that he placed a special emphasis on the way he said it. (There was continuing racial violence in the South. The month before, several black children were killed in the bombing of a Birmingham church. *The Worker*'s position was that the president and the attorney general weren't taking a strong enough stand against the racists.) Eventually an older man interrupted their discussion, and he and Oswald talked about civil rights and Cuba. Before the meeting ended Oswald went to speak to the man who had operated the movie projector that night and asked him how the projector worked. Then he picked up an application form for membership in the ACLU. As they were going out the door, Krystinik joked to Paine, "We are going to have to set this boy up in business and convert him," and Oswald answered lightly, "The money might corrupt me."

On the drive home Paine explained that the function of the ACLU was to protect civil liberties. Oswald told him that he couldn't join such an organization because it didn't have political objectives. He asked Michael if he knew the older man he had been talking to. Paine recalled, "I think he said the man seemed to be friendly to Cuba, or rather he said, 'Do you think that man is a Communist?' And I said 'No.' And then he said something, 'I think he is.' Then I asked him why and I think he said something in regard to Cuba or sympathy with Cuba, and then I thought to myself, well, that is rather feeble evidence for proving a Communist.

"But he seemed to have the attitude of, felt he wanted to meet that man again and was pleased to have met him." And once again Paine thought, "If this is the way he has to meet his Communists, he has not yet found the Communist group in Dallas."

Oswald now considered how he might use the American Civil Liberties Union. On November 1 he mailed in the ACLU application form he had taken with him and rented a post office box, giving the ACLU and the Fair Play for Cuba Committee as organizations that might receive mail at that box. On the same day he sent another letter to Arnold Johnson, the Communist party official in New York. Even allowing for Oswald's deviousness, it doesn't sound like someone actively planning an assassination:

> . . . I have settled in Dallas, Texas for the time.
>
> Through a friend, I have been introduced into the American Civil Liberties Union local chapter, which holds monthly meetings on the campus of Southern Methodist University.
>
> The first meeting I attended was on October 25th, a film was shown and afterwards a very critical discussion of the ultra-right in Dallas.
>
> On October 23rd, I had attended a ultra-right meeting headed by General Edwin A. Walker, who lives in Dallas.
>
> This meeting preceded by one day the attack on A. E. Stevenson at the United Nations Day meeting at which he spoke.
>
> As you can see, political friction between "left" and "right" is very great here.
>
> Could you advise me as to the general view we have on the American Civil Liberties Union?
>
> And to what degree, if any, I should attempt to heighten its progressive tendencies?
>
> This Dallas branch of the A.C.L.U. is firmly in the hands of "liberal" professional people, (a minister and two Law professors conducted the Oct. 25th meeting.) However, some of those present showed marked class-awareness and insight.

Oswald seemed about to launch another campaign of "aboveground" political work involving the Fair Play Committee and the ACLU. But when he arrived at the Paine house that afternoon, he learned that the FBI had been there looking for him.

During October, William Attwood continued his effort to open a line of communication with Cuba. So far, he had gotten little response from Cuban officials. In mid-October Attwood and the president's friend Ben Bradlee, then with *Newsweek,* urged Kennedy to meet with Jean Daniel, a French journalist who was on his way to Havana to speak with Castro—perhaps the president could convey a personal message to Fidel. Kennedy saw Daniel on October 24, and gave him his views on Cuba. He told Daniel that he understood the Cubans' desire for a genuine revolution after the Batista regime, which the Americans had wrongly supported, but that the United States couldn't tolerate Communist subversion in Latin America. The problem, he said, was that Castro had betrayed the revolution by becoming "a Soviet agent in Latin America." Kennedy asked Daniel to come back to see him after he talked with Castro, and Daniel understood that he was to be an "unofficial envoy."

Meanwhile, CIA officials again met with AM/LASH. The Cuban was told that his proposal for a coup was under consideration. AM/-LASH requested a meeting with Robert Kennedy to obtain assurances of high-level American support. Instead, Desmond Fitzgerald, the senior official of the CIA section handling Cuba, decided to meet with AM/LASH personally on October 29. Fitzgerald used an alias and was introduced as a "personal representative" of the attorney general. Fitzgerald indicated that the United States would support a coup but drew the line at providing a high-powered rifle with a telescopic sight, the assassination weapon AM/LASH had requested.

But in early November AM/LASH's case officer was directed to inform the Cuban he would be given the rifles and explosives he had asked for.

14...November—The Decision

FBI agent James Hosty wanted very much to speak to Lee Harvey Oswald. The FBI had lost track of him when he left New Orleans. On October 3 the New Orleans office advised Hosty that Marina had recently left town in a station wagon with a Texas license plate "driven by a woman who could speak the Russian language," and that Lee Oswald had remained behind and then disappeared the next day. (This information apparently came from a neighbor.) Hosty was asked to try to locate Lee and Marina Oswald. He had then checked their old neighborhood in Dallas and contacted Robert Oswald, but came up empty.

On October 25 his interest in Oswald intensified considerably when New Orleans advised him that it had been informed by the CIA that Oswald had been in touch with the Soviet Embassy in Mexico City in early October. Hosty's worry now was that the Russians might have recruited Oswald for espionage. Four days later, New Orleans sent him the forwarding address Oswald had left with the post office —2515 West Fifth Street in Irving, Ruth Paine's home. Hosty immediately checked out the Paines and found that they were reputable. Ruth was said to be a Quaker and a "kindly" lady.

On November 1 Hosty went to her house to find Oswald. Ruth was cordial and invited him in, but she didn't know Oswald's rooming house address. She knew the phone number, but didn't think to offer that, and Hosty didn't request it. When Hosty asked if she knew where Oswald worked, Ruth hesitated. She explained that Lee had told her the FBI had gotten him fired from jobs in the past. Hosty assured her that this wasn't so, that the agency never interviewed people at their jobs, and that he wanted to know where Oswald worked to see if he was employed in a sensitive industry. Ruth told him, and when Hosty realized that Oswald was a laborer in a warehouse, he was relieved—Oswald wasn't in a position to commit espionage at work.

While they were talking, Marina walked into the room. When Ruth introduced Hosty as an FBI agent, Marina looked alarmed. Hosty thought she reacted like other people he had interviewed from Soviet bloc countries who seemed to be afraid of any kind of police. But this was only part of the reason. Marina knew her husband's attitude toward the FBI, and something of that attitude had rubbed off on her. Using Ruth as an interpreter, Hosty tried to reassure her. He told her that his duty was to protect people and that if anyone should ever try to put pressure on her by threatening her relatives in Russia she could come to the FBI for help.

Hosty mentioned Oswald's pro-Cuba activities in New Orleans, but gave nothing away regarding his knowledge of the trip to Mexico. Marina recovered her composure enough to tell him that Lee was no longer passing out his pro-Castro leaflets. As Ruth remembered it, Marina also told Hosty that she thought Castro wasn't getting fair treatment in the American press. Before he left, Hosty gave Ruth his office address and telephone number, which she would give to Oswald that day.

When Oswald arrived a few hours later, Marina told him an FBI agent had been there looking for him. Irritated and upset, he questioned her in private, going over exactly what had been said. He was especially concerned and suspicious about Hosty's remark that Marina could go to the FBI for help if she needed it. McMillan reports that he told Marina, "You fool. Don't you see? He doesn't care about your rights. He comes because it's his job. You have no idea how to talk to the FBI. As usual, you were probably too polite. You can't afford to let them see your weaknesses." Oswald warned her that if she ever agreed to let the FBI "protect her rights," she would get into trouble with the Soviet Embassy. Even as he spoke Marina could tell that he was inwardly calculating at great speed and trying to conceal his anxiety. Oswald instructed his wife that if Hosty returned, she should take down his license plate number. That way, if Oswald saw his car parked near Ruth's house, he would be forewarned. He now had to think of some way to handle the FBI.

One should keep in mind Oswald's attitude toward authority, as he had demonstrated in the past. Oswald evidently felt he should be able to do whatever he wanted without interference. When he was interfered with, he considered it a personal affront and often took his complaint to a higher authority. He believed that what he was doing was right, even when his actions were "illegal." Thus, for example, he could threaten to give away military secrets in one breath and charge that his legal right to expatriate himself was being denied him in the next—and tell the American ambassador he was going to ask his new government to lodge a formal protest. After deciding to leave Russia, he expected the Americans to do everything they could to help him. In his logic, there was no inconsistency in any of this. Since he was always right, anyone who opposed him was wrong.

On that weekend there was a crisis in South Vietnam. On November 2 an army coup ousted President Diem, and Diem and his brother were assassinated. At home, a front page *Morning News* headline on November 4 announced, "President in Dallas." The story said that the president was tentatively scheduled to attend a noon luncheon in Dallas on November 21 or 22.

On November 5, Hosty passed through Irving with another agent en route to Fort Worth and stopped by to speak briefly with Ruth. She still hadn't found out Oswald's address in Oak Cliff, but she told him that when the Oswalds moved into an apartment again, as she expected, she would be perfectly willing to give him that address. During their conversation Ruth commented that she thought Oswald was a Trotskyite. When Hosty asked her if she thought this was a mental problem, Ruth said that she didn't understand the mental processes of a Marxist, but that "this was far different from saying he was mentally unstable or unable to conduct himself in normal society." Ruth later testified, "I was not at all worried about ideology contrary to my own or with which I disagreed, and it looked to me that he was a person of this ideology or philosophy which he calls Marxism, indeed nearly a religion," but that she didn't think him dangerous because of these beliefs.

While Ruth was speaking with Hosty, Marina slipped out the back door and memorized the license number of his car. She had also overheard and understood a part of their conversation. Ruth testified that during that day or the next, while they were doing dishes, Marina told her "she felt their address was their business. . . . and she made it plain that this was a matter of privacy for them. This surprised me. She had never spoken to me this way before, and I didn't see that it made any difference."

When Oswald returned to Irving on Friday the 8th, he was greeted with the unwelcome news of Hosty's return visit. When Ruth told him Hosty had asked if this was a mental problem Lee "gave no reply but more a scoffing laugh, hardly voiced." He said, "They are trying to inhibit my activities." Ruth replied, "You have your rights to your views, whether they are popular or not." She was thinking in terms of his handing out pamphlets or expressing a belief in Fidel Castro. But privately she also thought that with his background as a defector he ought to expect the FBI to be interested in him. She suggested that he go see Hosty and tell him whatever he wanted to know. Of course, this was exactly what he could not do. But he said that he had stopped at the downtown office of the FBI and left a note.

The front-page story that day was again the president's trip to Dallas. Two luncheon sites, one of them the Trade Mart, were under consideration, but no parades were yet being planned.

Years later, Hosty's receptionist, Nanny Lee Fenner, recalled that Oswald had come into the FBI office on Commerce Street two or three weeks before the assassination. He looked "fidgety" and asked to speak with Hosty. Informed that he wasn't in, Oswald handed her a business-size envelope with the word "Hosty" written on it and walked out. Hosty later admitted that he had destroyed the note inside after Oswald's death, on orders from his Dallas superior, J. Gordon Shanklin. (Shanklin was evidently concerned that the note would suggest that the FBI hadn't kept a careful enough eye on the president's assassin.) In 1975 Hosty told the Church committee that the unsigned note read, roughly:

> If you have anything you want to learn about me, come talk to me directly. If you don't cease bothering my wife, I will take appropriate action and report this to proper authorities.[1]

Hosty put the note in his workbox, where it remained until the day of the assassination.

On Saturday the 9th Oswald borrowed Ruth's typewriter to compose a letter to the Soviet Embassy in Washington. It was a characteristic mixture of guile and ingratiation.

> This is to inform you of recent events since my meetings with comrade Kostin in the Embassy of the Soviet Union, Mexico City, Mexico.
>
> I was unable to remain in Mexico indefinitely because of my Mexican visa restrictions which was for 15 days only. I could not take a chance on requesting a new visa unless I used my real name, so I returned to the United States.
>
> I had not planned to contact the Soviet Embassy in Mexico, so they were unprepared, had I been able to reach the Soviet Embassy in Havana as planned, the Embassy there would have had time to complete our business.
>
> Of course the Soviet Embassy was not at fault, they were, as I say unprepared, the Cuban [consul] was guilty of a gross breach of regulations, I am glad he has since been replaced.
>
> The Federal Bureau of Investigation is not now interested in my activities in the progressive organization "Fair Play for Cuba Committee," of which I was secretary in New Orleans (state Louisiana) since I no longer reside in that state. However, the FBI has visited us here in Dallas, Texas, on November 1st. Agent James P. Hosty [sic] warned me that if I engaged in F.P.C.C. activities in Texas the F.B.I. will again take an "interest" in me.
>
> This agent also "suggested" to Marina Nichilayeva that she could remain in the United States under F.B.I. "protection," that is, she could defect from the Soviet Union, of course, I and my wife strongly protested these tactics by the notorious F.B.I.

Please advise us of the arrival of our Soviet entrance visas as soon as they come.

Also, this is to inform you of the birth, on October 20, 1963, of daughter, AUDREY MARINA OSWALD in DALLAS TEXAS to my wife.

Several points should be made. On his application at the Cuban Embassy, Silvia Duran had written, "He appeared at the Embassy of the U.S.S.R. in this city and requested that his visa be sent to the Soviet Embassy in Cuba"—thus Oswald's reference to completing their business in Havana.

Second, Oswald went out of his way to assure the Russian officials in Washington that he didn't hold the Soviet Embassy responsible for his difficulties in Mexico City. It was as though he was afraid they might have gotten the "wrong" impression. In Mexico he had contacted the Soviet Embassy several times after learning there would be a four-month delay in getting a visa. He probably showed his anger there as he had at the Cuban Embassy. Thus, he may have had some fence-mending to do: "They were unprepared," "Of course the Soviet Embassy was not at fault," and so on.

Consul Azcue had been replaced before Oswald's in-transit visa was conditionally approved on October 15—but how did Oswald know this? Azcue's replacement, Alfredo Mirabal, had been in the consul's office when Oswald had his quarrel with Azcue, and it's quite possible he picked up the information that Azcue was leaving from Duran or someone else at that time. But it's also conceivable that Oswald checked back with Duran about his visa after he returned to Dallas —she said she couldn't remember if he had ever called her or not— and learned that Azcue was no longer there. Although there's admittedly no evidence of a phone call or other communication, this slim possibility might explain why he was now renewing his request for Soviet visas. Obtaining them would clear the path to Cuba. In any case, Oswald said nothing to Marina about this new request for Soviet entrance visas. Perhaps he wanted no arguments from her until the arrangements were an accomplished fact. With the FBI pursuing him, he may have wanted an exit out of the country, if he needed it.

Finally, Oswald had given his own interpretation to what Hosty told Marina. Hosty hadn't suggested that she "defect,"[2] and he hadn't "warned" Oswald of anything—Hosty hadn't, of course, even seen Oswald on November 1. But Oswald had found a way to use even the FBI's renewed interest in him to his advantage. By making it appear that a Soviet citizen was being harassed, he could perhaps speed up those long-awaited visas.

On the day he began working on this letter, Ruth drove Lee, Marina, and the children to a shopping center where Oswald could apply for a learner's permit to drive a car. But since it was an election day, the driver's license bureau was closed. Ruth recalled that on the way home, "Lee was as gay as I have ever seen him. . . . He sang, he joked, he made puns, or he made up songs mutilating the Russian language, which tickled and pained Marina, both at once."

Oswald stayed over an extra night on that Veteran's Day weekend, and when he called Marina the following Thursday she suggested he not come out that week—he may have overstayed the last time, and besides, Ruth was giving one of her children a birthday party on Saturday. Oswald agreed. On Saturday morning he went back to the license bureau alone and filled out an application for a learner's permit.

There was still no indication that Oswald was planning the president's assassination. On the same morning, November 16, the *Morning News* announced that the president would "drive west on Main Street at noon next Friday while en route to a luncheon at the Dallas Trade Mart beside Stemmons Freeway." From this a reader familiar with the downtown streets might have deduced that the motorcade would have to pass by the Depository, but the president's route was not explicit. Another front-page headline the next day said, "Incident-Free Day Urged for JFK Visit." Dallas leaders were anxious to avoid any right-wing demonstrations that might embarrass the city as it had been embarrassed by the Adlai Stevenson incident.

That Sunday afternoon, June was playing with Ruth's phone dial and Marina said, "Let's call papa." Ruth called the rooming house number and asked for Lee Oswald. The man who answered told her there was no Lee Oswald at that address. Oswald had registered as

O.H. Lee—a circumstance he had forgotten when he gave Ruth the phone number during Marina's last stage of pregnancy. On Monday, November 18, Oswald called Marina as he usually did after work. Marina testified, "I told him that we had telephoned him but he was unknown at that number."

> Then he said that he had lived there under an assumed name. He asked me to remove the notation of the telephone number in Ruth's phone book, but I didn't want to do that. I asked him then, "Why did you give us a phone number, when we do call we cannot get you by name?"
>
> He was very angry, and he repeated that I should remove the notation of the phone number from the phone book. And, of course, we had a quarrel. I told him that this was another of his foolishness, some more of his foolishness. I told Ruth Paine about this. It was incomprehensible to my why he was so secretive all the time.
>
> Q. Did he give you any explanation of why he was using an assumed name?
>
> A. He said that he did not want his landlady to know his real name because she might [have] read in the paper of the fact that he had been to Russia and that he had been questioned.
>
> Q. What did you say about that?
>
> A. Nothing. And also that he did not want the FBI to know where he lived.

Ruth overheard Marina's side of the argument, and afterward Marina, who was obviously upset, told her it wasn't the first time she had felt caught between "two fires." But she didn't mention to Ruth that Oswald wanted her to cross out the phone number. Oswald was clearly afraid that Ruth might give the number to the FBI, which could then use it to determine where he lived.

That evening President Kennedy gave what was to be his last major address. Appearing in Miami, the president spoke on Latin America, and his remarks on Cuba were similar to the message he wanted Jean Daniel, who was now in Havana, to deliver to Castro.

> . . . The genuine Cuban Revolution, because it was against the tyranny and corruption of the past, had the support of many whose aims and

concepts were democratic. But that hope for freedom and progress was destroyed. The goals proclaimed in the Sierra Maestra were betrayed in Havana. It is important now to restate what now divides Cuba from my country and from the other countries of the hemisphere. It is the fact that a small band of conspirators has stripped the Cuban people of their freedom and handed over the independence and sovereignty of the Cuban nation to forces beyond the hemisphere. They have made Cuba a victim of foreign imperialism, an instrument of the policy of others, a weapon in an effort dictated by external powers to subvert the other American republics. This, and this alone, divides us. As long as this is true, nothing is possible. Without it, everything is possible. . . . Once Cuban sovereignty has been restored we will extend the hand of friendship and assistance. . . .

The speech was written in part by McGeorge Dundy, who knew of Daniel's current trip to Havana, and its evident intent was to let Castro know that the United States could reach an accommodation with Cuba if Cuba backed away from the Soviet Union and ceased its interference in other Latin American countries. But the message was capable of being read another way.

On November 19 both Dallas newspapers reported on the president's speech. The afternoon *Times Herald* said that President Kennedy had "all but invited the Cuban people . . . to overthrow Fidel Castro's Communist regime and promised prompt U.S. aid if they do." The headline was "Kennedy Virtually Invites Cuban Coup." Under its front-page article about the speech, the *Morning News* gave a street-by-street layout of the motorcade route, making it clear that the president would travel down Elm Street past the School Book Depository. The afternoon paper carried a comparable story on the motorcade route. Thus, on Tuesday Oswald could have known the unique vantage point his workplace had given him, and in the same issue he may have read an article suggesting that the president was calling for a coup against Fidel Castro.

Late that afternoon there was a change in Oswald's routine—he didn't call Marina after work, or on Wednesday. Marina attributed this change to the quarrel they'd had on Monday, and that seems to be a reasonable explanation. But there was something else—a small slip of the mind that suggests he was no longer thinking about eluding the FBI and had turned his attention to some other matter. On Monday Oswald had been extremely anxious for his wife to remove his number from Ruth's phone book. He was furious with Marina for refusing to do it. But after Monday he said no more about the phone number, and when he next went to Irving on Thursday, he didn't remove the number himself, as he might have done.

At the Depository on November 20 a textbook salesman brought in a new hunting rifle to show Roy Truly and some of the employees who happened to be in Truly's office, Lee Oswald among them. Oswald filed this incident away for future use—he would refer to it later that week.

On the morning of Thursday, November 21, Oswald approached Wesley Frazier at work and asked him for a ride to Irving that afternoon. Frazier readily agreed, but asked him why he was going home on a Thursday. Oswald said, "I am going to get some curtain rods. You know, put in an apartment." Later that afternoon Ruth came home from the grocery store and saw Oswald with Marina and June on her front lawn—"I was surprised to see him. . . . I had no advance notice and he had never before come without asking whether he could." As they all went inside, Ruth said to him, "Our President is coming to town." Oswald replied, "Ah, yes," and walked on into the kitchen.

Oswald told his wife he had come home to make up with her. That night he watched TV, helped Marina fold diapers, and talked about getting an apartment in Dallas right away. Before Marina got up the next morning, Oswald tucked $170—almost all the money he had— into a wallet they kept in a drawer and left his wedding ring in an antique Russian cup on top of the bureau. When she woke he told her to buy something for herself and the children, and she wondered why he was being so kind all of a sudden. In the garage he picked up the disassembled rifle he had secretly wrapped in brown paper the night before. Then he rode into work with Frazier. After the Depository workers broke for lunch and most of them went outside to see the president pass by, he would have the sixth floor to himself.

In Fort Worth early that morning President Kennedy addressed four thousand people who had assembled in a misting rain at his hotel parking lot. Like the crowds in San Antonio and Houston the day before, they gave him an enthusiastic welcome. "Where's Jackie?" someone shouted, and Kennedy joined in the laughter. "Mrs. Kennedy is organizing herself," he said. "It takes longer, but, of course, she looks better than we do when she does it. We appreciate your welcome." During a breakfast speech later on, the president answered his right-wing critics by pointing to his efforts to improve the national defense. Afterward, at his hotel suite, he looked through the Dallas *Morning News* and saw a full-page advertisement that accused him of selling out to the Communists. Entitled "Welcome Mr. Kennedy" and bordered in black, the ad asked twelve impertinent questions, among them, "WHY do you say we have built a 'wall of freedom' around Cuba when there is no freedom in Cuba today? Because of your policy, thousands of Cubans have been imprisoned, are starving and being persecuted—with thousands already murdered and thousands more awaiting execution and, in addition, the entire population of almost 7,000,000 Cubans are living in slavery?" And, "WHY have you scrapped the Monroe Doctrine in favor of the 'Spirit of Moscow'?" Referring to the ad he told his wife, "Oh, you know, we're heading into nut country today." It reminded him of something he had realized since he took office. Despite Secret Service protection, anyone who was willing to exchange his life for the president's could do so. Now, to his aide Kenneth O'Donnell he said lightly, "Anyone perched above the crowd with a rifle could do it." Always fatalistic, and having a fine sense of irony, Kennedy put himself in the assassin's place—he pantomimed the imagined action, extending a forefinger like a weapon.

At 11:40 that morning, *Air Force One* brought the presidential party to Love Field, where Kennedy greeted a crowd of well-wishers. An open limousine driven by a Secret Service agent was waiting. The president and Mrs. Kennedy sat in the back, and Governor and Mrs. Connally took the jump seats in front of them. With another limousine carrying armed Secret Service agents behind them, the motorcade formed and left for downtown Dallas.

At 12:30 P.M., Lee Harvey Oswald entered history. Three shots from a sixth-floor Depository window hit Governor Connally once and the president twice. Oswald fled the building minutes later, caught a bus, and, when it got stalled in traffic, got out and took a cab to his rooming house. He picked up his revolver and a jacket and rushed out—on his way, Albert Newman believes, to try to assassinate Walker, too.[3] At approximately 1:15 P.M., he was stopped by Patrolman J.D. Tippit, who had been cruising the area in a squad car. When Tippit got out to question him, Oswald shot and killed him. Within minutes, the manager of a shoe store a few blocks away heard police sirens and saw a disheveled young man outside his front window glancing back over his shoulder. The manager watched as he ducked into the lobby of a nearby movie theater.

15...The Arrest

REPORTER Seth Kantor had been waiting at the Trade Mart for the motorcade to arrive. Upon learning of the assassination attempt, he joined the general scramble for transportation to the hospital where the president had been taken. Kantor's first emotion was revulsion toward Dallas right-wing extremists. Running toward a station wagon, he wanted to scream, "God damn you, Dallas. Smug Dallas. God damn you."

At that hour AM/LASH was meeting with his case officer in Europe. The CIA man referred to President Kennedy's November 18 speech and told AM/LASH that he could take Kennedy's remarks on Cuba as a signal that a coup against Castro would receive American support—the CIA man was asking the Cuban official to read between the lines of the president's speech. He told AM/LASH that the weapons he had asked for would be provided, and to establish his credibility he handed him a poison-pen device. As they were coming out the door from their meeting, they were told that President Kennedy had been shot.

Fidel Castro was meeting with Kennedy's unofficial envoy, Jean Daniel. When he received word of the shooting, Castro slumped in his chair and said, "Es un mala noticia" ("This is bad news"). After Kennedy's death was confirmed, Castro said, "Everything is changed. Everything is going to change. . . . I'll tell you one thing: at least

Kennedy was an enemy to whom we had become accustomed. This is a serious matter, an extremely serious matter."

Michael Paine was at work. Someone turned on a radio, and when he heard the Book Depository mentioned, his heart jumped. Frank Krystinik asked, "Isn't that where Lee Oswald works?" Krystinik thought Paine should call the FBI, but Michael resisted. He didn't want to accuse Oswald unjustly. Even so, when he went back to his job, his hands trembled so badly he was unable to assemble a vibration meter he'd been working on. Then an eyewitness who had seen the assassin in the window came on the radio. He said that the rifleman fired "coolly," that he took "his jolly good time," and then drew his rifle back "just as unconcerned as could be." Paine thought it sounded like Oswald.

Oswald was arrested at the Texas Theater in Oak Cliff at 1:40 P.M. After a struggle, an officer took from his hand the Smith & Wesson with which he had shot Patrolman Tippit. As he was hauled through the lobby, Oswald was heard to shout, "I protest this police brutality," and "I am not resisting arrest." A large crowd of people had gathered outside the theater, and when they saw the policemen emerge with Oswald in tow some of them yelled, "Kill the s.o.b." and "Let us have him." The lawmen hustled him into a patrol car and drove away.

Oswald wasn't visibly shaken. When one of the men in the car asked him if he had killed Tippit because he was afraid of being arrested, Oswald said he wasn't afraid of anything, and asked, "Do I look like I am scared now?" As they drove into the police department basement, Oswald was asked if he wanted to conceal his face from the photographers. "Why should I cover my face?" he asked. "I haven't done anything to be ashamed of."

From the written reports and testimony of the police detectives, FBI agents, and Secret Service agents who questioned Oswald at the police station, we have the following account.

His chief interrogator was homicide captain Will Fritz. Fritz recalled that Oswald would talk to him readily "until I asked him a question that meant something, that would produce evidence," and then Oswald would immediately tell him he wouldn't answer. Fritz thought he seemed to anticipate what he was going to ask. Others who were there also got the impression that Oswald was quick with his answers and that he appeared to have planned what he was going to say. The one thing Oswald discussed willingly was his political beliefs —he said he was a Marxist and gave his views on civil rights. He said he supported the Cuban revolution.

On Friday afternoon Fritz apprised Oswald of his rights—his immediate response was to say he didn't need a lawyer. Fritz had just begun asking some general questions about his background when FBI agents Hosty and James Bookhout came in. When Hosty introduced himself Oswald reacted angrily and said, "Oh, so you are Hosty. I've heard about you." He accused Hosty of "accosting" his wife and called the FBI a gestapo. According to one report he added, "I am going to fix you FBI." During this scene Hosty became 100 percent certain that the unsigned note in his workbox came from Oswald. Unable to calm him down, Hosty took a seat in the corner with Bookhout and let Fritz continue with his interrogation.

In the past, when Oswald was questioned by agents Fain and Quigley and Lieutenant Martello, he had told many calculated lies. Some of his responses now showed the same calculation. When Fritz asked Oswald if he owned a rifle, he replied that he had seen his superviser, Mr. Truly, showing a rifle to some other people in his office on November 20, but he denied owning a rifle himself. He maintained that he had been eating his lunch when the motorcade passed by and that afterward he assumed there would be no more work that day, so he went home and decided to go to a movie. When he was asked why he took his pistol with him, he said it was because "he felt like it." He claimed that he had bought the pistol from a dealer in Fort Worth. At one point, when Hosty spoke up and asked him if he had ever been to Mexico City, Oswald again displayed anger. According to Fritz, he "beat on the desk and went into a kind of tantrum." He said he had never been in Mexico City. The interview was interrupted several times for identification lineups in which witnesses identified Oswald as the man they had seen shooting Tippit or running away from the scene.

Sometime that day FBI agent Manning C. Clements asked Oswald for some routine background information, including his previous residences. In his reply Oswald mentioned the addresses of every place he had lived since he returned from Russia—*except* the Neely Street apartment in Dallas, where Marina had taken pictures of him holding a rifle in the backyard. Instead, he claimed that he had lived on Elsbeth Street for about seven months, that is, the entire time he had been in Dallas in early 1963.

At 7:10 P.M. Oswald was arraigned for Tippit's murder. Around midnight he was taken downstairs for an interview with the press corps, which had been clamoring to see him. There Oswald said of his arraignment, "I protested at that time that I was not allowed legal representation during that very short and sweet hearing. I really don't know what the situation is about. Nobody has told me anything except that I am accused of, of murdering a policeman. I know nothing more than that and I do request someone to come forward to give me legal assistance." A reporter asked, "Did you kill the President?" He answered, "No. I have not been charged with that. In fact nobody has said that to me yet. The first thing I heard about it was when the newspaper reporters in the hall asked me that question."

Among the observers crammed into the room was Jack Ruby, the owner of a nightclub featuring stripshows. A well-known character in Dallas, a habitual gladhander and publicity-seeker, Ruby was a police buff who knew several dozen members of the local force. He also had an old arrest record for disturbing the peace, carrying a concealed weapon, and assault, and he knew several individuals in the Mafia. Perhaps because of the nature of his business, Ruby often carried large sums of money and a pistol. Despite his rough background, acquaintances had noticed that Ruby, like many other people, seemed greatly affected by the president's murder.

At approximately 10 o'clock on Saturday morning the interrogation resumed. Oswald denied that he had told Wesley Frazier he was going to Irving to pick up curtain rods. He said the package he brought to work contained his lunch. He said he had gone to Irving on Thursday because Mrs. Paine was planning to give a party for the children that weekend and he didn't want to be there then. In fact, the party had been held the weekend before, but if Ruth were questioned about it, he could say he had simply misunderstood. As so often happened, Oswald was twisting the truth to fit his own purposes—it was almost as though he saw reality itself as nothing more than raw material to be shaped and used. Oswald said that when the motorcade passed the building he had been in the second-floor lunchroom with some of his co-workers, one of them a Negro named Junior. In fact, Junior Jarman didn't see Oswald in the lunchroom that day. Jarman finished eating before noon and went up to the fifth floor to watch the motorcade with Harold Norman and Bonnie Ray Williams. They heard the shots going off over their heads. Norman was at the window directly beneath the sniper and could hear the ejected shells hitting the floor above him.

According to a Secret Service report, Oswald refused to answer any more questions concerning the pistol or rifle until he had seen a lawyer.

. . . He stated that he wanted to contact a Mr. Abt, a New York lawyer whom he did not know but who had defended the Smith Act "victims" in 1949 or 1950 in connection with a conspiracy against the Government; that Abt would understand what this case was all about and that he would give him an excellent defense. . . .

Upon questioning by Captain Fritz, he said, "I have no views on the President." "My wife and I like the President's family. They are interesting people. I have my own views on the President's national policy. I have a right to express my views but because of the charges I do not think I should comment further."

Oswald was returned to his cell before noon.

Seth Kantor had joined the horde of reporters inside the jail, and at one point he saw the prisoner being led through the hall. Reporters were shouting, "Why did you kill the President?" One asked if he blamed the wounded Governor Connally, a former secretary of the navy, for his dishonorable discharge, and Oswald shouted back over his shoulder, "I don't know what kind of newspaper reports you are getting but these are not true." Kantor's impression of Oswald was visceral: "He was defiant. He looked alert at all times. In his profile, he was sharp-featured. Full-faced, he had a cunning look." He reminded Kantor of the demonstrators who had disrupted a House Un-American Activities Committee hearing in September. The demonstrators had seemed to time their actions to get the best camera angles when the police dragged them out of the room. "This was Lee Harvey Oswald," Kantor wrote in his notes. "He was living the part of a martyr." Oswald also told the reporters, "I'm just a patsy."

On November 23 Aline Mosby picked up a newspaper and saw a photograph of the young defector she had interviewed in 1959. The picture, taken after his arrest, had a caption that said he was "glaring at photographers defiantly." Looking at his face, Mosby disagreed. She thought Lee Oswald was probably enjoying every minute of it.

That morning the police had returned to Ruth's house armed with a warrant for a more thorough search than they had conducted the day before, and they found copies of the photographs showing Oswald holding a rifle, and one negative. In the meantime Michael Paine had been questioned about Oswald's previous residences and mentioned the Neely Street apartment. After lunch Fritz asked Oswald about the Neely address and found that he was "very evasive about this location."

Afterward Oswald was allowed to speak with his wife. Marina had been apprehensive ever since she first heard from Ruth that the shooting took place near the Depository. She hadn't known the motorcade would pass by her husband's place of work. Even if she had, she wouldn't have suspected he would kill the president—Walker, yes, but not Kennedy. When the police came on Friday she showed them where Oswald kept his rifle. The blanket was still there, neatly tied, but when a policeman picked it up the ends fell limp and she turned ashen, realizing the rifle was gone. That night she had found the two pictures of her husband in June's baby book. Marguerite had by that time arrived at the Paine house, having heard that her son had been arrested. Marina showed her one of the photographs of Lee brandishing a rifle, and Marguerite groaned and shook her head to indicate that she shouldn't tell anyone.

Before she went to see Lee that afternoon Marina folded the pictures and stuffed them inside her shoe. She wanted to ask him what she should do with them. Separated by a glass partition they spoke over a pair of telephones. Thinking of the pictures, she asked him, "[C]an we talk about anything we like? Is anybody listening in?"

"Oh, of course," he said. "We can speak about *absolutely* anything at all." And she knew from his tone that he was warning her not to say anything significant.

He assured her everything would work out fine, but she didn't believe him. He told her she had friends who would help her, and if necessary she could get help from the Red Cross. Marina could tell that he was guilty. If he hadn't been, she thought, he would have been loudly protesting his arrest, and besides, she sensed that he was saying goodbye to her with his eyes. McMillan has written that Marina didn't know if he would confess or not: he might claim that his act had been justified, or he might insist that he was innocent. Either way, he would take the opportunity to proclaim his ideas.

Concerning their conversation, Marina testified, "He spoke of some friends who supposedly would help him. I don't know who he had in mind. That he had written to someone in New York before that. I was so upset that of course I didn't understand anything of that. . . . I told him that the police had been there and that a search had been conducted, that they had asked me whether we had a rifle, and I had answered yes. And he said that if there would be a trial, and that if I am questioned it would be my right to answer or to refuse to answer."

Oswald was perhaps referring to the lawyer in New York, John Abt, who had represented Gus Hall and Ben Davis. Oswald hadn't written to him, but he had written a letter to the Hall Davis defense committee in 1962. Abt, an attorney for the Communist party, had never heard of him and would undoubtedly have been horrified to be asked to take this case. The Left certainly had no intention of rallying to Oswald's cause, even if he claimed he was innocent. Since John Abt's name had appeared several times in *The Worker* during the months Oswald was planning his attack on Walker, it's probable that this was the lawyer he had intended to ask for if he had been arrested after shooting Walker. In any event, it's clear that Oswald was now planning ahead for his trial, and it's likely he had already given it considerable thought. Evidently he intended to charge the FBI with harassment and say he'd been framed because of his political beliefs. Even from his jail cell, he still expected to manipulate events. He would try to turn his trial into a political cause célèbre like the Rosenberg case, thus making propaganda and ensuring his place in leftist history.

If this was Oswald's plan, it was typical of his thinking—grandiose, perverse, manipulative, unrealistic.

Sometime that afternoon Robert Oswald visited his brother and found him "completely relaxed"—he talked "matter-of-factly, without any sign of tension or strain." As soon as they picked up the telephones in the visiting room, Oswald said, "This is taped [sic]." (When Marguerite spoke with Robert alone at the police station, her first words were, "This room is bugged. Be careful what you say.") As with the police, Oswald seemed willing to discuss anything but the assassination. Robert later wrote that he asked, "Lee, what the Sam Hill is going on?"

"I don't know," he said.

"You don't know? Look, they've got your pistol, they've got your rifle, they've got you charged with shooting the President and a police officer. And you tell me you don't know. Now, I want to know just what's going on."

He stiffened and straightened up, and his facial expression was suddenly very tight.

"I just don't know what they're talking about," he said, firmly and deliberately. "Don't believe all this so-called evidence."

Robert stared into his eyes, trying to find the truth, and Oswald said quietly, "Brother, you won't find anything there."

Although Oswald was uncommunicative, he made two statements to Robert that suggest he saw the assassination as an act similar to both his defection and the attack on General Walker. When Robert asked him what he thought was going to happen to Marina and his children, he said, "My friends will take care of them," and indicated that he meant the Paines. He was depending on other people to look after his family, just as he had done when he tried to kill Walker. Shortly before Robert left, Oswald told him not to get involved in his case, or he might get in trouble with his boss and lose his job. He had said the same thing in Moscow. He told Aline Mosby, "I don't want to involve my family in this," and "My brother might lose his job because of this."

After talking with his brother, Oswald telephoned Ruth and asked her to call John Abt for him, giving her two numbers he had gotten from information. He had already tried to reach the attorney himself. He made no reference to the reason he was in jail, and Ruth was appalled and irritated that he sounded so apart from the situation. He sounded to her "almost as if nothing out of the ordinary had happened." Later she tried to reach Abt, but he was out of town.

Meanwhile the president of the Dallas Bar Association, H. Louis Nichols, had been getting long-distance calls from other attorneys who had seen Oswald's press conference and were afraid his legal rights weren't being protected. Nichols decided to offer Oswald his assistance. When he saw Oswald in his cell that afternoon, the prisoner seemed calm and appeared to know "pretty much what his rights were." Oswald told him he wanted Abt or a member of the American Civil Liberties Union. If he couldn't get either one, Oswald said, and if he could find a lawyer in Dallas who "believes as I believe, and believes in my innocence—as much as he can, I might let him represent me." Oswald told Nichols he didn't think he would need his assistance but that he "might come back next week." Nichols left, having satisfied himself "that the man appeared to know what he was doing. He did not appear to be irrational."

By this time the police lab had enlarged one of the backyard photographs and Fritz had Oswald brought in at six o'clock to confront him with this evidence. Oswald claimed that the photographs were fakes and that he had never seen them before. He said he knew all about photography and that the small picture was a reduced copy of the large one. Fritz reported, "He further stated that since he had been photographed here at the City Hall and that people had been taking his picture while being transferred from my office to the jail door that someone had been able to get a picture of his face and with that, they had made this picture. He told me that he understood photography real well, and that in time, he would be able to show that it was not his picture, and that it had been made by someone else. At this time he said that he did not want to answer any more questions and he was returned to the jail about 7:15 P.M."

This was probably the line Oswald intended to pursue had the backyard photographs been found after he shot Walker. For years to come there would be a controversy about the authenticity of these pictures. The House Assassinations Committee had a panel of photographic specialists examine the recovered photos and negative. Using sophisticated analytical techniques, the panel could find no evidence of fakery. In addition, the panel used similar techniques to uncover a unique mark of wear and tear on the rifle in the photos that corresponded to a mark on the weapon found in the Depository, and concluded that the two weapons were identical.

On Sunday morning the accused assassin was questioned for the last time by Fritz, two Secret Service men, and a Dallas postal inspector, Harry Holmes. During this interview Oswald denied knowing anyone named A.J. Hidell, the name on an I.D. card in his wallet and on his post office box application, and denied using the name as an alias. He began talking politics again, and said that Cuba should have full diplomatic relations with the United States. Asked if he was a Communist, Oswald said, "No, I am a Marxist but I am not a Marxist Leninist." When Fritz asked him the difference, Oswald said it would take too long to explain it to him. When a Secret Service inspector asked him if he thought the assassination would have any effect on the Cuban situation, Oswald at first responded with a question. "I am filed on for the President's murder, is that right? Under the circumstances, I don't believe that it would be proper [to respond]." Nevertheless, he went on to say that he thought there would probably be no change in America's attitude toward Cuba with Vice-President Johnson becoming president "because they both belonged to the same political party and the one would follow pretty generally the policies of the other."

Detective J.R. Leavelle was also present that morning. Oswald gave him the impression "of being a man with a lot better education than his formal education indicated. . . . for instance the long elaboration that he went into on the Cuba deal would tell—indicate that he had a fairly better than high school education that he was reported to have had." Leavelle told the Commission the prisoner seemed very much in control of himself at all times and added, "In fact, he struck me as a man who enjoyed the situation immensely and was enjoying the publicity and everything [that] was coming his way."

Inspector Holmes later reported:

Oswald at no time appeared confused or in doubt as to whether or not to answer a question. On the contrary, he was quite alert and showed no hesitancy in answering those questions he wanted to answer, and was quite skillful in parrying those questions which he did not want to answer. I got the impression he had disciplined his mind and reflexes to a state where I personally doubted if he would ever have confessed. He denied, emphatically, having taken part in or having had any knowledge of the shooting of the policeman Tippit or of the President, stating that so far as he is concerned the reason he was in custody was because he "popped a policeman in the nose in a theater on Jefferson Avenue."

Priscilla Johnson also believed he would never have confessed. Soon after the assassination she wrote that if there was one thing that stood out in the conversation she had had with him in Moscow, "it was his truly compelling need . . . to think of himself as extraordinary. A refusal to confess, expressed in stoic and triumphant silence, would have fitted this need. In some twisted way, it might also have enabled him to identify with other 'unjustly' persecuted victims, such as Sacco and Vanzetti and the Rosenbergs."

Oswald was scheduled to be transferred to the county jail at ten o'clock. The questioning ran longer than expected, past eleven, but yielded nothing further. Oswald chose a black sweater from among those offered to him from his clothes and put it on over his T-shirt. He was now dressed entirely in black, as he had been in the rifleman photographs Marina had taken. To the end, he was playing out the role he had created for himself and had been rehearsing, in one way or another, for most of his life. Then he was handcuffed to Leavelle's left wrist and walked to the elevator. Outside the building a large crowd waited, and the basement was packed with police and reporters. At 11:17 Jack Ruby was at the Western Union office across the street sending a money order to one of his strippers. He walked out and went to the police station. Less than four minutes later, as television cameras followed Oswald being brought out toward a waiting car, Ruby rushed forward and shot him once in the abdomen. Ruby was immediately wrestled to the floor by several policemen, to whom he said, "You all know me. I'm Jack Ruby." When the crowd outside heard what had happened, it let out a cheer.

Police detective Billy Combest had the presence of mind to try to get a statement from Oswald before he died. The author of *Conspiracy,* Anthony Summers, interviewed Combest in 1978. Combest told him, "I got right down on the floor with him, just literally on my hands and knees. And I asked him if he would like to make any confession, any statement in connection with the assassination of the President. . . . Several times he responded to me by shaking his head in a definite manner. . . . It wasn't from the pain or anything—he had just decided he wasn't going to correspond with me, he wasn't going to say anything."

In a footnote Summers added something he had left out of the text. Combest had told him that Oswald accompanied his headshaking with "a definite clenched-fist salute." Summers then argued, "This cannot be taken as good evidence of a political gesture, given Oswald's condition at that moment. It may indeed have been an expression of pain." He added that Combest had said nothing about the clenched-fist salute in his statements to the Warren Commission. Two comments can be made on Summers' argument. When Combest testified in 1964 he probably didn't know what a clenched-fist salute was. Although the gesture had been a socialist salute in Spain in the 1930s, it didn't become a widely recognized symbol of political militancy in this country until the late 1960s. It was probably then that Combest reinterpreted Oswald's gesture as a political statement. Second, a news photograph taken of Oswald after his arrest shows him raising one manacled arm in what appears to be a clenched-fist salute.

In any event, a raised fist was Oswald's last comment.

16 . . . Reactions

> I really look with commiseration over the great body of my
> fellow citizens who, reading newspapers, live and die in the
> belief that they have known something of what has been pass-
> ing in the world in their time.   —Harry Truman

A STUNNED nation groped for a meaning. Trying to assimilate the
president's death into the only context they knew, many saw it as a
continuation of the violent opposition to the civil rights movement in
the South—the murder of Medgar Evans, the bombing of the Birmingham church. Editorial writers and television commentators
immediately blamed the anti-Kennedy environment in Dallas or
American violence in general.

As more information came out, the possibility that Oswald had a
political motive became ever more remote. When reporters learned
that Oswald had once tried to join Carlos Bringuier's organization in
New Orleans, this was taken as an indication that he was politically
erratic. In December the discovery that Oswald had tried to murder
Walker—whose political philosophy was radically different from
Kennedy's—produced a similar impression.

An accepted picture of Oswald gradually emerged. He was seen as
a confused drifter who acted out of personal frustration—he couldn't
hold a job and his wife didn't want to live with him. The assassination

had no political significance, except as a timely lesson about right-wing extremism and its consequences.

Fidel Castro's first reaction was given in a *New York Times* headline: "Castro Mourns 'Hostile' Leader: Deplores Slaying But Says Kennedy Courted War." Later, however, after details of Oswald's background were revealed, Castro began to suspect "a Machiavellian plan against Cuba." In a speech in late November he declared:

> Oswald never had contacts with us—we have never heard of him. . . . We have searched through all our files and this man is not listed as president of any committee. Nowhere is there any mention of any Fair Play for Cuba Committee in Dallas or New Orleans. . . . Oswald is an individual expressly fabricated to begin an anti-Communist campaign to liquidate the President because of his policy. This plan to call Oswald a Castro Communist is designed to pressure the new Administration. All people, including the U.S. people, should demand that what is behind the assassination be clarified. Those who love peace and the United States intellectuals should understand the gravity of this campaign.

Apparently Castro sincerely believed this. He was afraid a public clamor about Oswald's politics might lead to war. American government officials were also aware of this danger, and they too were worried. There was a general fear among cabinet members that the American people might demand retribution from Russia or Cuba or both. When the new president, Lyndon Johnson, asked Chief Justice Earl Warren to head up the investigation, he stressed that rumors about Oswald's foreign connections had created a grave international situation. He made Warren understand that it was his duty to head up a responsible investigation to dispel these rumors, and Warren reluctantly accepted the assignment.

When the Warren Commission began taking testimony a few months later, some of the witnesses who knew Oswald were asked what they thought his motive might have been. None of these witnesses thought Oswald acted because he was irrational or because he had personal problems. Several said they believed his motive was somehow political. Their opinions are remarkable in that they ran counter to the contemporary news media interpretation and popular belief.

Michael Paine had initially doubted that Oswald was guilty because he "didn't see how this could fit, how this could help his cause, and I didn't think he was irrational." Paine came to believe that the president was a target of opportunity: "I thought it was a spur of the moment idea that came into his head when he realized that he would have the opportunity with sort of a duck blind there, an opportunity to change the course of history, even though he couldn't predict from that action what course history would take, that in my opinon would not have deterred him from doing it."

John Hall, Elena Hall's husband, said he wasn't surprised when he heard that Oswald had been arrested because he thought Oswald was the "kind of guy that would do something like that." Not that he believed Oswald was insane—"He was pretty sharp. If he had the right training in the right direction, he could have done something with his life." Hall thought the assassination was a violent expression of Oswald's resentment not only of the American government but of "our whole way of life." Max Clark, the Fort Worth attorney, also said he didn't think Oswald was mentally unstable. But he thought Oswald was capable of assassinating Kennedy in order "to go down in history, because he seemed to think he was destined to go down in history some way or another."

Lee's cousin Marilyn disagreed with the news media explanations, as well. She didn't think he acted because he was "jealous of Kennedy and all that Kennedy stood for," or because he wanted to "be somebody." In her view, Lee Oswald already thought he *was* somebody and always seemed perfectly satisfied with the way he was. She thought his motive might have been "to discredit America in the eyes of the world"—or "perhaps because he was turned down by Russia and then turned down by Fidel, that perhaps he wanted to show them that he could commit such a great act without the help of any others."

Marina gave several contradictory opinions about her husband's motive, but at one point she testified that her first impression had been that he wanted "by any means—good or bad, to get into history."

Then she added, "But now that I have heard a part of the translation of some of the documents, I think that there was some political foundation to it, a foundation of which I am unaware."

Police Captain Fritz seems to have come closer to the truth than anyone else. He testified: "I got the impression he was doing it because of his feeling about the Castro revolution, and I think that . . . he had a lot of feeling about that revolution. I think that was the reason. I noticed another thing. I noticed a little before when Walker was shot [sic], he had come out with some statements about Castro and about Cuba and a lot of things and if you will remember the President had some stories a few weeks before his death about Cuba and about Castro . . . and I wondered if that didn't have some bearing. I have no way of knowing that other than just watching him and talking to him." Asked if Oswald acted afraid, Fritz said, "No, sir; I don't believe he was afraid at all. I think he was a person who had his mind made up what to do and I think he was like a person just dedicated to a cause. And I think he was above average for intelligence. I know a lot of people call him a nut all the time but he didn't talk like a nut. He knew exactly when to quit talking."

Oswald's death left Marina in a predicament. The FBI and Secret Service now turned to her for the answers to their questions, and although Marina had no foreknowledge of the assassination, she did have knowledge of some of Oswald's past activities that she was afraid to admit. On November 27, when FBI and Secret Service agents confronted her with the backyard photographs showing Oswald with his rifle, she admitted taking them, but said nothing about his attack on Walker. Instead, she said that before the assassination "she had never had any inkling that he would be so violent to anybody"—she must have realized that she would be blamed for not going to the police after the Walker shooting. At the end of the interview she volunteered the information that when Oswald came to Irving on Thursday he told her he wouldn't be coming back that weekend because "he had something very important to do." Asked about this statement a few weeks later, Marina said she couldn't remember, and the matter was dropped.

A Secret Service report of November 28 quotes her as saying that at "one time she became so exasperated with Lee Oswald she asked him 'What are you trying to do, start another revolution?' " Interviewed again the next day, Marina said that when she left New Orleans with Ruth no arrangement had been made for Oswald to go to Mexico City. The interviewer noted, "Inasmuch as Mexico City had not been mentioned, she was asked why she had said no arrangements had been made. . . . She replied she had been looking at television the past few days and had seen or heard that Oswald had been in Mexico City." Later she admitted she had known about his visits to the Cuban and Russian embassies.

And yet, despite her evasions, it does appear that Marina was trying to convey the truth, but in such a way that she could avoid getting into any trouble. On November 30, when Oswald's attack on Walker still hadn't been discovered, she told the FBI that Oswald had once told her "Hitler needed killing," since by killing Hitler many lives could have been saved. But Marina didn't mention the shooting incident that had inspired that remark until she had to—after the note Oswald had left her was discovered by the Secret Service on December 2, tucked inside her Russian "Book of Useful Advice." She then admitted that he had told her Walker was the leader of the fascist organization in Dallas "and it was best to remove him." She explained that she had saved the note so that she could threaten to take it to the police if Oswald ever spoke of doing such a thing again.

After she appeared before the Warren Commission in February, the Commission lawyers weren't satisfied with her testimony. Wesley J. Liebeler thought she might have been approximating the truth in order to tell the Commission what she believed it wanted to hear. In 1978 Marina explained the inconsistencies in her testimony when she appeared before the House Assassinations Committee:

> At the beginning, if it is possible to understand . . . I am just a human being and I did try to protect Lee—that was my natural instinct that I followed. Some things I did not want to talk about because I tried to protect Lee. So they can hold this against me, there is nothing I can do about it.
>
> I had to protect myself, too. I didn't have any home to turn back to. I was not eligible or qualified to live right here so I really was trying to

save my skin, to put it bluntly, but it was not for the reasons that I was protecting somebody, that I was part of any crime, that is not so. That was just a very human mistake that you make but it was not—maybe legally you call this perjury, I don't know. But it was not because I was afraid that I might betray some secrets that I knew in order to be punished for . . . I was not aware of the crime that he was planning and I am sorry that all this happened like the rest of us suffer. So I don't think I can add any more.

It was within this context that Marina told the Commission a story that led to one of the earliest and most often repeated theories about Dallas—that on the night before the assassination Oswald begged his wife to live with him and she refused.

Q. Did your husband give any reason for coming home on Thursday?
A. He said that he was lonely because he hadn't come the preceding weekend, and he wanted to make his peace with me.
Q. Did you say anything to him then?
A. He tried to talk to me but I would not answer him, and he was very upset.
Q. Were you upset with him?
A. I was angry, of course. He was not angry—he was upset. I was angry. He tried very hard to please me. He spent quite a bit of time putting away diapers and played with the children on the street.
Q. How did you indicate to him that you were angry with him?
A. By not talking to him.
Q. And how did he show that he was upset?
A. He was upset over the fact that I would not answer him. He tried to start a conversation with me several times, but I would not answer. And he said that he didn't want me to be angry at him because this upsets him.
On that day, he suggested that we rent an apartment in Dallas. He said that he was tired of living alone and perhaps the reason for my being so angry was the fact that we were not living together. That if I want to he would rent an apartment in Dallas tomorrow—that he didn't want me to remain with Ruth any longer, but wanted me to live with him in Dallas.
He repeated this not once but several times, but I refused. And he said that once again I was preferring my friends to him, and that I didn't need

him. . . . And I told him to buy me a washing machine, because two children it became too difficult to wash by hand.
Q. What did he say to that?
A. He said he would buy me a washing machine.
Q. What did you say to that?
A. Thank you. That it would be better if he bought something for himself—that I would manage.

Ruth Paine, who saw them together that night, saw nothing of this. She thought they seemed "cordial," "friendly," and "warm"—"like a couple making up after a small spat." Ruth also testified that shortly after Oswald's arrest, Marina let her know she was bewildered and hurt that he should do such a thing when just the night before he had talked of their getting an apartment soon.

Marina later admitted to McMillan that she had never asked her husband to buy her a washing machine, and that it was Lee who had brought that subject up on November 21. McMillan concluded, "Lee and Marina did not fight that evening about a washing machine." Nor, apparently, did they fight about anything else. When Marina appeared before the Assassinations Committee and was questioned for perhaps the twentieth time about the events of November 21, she showed her impatience. She was asked what her husband said to her when he arrived. "Did he say hello?" someone asked, and she replied, "Isn't is usually people say hello when they see each other? Probably." But the way she eventually described that evening was quite different from the story she had told in 1964:

He was more in [a] peaceful mood . . . and was willing to listen.
Well, like, for example, if maybe before I would say I would like for us to be together, and he would tell me to, oh, just stop dreaming, or just cut me off, or not listen at all, but now at least he was listening at what I had to say. . . .
[W]e were looking forward and talking about him renting [an] apartment for us . . . it was a very big imposition to live with Mrs. Paine, and I thought we . . . should live as a family. . . .

In the earlier version Oswald had begged her to live with him and *she* had refused to listen; now, it was Marina who was repeating her request that they be together, and Oswald for the first time seemed willing to hear her out. No wonder, then, that she was bewildered and hurt when he was arrested for the president's assassination the following day. Oswald had led her on about their future together—because, I believe, he wanted to ensure that she wouldn't guess what he planned to do and tell Ruth, who would have instantly called the police. "You and your long tongue," Oswald had once chided Marina, "they always get us into trouble." It would not have been the only instance that Oswald had manipulated her shamelessly to get what he wanted.

And yet, Marina's initial story was not entirely a fiction. McMillan believes that Oswald did in fact ask her to move into an apartment, not once but three times, and that each time Marina said no, saying that she preferred to wait until they had saved some money. But as McMillan wrote:

> He knew how to get his wife back—indeed, he had done so one year before when she ran away from him and he wanted her back in time for Thanksgiving at Robert's on November 22, 1962. Had Lee, on November 21, 1963, genuinely wanted Marina back, he knew how to arrange it —the telephone call in advance, a little cajoling, believable tenderness. It seems a fair guess that, unhinged as he must have been, Lee still, on November 21, knew how to obtain the answer "Yes."

The story that Oswald was rejected by his wife on the eve of the assassination has been so widely accepted that it seems almost perverse to challenge it. But I believe Marina's account was part of an understandable impulse to distance herself as much as she could from the president's assassin. Consider the situation. On November 21 she knew that her husband had attacked Walker, that he continued to keep a rifle, and that he was using an alias. If she told the Commission she was still warm and friendly, how would it look? How did you treat him that night, Mrs. Oswald? I was angry, of course; I wouldn't have anything to do with him. And this was probably not even a calculated lie—it just came out that way. It was not only a facesaving answer, it was probably also what she fervently *wished* she had done, instead of falling for another one of Oswald's deceptions.

Furthermore, it was a story that was readily accepted and never questioned. It was exactly the kind of thing everyone wanted to believe—that the assassin was such an obvious miscreant, even his own wife spurned him. It was Ruth Paine who warned the Commission that if people thought that Oswald was someone who would be instantly recognized as a potential assassin, someone who would stand out in a crowd as being unusual, then they didn't know this man and had no way of recognizing such a person in the future.

Marina may have reasoned that her marital relationship was not important and not the Commission's business—as indeed it wasn't, except insofar as it related to the cause of the assassination. But by maintaining that she had coldly rejected Oswald, she inadvertently distorted the perception of his motive.

George de Mohrenschildt's testimony to the Commission reflected his own difficult situation. By the time he appeared, Marina had revealed that he had guessed, after the fact, that Oswald might have been the unknown sniper who shot at Walker. (When de Mohrenschildt and his wife had stopped by the Oswalds' apartment a few days after the incident, George had said jokingly, "How did it happen you missed?" Both Marina and the de Mohrenschildts reported that Oswald had turned pale and quickly changed the subject.) In his manuscript on Oswald, de Mohrenschildt confessed that because he had felt intimidated and wanted to clear his name, he said untrue things about Oswald in his testimony that he later regretted, such as that he was "a poor loser" who was envious of other peoples' success and money. He wrote that he believed Oswald had been framed: "Lee, an ex-Marine trained for organized murder, was capable of killing but [only] for a very strong ideological motive or in self-defense."

By coincidence, de Mohrenschildt had known Janet Auchincloss, Jacqueline Kennedy's mother, and Jackie herself as a child. De Mohrenschildt claimed that after he gave his testimony in Washington, he was invited to the Auchincloss house in Georgetown. He said that he suggested to Jackie's mother that the family should finance a real investigation of Kennedy's murder, because he doubted Oswald's guilt, and that Mrs. Auchincloss said, "He's dead, nothing can change that." De Mohrenschildt then speculated that Kennedy's relatives may have suspected anti-Castro Cubans were involved and didn't want his death associated with the Bay of Pigs, "his biggest mistake."

Despite that story there is reason to believe that de Mohrenschildt actually felt guilty, perhaps believing that he might have somehow prevented Kennedy's death. According to Edward Jay Epstein, de Mohrenschildt told a friend in Houston in 1964 that he had inadvertently given Marina the money Oswald used to buy his rifle. Marina supposedly said to him, "Remember the twenty-five dollars you gave me? Well, that fool husband of mine used it to buy a rifle."

In 1967 de Mohrenschildt revealed that he owned one of the backyard photographs showing Oswald with his rifle. His copy had a signed inscription on the back in Oswald's hand, "To my dear friend George, from Lee," with a date written Russian-style: "5/IV/63"— that is, April 5, 1963, or five days before the Walker shooting.[1] There was a second inscription in Russian that McMillan believes Marina wrote: "Hunter of fascists ha-ha-ha!!!" De Mohrenschildt explained that he had discovered this photograph among his stored belongings when he returned to Dallas in 1967 from Haiti, where he and his wife had lived since May 1963. He said that it was inside an unopened package of records Marina had returned to him by mail shortly before the de Mohrenschildts left Texas that April. But when Marina was shown this photograph during her Assassinations Committee testimony, she indicated that she had seen her husband show the picture to George, presumably in April 1963. At that point in the transcript she seemed flustered, and the Committee didn't pursue the question further. In his manuscript de Mohrenschildt wrote that this photograph demonstrated that Oswald "might have been considering hunting fascists—and in his mind General Walker was one—but certainly not our President Kennedy."

De Mohrenschildt also wrote that the Warren Commission investigation had virtually ruined his life. He claimed that he had lost work because of the FBI's interest in him and that the subsequent conspiracy theories produced "strange idiocies"—that he was Oswald's "CIA handler," for example—that made him seem "controversial and even gruesomely threatening." He began getting strange phone calls, apparently from assassination buffs who believed he was part of a CIA conspiracy. (The Assassinations Committee investigation found no evidence that he had ever worked for the CIA.)

In later years, de Mohrenschildt became depressed and voluntarily underwent treatment in a sanitarium. In 1977, shortly before he was to be questioned by the Assassinations Committee, he fatally shot himself.

Our perception of what happened in Dallas was distorted, for several reasons. Since Oswald was highly secretive, his motivation had to be pieced together as one would reassemble a shredded document. In 1963 his political motive was invisible, largely because the public lacked knowledge of the context in which he had operated—it didn't know about the attempts to kill Castro. If Oswald were alive and on trial today, he might be seen as a revolutionary terrorist.

Another circumstance blocked our view of this event. The president's murder had aroused Washington's fears of a dangerous international crisis. As a result, the overriding concern of the official investigation was to prevent the situation from getting out of control. As the Church committee amply demonstrated, the CIA and FBI downplayed the possibility of a Cuban connection from the beginning.

At 5:00 P.M. on November 23, 1963, CIA headquarters learned that the Mexican police were about to arrest Silvia Duran, the Cuban Embassy employee who had dealt with Oswald. Agency personnel telephoned the Mexico station and asked them to stop the arrest. After discovering that this couldn't be done, Richard Helms's deputy, Thomas Karamessines, cabled the station that her arrest "could jeopardize U.S. freedom of action on the whole question of Cuban responsibility." When the Church committee asked him about this statement in 1976, Karamessines

speculated that the CIA feared the Cubans were responsible, and that Duran might reveal this during an interrogation. He further speculated that if Duran did possess such information, the CIA and the U.S.

Government would need time to react before it came to the attention of the public.

On November 24 the FBI legal attaché in Mexico cabled headquarters that the American ambassador there believed that the Cubans were unsophisticated and militant enough to have directed Oswald's action, and he suggested that the bureau might want to poll its Cuban informants in the U.S. "to confirm or refute this theory." But in Washington an FBI supervisor wrote a note on the cablegram: "Not desirable. Would serve to promote rumors." This view was shared by the CIA and the State Department. On November 28 Helms notified the CIA in Mexico:

> For your private information, there [is a] distinct feeling here in all three agencies that Ambassador is pushing this case too hard . . . and that we could well create flap with Cubans which could have serious repercussions.

In the months ahead, the CIA repeatedly failed to follow up leads that seemed to point toward direct Cuban involvement. Its investigation of this area became "passive in nature," as did that of the FBI. The CIA and FBI had both laudable *and* self-serving reasons for wrapping this case up quickly, like spoiled fish. Each was aware that a flap with the Cubans might lead to a nuclear confrontation like the 1962 missle crisis. But at each agency, there were private considerations as well.

J. Edgar Hoover pushed for a quick solution. He was convinced that Oswald acted alone. But he was eager to avoid public criticism that the bureau neglected its job by not keeping Oswald under closer surveillance after he returned from the Soviet Union. If a foreign conspiracy were found, the FBI would look even worse. Although he publicly defended the agents handling Oswald's case, Hoover secretly disciplined seventeen employees, including James Hosty, for not pursuing Oswald more aggressively.

A full investigation of a possible Cuban involvement might have proved even more embarrassing to the CIA. Warren Commission member Allen Dulles, who resigned as the agency's director in 1961, knew about the Mafia plots and withheld this information from the other members. Perhaps he reasoned that it wasn't relevant, since these plans ended well before the assassination. But the few CIA officials who were aware of the AM/LASH operation took steps to make sure that the Commission never got wind of it.

Although the Commission was kept in the dark, it seemed reluctant to raise the Cuban issue on its own: Castro's warning and Oswald's alleged threat at the Mexico Embassy were omitted from its report. Even fourteen years later the House Assassinations Committee found this subject hot to the touch. With remarkable frankness, its chief counsel, G. Robert Blakey, has written that one reason the Committee formally concluded that Cuba was not involved in Dallas was that "the Committee, as a responsible body of government, had an obligation to determine that the Cuban government was not involved in the assassination, if it could not find convincing proof that it was." In other words, if it couldn't *prove* Cuba was involved, it had to say Cuba was not involved.

Blakey was referring to the question of direct Cuban responsibility, but the same rule seemed to apply to the question of indirect involvement, that is, Castro's influence on Oswald, a possibility that was never discussed in the Committee's report. When members of the Committee interviewed Castro and showed him the passage in Daniel Schorr's book dealing with the Comer Clark interview, Castro denied that Oswald had threatened Kennedy at the Cuban Embassy. Counsel Blakey didn't believe him—he suspected that Oswald probably did make the threat and that Castro felt it was in Cuba's interest to deny it. But the Committee not only decided to accept Castro's denial, it went further. Although its report discussed Castro's warning and Oswald's alleged threat a few weeks later, it said nothing about Schorr's theory that the one event inspired the other. The report didn't mention that Castro's warning appeared in Oswald's local newspapers. Moreover, the report dealt with the warning and the threat in separate sections, thus stripping away the connective tissue that would have been provided by a simple chronology.

Finally, there may be one other reason that our perception of Dallas was flawed. After a traumatic event, people naturally seek a reassuring explanation, not one that is disturbing or painful. To believe that Lee Oswald was a drifter with no motive or the victim of a high-level conspiracy is easier to bear than the idea that American-backed murder plots helped bring about the assassination of President Kennedy.

17...Conspiracy Thinking

It is wiser, I believe, to arrive at theory by way of the evidence rather than the other way around. . . . It is more rewarding, in any case, to assemble the facts first and, in the process of arranging them in narrative form, to discover a theory or a historical generalization emerging of its own accord.

The very process of transforming a collection of personalities, dates, gun calibers, letters, and speeches into a narrative eventually forces the "why" to the surface. It will emerge of itself one fine day from the story of what happened. It will suddenly appear and tap one on the shoulder, but not if one chases after it first, *before* one knows what happened. Then it will elude one forever.   —Barbara W. Tuchman, *Practicing History*

BUILDING a conspiracy theory is easy. One might say, it's what the mind does best. Consider this hypothetical example. According to a 1982 ABC television documentary, J. Edgar Hoover once ruined an important investigation of Soviet espionage by publicizing the case too soon. And for years Hoover put his faith in a Soviet defector who later turned out to be a phony, a KGB plant. After a pattern such as this has been noticed, additional information tends to be filtered through the screen of that pattern. Thus, if one examined Hoover's career in detail, one would undoubtedly find other instances in which decisions he made turned out badly and helped the Soviet cause. Upon such documented evidence one might build a theory that Hoover was a high-level mole working for the KGB. But to make the theory stick, one would have to ignore two things: alternative explanations for those "pro-Soviet" actions (publicity seeking, bad judgment), and the entire context, that is, everything else we know about J. Edgar Hoover. Still, the notion that Hoover might have been a KGB agent is titillating—and who can prove that he wasn't? All the conspiracy books about Dallas are constructed in this way.

The paperback edition of David S. Lifton's *Best Evidence* cites reviews that called the book "a meticulously detailed detective story," "rigorously documented." The author's theory began, he tells us, when he saw the Zapruder film of the assassination for the first time and saw Kennedy's body fall violently backward and to the left after the fatal head shot. Having been a physics major, Lifton understood Newton's laws. He concluded that the backward movement of Kennedy's body could only be explained by a bullet striking him from the opposite direction—the direction of a grassy knoll west of the Depository. (Even his later discovery that Kennedy's head moved *forward* two inches before he fell back didn't change his mind.) Many witnesses thought shots came from the knoll, and some of the doctors who examined Kennedy in Dallas described wounds consistent with a shot from the front. Yet the autopsy X rays and report clearly indicated that Kennedy was struck only from the rear. How could this be?

Unable to accept that the grassy knoll theory might be wrong, Lifton reconciled the conflicting versions in an original manner. He decided both versions were true: the Dallas witnesses were right and so were the autopsy surgeons—they saw different things because *someone altered the president's body before the autopsy.*

Stated baldly, Lifton's theory is preposterous. He contends that all the bullets that struck Kennedy were fired from the front, and that to conceal this fact a large group of unnamed conspirators managed to steal Kennedy's body from its casket aboard *Air Force One,* slip it aboard a helicopter after the president's plane reached Washington, alter the body so that it appeared that Kennedy was shot from the rear by Oswald, and then sneak the altered body into Bethesda Naval Hospital for the official autopsy. That much is complex enough, but after Lifton began interviewing people who had been at Bethesda Hospital that night he found new conflicts in the testimony. Most of the witnesses said the body arrived in an expensive casket, and was wrapped in a sheet with a plastic mattress cover laid underneath. This was how the body left Dallas. But three hospital employees thought they remembered seeing Kennedy's body arrive wrapped in a body bag inside a plainer casket. Most witnesses put the time of arrival at about 7:15, but one written report said 8 o'clock. As he had before, Lifton now attempted to reconcile these differences. As he put it, "Had this been an ordinary case, the choice of which witnesses to believe would have been left to the jury. But this was no ordinary case." He decided that the body must have entered the hospital *twice* —once in the plain coffin/body bag, and later in the bronze coffin/sheet. This is comparable to saying that if some witnesses say the robber wore a black hat and others say he wore a red hat, there must have been two robberies.

But how could witnesses recall a body bag, if there wasn't one? Elizabeth Loftus is a psychologist who specializes in eyewitness testimony. Loftus says, "No matter how well meaning or how well trained observers are, there are ways to make people see, hear, and even smell things that never were." Over time, she explains, memory doesn't fade, it grows. "What may fade is the initial perception, the actual experience of the events. But every time we recall an event we must reconstruct the memory, and so each time it is changed—colored by succeeding events, increased understanding, a new context, suggestions by others, other people's recollections. We can get people to conjure up details that are pure fantasy."

When Lady Bird Johnson testified before the Warren Commission, she vividly described ascending and descending a flight of stairs when she went to pay her condolences to Jacqueline Kennedy at the Dallas hospital. But there were no stairs—the two women were on the same floor. Mrs. Johnson had apparently confused this incident with another—when she went upstairs to visit Mrs. Connally.

The first witness who remembered a body bag, Paul O'Connor, told

Lifton his story thirteen years after the event. During the intervening time, body bags had been shown repeatedly in newscasts out of Vietnam. In his reconstruction, O'Connor may have transmuted the plastic mattress cover into a body bag, or he may have confused two separate events. Lifton was able to find two other witnesses who "remembered" a body bag and/or cheap casket, but only after he asked them leading questions. For instance,

> LIFTON: . . . was he in any kind of bag or anything, or in a sheet?
> REIBE: I think he was in a body bag.

Reibe said that his recollection was "vague."

Lifton knew, of course, that memories fade and that witnesses make mistakes. But he apparently never realized how often witnesses recall images they never saw—nor did I, until I read *Best Evidence.* This failing leads him into extending the labyrinth of his theory, time after time:

> I found O'Connor perfectly credible when he said the throat wound was unsutured when the body arrived. I also found Ebersole credible when he said it *was* sutured at what *he* thought was the outset of the autopsy. I thought they made their observations at different times.

Similarly, the chief of surgery at Bethesda recalled seeing an intact bullet "roll out from the clothing of President Kennedy and onto the autopsy table." Nobody else saw this, and it is beyond dispute that Kennedy's body was unclothed. Yet Lifton accepted this testimony and used it to build another corridor in his theory. He concluded that the bullet the chief "saw" must have been the same bullet the conspirators had earlier planted on a hospital stretcher in Dallas (before they changed their plans, brought the bullet to Bethesda, then decided to go with their original plan).

In *The Mechanism of Mind,* Edward de Bono has said, "Ideas must advance and if they miss the right direction they move further and further in the wrong direction." De Bono was describing the weaknesses of what he calls vertical thinking, which he defined as the sequential development of a particular pattern. As soon as a pattern is recognized, it provides the framework for processing incoming information. The established pattern in fact *selects* the new information. This method of thinking is extremely efficient when the perceived pattern coincides with reality. But when it doesn't, it leads to the creation of a myth.

When a perceived pattern is firmly established, alternative explanations are ignored or rejected. If Kennedy was struck from the rear, why was his body propelled backward? Three alternative explanations have been given, none of which violates the laws of physics: (1) Neuropathologist Richard Lindenburg told the Rockefeller Commission that the movement could have been caused by a violent neuro-muscular reaction resulting from "major damage inflicted to the nerve centers in the brain." (2) Physicist Luis Alvarez experimented by firing a rifle into melons wrapped with tape. Each time, the melon was propelled backward in the direction of the rifle. Alvarez cited the law of conservation of momentum—as the contents of the melon were driven forward and out by the force of the bullet, an opposite force was created similar to the thrust of a jet engine, propelling the melon in the opposite direction. (3) In a documentary on the assassination, CBS pointed out that the Zapruder film showed Mrs. Kennedy touching her husband's left arm at the moment the fatal bullet struck, and that in her shocked reaction she may have caused the president's backward movement by a pressure on his arm. Any of these explanations, or a combination of any of them, might explain the backward motion.

When Lee Harvey Oswald's body was exhumed in October 1981, reexamined by pathologists, and reburied, a conspiracy theory put forward by British author Michael Eddowes was buried with it. In a book called *The Oswald File* Eddowes had argued that the man killed by Jack Ruby was not Lee Harvey Oswald but a Russian impostor. Eddowes's theory was never very popular, but since it has now been conclusively disproved, it may serve as an undisputed example of the way a conspiracy theory can go wrong.

There is usually a predisposition toward a certain point of view. The introduction to Eddowes's book says that the author had suspected Russian involvement even before he began investigating the assassination. When the Warren Hearings and Exhibits were published, Eddowes and several assistants began looking for evidence to support his suspicions—and found it. As it always happens in conspiracy theories, Eddowes ignored the larger pattern of Oswald's life and zoomed in on some tiny but puzzling anomalies in the record. Just before Oswald left the Marines in 1959, his height was measured twice—once by a doctor—and recorded each time as 5 feet 11 inches. Yet after Oswald was arrested in Dallas, his height was measured as 5 feet 9½ inches, and the autopsy report later recorded his height as 5 feet 9 inches. Furthermore, at age 6 Oswald had undergone a mastoidectomy, and the Marine medical records noted the resulting scar behind his left ear. But the postmortem on Oswald didn't mention a mastoidechtomy scar. (In conspiracy theories, people don't make mistakes.) There was more. Oswald's brothers noticed changes in his appearance after his stay in Russia: thinner hair, a ruddier complexion, a slimmer build. Asked about this difference, John Pic testified, "I would never have recognized him, sir." Pic also noticed that, after coming back, Lee referred to him for the first time as his *half*-brother. Of course, Pic knew perfectly well that the man *was* Oswald, but on the basis of these inconsistencies Eddowes constructed a theory that the man who returned from Russia wasn't the young defector but a shorter Russian look-alike who was working for the KGB.

Once this theory was in place, everything else was interpreted to fit it. Oswald's Marine Corps fingerprints inconveniently matched those of the man killed in Dallas. Undeterred, Eddowes concluded that the KGB must have somehow replaced the authentic Oswald's fingerprints in the Marine files with those of the Russian. But the results of the exhumation prove that Eddowes was wrong. The team of pathologists unanimously concluded that the body in Oswald's grave was beyond all doubt that of Lee Harvey Oswald. The dental X rays matched, and they located the mastoidectomy scar the original autopsy surgeons had overlooked.

Although the solutions proposed by Lifton and Eddowes are more farfetched than some, they use the same style of reasoning found in other conspiracy books. All these theories are based on unexplained discrepancies in the record. As in the J. Edgar Hoover analogy, alternative explanations and the overall pattern of the evidence are given little attention, if any.

Significantly, in these books, Oswald is almost always offstage. Lifton scarcely mentions him. Eddowes left him trapped in Russia, not even present at the murder scene. The odd thing is, we never get a good view of Oswald in the other conspiracy books, either. This is their major flaw, for although it is easy to point to anomalies in the mountain of evidence the Warren Commission accumulated, it is something else again to weave those anomalies into a credible scenario that illustrates how a conspiracy might actually have been carried out. The few authors who have attempted to do so have presented stories that are grotesquely improbable.

In *Betrayal,* for instance, Robert D. Morrow casts Oswald as an American intelligence agent who was sent to Russia as a bogus defector. On returning to this country, he continued his clandestine work, taking orders from Jack Ruby, the CIA, and an anti-Castro group while working as an FBI informer on the side. Among other things, Oswald was supposedly directed to fire a shot over General Walker's head and to establish a left-wing reputation by writing letters to the Communist party and making himself conspicuous at an ACLU meeting. On November 22, according to Morrow, Oswald completed his last assignment: bringing his rifle to the Depository and arranging a sniper's nest on the sixth floor. After neatly stacking a pile of boxes near the window, "Oswald went to the men's room on the second floor, opened the window slightly, and sat quietly in a stall to wait." Having explained Oswald's whereabouts at the critical moment, Morrow now faced another hurdle—Oswald was arrested with the Tippit murder weapon in his hand. How to explain this? As Morrow tells it, an Oswald look-alike shot Tippit with a similar gun, after which the team of conspirators arranged for the gun, bullets, *and* shell casings to be switched—by Jack Ruby, the FBI, and the Dallas police, respectively.

Most conspiracists wisely eschew the narrative method. My point is that the wild implausibilities in *Betrayal* are implicit in every other conspiracy book. If the others seem more persuasive, it is largely because they do not present a scenario of the events, but simply point to one suspicious-looking anomaly after another. The reader will understand the difficulty these writers have sidestepped if he or she tries to invent a story that explains why an *innocent* Oswald went to Irving for "curtain rods," left his wedding ring behind the next morning, brought a package into the Depository, and so on. Because the evidence against Oswald is strong, any detailed reconstruction that argues a frame-up will inevitably sound less plausible than one that argues his guilt.

It is not surprising, then, that most conspiracists now concede that Oswald was at least involved in the assassination. But they contend that he was the instrument of others, typically a renegade element of U.S. intelligence, anti-Castro activists, or the Mafia. This hypothesis also lacks a credible story line, mainly because its proponents imply that Oswald was either a closet right-winger who participated willingly or a gullible Marxist who was tricked into it. These writers turn aside the plentiful evidence about Oswald's politics and nature and create, by implication, a different person entirely. As before, Morrow made the problem explicit when he tried to illuminate Oswald's motivations for his "intelligence work":

> If Oswald had any misgivings about the things he was asked to do he put them aside, pleased to be gainfully employed and able to do things for Marina. Bizarre as some of his assignments were, he cooperated without question.

This is not Lee Harvey Oswald, but a fictional character.

Virtually every argument the critics make looks weak when its hidden implications are stated openly. For example, many writers suspect that someone impersonated Oswald at the Cuban Embassy. In 1978 Consul Azcue insisted that the man he dealt with "in no way resembled" the president's accused assassin. But to accept this, one must assume the following. The impostor presented a photograph of Oswald for the visa application and forged his signature. Silvia Duran didn't notice that the picture looked nothing at all like the person who handed it to her. Duran and Alfredo Mirabal were mistaken when they later identified the applicant as Oswald. Back in Dallas, someone forged Duran's phone number in Oswald's notebook.

One might be able to swallow this story, however improbable, were it not for Oswald's November 9 letter to the Soviets in Washington —in which he talked about his run-in with the Cuban consul. Ruth Paine and Marina observed him writing this letter, and Ruth found a copy of it lying on her desk later that day. One is faced with two incredible alternatives: either Ruth and Marina were involved in the forgery/impostor scheme, or Oswald wrote about events that happened to his impersonator. As might be expected, the conspiracists say little, if anything, about the November 9 letter. Anthony Summers mentions it, but he omits entirely Oswald's reference to the Cuban Embassy. To do otherwise would have made his impostor theory sound ludicrous.

The conspiracists' methods produce a surreal world. Every discrepancy is interpreted as a crack in the official stone wall through which one may glimpse the ugly truth of what happened. Behind the wall are disconnected scenes, each with its own set of conspirators. On close examination, many of these scenes evaporate.

On November 24 one of the policemen who arrested Oswald at the movie theater, N. M. McDonald, told a reporter, "A man sitting near the front, and I still don't know who it was, tipped me the man I wanted was sitting in the third row from the rear." Robert Sam Anson takes this statement to mean that a stranger in the audience stood up, "fingered" Oswald, and then quietly slipped away. Typically, this interpretation evokes a striking mental image: a conspirator materializes. But in fact, there was no mystery man. McDonald later recognized his informant as Johnny Brewer, the shoe store manager who had followed Oswald after noticing his suspicious behavior. It was Brewer who pointed him out, as he testified.

A story told by Summers conjures up another spooky image. A switchboard operator at the Dallas jail named Mrs. Troon has said that on the evening of November 22 two law officers—apparently Secret Service men—arranged to listen in on a telephone call they expected Oswald to make. After they took their positions in an adjoining room, the switchboard lit up. Troon and fellow operator Mrs. Swinney plugged in, after alerting the eavesdropping agents. Troon continued, "I was dumbfounded at what happened next. Mrs. Swinney opened the key to Oswald and told him, 'I'm sorry, the number doesn't answer.' She then unplugged and disconnected Oswald without ever trying to put the call through. A few moments later Mrs. Swinney tore the page off her notation pad and threw it into the wastepaper basket." Troon retrieved the page as a souvenir—it listed a Raleigh, North Carolina, number and a name spelled "Herty" or "Hertig." So far as the record shows, Oswald had no such acquaintance and had never set foot in North Carolina.

But Summers pointed out that during the year Oswald defected, naval intelligence was reportedly training several dozen young recruits to be sent to Eastern Europe in hopes the KGB would spot them as potential agents. The major training base was said to be at Nag's Head, North Carolina, which Summers notes is in "the same general area" as Raleigh. In fact, they are 201 miles apart.

And yet, how quickly one sees a connection: "Herty" may have been Oswald's naval intelligence officer. Furthermore, since neither the agents nor the Dallas police reported this attempted call, there must have been a cover-up.

Hurtling along this conspiracy track, one might not notice that Troon's story makes no sense. Why would Swinney hang up on Oswald? Why didn't the agents rush in to demand an explanation, or confiscate her note? Her behavior and theirs are inexplicable—unless the caller was not Oswald, but *some other prisoner who was about to tie up the line.* Assume that, and the rest falls into place. The caller may have given his name and Troon missed it. Realizing her mistake, Swinney aborted the call and threw away the note—which was of no interest to the agents. Oswald's strange phone call wasn't reported because it didn't occur.

Human errors needn't be momentous to generate an elaborate plot. Summers turns one word into a sinister link between Oswald and *army* intelligence. After questioning him in August 1963, the New Orleans police sent a report to the army's regional headquarters in San Antonio, Texas, where a file was opened on Oswald as a potential "counter-intelligence threat." Eight years later word leaked out that the army had been routinely collecting data on thousands of American "subversives." After a furor in the press, the Department of Defense ordered that all civilian files—no exceptions—be destroyed. In 1973, army records say, a civil service file clerk in San Antonio marked Oswald's dossier for destruction, together with many others. The available evidence, including statements from witnesses who had seen the file, indicates that his dossier contained what one would expect: newspaper clippings about his defection, Marine records, copies of FBI reports. Nevertheless, the destruction of the file aroused the direst suspicions.

Shortly after the assassination, the army officer in charge, Lieutenant Colonel Robert Jones, telephoned the FBI in Dallas and, with Oswald's file open in front of him, volunteered the information he had. FBI records show that he described "A. J. Hidell" as an *associate* of Oswald's—which is what Oswald had told the New Orleans police. The investigation soon established, however, that "Hidell" was actually an alias.

In 1978, fifteen years later, Jones explained the file's history to the Assassinations Committee, which found him to be a credible witness. But Summers thought it was significant that, during his testimony, Jones said that "A. J. Hidell" had been listed in his records as Oswald's *alias*. Summers pounced on this inconsistency because Oswald's only known use of the name *as an alias* was in purchasing his pistol and rifle through the mail. "If Jones' testimony is correct," Summers concludes, then the army may well have learned of these weapons purchases months before the assassination—either by monitoring Oswald's post office box or through "some human informant, conceivably Oswald himself." He suspects that the file was destroyed because it would have revealed Oswald's dealing with army intelligence.

One has to look twice to notice that the only clue to this clandestine relationship came from the man who would necessarily have been a central figure in the cover-up. If Jones lied to the FBI in 1963, it was to conceal the army's knowledge of Oswald's alias. When he prepared to face the Committee, is it probable that he would have overlooked this crucial detail? More likely, the word "associate" came from the New Orleans police report and Jones later misremembered "Hidell" as Oswald's alias because that fact had been firmly established long before.

Were others involved in the assassination? The House Assassinations Committee believed that a tape recording of a police motorcycle radio transmission contained the faint sounds of four shots and that one of them came from the grassy knoll. It concluded that another gunman in that area had fired a shot that missed the motorcade completely. But in 1982 a new panel of acoustical experts reexamined the tape for the National Research Council and unanimously concluded that the sounds on the tape had been recorded about one minute *after* the shooting and that there was thus no evidence for a second gunman. And that is where the matter stands as of now. In any event, the bulk of the evidence about Oswald clearly suggests that if there had been a conspiracy, Oswald would not have been a patsy, but the ringleader. If he had any accomplices, which seems doubtful, I would nominate the two unknown men who helped him try to gull Sylvia Odio.

As the Assassinations Committee said, a conspiracy involving Oswald and someone else, "possibly a person akin to Oswald in temperament and ideology, would not have been fundamentally different from an assassination by Oswald alone." In a footnote it added, "If the conspiracy was, in fact, limited to Oswald, the second gunman, and perhaps one or two others, the committee believes it was possible they shared Oswald's left-wing political disposition. A consistent pattern in Oswald's life was a propensity for actions with political overtones. It is quite likely that an assassination conspiracy limited to Oswald and a few associates was in keeping with that pattern." Conspirators are usually allies, not political enemies.

But there's no compelling reason to believe anyone else was involved. The police-tape theory overshadowed the other work done by the Committee that strengthened the case for Oswald's guilt. Having examined the Warren Commission's evidence, as well as new evidence it developed on its own, the Committee reached the following conclusions. President Kennedy was struck by two rifle shots fired from the sixth-floor window on the southeast corner of the Texas School Book Depository. All the wounds inflicted on President Kennedy and Governor Connally were caused by two bullets fired from the Mannlicher-Carcano rifle found on the sixth floor of the Depository, and this rifle belonged to Lee Harvey Oswald. Oswald was present on the sixth floor shortly before the assassination. A paper bag suitable for containing a rifle found in the sniper's nest bore a fingerprint and palmprint of Oswald's. Oswald had no alibi for the time of the assassination. Oswald shot and killed Patrolman J.D. Tippit. The evidence "strongly suggested that Oswald attempted to murder General Walker and that he possessed a capacity for violence." Considering this and other evidence against him, the Committee concluded that Oswald assassinated President Kennedy. As Anthony Summers said, "If Oswald really was just a fall guy, he had been bewilderingly well framed."

Much of the controversy about Dallas derives from the Warren Commission's analysis of an 8-millimeter film of the motorcade taken by spectator Abraham Zapruder, who was standing west of the Depository near the spot where Kennedy was killed. His movie, often blurry, tracked the president's limousine at 18.3 frames per second as it turned onto Elm Street in front of the Depository and came toward Zapruder's position, 200 feet away. At frame 210 the president disappeared from Zapruder's view as the car passed behind a road sign. When he reappeared at frame 225, he had obviously been wounded, his fists clenched in front of his throat, elbows extended. Roughly a second and a half later Connally reacted dramatically to being hit.

The Commission's test of Oswald's rifle found that 2.3 seconds were required between shots if the telescopic sight was used. This finding resulted in an apparent dilemma: either Connally and Kennedy were wounded by the same bullet and Connally's visible reaction was delayed—or there were two gunmen. Eventually the Commission concluded that one shot missed; another hit Kennedy in the upper back and exited his throat to wound Connally in the upper torso, wrist, and thigh; a third struck Kennedy's head between Zapruder frames 312 and 313. A whole bullet recovered from a stretcher at

Parkland Hospital was said to have transited both men; it was soon called "the magic bullet" by critics who insisted that it could not have caused so much damage and remain virtually intact. But neutron activation tests have now linked this missile rather firmly with fragments removed from Governor Connally's wrist, thus supporting the one-bullet hypothesis.

One shot had clearly been fired *before* the limousine reached the road sign. Connally has said that when he heard a rifle report shortly after the car turned onto Elm Street, he immediately shouted "No, no, no" while attempting to look at Kennedy behind him. The Assassinations Committee located the start of the movement he described at frames 162–167, that is, eight seconds before the fatal shot. Mrs. Kennedy recalled that she had been looking left at the crowd when she heard Connally cry out, and that she too turned toward the president. Up until frame 183, she is facing the crowd; by frame 193, she has swung completely around to stare at her husband. Her position is unmistakable. If the first shot occurred at frame 161, Oswald had eight seconds to aim and fire two more. The Committee found that it was possible to fire the Mannlicher-Carcano twice within 1.66 seconds, using the open iron sights.

All the hard evidence points to a sixth-floor assassin and points away from a gunman firing from any other location. Minutes before the assassination, several spectators saw a young male fitting Oswald's description in the sixth-floor window. Another witness, who saw him aim his last shot, ultimately identified the man as Oswald. Three others looked up in time to see the rifle being withdrawn from the window. No one saw a sniper or a weapon at any other location. A large bullet fragment recovered from the car has been connected by neutron activation analysis to Kennedy's head wound and, like the stretcher bullet, by ballistics tests to Oswald's rifle. No fragments of a third bullet were indicated. In the autopsy X rays of Kennedy's skull, the dispersal of metal fragments extends from back to front. The trajectory of all wounds ranged downward from back to front. Thus, there is no evidence whatsoever of a bullet striking either man from any other weapon or any other direction. A bullet from the grassy knoll that hit Kennedy and disappeared without a trace (along with

the gunman) would indeed have been a "magic bullet."
Why, then, did many witnesses believe that shots came from the
grassy knoll? Some of these people made the same mistake David S.
Lifton made: they saw Kennedy fall backward and *assumed* he had
been shot from the front. For instance, a witness quoted by the Dallas
Times Herald said he thought "the shots came from in front of or
beside" the president because Kennedy "did not slump forward as he
would have after being shot from the rear." William Newman, standing in front of the knoll, believed that the shot hit Kennedy "in the
side of the head," adding that Kennedy's head was pushed back and
to the left.

Probably the strongest evidence the proponents of a Mafia or anti-
Castro conspiracy have ever found is Oswald's alleged association
with David Ferrie in New Orleans during the summer of 1963. Ferrie
was a strange character who was violently anti-Kennedy and anti-
Communist. After a disease caused the loss of his body hair, he began
wearing a reddish mohair wig and fake eyebrows. He was also a
homosexual and had been fired from his job as an Eastern Airlines
pilot after he was charged with extortion and with molesting young
males. In 1963 he worked as a private investigator, both for the lawyer
of Carlos Marcello, the New Orleans Mafia boss, and for Guy Banister, another militant anti-Communist who ran a detective agency.
Both Banister and Ferrie had connections with anti-Castro groups.
On November 22, Ferrie was in a New Orleans courtroom with
Marcello and his lawyer.

The office of Banister's detective agency was in a building near the
coffee company where Oswald worked until mid-July. The building
had two entrances, and the address of the one around the corner from
Banister's office was 544 Camp Street. Anyone who has read a conspiracy book should be familiar with that address, because it was
stamped on some of Oswald's "Hands Off Cuba" leaflets.

So, the plot thickens. The conspiracists believe that Oswald's pro-
Castro activities in New Orleans were a scam being run by the anti-
Castroites Ferrie and Banister in order to discredit the Fair Play for
Cuba Committee. This is highly unlikely. Even if we knew nothing

about Oswald, the fact that his first pro-Castro demonstration occurred before he got to New Orleans would seem to rule that out. Although the owner of the Camp Street building denied that he ever rented space to the president's accused assassin, Oswald may have used an alias or an intermediary. (In a letter to Vincent Lee, he claimed that he had rented an office somewhere but was evicted on a pretext three days later.) However, I suspect that Oswald may have had some contact with Ferrie and perhaps with Banister as well, but I believe it had nothing to do with the events in Dallas—which, at that point, no one could have foreseen.

Oswald may have approached Ferrie or Banister, as he approached Carlos Bringuier, with a plausible cover story and with an eye to pursuing his own ends. It's possible that, after he lost his job at Reily's, he went to see Banister; working for a detective agency might have appealed to him.

The best evidence that Oswald knew Ferrie, and possibly Banister, comes from the testimony of several credible witnesses who told the Assassinations Committee that they saw Oswald in Clinton, Louisiana, during late August or early September with a man who looked like Ferrie and another man whom they identified as Clay Shaw, the businessman involved in the Garrison investigation. The second man was almost certainly not Shaw—but Shaw looked very much like Guy Banister. According to these witnesses, Oswald was first seen in nearby Jackson, where he asked a barber how he could get a job as an electrician at the local mental hospital. (Oswald had no training as an electrician.) The barber referred him to a state representative, who advised him to register as a voter to establish residency. Two secretaries said that Oswald applied for work at the hospital, and afterward he was seen standing in line at the Clinton voter registrar's office while Ferrie and the other man, presumably Banister, waited outside in a Cadillac. As it happened, blacks in the parish were conducting a voter registration drive that month, and there was a long wait. The registrar, Henry Palmer, testified that when it came his turn Oswald handed him a U.S. Navy ID card with his name and a New Orleans address on it, and Palmer told him he hadn't been in the area long enough to register.

Summers believes that Ferrie and Banister may have brought Oswald to Clinton as part of a U.S. intelligence scheme to discredit the civil rights movement. Just how Oswald could have discredited the movement by standing quietly in line isn't clear. The chronology suggests that the right question is not why this man identified as Oswald was at the registrar's office, but why he wanted to get a job at the East Louisiana State Hospital. It's conceivable that he wanted to get inside the hospital as an employee to photograph someone's psychiatric records for the detectives Banister and Ferrie. This interpretation is, of course, highly speculative, but if this was indeed Oswald, it might explain why Ferrie always denied knowing him in 1963, if in fact he did.

On the other hand, the proposition that Oswald was in Clinton rests entirely on the testimony of these witnesses who didn't come forward until 1967, during the Garrison investigation. If some of them misidentified Banister as Clay Shaw, they may have been mistaken about Oswald as well.

How can we be certain, even so, that Oswald wasn't working for American intelligence or a similar group all along? I return to the principle that, in order to be plausible, a theory must fit the available evidence into a reasonable chronology of events. As we have seen, Oswald was capable of playing a double role for his own purposes and of risking his life for his beliefs. This inner-directedness gives us no reason to think that he would have staked his life for the beliefs of anyone else. To argue, as some critics have, that Oswald was merely *posing* as a leftist from the time he was 16 until, literally, the day he died, one must unravel the story of his life presented in this book and attempt to reweave it into an entirely new pattern. I can't say that it is impossible to do so, but thus far it hasn't been done.

No event aroused more skepticism about the lone assassin theory than Jack Ruby's murder of Oswald. Immediately after his arrest, Ruby said that he shot Oswald because he had been upset by the assassination and wanted to spare Jacqueline Kennedy the ordeal of returning to Dallas to testify at Oswald's trial (as news reports had indicated that she would have to do). Ruby added, "I also want the world to know that Jews do have guts."[1]

To many, Ruby's professed grief looked suspicious. At the apartment of his sister, Eva Grant, a few hours after Kennedy's death, he telephoned numerous acquaintances to bemoan the assassination. He tried to eat supper but threw up in the bathroom. As he was leaving, Eva thought he looked "broken." He told her, "I never felt so bad in my life, even when Ma or Pa died." Several other people who talked with Ruby that day or the next remembered that he expressed concern for the president's wife and children, saying in one instance, "those poor people, those poor people." These sentiments may seem excessive, or phony, but they were not unusual.

Before the end of November the National Opinion Research Center completed a poll on the public's reactions to the assassination. In 1964 the Center reported:

> The majority of all respondents could not recall any other time in their lives when they had the same sort of feelings. . . . Of those who could think of such an occasion (47%) the majority referred to the death of a parent, close friend, or other relative. . . .
>
> The first reactions of nine out of ten Americans were sympathy for Mrs. Kennedy and the children and deep sorrow that "a strong young man had been killed at the height of his powers."

During the four days following the event, 68 percent of those interviewed were "very nervous and tense," 57 percent felt "dazed and numb," 43 percent "didn't feel like eating," 22 percent had upset stomachs. Many felt a need to talk to someone they knew, and the nation's telephone lines were clogged with calls. One person in nine hoped that Oswald would be "shot down or lynched."

This intense outpouring of emotion had little to do with politics. Clearly some psychological nerve had been touched. Perhaps these people had unconsciously identified with John Kennedy—at any rate, his death was a sharp reminder of personal mortality. Whatever the underlying cause, Ruby's reaction was within the mainstream.

But more important for our purposes is Ruby's remark that he wanted to prove "that Jews do have guts." This is the kind of statement that appears nonsensical at a distance but has a surprising relevance on closer inspection. It turns out that Ruby himself was a conspiracy theorist and that his crime, like Oswald's, was the result of a deadly interplay between his past and the accidental circumstances of the moment.

Born in Chicago in 1911 as Jacob Rubenstein, Ruby was the fifth child of an alcoholic father and a mentally ill, delusional mother. As a young boy, he was said to be "quick tempered" and "egocentric." Growing up in a ghetto surrounded by other ethnic groups, Ruby became a street fighter who reacted to anti-Semitic slurs with his fists. Before World War II, Ruby and his neighborhood friends disrupted several pro-Nazi rallies of the German-American Bund, "cracking a few heads" in the process. Although he took no other interest in politics, Ruby was described by an acquaintance as a "cuckoo nut" on the subject of patriotism; he cried openly on learning of President Roosevelt's death in 1945.

In 1947 Ruby moved to Dallas to help his divorced sister, Eva, manage a nightclub. Over the next decade Ruby got into numerous fistfights with his employees and unruly patrons. According to Buddy Turman, a prizefighter friend, he "picked his shots": his victims were often drunk, female, or otherwise unable to defend themselves. By the fall of 1963 Ruby was running two striptease joints and having financial problems. He was also taking Preludin diet pills, commonly known as "uppers."

On the morning of November 22 Jack Ruby noticed the black-bordered "Welcome Mr. Kennedy" page in the Dallas *Morning News.* He telephoned Eva to call her attention to it—he was annoyed that a message attacking the president bore a Jewish name, Bernard Weissman, as chairman of the sponsoring committee. At about 11 o'clock Ruby made his customary visit to the *Morning News* building to place weekend ads for his nightclubs. After he completed his business, a newspaper employee, John Newnam, saw him sitting at a desk leafing through the day's paper, "killing time, as he always did." Ruby made a comment criticizing the "lousy taste" of the anti-Kennedy advertisement. "Who is this Weissman?" he wanted to know. Privately he suspected that someone had used a false name "to make the Jews look bad." (Actually, Weissman was a young conservative who had recently moved to Dallas.)

Five minutes later, another employee ran into the office and said, "Kennedy's been shot." Newnam saw Ruby respond with a look of "stunned disbelief." Soon telephone calls came in from people canceling weekend advertising—a development that Ruby interpreted as a protest against the "Welcome Mr. Kennedy" page. A few minutes later he used an office phone to call Eva again—and put the receiver to Newnam's ear so that he could hear her anguished reaction to the shooting. Ruby later explained that he wanted Newnam to know that he and his sister were "emotionally disturbed [by the assassination] the same way as other people." It had never occurred to Newnam that they weren't, but Ruby was clearly worried that Weissman's untimely criticism of the president might provoke a backlash against other Jews.

Later that afternoon, Ruby checked the Dallas phone book: Weissman's name wasn't in it. Driving across town on November 23, Ruby noticed a billboard saying "Impeach Earl Warren" that listed a post office box number similar to the one given in the right-wing advertisement. Ruby wasn't sure who Earl Warren was, but he suspected a plot involving "the John Birch Society or the Communist Party or maybe a combination of both." After reaching his apartment, Ruby called Larry Crafard, an employee of his who had a Polaroid camera, picked Crafard up, and drove back to the sign and took pictures of it. Ruby's roommate, George Senator, went along. Ruby acted as though he had uncovered something important. Next the trio went to the Dallas Post Office, where Ruby tried unsuccessfully to find out who had rented the box indicated on the billboard. The men went to a nearby coffee shop, where Senator noticed that Ruby's voice sounded "different" and that "he had sort of a stare look in his eye."

When Ruby stopped by Sol's Turf Bar that afternoon, a patron, Frank Bellochio, began blaming Dallas for the assassination and pulled out a copy of the anti-Kennedy page as evidence. Ruby became "upset and loud" and said that he didn't believe there was such a person as Bernard Weissman, that the ad was the work of a group trying to create anti-Semitic feelings. An hour later Ruby was telling a friend that the black border was a "tipoff" that whoever placed the ad "knew the President was going to be assassinated." Thus, Ruby suspected a scheme to murder Kennedy and use the Jews as scapegoats.

After he shot Oswald the following morning, Ruby expected to get out of jail on bond and be interviewed by reporters as a hero. Instead, he found himself under suspicion of being involved in a plot to kill the president. Every aspect of his life was investigated, and reports of his past acquaintance with underworld figures made it appear that he was a Mafia hit man. Ruby assimilated this turn of events into the pattern that had already formed in his mind. He interpreted it as the work of the same people responsible for the Weissman advertisement.

For Ruby, the irony was nightmarish. His act was supposed to *absolve* the Jews, by removing any possible doubt about where their sympathies lay. But in his mind, it had done just the opposite. He now believed that he had unwittingly played into the conspirators' hands.

By the time Ruby testified to the Warren Commission in June 1964, his conspiracy theory was full-blown. As he imagined it, the John Birch Society had convinced President Johnson that he was involved in Kennedy's murder. Believing that, Johnson had "relinquished certain powers" to the organization, which was now beginning a widespread pogrom against American Jews. Speaking in his jail cell, Ruby insisted that he had shot Oswald on his own.

And I have never had the chance to tell that, to back it up, to prove it. Consequently, right at this moment I am being victimized as a part of a plot in the world's worst tragedy and crime.

The bewildered Warren listened as Ruby tried to explain this plot:

There is an organization here, Chief Justice Warren, if it takes my life at this moment to say it . . . there is a John Birch Society right now in activity. . . .

Unfortunately for me, [by my] giving the people the opportunity to get in power, because of the act I committed, [this] has put a lot of people in jeopardy with their lives.

Don't register with you, does it?
WARREN: No; I don't understand that.
RUBY: Would you rather I just delete what I said and just pretend nothing is going on?
WARREN: I would not indeed. I am only interested in what you want to tell this Commission.

Ruby also said that his sister and brothers were going to be killed. Although he sounded completely irrational, his explanation for the shooting was virtually the same one that he had given after his arrest. He mentioned his use of diet pills and suggested that this might have been a "stimulus" on the morning of November 24, when

suddenly I felt, which was so stupid, that I wanted to show my love for our faith, being of the Jewish faith . . . the emotional feeling came within me that someone owed this debt to our beloved President to save [Mrs. Kennedy] the ordeal of coming back. . . .

I drove past Main Street, past the [jail], and there was a crowd already gathered there. And I . . . took it for granted [that Oswald] had already been moved. . . . So my purpose was to go to the Western Union—my double purpose—but the thought of committing the act wasn't until I left my apartment. . . .

I realize it is a terrible thing I have done, and it was a stupid thing, but I just was carried away emotionally. . . . I had the gun in my right hip pocket, and impulsively, if that is the correct word here, I saw him, and that is all I can say. And I didn't care what happened to me.

Throughout the interview, Ruby returned to the plot against him, begging Warren to take him to Washington for a lie detector test.

I am as innocent regarding any conspiracy as any of you gentlemen in the room, and I don't want anything to be run over lightly. I want you to dig into it with any . . . question that might embarrass me, or anything that might bring up my background, which isn't so terribly spotted— I have never been a criminal. . . .

I am making a statement now that I may not live the next hour when I walk out of this room. . . . it is the most fantastic story you have ever heard in a lifetime. I did something out of the goodness of my heart.

Unfortunately, Chief Earl Warren, had you been around 5 or 6 months ago . . . and immediately the President would have gotten hold of my true story . . . a certain organization wouldn't have so completely formed now, so powerfully, to use me because I am of the Jewish extraction, Jewish faith, to commit the most dastardly crime that has ever been committed. . . . The Jewish people are being exterminated at this moment.

A few minutes later, Ruby said:

It may not be too late, whatever happens, if our President, Lyndon Johnson, knew the truth from me. . . . But he has been told, I am certain, that I was part of a plot to assassinate the President. . . . I have been used for a purpose, and there will be a certain tragic occurrence happening if you don't take my testimony and somehow vindicate me so my people don't suffer because of what I have done. . . . All I want is a lie detector test. . . . And then I want to leave this world. But I don't want my people to be blamed for something that is untrue, that they claim has happened.

Some conspiracy theorists have taken Ruby's remark "I have been used for a purpose" to mean that he was "used" to kill Oswald. Others think that he was speaking in a sort of code and that the "certain organization" he referred to was really the Mafia. For some reason, it is extremely difficult to take Ruby's testimony at face value. Suspicious of his motives, one tends to focus on isolated details and give them a sinister interpretation. One naturally feels that there is "more to it" and that one must probe beneath the surface to get at it. This is a symptom of conspiracy thinking, the same human malady that afflicted Ruby in a more virulent form.

But how can we be sure that Ruby wasn't faking mental illness in order to conceal his role in a plot? Consider the implications of that hypothesis. If Ruby's grief and delusions were sham, one must accept that prior to November 22 Ruby was persuaded to feign an obsession with the Weissman advertisement in order to legitimize the bizarre, puzzling explanation he would give after his arrest. Try to imagine a conspirator actually giving Ruby those instructions.

In 1965 Ruby was seen briefly on television after he left jail for a court appearance. As he walked along a corridor he was heard to say, "complete conspiracy . . . and the assassination too . . . if you knew the facts you would be amazed." Ruby's vision of the forces against him eventually grew to include President Johnson. In a letter from jail he wrote, ". . . they alone had planned the killing, by they I mean Johnson and the others." These disjointed comments, and others like them, have been offered in support of the very allegation Ruby desperately wanted to disprove. These writers have never considered the possibility that Ruby was talking about a *different* conspiracy—not one in which he silenced Oswald on orders, but one *that tried to make it look as if he had.*

In December 1966 Ruby was diagnosed as having terminal cancer; he died less than a month later. In a tape recording made two weeks before the end, Ruby reiterated that his shooting of Oswald was pure chance and that he acted alone, not as part of a conspiracy. Sol Dann, one of his attorneys, told the press, "Ruby did not want to live. His death was a merciful release."

18...Oswald's Game

IN large part, the assassination of President Kennedy was the tragic result of a steady accumulation of chance happenings, the elimination of any one of which might have spared Kennedy's life.

The chain of circumstance began in Oswald's childhood, when someone innocently handed him a political pamphlet that gave his anger and resentment a direction. Six years later, he failed in an attempt to sign away his citizenship, which meant that he would be able to go back to the United States in 1962. Less than a year after he returned, a bullet intended for General Walker missed. Then in September 1963, when he was trying to build a record to impress the Cubans, Castro's warning appeared and gave him a new target. Finally, after his trip to Cuba was blocked, a neighbor of a friend suggested a job at a school book warehouse.

Ultimately, these coincidences came to have a horrible significance, but only because they happened to a particular dangerous individual. The root cause of the assassination wasn't blind fate, but Oswald's sociopathic nature.

As a child, Oswald isolated himself from other people. Raised by a mother who was monstrously self-centered, he grew to resemble her. He came to feel as if there were a veil separating him from everyone else, a barrier that he preferred to remain intact. As Evelyn Strickman said, he withdrew into a solitary and detached existence in which he didn't have to obey any rules. Marguerite encouraged this tendency. Her constant defense of his rule-breaking fed his belief that he was a superior being who could do no wrong. Lee Oswald saw himself as an outsider, and he relished this role. (He would play it from youth onward, as Marxist Marine, American defector, Russian-speaking returnee.)

With no personal relationships to anchor him in everyday life, Oswald created "his own world." Robert noticed his "love of fantasy," recalling that his kid brother would listen to children's stories on the radio and hours later would still be pretending to be one of the characters. It would have been an innocent pastime, but Lee's daydreams included visions of power and violence.

Early on, his imagination drew him to the larger world reflected in news reports—an arena that must have seemed more meaningful, more *real,* than his daily existence. As Marguerite recalled, he would stop whatever he was doing to listen to the news, because he considered it important.

Edward Voebel's testimony reveals where his fantasy life was leading him. From local press reports, Oswald had gotten the idea of stealing a pistol. One can turn this incident and see Oswald's ambitions reflected in it. He wanted to imitate the robbers—who had defied authority and gotten away with it. The theft would be dangerous and therefore exciting. Oswald made plans, obtaining a glass cutter and toy gun—the gun would be left in place of the stolen weapon, as a subterfuge. By outwitting his adversaries, he would assert his power over them.

Oswald's tactics and goals changed in the years ahead, but his psychological motivations did not. It would be for similar reasons that he tried to deceive Sylvia Odio, in another scheme inspired by a news report. In fact, the patterns seen in his robbery plan would be repeated in the three most dramatic episodes in his life. The defection, his attack on Walker, and the president's murder were all daring acts that allowed him to strike back at authority and put himself in control. In a literal sense, Oswald lived in his fantasies—he acted them out. As George de Mohrenschildt put it, he played with his life.

A few months after Voebel lost contact with him, Oswald discovered Karl Marx. He believed that Marxism gave him the "key" to his environment on an ideological level. But the system had a subconscious appeal. By redefining himself as the victim of an evil society, defiance of authority suddenly became not only legitimate, but heroic. He began thinking of himself as an idealist who acted on lofty principles. He immediately wanted to join the Communist party, a group of political outsiders, and achieve great things. By the time Kerry Thornley met him, Oswald saw Marxism as his religion, a means of justifying his life and obtaining a place in history.

After converting to Marxism, Oswald's conscious motives were political. He considered his defection to be a courageous protest against American military imperialism. His explanation for attacking Walker was also ideological: he would be eliminating a potential Hitler, thereby saving lives. Each time, he expected to be recognized as a fighter for justice. But his inner compulsions were the same as they had been. On learning that the Walker bullet had missed, he was disappointed, but Marina believed that he was also pleased "with the clever fellow he was" in getting away with the attempt. He had put one over on the police.

Strip away the politics, and Oswald's antisocial personality is evident. He resembles the typical St. Elizabeths criminal seeking power, control, and excitement. At Youth House he had been diagnosed as a "passive-aggressive" individual, someone whose outward compliance masked deep anger. This characteristic shows up in his political writings, where Oswald cast himself as a silent observer who waited in "stoical readiness" for the opportune moment to act.

This complex of motivations reverberated in the Kennedy assassination. It would be a violent protest against American imperialism toward Cuba and a retaliation for the plots against Castro. But beneath Oswald's rationalizations, there was a continuing self-aggrandizement and a desire for vengeance that came from something *other* than politics.

Each of these incidents was also derived, in some way, from Oswald's reading of press reports. His ideas were never entirely original. Oswald's defection was preceded by that of Guy Burgess and Donald Maclean, a famous case that Oswald alluded to in a conversation with

Nelson Delgado. It wasn't so much that news stories "put ideas in his head." It was almost the other way around: Oswald's grandiose self-image drove him to project himself onto the world stage. The international political scene was the reality that mattered to him, and he was determined to make his mark on it.

As each of his efforts was frustrated, Oswald's schemes became progressively more violent. His defection resulted in a week's publicity and two and a half years of obscurity. The Walker incident gained only a brief, anonymous attention. Then his plan to reach Cuba was thwarted by red tape—moreover, the Cubans didn't take him seriously. His repeated attempts to join a revolutionary movement had failed, leaving him as isolated and unrecognized as ever.[1]

After Oswald returned to Dallas in October 1963, events continued to narrow his path. His perception of the plots against Castro had already led him to threaten President Kennedy's life on two occasions. On October 19th, a double feature about assassinations reminded him of "the actual situation" that existed in Cuba. The following evening his preoccupation was such that he didn't think to ask about the birth of his second child.

Having failed to get Russian visas, Oswald was stranded in Dallas. He made plans to renew his political activities. By "reading between the lines" of leftist newspapers, he would determine which line to follow. But in November there were new developments. His visit to the Soviet Embassy in Mexico had understandably reawakened the FBI's interest in him. Cornered, feeling unjustly persecuted, Oswald wrote a note to Hosty and a letter to the Soviets in Washington protesting the FBI attention. At this juncture, he learned that the president's motorcade would pass the building where he worked.

It must have seemed to him that fate had spoken. All his past life was a rehearsal for the moment when he decided to act out his violent fantasies against President Kennedy. After his arrest, Oswald appeared calm, introspective, at peace with himself. He behaved as if he were now in control—as, in a real sense, he was, until Jack Ruby's own obsessions intervened. At long last, Oswald had achieved what he had always wanted: vengeance, power, and even an infamous immortality.

The assassination of John Kennedy was neither an act of random violence nor a conspiracy. It was carried out as a result of Oswald's character and background interacting with circumstance. It's likely that had there been no plots against Castro, Oswald would have eventually killed someone, but it would not have been President Kennedy. Castro's warning had simply deflected his aim.

A Selected Bibliography

BOOKS

Anson, Robert Sam. *"They've Killed the President!"* New York: Bantam Books, 1975.
Becker, Ernest. *Escape from Evil.* New York: Free Press, 1975.
Belin, David W. *November 22, 1963: You Are the Jury.* New York: Quadrangle Books, 1973.
Bishop, Jim *The Day Kennedy Was Shot.* New York: Funk & Wagnalls, 1968.
Blakey, G. Robert, and Richard N. Billings. *The Plot to Kill the President.* New York: Times Books, 1981.
Brener, Milton E. *The Garrison Case: A Study in the Abuse of Power.* New York: Clarkson N. Potter, 1969.
Damore, Leo. *The Cape Cod Years of John Fitzgerald Kennedy.* Englewood Cliffs, N.J.: Prentice-Hall, 1967.
De Bono, Edward. *The Mechanism of Mind.* New York: Simon and Schuster, 1969.
De Gramont, Sanche. *The Secret War.* New York: Dell, 1963.
Eddowes, Michael. *The Oswald File.* New York: Ace, 1978.
Epstein, Edward Jay. *Inquest: The Warren Commission and the Establishment of Truth.* New York: Viking, 1966.
———. *Counterplot.* New York: Viking, 1969.
———. *Legend: The Secret World of Lee Harvey Oswald.* New York: Reader's Digest Press/McGraw-Hill, 1978.
Halperin, Maurice. *The Rise and Decline of Fidel Castro.* Berkeley: University of California Press, 1972.
Hartogs, Renatus, and Lucy Freeman. *The Two Assassins.* New York: Zebra Books/Kensington, 1976.

Henderson, Bruce, and Sam Summerlin. *1:33*. New York: Cowles, 1968.
Kantor, Seth. *The Ruby Cover-up*. New York: Zebra Books/Kensington, 1978.
Kurtz, Michael L. *Crime of the Century: The Kennedy Assassination from a Historian's Perspective*. Knoxville: University of Tennessee Press, 1982.
Lane, Mark. *Rush to Judgment*. New York: Holt, Rinehart & Winston, 1966.
Lifton, David S. *Best Evidence: Disguise and Deception in the Assassination of John F. Kennedy*. New York: Dell, 1982.
Lockwood, Lee. *Castro's Cuba, Cuba's Fidel*. New York: Macmillan, 1967.
Manchester, William. *The Death of a President: November 20–25, 1963*. New York: Harper & Row, 1967.
Mankiewicz, Frank, and Kirby Jones. *With Fidel: A Portrait of Castro and Cuba*. Chicago: Playboy Press, 1975.
Martin, David C. *Wilderness of Mirrors*. New York: Ballantine Books, 1980.
McMillan, Priscilla Johnson. *Marina and Lee*. New York: Harper & Row, 1978.
Meagher, Sylvia. *Accessories after the Fact: The Warren Commission, the Authorities, and the Report*. New York: Vintage, 1976.
Morrow, Robert D. *Betrayal*. New York: Warner Books, 1976.
Navasky, Victor S. *Naming Names*. New York: Viking, 1980.
Newman, Albert H. *The Assassination of John F. Kennedy: The Reasons Why*. New York: Clarkson N. Potter, 1970.
Nizer, Louis. *The Implosion Conspiracy*. New York: Doubleday, 1973.
Oswald, Robert L., with Myrick and Barbara Land. *Lee: A Portrait of Lee Harvey Oswald*. New York: Coward-McCann, 1967.
Schlesinger, Arthur M., Jr. *Robert Kennedy and His Times*. Boston: Houghton Mifflin, 1978.
Stafford, Jean. *A Mother in History: Mrs. Marguerite Oswald*. New York: Farrar, Straus & Giroux, 1966.
Summers, Anthony. *Conspiracy*. New York: McGraw-Hill, 1980.
Warren, Earl. *The Memoirs of Earl Warren*. New York: Doubleday, 1977.
Wyden, Peter. *Bay of Pigs*. New York: Simon and Schuster, 1979.
Yochelson, Samuel, and Stanton E. Samenow. *The Criminal Personality*. Volume I: *A Profile for Change*. New York: Jason Aronson, 1976.

PUBLISHED ARTICLES

Anson, Robert Sam. "Congress and the JFK Riddle." *New Times* March 19, 1976.
Bergquist, Laura. "My Curious Row with Castro." *Look* December 12, 1967.
Branch, Taylor, and George Crile III. "The Kennedy Vendetta." *Harper's* August 1975.
Butler, Ed. "The Great Assassin Puzzle." *The Westwood Village Square* Summer 1968.

Committee on Ballistic Acoustics, National Research Council. "Reexamination of Acoustic Evidence in the Kennedy Assassination." *Science* October 8, 1982.
Daniel, Jean. "When Castro Heard the News." *The New Republic* December 7, 1963.
Janos, Leo. "The Last Days of the President: LBJ in Retirement." *Atlantic* July 1973.
O'Toole, George, and Paul Hoch. "Dallas: The Cuban Connection." *The Saturday Evening Post* March 1976.
Restak, Richard. "Assassin!" *Science Digest* December 1981.
Rodgers, Joann Ellison. "The Malleable Memory of Eyewitnesses." *Science 82* June 1982.
Schorr, Daniel. "The Assassins." *The New York Review of Books* October 13, 1977.

NEWSPAPERS AND NEWSWEEKLIES

The Dallas *Morning News,* Dallas, Texas, April, October, and November 1963, selected issues.
The Militant, December 1962–November 1963. Published in New York.
New Orleans *Times-Picayune,* April–September 1963.
Time, August 1962–November 1963, selected issues.
The Worker, April–June 1953 (when it was called *The Daily Worker*), selected issues. August 1962–November 1963. Published in New York.

OFFICIAL REPORTS

The Final Assassinations Report: Report of the Select Committee on Assassinations, U.S. House of Representatives. (New York: Bantam, 1979).
Hearings Before the President's Commission on the Assassination of President Kennedy. Testimony of witnesses, Vols. I–XV, and published exhibits, Vols. XVI–XXVI, (Washington, D.C.: U.S. Government Printing Office, 1964).
Report of the President's Commission on the Assassination of President Kennedy. (Washington, D.C.: U.S. Government Printing Office, 1964).
U.S., Congress, House, Select Committee on Assassinations, *Investigation of the Assassination of John F. Kennedy,* Hearings and Appendices, 95th Cong., 2nd sess., (Washington, D.C.: U.S. Government Printing Office, 1979), Volumes I–XII, Hearing #Y4.As7;K38.
U.S., Congress, Senate, *Alleged Assassination Plots involving Foreign Leaders: An Interim Report of the Select Committee to Study Governmental Operations with Respect to Intelligence Activities,* 94th Cong., 1st sess., (Washington, D.C.: U.S. Government Printing Office, 1975), S. Rept. 94–465, Serial Set # 13098-8.

U.S., Congress, Senate, *The Investigation of the Assassination of President Kennedy: Performance of the Intelligence Agencies, Book V. Final Report of the Select Committee to Study Governmental Operations with Respect to Intelligence Activities,* 94th Cong., 2nd sess., (Washington, D.C.: U.S. Government Printing Office, 1976), S. Rept. 94-755, Serial Set #13133-7.

Notes

The following abbreviations are used in citing official reports:

Report of the President's Commission (Warren Report)	WR
The published hearings and exhibits of the Warren Commission	Volume and page number only—e.g., II, 20
The final report of the Select Committee on Assassinations (House Assassinations Committee)	HACR
The hearings and appendices of the House Assassinations Committee	HACH (followed by volume and page number)
The interim report of the Church committee	Interim
The final report of the Church committee, Book V	Book V

INTRODUCTION

Page
14. Mrs. Kennedy's reaction: Manchester, 407.
Rifle ordered by Oswald: WR, 118–121.

14–15. Murder weapon in hand; "It's all over now": WR, 171, 178.

15. Wedding ring left behind: WR, 421.
 Warren Commission on motive: WR, 423–424, 22–23.
16. Butler on Oswald: "The Great Assassin Puzzle," 23, 24–28.
18–19. Ruby's testimony: Lane, 243, 244–245; V, 198–199, 210–212.
19. Lie detector test results: WR, 809–816.
20. Stuckey on Oswald: XI, 170–171.
22. President Johnson's suspicions: Janos, "Last Days of the President," 39;
 Means, King Features Syndicate column, April 24, 1975 (quoted by
 Schorr, "The Assassins," 22).
 Schorr on Oswald's threat: "The Assassins," 20–22.
23–24. Liebeler on Castro's warning: Lifton, 57; memo of September 16, 1964,
 from Liebeler to Rankin, "Re: Quote from New Orleans *Times-Picayune*
 of September 9, 1963, concerning Fidel Castro's speech," National Archives, Washington, D.C.
24. Hoover's letter: Schorr, "The Assassins," 21; letter dated June 17, 1964,
 from Hoover to Rankin (portions deleted), National Archives.
 Commission on Oswald's trip to Mexico: WR, 308.
 Slawson and Hoover's letter: Schorr, "The Assassins," 21.
24–25. CIA plots withheld from Commission: Book V, 5–6, 7.

CHAPTER 1. A MOST UNUSUAL DEFECTOR

29. Cape Cod meeting: Damore, 165.
 Oswald's activities in Moscow: WR, 690–693, 259–262; XVI, 96.
30. Handwritten note: WR, 261, 262.

Note 1: Oswald had a learning disability (dyslexia), which he largely over-
came but which left him a poor speller (XXVI, 812–817). In quoting Oswald's
writings throughout the book, I have corrected his spelling and minor punctu-
ation errors for the sake of clarity.

 Understood legal procedure: WR, 693, 262.
 "Wound up," "rehearsing for a long time": Epstein, *Legend,* 95.
31. Previous defector: V, 267.
 "Lonesome man," quizzed on Marxist theory: V, 290.
 Snyder's impressions: V, 272, 290; XVIII, 98, 100, 103.
 Offered military information to Soviets: XVIII, 98, 100; V, 265.
32. Tone of meeting: McMillan, 82.
 Snyder to State Department: WR, 748; XVIII, 98–103; Epstein, *Legend,*
 96.

Refused phone calls: Oswald, 105.
Robert Oswald's reaction: Ibid., 98–99.

33. Letter to American ambassador: WR, 262, 263.
November 8 letter to Robert: WR, 694–695.

33–35. Mosby interview and her reactions: XXII, 703–705; XXVI, 90; Epstein, *Legend*, 98–99, 292 n. 18; WR, 388, 695–696.

34.

Note 2: After a controversial trial in 1951, Julius and Ethel Rosenberg were convicted of conspiracy to commit wartime espionage and sentenced to death. They had been accused of transmitting atomic bomb secrets to the Russians. After several legal appeals were denied and President Dwight D. Eisenhower refused to commute their sentences to life imprisonment, they were executed in New York's Sing Sing prison on June 19, 1953. During the last months of their imprisonment, a Save the Rosenbergs campaign was mounted by leftist groups and others who felt their conviction, and especially the death sentence, was unjust.

35–36. Priscilla Johnson and Kennedy: McMillan, 3–4.

36–38. Johnson's interview of Oswald and her impressions: McMillan, 5, 83–85; XI, 448–449, 453; XX, 292–305 *passim;* HACR, 270.

38 Second letter to Robert: XVI, 815–822; WR, 391–392.

39. Third letter to Robert, Oswald sent to Minsk: WR, 697.

CHAPTER 2. MARGUERITE'S SON

(Except where noted, minor details of Oswald's early years are taken from the Warren Report, 377, 383, 669–679.)

41. Father's death and funeral: I, 225, 268; VIII, 47; XXI, 491, 505.
"The son of an insurance salesman": WR, 395; XVI, 285.

42. Marguerite's traits in Lee: Oswald, 23, 48.
Lillian on Marguerite: VIII, 98.
Marguerite's comments: Stafford, 30.
Insurance policy: VIII, 47.
Sneaking out of house: Oswald, 33.

43. Marguerite on babysitters: I, 254–255.
Oswald brothers at orphanage: Oswald, 34–35; I, 271; WR, 671.
Pic on Ekdahl: XI, 21.
Ekdahl marriage: WR, 672–673.

43–44. Marguerite and other woman: I, 250–251.

45. Robert on Lee's imagination and love of intrigue: Oswald, 46–47.
Ekdahl divorce: I, 251–252; XI, 29; Oswald, 39.
Evans on Marguerite and Lee: VIII, 50–51.

45–46. Marguerite on Lee and neighbor boy: Stafford, 51–52.

46. Oswald solitary: WR, 675; VIII, 52, 119, 121–122.
Marguerite on Lee's childhood: I, 225.
"Back down in lower class": WR, 674.
Robert on "burden": Oswald, 39, 42.
Marguerite's false affidavit: WR, 378.
Pic's comments on Marguerite: XI, 73–74, 75.
Pic's resentment and enlistment: Oswald, 42; WR, 378, 675.
Letters to Pic: XXI, 73, 74, 109–110.
Robert's enlistment and Lee's plans: Oswald, 49.

48. Move to New York: Oswald, 50; WR, 675.
Pic's impressions of Lee: XI, 39; Oswald, 51.
Mrs. Pic's recollections: XXII, 687.

48–49. Pic and Marguerite on knife incident: XI, 38, 40; I, 226–227.

49. Oswald's truancy and comments: XIX, 315, 189; VIII, 210.

50. Truancy court and hearing: XIX, 309.
Sokolow's report: WR, 381.

50–52. Evelyn Strickman's report: XXI, 485–509.

53. Strickman on Marguerite: XXI, 507.

54. Hartogs on Oswald: VIII, 214; VII, 223–224; Hartogs and Freeman,
318–320; XIX, 315, 317 (recommendation).
Oswalds' promise to cooperate: XIX, 317.
Canvass by The Worker's supporters: The Worker, May 21, 1953.

55. Mother's Day leafletting: The Worker, May 8, 1953.
The Worker on Rosenbergs as victims: Front-page articles, June 1 and June
21, 1953.
Oswald's view of people as cardboard figures: McMillan, 482 (quoting
Michael Paine).

56. "The key to my environment": XX, 300.

57. Thornley on Oswald's conviction: WR, 388.
Rosenberg and Mooney pamphlet: Nizer, 16.

58. Robert's visit: Oswald, 61–62; I, 301–302, 308–310.
Pic on psychiatrist: XI, 42, 43–44.
Teacher's report: XIX, 319.

59. Continuation of parole and Big Brothers: WR, 678–679; XIX, 321.

CHAPTER 3. DROPPING OUT, JOINING UP

61. Marguerite on averting a "tragedy": XXI, 83.
Oswald quiet and studious, read encyclopedias: VIII, 51, 55, 62, 63, 178.

61–62. Lillian's recollections: VIII, 124–125.

62. Bus incident: Oswald, 68; WR, 383; VIII, 15, 124, 159, 174.
Move to French Quarter: WR, 680.
Voebel's testimony: VIII, 7, 9–10.
Plans "military service": WR, 679.

62–63. Civil Air Patrol, Ferrie: WR, 679; VIII, 14; Oswald, 69.
Statements to Mosby: XXII, 703.
Marguerite's knowledge of Marxist books: I, 198.
Letter to school authorities, false affidavit: WR, 680, 681.

64. McBride's testimony: WR, 384; XXII, 710–711.
Eastland hearings and his comment: New Orleans *Times-Picayune,* April 6, 1956; *New York Times,* April 23, 1956, 40, and April 25, 25.

64–65. Wulf's testimony: WR, 384; VIII, 18–21.

65.

Note 1: As McBride recalled it, Oswald wanted them to join the Communist party to "take advantage of their social functions." But since neither Oswald nor the Party was known to be interested in "social functions," it's likely that McBride mistook his use of the word "socialist" for "social."

"I Led Three Lives": Oswald, 47; I, 200.
Weinstein and others on the typical assassin: Restak, "Assassin!" 80–82.

66. Yochelson and Samenow: For a summary of the book, see *Science,* February 3, 1978, 511–514; *Newsweek,* February 27, 1978, 91.
Samenow's comments, "wraps himself in . . . secrecy," and "sees himself as unique": Interview on "Good Morning America," ABC-TV, February 28, 1978.

67. "The criminal believes he has been wronged": Yochelson and Samenow, 488.
"Although he had broken the law": Ibid., 438.
"Although he may forcefully present himself": Ibid., 463.

68. Study rejected by many: *Science,* February 3, 1978.
Rode bike, visited museums: WR, 679; VIII, 125.
Tried to interest classmate in Marxism: VIII, 81.
B football team, Robert's comment: VIII, 83; Oswald, 56.

68–69. Letter to Socialist party: WR, 681; XI, 210.

69.

Note 2: Oswald's letter was discovered in 1964 at the Duke University library by an employee who was setting up a chronological file of a large consignment of Socialist party papers that had been turned over to the library in January 1959 (letter to the author from Virginia Gray, Assistant Curator of the William R. Perkins Library at Duke, February 27, 1970).

CHAPTER 4. THE MARXIST MARINE

71. Warren Report critics on enlistment: Summers, 143.
Robert and Pic on enlistment: Oswald, 49, 57; WR, 384.
Oswald's explanation: De Mohrenschildt manuscript, HACH, XII, 82; II, 399.
Basic training, reading and aviation scores: WR, 681–683.

71–72. Allen R. Felde's recollection: XXIII, 797.

72. U-2s at Atsugi seen by radar crew, briefings: Epstein, *Legend,* 55, 279–280 n. 1. (In the late 1970s Epstein interviewed dozens of the men who had served with Oswald in the Marines.)
Bristling at young officers: Epstein, *Legend,* 68.
Powers on Oswald: VIII, 288.
Bar girls: Epstein, *Legend,* 70–71.

72–73. Gunshotwoundandcourt-martial:Ibid.,72–73;WR,683;VIII,319–320.

73. Second court-martial: WR, 684; Epstein, *Legend,* 78–79.
Comment on getting out of brig: Epstein, *Legend,* 79.
Claimed met Communists in Japan: IX, 242–243; XI, 172–173.
Began studying Russian: WR, 684.

74. Guard duty incident: Epstein, *Legend,* 81–82; WR, 684.
Radar crew: WR, 684.
Donovan's comments on Oswald: VIII, 290–293, 297, 295, 293.

74–75. Delgado on officer-baiting: VIII, 265.

75. "Pursue Russian": VIII, 297.
Pro-Russian behavior: VIII, 322, 323, 315–316.
Subscriptions to Russian paper and *Worker:* VIII, 323, 315, 320, 242.
Critics on pro-Russian behavior: Anson, 158; Summers, 149.

75–76. Donovan on Oswald's politics: WR, 686.

76. Captain Block: Interview with Epstein reported in *Legend,* 86.
"Unjustly put upon": XI, 100.
Delgado on helping Castro: VIII, 233.
Exile raids on Dominican Republic, other countries: Halperin, 320–321.

Morgan's background: Epstein, *Legend*, 88, 285–286 n. 2.
Delgado on Morgan and leading expeditions: VIII, 240.
"Do away with Trujillo": VIII, 241.
Learning Spanish: WR, 687; VIII, 241.

77. Oswald on Cuban purges: VIII, 240, 243, 255.
"Be part of revolutionary movement": VIII, 241.
Contacted Cuban consulate?: VIII, 241–243.
Oswald on religion, *Das Kapital,* and *Animal Farm:* VIII, 262, 244, 255.

77–78. Delgado on Oswald's marksmanship: VIII, 235.

78. Rifle scores: WR, 681–682; *Time,* November 24, 1975, 37 (see also I, 233).
Thornley on Oswald: XI, 96, 87, 91–93, 97–98.

79. Extinction without meaning, "no wonder men go into a rage": Navasky, 426, 422; Becker, 64, 141.

80. "Come the revolution": XI, 94–95.

CHAPTER 5. THE DEFECTION

81. Commitment to Reserves: WR, 688–689; Epstein, *Legend,* 89.
Equivalency exam, college application: WR, 687; XVI, 621, 625.
Robert on cover story: Oswald, 99.

82. Oswald's trips to L.A.: VIII, 241, 251.
Extradition treaties, defection route: VIII, 260–261.
Oswald denies plan to go to Cuba: Epstein, *Legend,* 89; VIII, 244.
Letter to Robert, Marguerite's injury: Oswald, 93–94.
Letter to Marguerite: XVI, 581–582.
Marguerite's affidavits, Lee's discharge: WR, 688; HACR, 281–282.

83. Application for passport: XXII, 78.
Promise not to divulge secrets: Epstein, *Legend,* 90–91.
Claims involvement in "export": I, 201–202, 212; Oswald, 95; WR, 689.
Farewell letter to Marguerite: WR, 690.
On board the *Marion Lykes:* WR, 690; XI, 113, 117, Epstein, *Legend,* 92–93.

84. Arrival and departure at Southampton: WR, 690; XVIII, 162; XXVI, 32.

Note 1: Oswald evidently registered at a Helsinki hotel on October 10. However, the only direct flight between London and Helsinki that day landed at 11:33 P.M., too late to reach the hotel before midnight. Therefore, some critics believe that Oswald must have been flown to Finland by U.S. intelligence. (Ironically, the discrepancy they cite was first pointed out to the Warren Commission by the CIA's Richard Helms.) Oswald may have taken an *indirect* flight to Helsinki, or the hotel records may be wrong.

Moscow activities and "apparent suicide attempt": WR, 691–692; XVI, 94.
Hospital records: XVIII, 468; WR, 692.
Interviewed by new officials: XVI, 96.

85. Johnson on Soviets' suspicion: XX, 293.
Asked for credentials: XVI, 96.
Told to "go home": XVI, 94.
Embassy lost track of him: XVIII, 156, 120.
Suspicion of questioning by KGB: Epstein, *Legend*, 295 n. 4; Blakey and
Billings, 123.
Low security clearance: XXIII, 796; XVIII, 116.
Access to confidential information: VIII, 298.

86. Scientist defector and *Air Review* photograph: De Gramont, 354–355,
258.
"Will talk to a Marine about . . . drill": Dave Murphy, former head of CIA
Soviet operations in Berlin, quoted by Martin, 104, 157–158.
Application to Patrice Lumumba University, desire for education: WR,
705; McMillan, 104, 123–124; HACH, II, 217–218.
Thornley on Oswald's expectations: XI, 98.

86–87. Other defectors' work assignments: De Gramont, 349, 353.

87. "Serves him right": V, 294.
Given apartment and stipend: WR, 697, 698.
Disliked manual work: XVIII, 430; IX, 136; McMillan, 104.
First U.S. plans to assassinate Castro: Interim, 74, 80.
1961 State of the Union message: Quoted in Blakey and Billings, 136.

88. House of Representatives resolution: Ibid., 137.
Church on "rogue elephant": Baltimore *Sun*, July 16, 1975.
Church committee's conclusion: Interim, 6–7.
"Nailing Jello to a wall": Walter Mondale, quoted in the *New York Times*,
October 5, 1975.
Criticism of CIA and administration officials: Interim, 7.

89. Robert Kennedy briefing, Houston's comment: Ibid., 132–133.
Notes of November 4 meeting: Schlesinger, 476.
November 16 speech, MONGOOSE authorization and purpose: Interim,
139, 142.

89–90. January 19 meeting notes: Ibid., 141.

90. Helms testimony: Ibid., 149, 150.
Pressure from administration, McNamara's comment: Ibid., 159–160, 157–
158.
Smathers testimony: Ibid., 325–326.

91. Kennedy's habit to question: McMillan, 4.
Dinner party comment on Cuba: Interim, 326.

Tad Szulc interview: Ibid., 324–325.
Board of National Estimates conclusion: Ibid., 325, 136–137.
91–92. Becket situation and Mathias–Helms exchange: Ibid., 316, 149.
92. Date of first known plot: Ibid., 73.

CHAPTER 6. GETTING OUT

93. Letter to U.S. Embassy: WR, 752; XVI, 685.
Snyder's reply: XVIII, 135.
Dispatch to State Department: XVIII, 133–134.
State Department reply: XVIII, 136.
Fear of being arrested: McMillan, 126.

94. March 12 letter: XVI, 702–704.
Snyder's reply: XXII, 33–34.
First meetings with Marina: McMillan, 72–75, 93–94.
Conversation with Marina's relatives: Ibid., 95.
Marina's attraction to Oswald: Ibid., 96, 101.
"Fell in love with the man": HACH, XII, 375.
Pechorin as Marina's ideal: McMillan, 38–39, 584 n. 1.

95. April 18 meeting and marriage: Ibid., 97–98, 107.
Proposal to Ella German: WR, 699, 704.
Lies during courtship and Marina's reaction: McMillan, 97, 142.

96. "I'd love the danger": Ibid., 116.
Reaction to Bay of Pigs, comments on Castro: Ibid., 157; I, 24.
Cuban students and Oswald's view of Cuba: McMillan, 157; IX, 370.
May 16 letter: XVI, 705–708.
Letter to Robert: XVI, 826.
Letter to Marguerite: WR, 705.

97. May 31 letter to Robert: XVI, 828–829.
Fear of arrest, comment to Marina: McMillan, 127, 133.
Appearance at embassy, phone call to Marina: Ibid., 128, 129.
Embassy questioning of Oswald: XVIII, 137–138; XI, 200.

98. Warren Report on Oswald's responses: WR, 706.
Snyder on Oswald's anxiety about imprisonment and new attitude: XVIII, 138–139.

99. Marina's reaction to Snyder's comment: McMillan, 134, 591 n. 13.
Oswald's "Historic Diary": XVI, 94–105.

Note 1: Marina has said that she first saw her husband working on his diary in mid-July 1961, just after they returned from the American Embassy (McMillan, 144). Her recollection matches internal evidence in the diary. For instance, in describing his initial visit to the embassy in an October 1959 entry,

Oswald referred to "Richard Snyder, American Head Consular in Moscow at that time" and to his assistant, "(now *Head* Consular) McVickers [sic]" (XVI, 96). McVickar didn't take over from Snyder until July 1961 (V, 306) and left Moscow that September (V, 300; XVIII, 154). Thus the entry reflected the situation that existed only between those two dates.

"Future readers in mind": WR, 259, 691.
January 1961 entry and Report's conclusion: WR, 394–395.

101. Suggestion that Oswald return before Marina and his response: XXII, 90; XVI, 717–718.
"If it hadn't been for you" and Marina's reply: McMillan, 170.
Marguerite on discharge change: WR, 710.
January 30 letter to Robert: XVI, 865–867.

101–102. Letter to John Connally: WR, 710.

102. February 15 letter: XVI, 870–871.

102–103. Powers's trial and defense attorney's statements: De Gramont, 282.

103. Second letter to Robert mentioning Powers: XVI, 875.
Writing on board *Maasdam:* XVI, 110–120; McMillan, 194–195.

103–104. List of questions and answers: XVI, 436–439; WR, 399.

CHAPTER 7. HOMECOMING

105. Newspaper article on Oswald: IV, 415.
Oswalds' arrival and caution to brother: Oswald, 114–115.
Letter from *Fort Worth Press* writer: FBI document 102u, No. 2, National Archives.
Marina's first experiences in U.S.: Oswald, 118–119; XI, 53.
Oswald's complaints about Marina: III, 128; VIII, 135; II, 305.
106. Meeting with Peter Gregory: WR, 714.
Fluency in Russian: IX, 226, 259.
FBI interviewed defectors for CIA: HACR, 264–265.

Note 1: There is no evidence that the CIA itself ever debriefed Oswald. To investigate this possibility, the Assassinations Committee "reviewed the files of 22 other defectors to the Soviet Union (from an original list of 380 [sic]) who were born in America and appeared to have returned to the United States between 1958 and 1963. Of these 22 individuals, only 4 were interviewed at any time by the CIA. . . . Based on this file review, it appeared to the Committee that, in fact, the CIA did not contact returning defectors in 1962 as a matter of standard operating procedure" (HACR, 264–265).

Fain's interview and report: IV, 415–416, 422, 418.
Refused to take lie detector test: Book V, 88.

Job and apartment: WR, 715; IX, 226.
Subscription to *The Worker:* XXII, 271–272; Newman, 239–240.
Letter to Socialist Workers party: X, 113.

107. Wrote to Fair Play for Cuba Committee: XXIV, 341; Newman, 39.
August 16 FBI interview, Marina's recollections: I, 20; Book V, 88.
FBI's concern: Book V, 89; V, 105.
"Extreme allergy to FBI": IX, 458.
Refusal to give Robert his home address: XVI, 887; IV, 422; Newman, 242,
320; Oswald, 127.
"Nervous and irritable": I, 32, 49.
Fain closes case: V, 5.

Note 2: The Justice Department didn't prosecute Oswald for revealing
military information because the only evidence against him was his own
statement to Richard Snyder—a statement Oswald later retracted when he
was questioned by Snyder and by the FBI (HACR, 266–267).

Émigrés' desire to meet Oswalds: IX, 236, 267; VIII, 350–351.

107–108. Meeting Bouhe and Meller, Bouhe's comments: VIII, 358, 355, 360–
361, 371–372.

108. Bouhe at Oswald apartment: VIII, 384, 371
Meller's impressions: VIII, 382, 381, 384.
Refusal to let Marina learn English: II, 310; IX, 310, 357.

108–109. Paul Gregory and the Oswalds: IX, 145, 144, 155 157, 148; McMillan,
239; XXIII, 407.

109. John and Elena Hall: McMillan, 247; VIII, 407–408, 411, 409, 413, 402.

109–110. Oswald on émigrés: IX, 239, 250; I, 10.

110. De Mohrenschildt's background and personality: WR, 283; IX, 175, 181,
183–184, 268; VIII, 377; HACH, XII, 53, 56.
"Leftwing enthusiast": II, 327; IX, 266; X, 12.
Relationship with Oswald: IX, 277, 266; XXII, 783.
De Mohrenschildt's testimony: IX, 243, 241, 267.
"Looking for utopia": IX, 246, 312.

110–111. Oswald's political writings: XVI, 424, 426–427, 433–434, 436.

111. De Mohrenschildt manuscript, "a seeker for justice": HACH, XII, 81.

111–112. Oswald on defection and Russia: Ibid., 91, 86, 103.

112. On integration: Ibid., 127, 119–120, 133.
On world politics: Ibid., 121, 307.
On Hoover: Ibid., 121.
On death: Ibid., 151, 93.
On Marina and de Mohrenschildt's agreement: Ibid., 121, 261.

113. "Coup d'etat": Ibid., 147.
   On President Kennedy: Ibid., 146–147.
   Conversations on being a revolutionary and ideology: Ibid., 81, 144–145.
   Oswald "an idealistic Marxist": VIII, 436.

114. Oswald on Walker and Marines: I, 111.
   Walker's release and arrival at Love Field: *New York Times,* October 7, 1962, 1, and October 8, 14; Newman, 55.
   Émigrés' help and decision to move to Dallas: McMillan, 251–252; I, 5.
   Rented post office box: WR, 119.

115. Claim he had just gotten out of Marines: X, 179.
   Poster blowups to defense committee: X, 106.

CHAPTER 8. TAKING ACTION

117. "Like two friends meeting": IX, 86, 82.
   Oswald's striking Marina, rudeness: IX, 86, 313.
   Similar treatment of Marguerite: VIII, 55, 57.
   Marina's admiration of Castro: IX, 357; I, 24; XXIII, 390.
   Oswalds' disagreement on priorities: III, 128; XI, 130; IX, 311, 376; XXII, 763.

118. "Overblown opinion": IX, 357; I, 24; XXIII, 390.
   Katya Ford on Oswalds' relationship: II, 305.
   Marina's doubts Lee loved her: McMillan, 316, 393, 394, 395, 472–473.
   Alexandra Taylor's testimony: XI, 128–129.
   Gary Taylor and Oswald: McMillan, 256; IX, 82, 81.

118–119. Max Clark on Oswald's decision to leave Russia: VIII, 347, 350. See also VIII, 425; XXIII, 399; XI, 98.

119. Oswald's criticism of Kennedy: Epstein, *Legend,* 204.
   Attempt to join Socialist Workers party: X, 113; XIX, 576–578; Newman, 270–271.

120. Mrs. Tobias on Oswald: X, 235, 237, 248.
   Alexandra's comment: XI, 140.
   Marina on quarrel: XVIII, 621–622. See also I, 11.

120–121. Marina's moving out, émigrés' assistance: VIII, 386; McMillan, 263, 283–284.

121. Marina and Valentina Ray on reconciliation: XVIII, 622–623; VIII, 418.
   Only the de Mohrenschildts remained friendly: McMillan, 285–286; WR, 282; II, 307.
   "Living in another world": XVIII, 624; I, 4–5.

122. Political posters: XIX, 579; XI, 208–209 (Socialist Workers party); XXI,

674–677 (Hall–Davis committee); XXI, 721, XX, 269 *(The Worker)*.
Subscription to *The Militant:* X, 109.
The Militant on Kennedy's Miami speech: January 7, 1963, 1.

123. Walker's release and ordering of gun: Newman, 59; WR, 174; I, 16.
"Alek" nickname and James Bond: WR, 122; XXII, 82.
"Hidell" an "altered Fidel": I, 64; V, 401.
Hidell ID: WR, 723; McMillan, 319; Epstein, *Legend,* 316 n. 6.
Studying map and bus schedule: V, 417; WR, 404.

123–124. Pressuring Marina to return to USSR: I, 10, 12–13.

124. Letter to Soviet Embassy: XVI, 10; I, 35; Newman, 313.

124–125. Meeting Ruth Paine and Marina's comment: McMillan, 344, 606 n. 11.

125. February 1963 Marina's worst month: McMillan, 317.
Landlady's comments on Marina: X, 239, 244, 250.
Oswald's staying out late: I, 14; X, 18, 30–31; X, 243 (Tobias note); McMillan, 353 (call to de Mohrenschildt).
Decision to move, Mrs. Tobias's comment: McMillan, 329; X, 262–263.
Study in new apartment: McMillan, 330.

126. Pictures of Walker's house: WR, 185–186.
Notebook: Ibid., 404–405; XI, 292–293.
Rifle and pistol shipped March 20: WR, 723.
Renewed FBI interest: IV, 441–442; V, 5–6.
"Cooling off period," Hoover's later reaction: Book V, 90.
Oswald's case reopened: IV, 442.

127. Backyard photos with weapons: WR, 724; I, 15–16; XXIII, 420, 408; XI, 296; McMillan, 544.

127–128. Michael Paine, April 2 dinner: II, 393, 389–390, 402–403; XXIII, 502 (Michael's father); McMillan, 345–346.

128. Practice with rifle: McMillan, 347
Reasons for loss of job: X, 189, 190–191; XI, 479.
Sam Ballen interview: IX, 47–53; McMillan, 278; Epstein, *Legend,* 209–210, 319 n. 11.

129. Pro-Castro demonstration: XX, 511; XXII, 796.
Attack on Walker: WR, 183–187; McMillan, 608 n. 4; XI, 405–410; HACR, 59.

129–130. Oswald's note of instructions: WR, 183–185.

130. Marina on Oswald's explanation: I, 16; II, 315–316; XXIV, 47; HACH, XII, 391; HACH, II, 236, 232, 251.
Instructions kept in Marina's book: XXIII, 391.

131. Destruction of notebook: XI, 292–293.
   On Marina's failure to go to police: McMillan, 353–354, 607–608 n. 23.

132. Seeking asylum, "grandiose plans": Newman, 338–339; McMillan, 325–326; XI, 296.
   Nixon incident: WR, 187–189; V, 389–390, 392, 395; McMillan, 367–371; Newman, 349.
   Move to New Orleans: II, 457–463; McMillan, 381.

CHAPTER 9. THE ACTIVIST

135. Castro agents among refugees: *New York Times,* April 13, 1963, 41.
   Guerrilla attack in Venezuela: Newman, 269–270.
   MONGOOSE disbanded, Special Group under Bundy: Interim, 170.
   Opening to Cuba proposed, "separate track": Ibid., 173–174, 176 n. 1.

136. *Time* quotes administration official: February 15, 1963, 23.
   Kennedy news conference and White House estimate: *Time,* February 22, 1963, 21.
   Wall Street Journal quoted: *The Worker,* March 19, 1963, 2; *The Militant,* March 25, 1963, 7.
   Alpha 66 raid and official crackdown: *New York Times,* March 20, 1963, 2, March 30, 1; April 1, 1, and April 6, 1.
   Kennedy April 19 speech: McMillan, 611–612 n. 2.

137. No ongoing CIA assassination plots: Interim, 85–86, 84.
   Mafia not serious participants?: Summers, 269, 270; Blakey, 152.
   Oswald at home on April 21: McMillan, 369–370.

138. Standing Group and CIA on Castro's death: Interim, 171.
   Call to Lillian Murret: VIII, 133–134, 164.
   Unemployment benefits and job: WR, 725, 726.

139. Lillian's testimony: VIII, 136.
   Renting apartment: VIII, 59.
   Marina's discussions with Ruth and phone call: McMillan, 393, 394–395; II, 468.
   Oswalds' reunion: II, 470–472.

140. Card to Fair Play for Cuba and reply: XX, 531, 517.
   Oswald's response to Vincent Lee: XX, 512–513.

140–141. Newman on Oswald's plans: Newman, 42–43, 55–56, 71–72, 358.

141. Marina on purpose of pro-Castro activities: I, 24–25.
   Oswald's political résumé: XVI, 337–346.

142. "Subversion airlift": *Time,* March 29, 1963, 19. See also *Time,* March 8, 1963, 25.
President on travel ban defiance: *Time,* August 9, 1963, 31–32.

142–143. House Un-American Activities Committee chairman on travelers: New

143. Orleans *Times-Picayune,* July 24, 1963, 1.
Hijacking plans: I, 22, 23.
"There's a Cuban Embassy in Mexico": McMillan, 447.
Letter from Soviet Embassy: XVIII, 514–515.
Pressuring Marina to answer letter: McMillan, 410–411.
Marina's letter to Ruth: XVII, 88.
Handbills: XII, 796–798; WR, 728.

144. Letter from Vincent Lee: XX, 514–516.
Post office box rental: WR, 312.
Membership forms: XXII, 800–801.

144–145. Letter to Vincent Lee: XX, 518–521.

145. No response from Fair Play Committee: WR, 412.
June 10 letter to *The Worker:* XX, 257–258.
No evidence Oswald rented an office: WR, 292, 408. But see also Epstein, *Legend,* 321 n. 8.
Renewed FBI interest: XVII, 794; IV, 422–423.

146. Oswald at Dumaine Street dock: XXII, 806.
LeBlanc's testimony: X, 215.

146–147. At Crescent City Garage: X, 221.

147. Passport application: XVII, 666–667.

Note 1: Critics have expressed suspicion about the speed with which Oswald received his passport (Meagher, 336; Summers, 362). A July 21 story in the *Times-Picayune* headlined "Passports Are Now Easier to Obtain" pointed out that because of a new policy of decentralization, passports were being issued at New Orleans and other cities in 24 hours or less (Sec. II, p. 13).

Scene with Marina and letter to Soviet Embassy: I, 68; McMillan, 417–419; XVI, 30.
Ruth's offer to Marina: WR, 727–728.

148. Lost job, unemployment benefits: Ibid., 726–727.
Library books checked out: XXV, 929–931.
Subscriptions, *Agitator* a Party manual: WR, 743, 744; Epstein, *Legend,* 112.
Speech at Jesuit college: XXV, 923, 924, 919, 921, 926–927.

148–149. Robert Fitzpatrick's recollections: XXV, 924–925.

CHAPTER 10. "STREET AGITATION . . . RADIO SPEAKER AND LECTURER"

163. Size of New Orleans Cuban community: Blakey and Billings, 177.
DRE shelling of Havana: X, 34.
FBI raid: New Orleans *Times-Picayune*, August 1 and 2, 1963; Book V, 11–12.
Guerrilla camp disbanded: Brener, vii–viii, 69–70.

164. Notebook entry: XVI, 67.
DRE leader Bringuier, store window sign: X, 34; XXII, 823.

165. Young boys collecting for DRE: XXVI, 767.
Oswald's offer to Bringuier: X, 35–36.
Suggestions to anti-Castro boys: X, 83, 77.

166. "I infiltrated the Cuban Student Directorate": XIV, 280.

Note 1: Oswald may also have seen a July 17 *Times-Picayune* story that began, "Hundreds of anti-Castroites were arrested in northern Camaguey Province after a militiaman infiltrated their guerrilla ranks and reported them" (p. 14).

Bringuier incident seen as infiltration attempt: Newman, 379–380; Blakey and Billings, 162, 364; Epstein, *Legend*, 222–223; Meagher, 384, 386.
Bringuier and friends confront Oswald: X, 37–38; XVII, 761.

167.

Note 2: Some theorists contend that the exiles' attack on Oswald was a prearranged mock battle, citing an August 1 letter from Oswald to Vincent Lee that seems to describe this confrontation eight days before it occurred: "Through the efforts of some exile 'gusanos' [worms] a street demonstration was attacked and we were officially cautioned by police. This incident robbed me of what support I had leaving me alone . . ." (XX, 524–525; Summers, 302–303). But Oswald also wrote to Lee *after* his clash with Bringuier's group, presenting his arrest as a victory for Fair Play. It makes little sense that he would have given two versions of a staged incident. Actually, the August 1 letter suggests that there was another demonstration by Oswald in late July that a policeman quickly broke up and then failed to report. An oversight such as this wouldn't have been unusual, since the Warren Report doesn't mention that Oswald had distributed handbills on the city's Tulane University campus that summer. When a student called the FBI after the assassination to offer a copy, he was told it wasn't needed (Epstein, *Legend*, 222, 322 n. 15; XXVI, 575–576).

Marina checks rifle in closet: McMillan, 433.
"Hidell" an "altered Fidel": I, 64; V, 401.

Questioning by Martello and Quigley: X, 53, 56, 59; XVII, 758; IV, 436–438; Newman, 383.

168. Thornley on Oswald's definition of democracy: XI, 92.

168–169. Murret visit and Oswald's reaction: VIII, 146, 187; I, 25.

169. Bringuier on court appearance: X, 41.
Oswald pleased by his arrest: McMillan, 433; I, 24–25.
Newspaper clippings: XX, 261 (Arnold Johnson); XX, 526–528 (Vincent Lee); WR, 730 (pro-Castro file).

170. Purpose of pro-Castro activities: I, 24–25.
Trade Mart demonstration: WR, 729.
Bringuier's friend and Oswald: X, 41–42; I, 25.

171. Oswalds' improved relationship: McMillan, 446, 453.
Marina's comments and his replies: Ibid., 436–437; I, 22, 23.
Marina on "games" with the rifle: XVIII, 631.
Stuckey's impression of Oswald: XI, 162, 170–171.

171–174. Transcript of radio interview: XXI, 621–632.

174. Cuban literacy campaign: Newman, 197, 392.
Cuban friend Alfred: XXIII, 477, 484; Epstein, *Legend*, 113.
Refugees "no better source": HACH, XII, 182.
Oswald invited to debate and appearance: XI, 166, 168.
Stuckey learns of defection: McMillan, 439–440, 615–616 n. 7.
Debate transcript: XXI, 633–641.

175. "I would not agree with that particular wording": XXI, 641.
Castro on Kennedy as ruffian: New Orleans *Times-Picayune*, July 27, 1963, sec. I, 3.
Marina on Oswald's view of Kennedy: McMillan, 413–414, 571.
Considered Marina unqualified, knew she admired Kennedy: HACH, XII, 408; McMillan, 414.
Stuckey, "We finished him on that program": WR, 410.

176. Stuckey and Oswald at bar: XI, 171–175; XVII, 764.

176–177. Letter to Central Committee, Johnson's reply: XX, 262–264, 265.

177. Admiration of U.S. Party members, letter: McMillan, 438; I, 23.
Dry-firing of rifle and explanation: I, 21–22; McMillan, 452.

177–178. Andrews on Mexican and Oswald's discharge: WR, 325, 727; XI, 329; Epstein, *Counterplot*, 86.

178. Oswald and the Habana Bar: XI, 341–342, 347, 351, 361.

178–179. Résumé description and contents: WR, 731; XVI, 337–346; Newman, 411–413.

180. Microdots: Epstein, *Legend,* 194–196; XVI, 53, 346.
Cuba as "last escape hatch": WR, 414; Newman, 413.
181. Covert operations stepped up in June: Interim, 173.
Paramilitary operations and purpose: Ibid., 13.
Ray Cline and Cuban raider on plots: Branch and Crile, "Kennedy Vendetta," 61.
Renewed contact with AM/LASH, CIA cable: Interim, 86–87; Book V, 3, 13, 14, 100.
182 Attwood's efforts, comments by Robert Kennedy and Bundy: Interim, 173.
Administration not informed of AM/LASH: Ibid., 173–175.
183. Church committee on exile assassination talk: Book V, 14.
Raymond Rocca's comment: Ibid., 15 n. 21; Blakey and Billings, 143–144; CIA memorandum dated 30 May 1975 obtained from the CIA under the Freedom of Information Act, portions deleted.
184. Oswald eager for Ruth Paine's arrival: McMillan, 452.
Oswald's travel plans: Ibid., 448, 461.
Concealment of destination from Ruth: III, 10, 27; WR, 413, 730.
Oswald seen leaving apartment and on bus: WR, 730, 732.

CHAPTER 11. THE TROUBLING TESTIMONY OF SYLVIA ODIO

185–188. Odio's testimony: XI, 368–382; HACH, X, 26–27; Summers, 411–414; Blakey and Billings, 163.
189. Odio a credible witness: HACH, X, 29, and Summers, 589 n. 96 (doctor); XX, 690 (father's letter); Staff Report to the Warren Commission by William T. Coleman, Jr., and W. David Slawson, pp. 109–110, National Archives.

Note 1: Odio's description of "Leon" matched Oswald even in certain details the Warren Commission didn't notice. Odio recalled that "Leon" was unshaven, and McMillan mentions that during the preceding summer Oswald became slovenly in his appearance and "by mid-July shaved only every other day." During August he also lost considerable weight—and Odio remarked that the shirt the American had on looked too big for him (McMillan, 415–416, 459; XI, 371).

Efforts to establish Oswald's whereabouts: Epstein, *Inquest,* 104.
190.

Note 2: The Warren Report and its supporters argue that after reaching Houston on this bus at about 10:50 P.M., Oswald called the home of Horace

Twiford, a member of the Socialist Labor party and therefore couldn't have been at Odio's apartment that evening. (In 1962 Oswald had requested literature from the New York office of the SLP, which forwarded his name and address to Twiford. On September 11, 1963, Twiford sent him a copy of the Party newspaper with his return address on it.) The report's claim that Oswald made this call on September 25 isn't supported by the affidavits of Twiford and his wife, who spoke with Oswald in her husband's absence. Neither mentioned a specific date, placing the incident only in "late September" or "during the week" prior to September 27 (XI, 179–180). Moreover, Mrs. Twiford felt certain that Oswald telephoned between 7 and 10 P.M., and made the reasonable point that a call at a later hour would have been memorable. She stated that "Oswald inquired as to how my husband had his address. He also said that he had hoped to discuss ideas with my husband for a few hours before he flew down to Mexico." She assumed it was a local call (XXIV, 726–727; WR, 323, 731). If Oswald left for Houston by car on September 24, he could have called the Twiford residence before 10 P.M. and still had almost twenty-four hours to reach Dallas, 245 miles away.

Unemployment check: WR, 323; XXIV, 716, 388.

Not seen on Houston bus, but on other buses: WR, 323, 732–733, 736; XXIV, 717; XXV, 607; Meagher, 381.

Marina on when checks were picked up: XXIII, 388.

Check cashed on Tuesday, September 17: WR, 308.

Liebeler, "Odio may be right," and Rankin's response: Epstein, Inquest, 105; memorandum from Liebeler to Howard P. Willens, September 14, 1964, pp. 4–6, National Archives.

191. Rankin's letter to J. Edgar Hoover: XXVI, 595–596.

FBI explanation and Commission's conclusion: XXVI, 834; WR, 324.

Collapse of FBI explanation: Meagher, 387; Summers, 416–417; HACR, 165.

192–193. Meagher on Odio incident: Meagher, 386–387, 377.

194. Odio considered truthful: Anson, "Congress and the JFK Riddle," 29 (Church committee); Blakey and Billings, 364 (House Assassinations Committee).

Assassinations Committee conclusion: HACR, 166–167.

Blakey on Odio incident: Blakey and Billings, 165.

195. Marina on Oswald's boast he was a good shot: XXIII, 409.

198. Veciana and Gonzales plot: O'Toole and Hoch, "Dallas: The Cuban Connection," 96.

Castro on plot: New York Times, October 24, 1961, 14.

199. Odio's referral of Martin to Miami leader: XI, 375.

Odio on how she could have been located: XI, 380.

Rodriguez contacted by Oswald: Summers, 318, 575.
Denials by JURE leaders and Amador Odio: WR, 324; HACH, X, 29.

200. Assassinations Committee on Cuban intelligence agents: HACR, 150–151 n. 19.

201. "As far as taking orders . . .": HACH, XII, 405.
Oswald on Marine training: VIII, 278.
Oswald legalistic: XI, 171, 477; XVIII, 98; XIX, 264.

202. Marina on Oswald's masquerading: HACH, XII, 430.
De Mohrenschildt on Oswald: HACH, XII, 310.

CHAPTER 12. CASTRO'S REVELATIONS

205. McFarland testimony: XI, 214–215.
At the Hotel Comercio and Soviet Embassy: WR, 733, 301.

205–206. Marina on Oswald's travel plans: I, 23.

206. Application for Cuban visa: XXV, 814–815.
Silvia Duran in Oswald's notebook: XVI, 54.

206–207. Duran's statement: XXIV, 588–590.

207. Return visits to embassies: HACR, 147, 322.

208. Conditional approval of visa: XXV, 817.
"Confidential sources" in Mexico: WR, 305.
Phone call overheard by CIA: New York Times, September 21, 1975, 1; Washington Post, November 26, 1976, 1.

208–209. CIA photographs, notification of other agencies: Epstein, Legend, 238; Summers, 380, 384, 374.

209. Phillips on phone call: Summers, 388–389.
Oswald's finances: WR, 745.
Ernesto Rodriguez's story: Summers, 389 (quoting a Los Angeles Times syndication in the Dallas Morning News, September 24, 1975).

210. Duran and philosophy professor, Contreras's account: HACR, 145–146; Summers, 377–378.

Note 1: Contreras first told his story in 1967 to a U.S. consul in Mexico, who reported it to the CIA, which confirmed that Contreras was a student in 1963 and a strong supporter of Castro. When Summers spoke to him in 1978, Contreras claimed that the man who identified himself as Oswald didn't resemble the president's assassin, but this was not what he had told the consul (HACR, 144, 146 n. 17).

211. Hoover's letter to Rankin, unseen by Slawson and Belin: Schorr, "The Assassins," 21; New York Times, November 14, 1976, 30.

211–212. Garrison investigation, Ferrie in poor health: Epstein, *Counterplot*, 71, 104–106, 119, 128; Brener, 80–81; Blakey and Billings, 48–49; *New York Times*, May 11, 1967, 35 (Helms subpoenaed).

212. Bergquist interview: Bergquist, "My Curious Row With Castro," 33–34, 50–51.
Turner Catledge on Castro: Wyden, 26.

213ff. Clark interview: Schorr, "The Assassins," 21–22; Summers, 391 (quoting Comer Clark, "Fidel Castro Says He Knew of Oswald Threat to Kill JFK," *National Enquirer,* October 15, 1967).

214. Castro on assassination: Mankiewicz and Jones, 67.

216. Assassinations Committee meeting with Castro: HACR, 149, 142–144; Blakey and Billings, 143–148.

217. Castro "a disciple of Machiavelli": Halperin, 48, 60.

218. Castro on difficulty in getting an interview, public restaurants: HACH, III, 209, 208.
At Arab restaurant: Mankiewicz and Jones, 34–35.
At all-night pizzeria: Lockwood, 243.
"A former trial lawyer": Mankiewicz and Jones, 13.

CHAPTER 13. OCTOBER 1963—READING BETWEEN THE LINES

219–220. Activities on returning to Dallas: WR, 737.

220. "They're such bureaucrats": McMillan, 471.
Jaggars-Chiles-Stovall recommendation: XI, 478–479; XX, 3.
Landlady's comment: VI, 406.
Registers as O.H. Lee: X, 294; VI, 436.
Ruth Paine's letter: XVII, 150–153.

220–221. Suggestion of job at Depository: III, 33–35; I, 29; WR, 738.

221. Truly's comment: XXII, 527.
Reading newspapers: VI, 352; III, 164–165, 218, 116.
Kennedy and Russian troops, Venezuelan attacks: Newman, 441, 440, 446–447.
Oswald on exploitation: II, 400–401, 411.

222. People "like cardboard" to him: McMillan, 482; XI, 402.
Disliked Kennedy less than politicians to right: II, 414.
Oswald's view of Michael: V, 395.
Paine on Oswald as a revolutionary: XI, 402, 403, 411; II, 411.
Lawrence of Arabia comparison: II, 401, 410.

222–223. Michael and bundle containing rifle: II, 414–418; IX, 437–448.

223. Newspapers and magazines at Ruth's: III, 114–116, 418.

"Reading between the lines": II, 418–419; IX, 455–456.

224. Castro speech: *The Militant,* October 14, 1963.
Birthday party, Oswalds' improved relations: McMillan, 474; II, 422; I, 68.

224–225. Movies and Oswald's reactions: McMillan, 475–476; XXIII, 403; I, 71–72.

226.

Note 1: Macmillan interpreted Oswald's remarks as a reference to the *Machado* revolution. This view isn't suggested in Marina's testimony and wouldn't explain either Oswald's excitement or Marina's reporting the incident to the Secret Service. (McMillan, 476).

Oswald on Sunday night: III, 39–40; McMillan, 477.
Oswald at Walker rally and ACLU meeting: II, 412, 403, 408.

227. Krystinik's impressions: IX, 463.
Discussion after meeting: IX, 464–465, 468; II, 408; XXII, 714 (projectionist).

228. Conversation during drive home: II, 409, 408.
ACLU application, post office box: XVII, 671; XX, 172; WR, 312.

228–229. Letter to Arnold Johnson: XX, 271–273.

229. Attwood's efforts, Kennedy–Daniel meeting: Summers, 423–424.

230. CIA–AM/LASH meeting, weapons promised: Book V, 17–18, 101.

CHAPTER 14. NOVEMBER—THE DECISION

231. FBI attempts to locate Oswald: IV, 446–448; XI, 461–462.

231–232. Hosty visits Ruth and Marina: IV, 452, 449; III, 15; I, 49; McMillan, 494–495.

232. Marina's remarks to Hosty: I, 57, 357; III, 103.
Hosty's address and phone number: III, 18.

232–233. Oswald's reaction to FBI visit: McMillan, 499; III, 101; XXII, 786.

233–234. Second Hosty–Ruth Paine conversation: IV, 453; III, 96, 102, 104, 129.

234. Marina memorizes license number: McMillan, 498.
Marina on "a matter of privacy": III, 100.
November 8 conversation with Ruth: III, 102, 18–19, 101. See also I, 57.

234–235. Oswald's note to Hosty: Book V, 95–97.

235.

Note 1: Hosty's receptionist claimed that the note was partly visible inside the unsealed envelope and that it contained a threat to blow up the FBI and

Dallas Police Department, but this is unlikely. Hosty said the note was folded so that the writing couldn't be seen, and it would have been uncharacteristic of Oswald to put an incriminating statement on paper. Hosty's version also sounds more like Oswald, who frequently took his complaints to "proper authorities." Finally, Hosty's reaction—putting the note aside—suggests that Oswald made no violent threat.

235–236. Letter to Soviet Embassy: XVI, 33; III, 13; WR, 309–311.

236. Oswald's knowledge of Azcue's replacement: Newman, 495; WR, 310; XXV, 817 (October 15 letter from Cuba regarding Oswald's visa, addressed to Alfredo Mirabal, consul of Cuba).
Marina unaware of new visa request: McMillan, 506.

237.

Note 2: In an earlier, handwritten draft Oswald had written, "The agent also 'suggested' that my wife could 'remain in the U.S. under FBI protection,' that is, she could refuse to return to the——" The last five words were crossed out and the sentence completed with "defect from the Soviet Union." Oswald clearly felt that Hosty's routine assurances to Marina somehow threatened his plans to send her back to Russia. Ruth discovered this draft lying on her desk on November 9 (III, 13–18, 51–52; WR, 309). Puzzled and disturbed by its contents, she made a copy, intending to show it to Hosty if he returned.

Trip to shopping center, Oswald's mood: III, 14; IX, 391, 394.
Oswald asked not to return on weekend, learner's permit application: I, 63; II, 515–517.
Marina's attempt to call Oswald: III, 43–44.

238. November 18 argument over alias: I, 46; III, 45; McMillan, 516–517.

238–239. President's Miami speech: Newman, 509; Summers, 425, 423.

239. Newspapers' coverage of speech and motorcade route: XXVI, 69; Newman, 511.
Marina on Oswald's failure to call: III, 45–46.

240. Hunting rifle in Truly's office: McMillan, 519; VII, 381–382, 387–388.
Conversation with Frazier: II, 222.
Ruth on Oswald's arrival: III, 46–48.
Oswald's activities at Ruth's house: McMillan, 521, 523–525.

240–241. President Kennedy in Fort Worth: Bishop, 25, 28, 61; Manchester, 114, 121, 137; VII, 455.

242. Oswald on his way to shoot Walker?: Newman, 47–49.

Note 3: There are other theories about where Oswald was headed. Commission lawyer David Belin believes that he was en route to a street at which he could have caught a bus to Mexico (Belin, 425–428). Congressman Harold Sawyer of the Assassinations Committee believes that Oswald was on his way to the home of an individual identified by the Dallas press as a Communist party defector who had helped the FBI destroy the Party in Texas. The news story had appeared on the same page as articles about John Abt defending Communists in New York and the president's proposed visit to Dallas. The informant's home was two blocks farther up the street in the direction Oswald was walking when Tippit stopped him (HACR, 673–674).

Oswald seen by shoe store manager: VII, 3–4.

CHAPTER 15. THE ARREST

243. Seth Kantor's reaction: XX, 410.
AM/LASH meeting with case officer: Book V, 19–20.

243–244. Castro's statements: Daniel, "When Castro Heard the News."

244. Michael Paine's reactions: McMillan, 540–541.
Oswald's arrest: VII, 40, 52, 73; VII, 54 (crowd); VII, 41, 59 (in police car); Belin, 27.

244–245. Fritz on Oswald's answers: IV, 239.
Other questioners' impressions: XXIV, 839, 844; VII, 135.

245. Oswald discusses political beliefs: WR, 610; IV, 224.
Oswald apprised of rights, declines lawyer: IV, 216.
FBI agents join questioning: IV, 209, 210.
Oswald meets Hosty: IV, 210, 466–467.
Hosty realizes note was from Oswald: HACR, 245.
Oswald's statements on rifle, whereabouts, and pistol: WR, 619; XI, 613; WR, 181.
Denial he was in Mexico City: IV, 210.
Witnesses identify Oswald: WR, 166.

246. Concealment of Neely Street address: WR, 617.
Oswald at press conference: IV, 166; Newman, 547.
Ruby's personality and arrest record: XXIII, 21, 22, 172, 356, 7, 125; WR, 796, 800.
Ruby's large sums of money and pistol: WR, 797, 805.
Ruby's reaction to assassination: WR, 335, 337–338.

247. Oswald's assertions, Jarman's location: WR, 182, 635, 250.
Jarman, Norman, and Williams on shooting: III, 204–207, 191–192, 175–176.
Secret Service report: WR, 635; Oswald asks for Abt: XX, 441; IV, 215; VII, 314.

247–248. Kantor and Oswald's remarks: XX, 416.

248. Aline Mosby's reaction: XXII, 710.
Search of Paine home, pictures found: WR, 628; VII, 215, 231.
Paine and Oswald on Neely Street residence: WR, 607.
Marina's first reactions, rifle missing: McMillan, 538–540; III, 79.
Pictures in June's baby book and Marguerite's response: McMillan, 544; I, 146, 148.

249. Marina's talk with Oswald: McMillan, 546–548; I, 77.

250. Marguerite, "This room is bugged": Oswald, 22.
Robert on brother's demeanor and statements: Ibid., 143, 144, 146.

251. Similar statements in Moscow: XXII, 706.
Phone call to Ruth and her reactions: III, 85–86.
Conversation with president of Dallas Bar Association: VII, 328–330.
Oswald's reaction to backyard photos: WR, 608–609.

252. Assassinations Committee on photographs: HACR, 52.
Sunday morning questioning: VII, 298–299, 267; IV, 228, 240; XX, 444; WR, 610, 629.

252–253. Leavelle's impression: VII, 269.

253. Holmes's statement: WR, 633.
Priscilla Johnson's comment: XX, 310.
Transfer to county jail delayed: XV, 148–149; Belin, 463–465.
Dressed in black: WR, 636; McMillan, 555.

254. Ruby at Western Union office: WR, 354, 357; XIII, 226.
"I'm Jack Ruby": Kantor, 149.
Crowd's cheer: VII, 589; XX, 419.
Clenched fist: Summers, 137, 547 n. 35.

CHAPTER 16. REACTIONS

255. Oswald seen as politically erratic: New York Times, November 23, 1963, 1, and December 7, 1963, 1.

256. Castro's reaction reported: Ibid., November 24, 1963, 10.
Castro speech: The Worker, December 1, 1963, 8.
Castro's fear of war: WR, 309; HACH, III, 225.
U.S. officials' concern: Manchester, 333, 359.
Lyndon Johnson persuades Warren: Manchester, 630; Warren, 358.

256–258. Witnesses on Oswald's motive: II, 392, 424; XI, 402 (Paine); VIII, 413–414 (Hall); VIII, 354 (Clark); VIII, 176–177, 179 (Marilyn); I, 123 (Marina); IV, 239–240 (Fritz).

258. Marina on backyard photos, "something important": XXIII, 408–409, 479.

259. "Start another revolution?": XXIII, 385.
Denies knowledge of Mexico trip, later admission: XXIII, 388, 511.
"Hitler needed killing," note's discovery: XXIII, 413, 391; IX, 393–394.
Explanation for saving note: McMillan, 369, 370, 373; WR, 405.
Marina approximating the truth: Epstein, *Inquest,* 99.

259–260. Marina explains inconsistencies: HACH, XII, 433.

260–261. Marina's testimony about November 21: WR, 420–421.

261. Ruth's observations: XI, 391–393; McMillan, 523, 544–545.
Marina denies quarrel: McMillan, 628 n. 13.
Marina's later testimony about November 21: HACH, II, 266–267.

262. "You and your long tongue": McMillan, 516.
McMillan on events of November 21: McMillan, 521, 523, 566.

263. Ruth Paine's warning about Oswald: II, 509.
De Mohrenschildt and Walker shooting: I, 18; IX, 249, 317.
De Mohrenschildt on his testimony and Oswald's motive: HACH, XII, 216, 241, 224.
De Mohrenschildt and Janet Auchincloss: IX, 179; HACH, XII, 226–227.

264. Money for rifle, guilt feelings: Epstein, *Legend,* 319 n. 10; McMillan, 570.
De Mohrenschildt's backyard photo: HACR, 52–53; HACH, XII, 52–53, 336, 241, and II, 315; McMillan, 362, 609 n. 9.

Note 1: McMillan believes that "5/IV/63" signified May 4, 1963, but Marina testified that the date on the photograph meant "Five-fourth month-1963" (HACH, II, 265–266). Oswald was surely familiar with the Russian style of writing dates, since two birthday gifts he received in the Soviet Union were inscribed in that fashion (WR, 691, 708).

264–265. De Mohrenschildt on investigation's effects: HACH, XII, 312, 301.

265. No evidence worked for CIA: HACR, 277; Epstein, *Legend,* 185–187; McMillan, 632 n. 5.
De Mohrenschildt's suicide: McMillan, 569–570.

265–266. CIA and FBI response to Dallas: Book V, 25, 40, 41, 60–67, 58, 38.

266. Hoover's push for quick solution: Ibid., 32–35, 38–42.
Concern for FBI's reputation: Ibid., 46–47, 51, 53.

267. CIA plots kept from Commission: Ibid., 67–75.
Assassination Committee's conclusion on Cuba: Blakey and Billings, 155.
Blakey's suspicion Castro's denial untrue: Ibid., 146, 147–148.

CHAPTER 17. CONSPIRACY THINKING

269. TV documentary: "J. Edgar Hoover," ABC News Closeup, June 3, 1982.

270. Origin of Lifton's theory: Lifton, 25–27, 80.

271. Witnesses on casket and sheet: Ibid., 775, 777, 786–787.
Body bag, plain casket: Ibid., 746–747, 785, 794.
Time of arrival: Ibid., 516, 604, 605, 728.
"Had this been an ordinary case": Ibid., 775.
Elizabeth Loftus on memory: Rodgers, "The Malleable Memory of Eyewitnesses," 32, 34.
Lady Bird Johnson's flight of stairs: Manchester, 236.

271–272. O'Connor and body bag: Lifton, 747.

272. Two other witnesses: Ibid., 794, 785.
Lifton on sutured throat wound: Ibid., 755.
Chief of surgery's recollection: Ibid., 804, 810.

272–273. On vertical thinking: de Bono, 7, 88.

273. Other theories on backward movement: Kurtz, 102–103.

273–274. Eddowes and assistants: Eddowes, x.

274. Varying heights: Ibid., 211, 213, 214.
Pic on Oswald's appearance: Ibid., 36–37.
"Switching" of fingerprints: Ibid., 139.

275. *Betrayal* scenario: Morrow, 108, 124–127, 176–177, 200–233 *passim*.

276. Morrow on motivations: Morrow, 127.

276–277. Evidence Oswald at Cuban Embassy, November 9 letter: Summers, 372, 374–376, 398; WR, 304–305, 309–310.

277. Man in movie theater: Anson, 38, 282, 353; Belin, 26, 35.

277–278. Mrs. Troon's story: Summers, 174–176.

278–279. Army intelligence file: HACR, 282–286; Summers, 91–93, 305–306.

280. National Research Council on shots: *Science*, October 8, 1982, 127–133.
Assassinations Committee on possible conspirators: HACR, 108 109, 109 n. 4.

281. Committee conclusions on Oswald's guilt: Ibid., 40, 46 47, 53–54, 57–59.
"Bewilderingly well framed": Summers, 86.
Commission on Zapruder film and rifle: WR, 96–117.
Stretcher bullet tested: HACR, 37.

282. Connally, Committee, and Mrs. Kennedy on first shot: IV, 132–133; *Life*, November 25, 1966, 48; HACR, 87; V, 180.
Committee test of rifle: HACR, 89.

Spectators see man or rifle in window: WR, 63–65, 143–147.
Evidence bullets fired from Oswald's rifle only: HACR, 37, 34–35, 42, 45.

283. Grassy knoll witnesses: Lifton, 70–72.
Ferrie's background: HACH, X, 106–111, 127.
Office at 544 Camp Street?: XX, 524–525 (letter); Epstein, *Legend,* 321 n. 8.

284. Oswald in Clinton?: HACR, 142; HACH, IV, 485; Summers, 334–335.
No training as electrician, HACH, XII, 400.

285. Clinton incident seen as intelligence scheme: Summers, 336–337.

286.

Note 1: During his trial Ruby passed a note to his attorney, Joseph Tonahill, concerning his first lawyer, Tom Howard:
> Joe, you should know this. Tom Howard told me to say that I shot Oswald so that Caroline and Mrs. Kennedy wouldn't have to come to Dallas to testify. OK? [HACR, 193]

This would seem to prove that Ruby's professed motive was a fabrication. But that isn't so—Ruby gave this reason for his action in a statement to a Secret Service agent, Forrest Sorrels, shortly after his arrest, *before* he talked to Howard (XIX, 440; Blakey and Billings, 321, 324). What Ruby may have meant was that Howard had advised him to stick to that particular part of his statement and omit the other reasons he had mentioned.

Ruby's reactions: WR, 338, 344, 349.
Opinion poll: Henderson and Summerlin, 202–205, 207, 216–217.

287. Ruby's background: WR, 779–806 *passim.*

287–289. Ruby's activities November 22–24: WR, 334–352; Kantor, 84–86, 105, 110; Henderson and Summerlin, 44.

288. Weissman a conservative: WR, 295.

289. Ruby's expectations after arrest: Kantor, 157, 224.

289–291. Ruby's testimony: V, 181–212 *passim.*

292. Ruby's statements on conspiracy, tape recording, Dann's remark: Meagher, 453, 452.

CHAPTER 18. OSWALD'S GAME

294. Oswald's "love of fantasy," radio program: Oswald, 46–47.

296.

Note 1: Oswald's history resembles that of another American assassin, McKinley's assailant, Leon Czolgosz. A self-taught radical with few personal relationships, Czolgosz tried unsuccessfully to join anarchist groups in Cleveland and Chicago. The anarchists were put off by his eagerness and suspected him of being a police agent. After being rejected by these groups, he shot McKinley. Before his execution Czolgosz said, "I killed the President because he was the enemy of the good working people."

Sources for other material in Chapter 18 have been cited in earlier chapters.

Index